BLOOD
BETWEEN
QUEENS

Books by Barbara Kyle

Blood Between Queens
The Queen's Gamble
The Queen's Captive
The King's Daughter
The Queen's Lady

BLOOD BETWEEN QUEENS

BARBARA KYLE

KENSINGTON BOOKS
www.kensingtonbooks.com

KENSINGTON BOOKS are published by

Kensington Publishing Corp.
119 West 40th Street
New York, NY 10018

All Kensington titles, imprints, and distributed lines are available at special quantity discounts for bulk purchases for sales promotion, premiums, fund-raising, and educational or institutional use.

Special book excerpts or customized printings can also be created to fit specific needs. For details, write or phone the office of the Kensington Special Sales Manager: Kensington Publishing Corp., 119 West 40th Street, New York, NY 10018. Attn. Special Sales Department. Phone: 1-800-221-2647.

Kensington and the K logo Reg. U.S. Pat. & TM Off.

ISBN-13: 978-0-7582-7322-2
ISBN-10: 0-7582-7322-3
First Kensington Trade Paperback Printing: May 2013

eISBN-13: 978-0-7582-9100-4
eISBN-10: 0-7582-9100-0
First Kensington Electronic Edition: May 2013

10 9 8 7 6 5 4 3 2 1

Printed in the United States of America

HISTORICAL PREFACE

In 1560 the young English queen, Elizabeth Tudor, in the second year of her reign, feared a French invasion through Scotland. To prevent it, she sent an army to back Scottish rebels who had risen up against their mighty overlords, the French. The nominal queen of Scotland was Mary Stuart, but she had gone to France as a child to marry the heir to the throne. He had become king and she, at seventeen, was queen of France. The leader of the Scottish rebels was Mary's half brother, the Protestant Earl of Moray, and with Elizabeth's help he and his fighters beat the French army, ending French domination in Scotland and putting a Protestant government in power. Elizabeth's victory over the French in Scotland was a turning point in her fledgling reign. By gambling on intervention she had defied the great powers of France and Spain, elevating her status at home and in the eyes of all Europe, whose leaders had to acknowledge her as a formidable ruler. She did this at the age of twenty-six.

Elizabeth could not have realized that her problems with Scotland had just begun. Mary Stuart had a claim to Elizabeth's throne. They were cousins: Henry VII was Elizabeth's grandfather and Mary's great-grandfather. The following year Mary's husband, the French king, died, and she, a widow at eighteen, came back to Scotland to take up her birthright as its queen. She also publicly maintained her claim to the throne of England. But first she had her own people to contend with. Her return upset the balance of power among the Scottish nobility, setting off an incipient civil war between Mary's supporters, who were mostly Catholic, and those of her Protestant half brother, Moray, the de facto head of the government. For six years this unrest smoldered. Mary infuriated Moray's party when she married a young Englishman, Lord Darnley. She gave birth to a son, but the marriage quickly turned sour and Mary began to rely on the tough, soldierly Earl of Bothwell; many whispered that the relationship was adulterous. In the winter of 1567 the rivalry between the power-seeking factions came to a head when Lord Darnley was killed in an explosion: The house he was staying in was blown up with gunpowder. Three months later Mary wed Bothwell. Suspicion for Darnley's death fell on them both. Moray acted quickly to take power. He indicted Mary for masterminding her husband's murder, took charge of her baby son, and imprisoned her. Bothwell fled. Mary, Queen of Scots, at age twenty-four, had lost her kingdom.

Mary's prison tower rose from an isolated fortress, a castle on an island in Loch Leven. She had been a captive for ten months when one of her young supporters helped her slip out of the castle dressed as a country woman. He rowed her the mile across the lake. Waiting on the other side were her loyal nobles.

All of Europe gasped at the news of Mary's escape. She was notorious for the scandals that had swirled around her: Was she a murdering adulteress who had deserved to be deposed, or an innocent victim horribly wronged? Everyone had an opinion—and waited to see what would happen next. It held enormous significance for every leader. The kings of Spain and France, fiercely Catholic, were eager to see Moray's Protestant government destroyed. If Mary ventured to reclaim her throne, it could start an international war. Elizabeth, once again, feared invasion.

Mary quickly gathered an army. So did Moray. They faced each other on the Glasgow moor near the village of Langside. As Mary looked on from a hilltop, her commander Lord Herries led a cavalry charge that forced Moray's men to retreat. But when another of the Queen's commanders led his infantry through the village's narrow street, they met close fire from hackbutters that Moray had placed behind cottages and hedges. Hundreds of the Queen's men fell under the gunfire. Moray's main force, moments ago in retreat from Herries's cavalry charge, turned and attacked. Mary's demoralized men began to flee, deserting. Moray's men chased them. The Battle of Langside was over in less than an hour. Mary had lost her kingdom for a second time.

She panicked. She galloped down the slope, terrified of being captured again. Lord Herries and a dozen others loyal to her rode after her. Herries begged her to take flight for France, but Mary galloped south. In her terror she wanted to put Scotland behind her as quickly as she could.

She rode for England.

PART ONE

The Scottish Queen

❧ 1 ❧

Alice

The night of the fireworks changed the course of many lives in England, though no one suspected the dark future as hundreds of courtiers stared, faces upturned in delight, at the starbursts of crimson and gold that lit up the terraces and pleasure grounds of Rosethorn House, the country home of Richard, Baron Thornleigh. That night, no one was more proud to belong to the baron's family than his eighteen-year-old ward, Justine Thornleigh; she had no idea that she would soon cause a deadly division in the family and ignite a struggle between two queens. Yet she was already, innocently, on a divergent path, for as Lord and Lady Thornleigh and their multitude of guests watched the dazzle of fireworks honoring the spring visit of Queen Elizabeth, Justine was hurrying away from the public gaiety. Someone had asked to meet her in private.

"Who is it, Timothy?" she had asked the footman when he reached her beside the goldfish pond. She was shepherding three of Lord Thornleigh's grandchildren in a game of tag and had to raise her voice above their squeals. They were a rambunctious trio, excited at being allowed to stay up late for the revels.

"I know not, my lady. She would not say. Just asked for you."

"Behave yourselves," she told the little ones. "Katherine, watch them, will you?" The eight-year-old took an instant tyrannical pleasure in ordering her brother and cousin to sit.

Justine hurried along the path through the knot garden crowded with strolling courtiers. She was hurrying because she wanted to get the interview over with quickly, whoever it was. She had something more exciting on her mind. She'd been told that Lord Thornleigh's nephew, Will Croft, was somewhere among the guests. An ambitious law student, Will was never far from his patron, Sir William Cecil, and Cecil, the Queen's most trusted councilor, was never far from her court. Tonight, most of the court was here at Rosethorn. Justine was determined that as soon as she had fulfilled her promise to entertain the children, and their nursemaid had taken them off to bed, she would find Will in the throng. One word from him, one look even, would thrill her more than all the fireworks in the kingdom.

Nevertheless she slowed, a little in awe, as she passed the open-air banqueting pavilion where the Queen was making merry with her hosts and closest courtiers. Justine had never spoken to Queen Elizabeth face-to-face, an honor she hoped one day to be worthy of, and it was thrilling to see her bantering with Lord and Lady Thornleigh. The three were old friends. Naturally, Justine thought with a glow of pride, for no monarch could ask for a more loyal nobleman than Lord Thornleigh. So commanding a man, tall, erect, with his close cropped iron-gray hair and the leather patch over his lost eye while his good eye, a blazing blue, missed nothing around him. Lady Thornleigh, elegant and gracious as ever, would always have Justine's affection and respect, but his lordship had Justine's love.

And what magnificent entertainment he had laid on for the Queen! The pavilion, built for her visit, was on a raised platform to give her the best view. Its canopy of scarlet silk rippled faintly in the breeze, and torches flared around it. The vista she looked out on was a dazzle of fire and water. On the terraces, fountains shot up bursts of wine that sparkled in the torchlight as if mimicking the fireworks. The man-made lake reflected the torch flames that ringed its shores. Windows in the four-story house appeared ablaze as they, in turn, reflected the burnished lake. Even the crowd shimmered,

Justine thought, all the lords and ladies in their satins and silks of every jewel hue. She hoped her own finery did justice to the family; she had carefully chosen a velvet gown of cornflower blue spangled with silver stars. Lady Thornleigh had approved it for the grand event and Justine knew the color set off her fair hair well. Yet she felt a pang of regret, as she often did, at looking so unlike a Thornleigh. Her ladyship and her daughter and stepson and all their children were dark-haired, and Justine often wished that her own hair was not so brightly blond nor her eyes so very blue. Still, she took a secret delight in sharing that blue trait with Lord Thornleigh. It made her feel as though she alone was his daughter.

Trumpeters blared a fanfare. Drummers rumbled a drum roll. A signal that the next fireworks fusillade would be the crowning event? Every guest looked to Queen Elizabeth, and so did Justine. Slender at thirty-four, dressed in lustrous black and white satin, her red hair studded with pearls, Elizabeth stepped closer to the pavilion's rose-wrapped railing to watch, a wineglass in her hand. The barrage that followed was stunning: twelve cannon boomed from earthen ramparts, shooting balls of fire high into the blackness. Justine felt the ground tremble from the blasts. People cheered. She caught the expectant looks of Lord and Lady Thornleigh standing beside their royal guest. Had this magnificent display they had arranged been worth the enormous expense?

The Queen quaffed back the last of her wine. She rapped the goblet against the railing and the bowl of the glass shattered. She stuck the broken stem in her mouth, then grinned. Sugar glass. Courtiers around her followed suit, smashing their glasses in a shower of brittle sugar and munching the shards that their servants scrambled to retrieve. The Queen threw back her head and laughed. Lord and Lady Thornleigh beamed.

Definitely worth the expense, Justine thought with a smile.

Once past the Queen's pavilion she hurried on up the crowded terrace steps, making for Lady Thornleigh's rose garden, where the unnamed guest was waiting. The rose garden lay at the far side of the terrace, beyond the torches, and she could make out no figure yet in its shadows. Who could want to see her? She recalled that a place for a lady-in-waiting to the Queen had recently opened up. Could this visitor be the widowed Lady Denny come to solicit her to get Lady Thornleigh to put her daughter's name before the Queen? Or could it be the scholar's wife from Oxford who had grabbed her sleeve on the Whitehall Palace wharf at Lent, asking her to recommend her son as a tutor to Lord Thornleigh's eldest grandson? Justine was determined to protect her guardians from excessive demands on their largesse. She would take Lady Thornleigh only the petitions of the deserving.

Another fusillade of fireworks burst behind her with such a mighty noise, a *whoosh* like a thousand arrows let fly, she stopped and looked up. Five enormous bursts of fire hung suspended for a moment, then rained down in a shower of gold. Justine had to admire the wild beauty of it. It was as if the stars were falling from the sky. It gave her goose bumps, for it seemed to herald success with her vow to speak to Will before the night was out. This time, she would let him know her heart. Unmaidenly behavior, no doubt, but she didn't care.

She had loved Will Croft from the moment she first saw him. Eight years ago when Lord Thornleigh had brought her into his London home, she was a frightened ten-year-old whose world had been devastated. Bewildered and withdrawn, she had responded to Lord and Lady Thornleighs' gentle questions with tight one-word answers, for although they were kindness itself, she had so much anxiety knotted up inside her, she was afraid to open her mouth lest her fears shoot out in words and turn these good people against her. They had taken her in, telling everyone she was the orphan of a distant Thornleigh relation. No one beyond the immediate family knew the truth: that she was the child of a traitor. One evening, creeping into the parlor as the family went into the great hall for supper, Justine had stood in lonely silence, trying to rouse courage to join them, to speak, to allow herself to hope that they really would accept her as one of them.

"I'm not too hungry myself," a voice said, startling her. She turned. He was sitting on the window seat tucked into an alcove, reading a book. A lad a few years older than Justine, thirteen or fourteen she guessed, lanky, his long legs stretched out along the window seat, perfectly at home. He glanced up at her, pushing aside a lock of his thick dark hair that had tumbled over his eyebrow. "Ever read Leland's histories?"

She shook her head. But said not a word. Who was he?

"He says there actually was a King Arthur of Camelot. Says there's evidence to reconstruct Arthur's lost tomb at Glastonbury Abbey. Ever been there?"

Another shake of her head.

"I haven't either. I'd like to, though. What's even more interesting, he identifies the hill fort of Cadbury Castle in Somerset as Camelot. Listen to this." He read: "At the south end of the church of South Cadbury stands Camalat, once a famous castle town, upon a tor or hill, wonderfully strengthened by nature. The people there have heard say that Arthur much resorted to Camalat."

Curiosity tingled her. "Isn't King Arthur just a fairy tale?"

He looked up at her over the page. She realized she had spoken her first sentence in weeks. The smile in his gentle brown eyes told her that he knew it, too. He said, "I like to have all the facts before I make up my mind."

Suddenly, so did she.

"Sit down," he said, "and I'll read you about Queen Guinevere. She was his love, you know. He would have laid down his life for her."

Shyly, Justine perched on the edge of the window seat.

He smiled. "I'm Will. They won't miss us in there." He flipped a page. "Listen to this."

And he read to her for maybe half an hour, maybe an hour, she was too enthralled to notice. By the time he closed the book Justine was curled up in the other corner of the window seat, dreaming of how, if Will ever should need it, she would lay down her life for him.

But the next day he was gone. To Oxford, she was told. Thirteen was when promising young gentlemen started their studies at the university, and Will Croft, Lord Thornleigh's nephew—for that's who they told her he was—was preparing for a life in the law. Justine thought about him often, and whenever she opened a book it was his voice she heard reading, but she did not see him again for eight years. Then, four months ago, at the Queen's Twelfth Night revels at Hampton Court, there he was. Justine's heart had leapt. He was a man now, twenty-one, almost as tall as Lord Thornleigh, but with the same boyish lanky limbs she remembered, the same gentle brown eyes, the same lock of thick dark hair tumbling over his eyebrow. He had looked at her in surprise, as though astonished to find her grown up, too.

"Did you get to Glastonbury and find King Arthur's tomb?" she asked, unable to mask the glow that radiated from her heart.

He smiled. He remembered! "Not yet. It's good to have a mystery or two waiting to be unlocked, don't you think?"

She had danced with him, and wished the music would never end. Not that he was the best dancer. Rather gangly, really. No, it was the way he answered her questions about the Inns of Court in London where he was now studying law—answered as if he were struggling to keep his mind off her. And the way he pushed back the curling lock of hair that kept falling in his eyes—pushed it as if annoyed at it for breaking his concentration on her. By the time he had made of point of dancing with her three more times that night, Justine was sure he felt as she did. Every day since then she had relived the thrill of his hand on her hip in the dance. But, maddeningly, they had seen each other only twice more, both times at Whitehall Palace, surrounded by people, no chance to talk. There might as well have been a wall between them. Tonight she was bursting to open a door in that wall.

She reached the rose garden and passed under its brick entrance arch. Inside, the trellised walls reached as high as her shoulders. The blooms, dusky red in the darkness, perfumed the air. The light was dim, the torches now so far away, but moonlight silvered the foliage. The voices and laughter on the terrace sounded fainter, and Justine's footsteps crunched softly on the gravel path. She stopped. Trellised alleys radiated out from the arch, but she saw no one. A bat flitted down the right-hand alley. In the distance behind her, musicians struck up a tune. *The Queen will be dancing,* she thought.

There was a rustling as from a satin gown. She looked down the left alley. At the far end a figure stood in shadow, her dark red satin cloak the color of claret, like the roses. Justine went to meet her, thinking how odd it was that the hood of the lady's cloak was pulled up, putting her face in even darker shadow. The night was warm; no need for a hood.

"You came," the lady whispered when Justine reached her. The two words carried surprise and relief. And a touch of fear, Justine thought.

"Madam? May I know your name?"

The lady threw back her hood and lifted her head so that the moonlight made her features clear. Justine gasped. Could it be? "Alice?"

A smile. "Justine."

It had been eight years! Justine had been ten when they'd parted, Alice twelve. But she would know Alice Boyer anywhere, the dearest friend of her childhood. "Good heavens!" she cried.

"Shh!"

Justine grabbed Alice's hands in delight, but was immediately shocked at the feel of her skin, as rough as a field worker's. From the time Alice was seven she had been a seamstress in the household of Justine's father. By twelve she was an expert needle-woman, the kind that ladies vied for. But recently, it seemed, her hands had been at work far harder than plying a needle.

Alice flinched at the reaction and pulled her hands free. Justine took in her friend's whole appearance. Under the fine satin cloak she wore a dress as brown as a burr and of a wool almost as coarse. It was frayed at the neckline and smelled faintly of bacon fat. She wore no jewelry. Nor needed any, Justine thought. Though a servant, Alice had a beauty that would put any great lady to shame. Lustrous auburn hair, skin like cream, full lips, and a statuesque figure that gave her the bearing of a duchess.

"I lifted this from the Marchioness," Alice said, fingering the fine cloak. "To get me in here." A sly smile. "What odds she never noticed? She has five others."

Justine was a little shocked but had to laugh. Alice, always the bold one. She remembered how, as a child in her father's great house, Yeavering Hall, she had followed Alice to the top of the bell tower. They had climbed through the window, hopped down to the roof of the great hall, then crawled out along the leads. On their stomachs, heads over the edge of the roof, they had gazed out on the moors that stretched over Northumberland, the cold wind in their faces. Justine had never felt so excited. And she would never have had the courage for such an adventure without Alice leading the way.

"Where have you sprung from?" she asked. "How did you find me? And why have—"

"Shh," Alice said again, imploring.

"Oh yes, of course," Justine whispered, realizing her mistake. She glanced over her shoulder to make sure they were alone. It would be dangerous for Alice if anyone saw her here, a common interloper and, regarding the satin cloak, a thief. The shadowy alley was vacant, no one around. Justine was relieved, and not just for Alice's sake. She had her own secrets to guard. If she were seen with Alice, questions could lead to trouble, for she was not who everyone here thought she was—not a distant Thornleigh relation but the daughter of a traitor. Her father, Sir Christopher Grenville, had helped plan an aborted uprising against Queen Elizabeth. Justine shivered at the thought of him. Eight years ago she had cut her former life adrift, gladly letting it sink under the sea of the Thornleighs' love and care as they gave her their name and brought her up like a daughter. Now, with Alice, that abandoned life had resurfaced.

Alice must have seen the shiver. "Forgive me," she said. "I would not have come if I . . . if I didn't need . . ."

"Need what? Alice, what's wrong?"

"You may as well ask what's right. That tale is shorter."

"Does the Marchioness mistreat you? In your last letter you made her sound a shrew." They had written to each other a few times a year. Justine had been careful to keep the correspondence secret, but she would not have lost the connection with Alice for the world. Though no scholar, Alice sent jesting letters that made Justine laugh. "Is she so hard a mistress?"

"She sacked me."

"Good heavens. When?"

"Christmas. Quite the gift."

"But why?"

"Her son. She didn't like the time he spent below stairs."

With Alice. That was the unspoken, damning detail.

"But how have you got on since then?" Alice's needlework had supported not just her but her sickly parents, too.

"Haven't, not really. Da's leg has festered. Mam prays a lot."

"And you, Alice?"

"Been taking in washing."

Of course, Justine thought in dismay. The chapped, rough hands. "You're far from home. How came you so far south?"

"A man. A silky-talking, honey-voiced bastard of a man. Brought me to London. To marry me, he said. Then left me in a tavern by Holborn Hill. If I never see him again, it'll be too soon." She gave a laugh, but it was all bravado, Justine saw, and it ended in a shudder that Alice could not hide. "Oh, Justine." Tears glinted in her eyes. Justine reached for her hand and squeezed it.

"All I need is a few shillings. Just to get me home. I hate to bother you, and I swear I'll never . . ." She swayed, unsteady on her feet. Justine grabbed her by the shoulders, afraid she might faint.

"Come. Over here." She guided Alice to a stone bench. "Sit down. You look exhausted." No, worse than exhausted, Justine thought in alarm. She looked weak. From hunger? "Where are you staying?"

"Staying?"

"Have you a bed for the night?"

"The stable at the village inn. Straw's bed enough for me."

This appalled Justine. "I'll send a boy to you with some money. In the morning." She would have to wait until breakfast to ask Lord Thornleigh's master clerk; he was in charge of the money she had access to for charities and gifts. Still, she could not ask for more than a few sovereigns. Everything she ever needed or wanted, from books to new clothes to jewelry, was handled by Lady Thornleigh. "I wish I could give you a hundred pounds, Alice. And more. But I'm afraid I have only—" She stopped. "No, wait." She lowered her head and unfastened the clasp of her necklace, a silver chain with a sapphire pendant. "Take this." She took Alice's hand and dropped the necklace in her palm. She pulled off her ring of lapis lazuli, too. "And this."

Alice gaped. "No . . . it's far too much. You can't—"

"Sell them." She folded Alice's fingers around the jewels. "Take the money to your family."

"Justine, I—"

"And you need a position. Let me think." She glanced back toward the festive lights. "I know! I shall speak to Lady Isabel. She's here with her children for the Queen's visit. I dare say she'll be glad to get an expert seamstress." It was a happy thought—until a darker one struck. "Unless . . . do you mind working again at Yeavering Hall?" When her father's treason had shattered Justine's young world, his property had been forfeited. The Queen had given Yeavering Hall and all its lands to the Thornleighs' daughter Isabel and her husband. They lived there now.

"Mind? No," Alice said, still overwhelmed by the jewels. "I'll be right glad to have work anywhere. Ghosts don't bother me."

"Good, then Lady Isabel shall employ you. I promise you, Alice. Leave it to me."

Alice gazed at her, gratitude shining in her eyes. "Your mother would be proud to see you now. So pretty. So kind." Justine waved away the compliment, though it pleased her. She remembered her French mother's quiet, calm ways. Justine had been named after her. She'd died when Justine was seven. Alice asked, "Do you still jabber in French like you did with her?"

"Little need for it," she answered with a shrug. "Only when there's a French diplomat to curtsy to."

Laughter sounded nearby. They both tensed and looked down the alley toward the brick entrance arch. A couple sauntered past, the lady giggling.

"I must go," Alice whispered.

"Yes."

"God bless you, Justine."

They clung to each other for a long moment. Then Alice was gone.

Justine made her way back across the crowded terrace and back to the children, shaken by Alice's plight. She would speak to Isabel first thing in the morning. Employment would go a long way to reducing her friend's woes.

When she reached the three children she was surprised to find Katherine and Robert's mother with them. Frances Thornleigh had kept to her room for the festivities. She was in a kind of mourning. Not officially; no fatal word had come about her husband, Sir Adam, Lord Thornleigh's son, but it had been over a year since he had sailed away in command of his ship, one of a small fleet making a trading voyage to the West Indies. Everyone was anxious about him, but everyone hoped for his return. Frances, however, dragged around as if she were already a widow. Justine felt sorry for her.

Yet she always felt uneasy around her, too. Frances, born a Grenville, was her aunt. She had married Adam Thornleigh long before Justine's father had tried to depose the Queen, and after that calamity Frances had been eager to avoid the taint of her brother's treason and so became a willing accomplice to the Thornleighs bringing up Justine as one of them. She lived in London and did not go out much in public. Justine wasn't sorry for that. Her aunt was a dark reminder of her true blood, and her father's crimes.

"I'm glad you decided to join us, madam," she said, trying to mean it, for she really did pity Frances. Sad and sallow, she looked almost too old to have children as young as Katherine and Robert. At the moment they and their little cousin Nell were poking sticks at the goldfish.

"I was hoping," Frances said, "to ask Sir William Cecil for news of Adam."

"Oh?" Justine's desire to see Will surged back. Cecil was his patron. "Did you find him?"

"No, he is gone."

"Gone?"

"Back to London. Something about the Austrian Archduke's suit for Her Majesty's hand, so I was told."

"At this hour?"

"Affairs of state," Frances said with a disinterested shrug.

Justine felt her hope plunge. If Cecil had gone, so had Will. She had missed her chance. It might be months before they would be in the same place again. His duties kept him in London, at White-hall or Hampton Court or wherever Cecil went. Her place was with Lord and Lady Thornleigh, and it could be weeks before they left Hertfordshire to return to their London house. She suddenly wished the Queen loathed fireworks and was calling for her carriage at this very moment to take her back to London. The longer the Queen stayed, the longer Justine would be away from Will.

"Justine's back!" cried six-year-old Robert. "Now can we go see the fun, Mama? Justine promised. One more hour."

The three small eager faces turned to Justine and she clamped down her disappointment about Will. "I did, didn't I." She turned to Frances, "All right?"

"Of course. Enjoy yourselves." Frances, an affectionate mother, kissed her two children on the tops of their heads, then turned and drifted away toward the house.

Justine looked at her charges. "Well, you lot, what shall we do?"

"To the acrobats!" Robert cried, pointing to the island in the lake where jugglers and tumblers, ringed by torches, performed their antics to an admiring crowd.

"No, storytellers!" his five-year-old cousin Nell insisted.

"Acrobats!" Robert tugged Justine's arm to pull her along the path to the lake.

"Storytellers!" Nell tugged her other arm to go the other way. Though the youngest, she was pulling the hardest.

Justine winced. "Ow!"

"Let her be," Katherine chastised the little ones, always ready to exert her power as the eldest. "I vote for storytellers. Grand-mamma hired them specially for us." On the terrace near the Queen's pavilion, a storyteller held forth under a tent, where several children sat on rugs, listening, like Persian princelings.

Robert broke away and started running down to the shore. "Robert!" Justine called. "Where are you going? Stop!"

"To the boat," he called over his shoulder.

She had to admire his initiative. He was voting with his feet.

"Come on," she said, beckoning the girls. "To the island." She picked up Nell and made for the path to the lake. Katherine accepted Justine's fiat and followed at her heels.

The path to the jetty was spread with pure white cockleshells for the Queen's visit. Justine and the girls passed the people strolling with goblets of wine. One lady led a pet monkey on a leash. Holding Nell, Isabel's youngest, Justine planned how she would approach Isabel in the morning about a position for Alice. She would praise Alice's mastery of the needle, and it would be no lie.

"Hurry," Robert cried as they reached the jetty.

"The last boat," Katherine pointed out.

Justine saw that she was right. Earlier, a half dozen boats had lined the jetty and servants had waited to row guests to the island's entertainments. Now only one boat remained; the rest were at the island. And there was no servant. Robert was untying the boat, about to climb in.

"Wait for us," Justine told him as Nell squirmed in her arms. Nell wriggled free and slipped to the ground and grabbed Justine's leg to hold her back, crying, "No! Storyteller!"

Robert fumbled the line and it slipped into the water. The boat began to drift.

"Catch it!" Justine called.

Robert flopped onto his stomach to try to grab the boat, but his arm was not long enough. Justine pried the little girl away from her leg and dashed to the jetty edge. She dropped to her knees and reached out over the water, stretching to reach the boat, and finally she snatched the bow. She handed the dripping line to Katherine, saying, "Hold this," then pried her skirt loose to get up off her knees. But before she could straighten up, Robert jumped onto her back with a laugh. "Horsey! Horsey!"

Nell plopped down on Justine's foot and hugged her shin. "*You* tell us a story!"

Weighted down with Robert, unable to budge her foot with Nell clamped on it, Justine struggled to keep her balance on the jetty edge, afraid she would tumble over the side, taking the children with her.

Suddenly, the burden lifted from her back. Then a hand pulled Nell off her foot. Free, Justine turned and looked up into the face of Will Croft.

"You are Atlas," he said with a wry smile. "The weight of the world on your back."

She could not think of a single word to say.

Will set Robert down, then said, "Katherine, make fast the boat. And you two," he told the little ones, "stop pestering Mistress Justine or there'll be no candied apricots before bed."

She found her voice. "Thank you, sir. In a moment I fear we would all have been swimming."

He smiled. The breeze toyed with the shirt lacings at his throat above his doublet of moss-green wool. Justine felt pulled into the warmth of his eyes. "You did not go to London," she said, wanting to stay like this, him smiling at her, forever.

He looked perplexed. "London?"

"With Sir William."

"Tonight?"

"About the Austrian Archduke?"

He shook his head, still perplexed. "No. We bide here with my uncle."

Thank goodness! "Only a rumor, then."

"Ah, I see. Yes, they spring up around Sir William like mushrooms in the night."

Again, he smiled, and again words fled Justine. To think that she had intended to tell him her heart. She could not collect enough wit to speak even of the weather.

The children were restless. Robert had climbed into the boat and was struggling with an oar. Katherine had got little Nell to sit still on the jetty edge, but Nell was fidgeting to climb aboard, too. More fireworks burst overhead. Some flew off at angles, skimmed the surface of the lake and sank below, then shot up again with garish flashes and bangs like gunshots.

"We're missing the acrobats," Robert complained.

Will looked at the island. "Is that your destination?" He looked back at Justine, clearly disappointed. "Now? I wanted . . . that is, I'd hoped . . . to speak to you."

Her heart leapt. "Oh?" She wished the children would evaporate. She yearned to hear what he had sought her out to say.

"Look, a fire-eater!" Robert cried, eyes on the island.

"Story," Nell pouted.

"Two competing claims on you, it seems," Will said. His tone turned serious, his voice low. "And I would make it three." He reached out and took her hand.

At his touch, her breath stopped. She felt as if her very heart might stop.

He said, "Mistress Thornleigh, we have not known each other long, but—"

"Long enough."

He looked startled. Happily so. "Long enough, indeed." He squeezed her hand.

"Jugglers! Look!"

Will did not take his eyes from Justine, nor she from him. "I know this is hardly the time nor place—"

"It's perfect," she said, a thrill coursing through her.

"Is it?" He looked eager, hopeful, but not quite trusting his luck. "I would wish perfection of time and place, indeed, if I were to ask you to be my wife. For I would be asking you to take a man who's far from perfect."

All she heard was *wife*. She blurted, "Yes!"

He seemed crestfallen. "Ah . . . I dare say you know my flaws."

She laughed. "No, I mean, yes I *accept*."

He understood then, and his eyes went wide. The air felt charged between them. Fireworks sizzled overhead. On the shore, three fire wheels as tall as trees spun showers of flame in green, gold, and purple. Justine felt sparks shoot through her as Will slipped his arm around her waist and pulled her close. "I love you, Justine," he whispered. She lifted her face to his, yearning for his kiss. He hungered for it, too, she knew. But people were everywhere. He withdrew his arm, clearly conscious that he should not compromise her.

"I'll go and find my uncle," he said, his voice intimate and low. "And get his consent."

"Oh, Will." She had never felt such happiness. Like fire wheels inside her.

He grinned. "And I'll ask for his assurance that we are not cousins, you and I. I don't want to wait for a church dispensation."

He was jesting, she knew. Only royalty required a dispensation. But it sent a shiver up the back of her neck. He thought she was a remote Thornleigh relation. He didn't know who she really was. *And never will,* she silently vowed. She would keep her past life banished forever. But marriage! Overjoyed though she was, this posed a wrinkle she would have to smooth out with Lord Thornleigh. "No, not just yet," she said. "It will be too much of a surprise for him. Let me speak to him first, prepare the way."

"If you think it best."

"I do."

"Can you talk to him tonight? Now?" His wry smile returned. "I told you, I don't want to wait."

Justine wanted him so much she was afraid she might kiss him, never mind the people all around.

"Master Croft?" a voice called.

They both turned. Frances was hurrying down the jetty toward them. "Will Croft, it *is* you," she said, reaching them. She looked pale and a little out of breath. "I come for news. I was looking for Sir William."

"Lady Frances." Will's bow to her was stiff. "How can I help you?"

His sudden coldness shocked Justine. He knew, as everyone connected with the family did, that Adam Thornleigh had been at sea for over a year. Was he really making Frances *ask?* It seemed cruel.

"Has Sir William any word yet of my husband?"

"Nothing." Another stiff bow. "Now, if you will excuse me." He stepped away from her as if from a felon, his face hard. Justine could not account for it. Why should he be so unkind to Frances? Then he said to Justine, his voice warm again, as if they were alone, "I leave you, Mistress Thornleigh, for I would not keep you from your task. And if—"

A man's shout made all three of them turn. It came from the Queen's pavilion. The words were indistinct, but the tone was one of alarm. There was a commotion at the pavilion, people rushing this way and that. "Make way!" a herald cried, and Justine glimpsed Her Majesty moving quickly down the stairs, making for the house. Her ladies rushed after her in a flurry of colorful silks.

What was happening? Was Her Majesty ill? Justine looked for Lord and Lady Thornleigh. In the moving mass of people she could not see them.

The crowd on the lakefront path, too, was suddenly abuzz. The cheerful mood had turned tense. A man leaving the pavilion area on the run came down the cockleshell path and passed the jetty.

"Sir Henry!" Will called to him. "What's amiss?"

The man stopped. "A messenger, Will. News from the north. Have you seen my wife?"

"Not bad news, I hope, sir?" Justine asked.

"You be the judge, mistress," was the enigmatic reply. "Mary, Queen of the Scots, has been routed in battle and has crossed our border. She has arrived in Cumberland with nothing but the clothes she stands up in. She has thrown herself on the mercy of Her Majesty!"

❧ 2 ❧

The Secret

Richard, Baron Thornleigh kept a tell-nothing card player's face as he made his way through the keyed-up crowd milling in his long gallery, his wife Honor at his side. At sixty-eight, Richard had plenty of experience keeping state secrets. The news was big, but he wasn't about to get caught up in the hubbub of his gossiping courtier guests, male and female, all abuzz about the messenger's report that had put a sudden halt to the fireworks: Mary, Queen of Scots, her army defeated, had fled across the Solway Firth in a fishing boat with a handful of supporters and stepped ashore in England as a royal refugee. Richard remembered how a year ago these same courtiers had been buzzing about whether Mary had been complicit in the murder of her husband, the swaggering Lord Darnley. Now he saw faces craning to get a glimpse of him and Honor as they passed, and the question in everyone's eyes was: What would Elizabeth do with her notorious cousin Mary? Well, they weren't going to get anything from him. He didn't know.

He glanced at Honor, proud of her elegant composure as she offered calm smiles and nods to all the inquiring looks he was ignoring. She was a decade younger than he was and still so beautiful he often thought she had scarcely changed since the day they had been married over thirty years ago. They were on their way to Elizabeth's suite. They had spared no expense in having the rooms specially prepared for her visit; now she had called for a hurried consultation there with her councilors, Richard among them. What a foolish uproar his household was in for, he thought. Every lordling and hanger-on was either rushing to get packed to follow Elizabeth, who had said she would leave on the morrow, or rushing about asking for more details *before* packing. Richard groaned inside, knowing his chamberlain would soon be faced with the monumental headache of moving dozens of people out of their rooms, and his master of horse with rousing the grooms and stable boys to make ready the scores of guests' horses. A couple of overeager young gents had already jumped into the saddle and were on the road in the moonlight, eager to be first to bring the gossip to London. Richard wasn't sorry this crowd would soon be gone. Honor might be chagrined that all her meticulous preparations for housing most of Elizabeth's court were coming to so abrupt an end, but it would save him the expense of feeding such an army.

"Our household folk have their work cut out for them," he said to her under his breath as they passed bearded old William Paulet, the Marquis of Winchester, his head cocked as he tried to catch Richard's words. They were approaching the door to Elizabeth's suite. Flanked by two of her palace guards, the door led to the tower where she had three chambers for herself and her ladies.

"As you have your work," she replied quietly. "Richard, you must warn Elizabeth of the danger she is in."

He glanced at her, knowing that beneath the tranquil countenance she put on for their guests, she was as anxious as if Elizabeth were their own daughter facing a highwayman intent on rape. The two of them knew, as their guests did not, of a second messenger who had arrived for Elizabeth, this one bearing a letter from Thomas Percy, Earl of Northumberland, the most powerful lord in England's north. He was claiming the right to take charge of Mary, Queen of Scots as his guest. "It's started," Honor had said grimly. "The faction readying to fight for Mary." Richard was sure she was overreacting—and sure they were not going to see eye to eye on this. But he knew her fears were heartfelt, making her calm front all the more impressive.

A front as false as mine, he thought, wincing at the pins and needles in his left foot. *Please, let it hold off until this meeting with the Elizabeth is over.* Twice this week his foot had gone so numb he had to drag it along the ground as he walked. Luckily, he had been alone both times, in the yard behind the stables. He hadn't told Honor. The numbness came and went, so he was hoping it would eventually just disappear the way the spell of blurred vision had last month. Thank God. With only one good eye, a patch over the one he'd lost three decades ago, he was careful of the other. He would be sixty-nine next month, and after an active lifetime on land and sea he cursed these signs that his body was no longer under his control. He had been captain and master of his own ships, an international trader in wool cloth and successful merchant in the commercial centers of Bruges and Antwerp. He was the owner of tin mines whose operations he oversaw with keen interest and had the lordship of thousands of acres on manors in Hertfordshire, Wiltshire, and Kent, where he took seriously the welfare of hundreds of farming tenants and their families. Decrepitude? Feebleness? It was a state beyond his ken, as foreign as the life of a slave. The prospect horrified him. The only way he could think to deal with it was to simply *not* think of it.

Besides, he had something else on his mind. Something he wasn't sure what to make of, a moment he had glimpsed this evening on the jetty. His ward, Justine, and his nephew, Will. It looked like they'd been about to kiss. It jarred Richard, the liaison so unexpected—yet he rather hoped it was true.

"Your lordship. Your ladyship," the guard said, bowing as he opened the door for them.

They started up the circular stairway. The great house, Honor's design, was barely a year old, and the tower, the last part to be built, was so new that Richard could still smell the masons' stone dust. In daylight it was bright with sunshine from the windows; now the light was from torches in brackets and it glinted off the gold and silver threads of the hanging tapestries. They were alone, climbing the steps, and as Richard heard the door at the bottom close, a tight sigh escaped Honor. *She's as relieved as I am at being out of the throng,* he thought. Yet her determined look told him that this was just the beginning.

"Mary must not be allowed to stay with Northumberland," she said. "Nor even stay in England. You must make that clear to Elizabeth."

"What would you have her do, truss the woman on a horse and slap its rump to bolt back to Scotland?"

"I only wish she would."

"Impossible. Mary is her cousin."

"A dangerous cousin. She must be sent back."

"Abandon her to the men who locked her up? Honor, she's a *queen*. Anointed by God."

She snorted. "A queen does not ride off and leave her supporters leaderless when they need her most. A queen does not think only of herself. Which is all Mary Stuart cares about."

"You are hard on her. And wrong about the power she wields. She's just a weak young woman, beaten, with no influence left. More to be pitied than feared."

"Do not underestimate her. She has been scheming for years to be proclaimed Elizabeth's heir."

"You cannot refute Mary's blood. She's a Tudor and has a claim."

"Which she never lets anyone forget. Northumberland certainly hasn't. He would like nothing better than to see Mary ruling England. A Catholic queen to overturn everything Elizabeth has done."

"Nonsense. England is a Protestant nation now. It's entrenched."

"What's built can be destroyed. Mary could decree an English Inquisition. Burnings, Richard. Never forget."

The old battle over religion. Richard was tired of it. Not that Elizabeth deserved any blame. Her first act on becoming queen nine years ago had been to forge a peace between the skirmishing Catholics and Protestants. She was the only monarch who had ever legalized religious tolerance. He admired that. Honor certainly did; she considered the religious peace more sacred than any tenet of *any* church. No wonder. Across the Narrow Sea the French were massacring Protestants, and the Spanish burned them in the hundreds every month just for refusing to say that the bread of the mass was Christ's actual body. Meanwhile here, despite Elizabeth's ban on the capital punishment of Catholics, the new Puritans could be vicious to any secret priest they hounded out of hiding, hell-bent on shredding his "papist" clothing. The older Richard got, the less patience he had with people fighting over asinine things.

It was why he took heart at what he'd seen pass between the young couple on the jetty. The opposite of fighting. Love. And yet, he wasn't sure he should allow it. Should he put a stop to it for his poor sister's sake? Joan's spirit had been broken by the horrors of the feud that had festered years ago between the houses of Thornleigh and Grenville. But that was the past, as dead as Christopher Grenville himself. Eight years ago, Richard had decided to make peace. It was the reason he had taken in Grenville's daughter. To make a new beginning.

"What do you know about Justine and Will?" he asked.

"Who?"

"Joan's boy. Has Justine talked to you about him?"

Honor looked exasperated. "What has your sister's son to do with the hazard Mary Stuart poses to Elizabeth?"

He let it go. After all, he could be wrong. He might have read too much into that moment he'd glimpsed on the jetty.

A jab in his foot made him clench his teeth. The foot was worse, the pins and needles now a painful grind. He and Honor had almost reached the top of the staircase and he hoped the damn thing would not go numb until he was in Elizabeth's chamber. When he wasn't moving he could hide the problem.

At the top, a landing led to the arched door of her suite. The door was open and he heard men's voices. Their words were indistinct, but it was clearly an argument. He recognized Cecil's voice, and that of Henry FitzAlan, the Earl of Arundel, who was louder. Elizabeth walked past the doorway, listening in silence to the men, her arms folded, head lowered in thought. Then she moved out of Richard's vision. Blanche Parry, a lady-in-waiting, bustled after her with a decanter of wine.

Honor laid her hand on Richard's arm to stop him before he took the last step. She spoke so quietly it was almost a whisper. "Don't pretend you don't understand the threat Mary poses, Richard. You have been Elizabeth's tireless champion. You stood up for her when she was a friendless princess who feared for her life. You fought for her rights. Stood by her at her coronation. You cannot now let Mary undo everything Elizabeth has wrought by claiming to be her heir."

"Then who shall inherit? Tell me that. Elizabeth refuses to marry and produce an heir of her body. Unless she does, her legitimate heir is the Queen of Scots."

"She would wrench the realm back to Catholicism."

"That's a lesser evil than civil war, which is the fate of a realm with no proclaimed heir. I remember, as a boy, the misery the warring, great houses of York and Lancaster left in their wake. Decades of misery. It could happen again. Over-mighty lords battling for power, spilling Englishmen's blood. If Elizabeth should die childless—"

"Die?" she said, vexed.

"It's possible."

"You men. You all want to force her into a marriage, however wretched."

"Nonsense. I want no such thing. But if she should die—"

"Again—die!"

"She cannot live forever."

"She is in her prime!"

He bit back a retort. It was pointless to argue. "You're right," he said with a weary sigh. "In her prime. Like me, eh?"

His sudden capitulation startled her. Then she smiled, amused—his reward for having offered the olive branch. She said warmly, "You have been in your prime for forty years, my love." Even her eyes smiled. He had always loved that. She had lived through perils that would have left a lesser woman a quivering husk, but nothing stopped Honor. Challenges fueled the inner flame that had always been the source of her beauty. Looking at her, he suddenly knew he wasn't wrong about his nephew and Justine. He had seen the way Will looked at the girl. He remembered the feeling, with Honor, that glorious hell of wanting.

"My lord?" Blanche Parry said, coming out to the landing. "Her Majesty thought it must be you. Do come in."

"Yes, we're coming," he said.

Blanche went back in, and Honor turned on the step to go down.

"You're not joining us?" Richard asked her. "She values your opinion as much as Cecil's."

"No, I must see to our household. Must impose *some* order on this decampment."

He was about to go on up the last step when she gripped his elbow. "Richard, I warrant she will refuse Northumberland's request to take charge of Mary. She'll have someone tame like Lord Scrope manage her for the moment. But after that, she'll need to send someone to Mary that she can trust. Someone with backbone. Ask her to send *you*."

The decampment, as Lady Thornleigh called it, took days. It was the most frustrating week Justine had ever spent. Will's marriage proposal still had her atingle, and she didn't know how she had managed to keep quiet about it for so long. That night under the fireworks she had been almost jumping out of her skin wanting to tell Lord Thornleigh and get his blessing, but the blast of news about the Scottish queen had ruined everything. Everyone had gone slightly mad, as though Mary were some tempestuous goddess who had sailed down from the clouds to bedazzle Englishmen. Lord Thornleigh got caught up in meetings with Elizabeth, and when Elizabeth left the next morning Will left, too, with Sir William Cecil. For days Rosethorn House was in a commotion as courtiers and their entourages left, one after another, their baggage packhorses following, and then, once they had all gone, the household workers, under the direction of Lady Thornleigh, began packing up to remove to the Thornleighs' London house. Justine had watched the bustle in aggravated silence. With affairs of state on her guardians' minds, plus the domestic upheaval, it had been impossible to talk to them of what mattered most urgently to her: Will.

She wanted to blurt it out to them, and might have rashly done so at one of the rushed meals if it hadn't been for her promise to Alice. That task—getting Alice settled—had kept her busy, thank goodness. She had spoken to Lady Isabel, the Thornleighs' daugh-

ter, praising Alice's needlework skills so highly she had easily convinced Isabel to hire her. She'd even managed to sneak a brief
meeting with Alice in the village, by the pond behind the inn, to
tell her the good news. They had shared a hug, and a laugh, then a
tear at parting yet again, and had promised to write. When Isabel
and her husband and their children had set out for the Great North
Road to make the journey back to Yeavering Hall, Alice was
among the servants who went with them. Justine felt very satisfied
at having arranged it all so cleverly.

Now she meant to get satisfaction in her own affairs. She had
been patient, but she could wait no longer to tell Lord Thornleigh.
He and her ladyship were comfortably settled back in London at
their house on Bishopsgate Street, and this morning at breakfast
Justine had got a lovely note from Will urging her to speak to his
uncle or else *he* would. His impatience excited her. It was time.
Past time, in fact, for Lord Thornleigh would be leaving soon for
the north. Elizabeth was sending him as her emissary to Mary. Justine wondered if he really was well enough to make the journey.
She had been worried about him ever since she had noticed him
leaving the solar one morning during the decampment from
Rosethorn. He had been walking with a limp.

"Have you hurt your foot, sir?" she had asked.

"What?" He'd stopped, startled to see her in the corridor. "No,
I'm fine. Foot fell asleep when I was reading." He didn't move,
as though waiting for her to carry on down the stairs. "Off you
go, now."

It sounded like he was hiding something. She went down the
staircase, but at the bottom she glanced back at him. He was moving toward the top step, dragging his foot. It made her gasp. It
looked horrible.

She hurried back up to him. "Are you ill, my lord?"

He heaved an angry sigh. She knew the anger was not for her,
but himself. "It comes and goes. Could be this changeable weather. Or more likely too much wine." He waved her away. "Go on.
It'll pass."

She obeyed, but not because she believed him. She saw his humiliation and would not increase it for the world. He had been so

kind to her, from the very first day when he had found her hiding in the tithe barn at Yeavering Hall. She had been there since the fire that had burned down the mill, the calamity that had devastated her life. Her father had been in the mill. Terrified by what she'd seen that night, she had hidden in the cavernous stone barn, for how many days she wasn't sure. Then one morning she awoke in the straw roused by the sound of the huge door creaking open. She blinked in the shaft of sunshine where dust motes danced in the air and saw a man stride in, a man older than her father. He found her. He looked like a dark angel, tall and still, standing over her in his fine black cape and his leather eye patch, his sword agleam. He told her his name was Thornleigh and gave her a sad smile and said, "Don't be frightened, child."

She was halfway down the stairs by the solar when he called softly after her, "Justine." She turned. He said, "Don't mention my foot to her ladyship, will you."

He *was* hiding it. That made her more anxious, even as she curtsied and said, "As you wish, sir." Leaving him, she wondered why Lady Thornleigh, who was devoted to him, had not noticed his malady. Perhaps the thought of her vigorous husband failing had never crossed her mind. After all, Justine herself had never seen him even sick.

And, indeed, now that they were back in London she had seen no sign of his malady since that episode outside the solar. He was his usual self: active and engaged. The problem must have cleared up, she thought. Thank goodness. She needed him engaged about Will.

She had chosen the hour carefully, a drowsy afternoon, the quiet broken only by the spattering of a cold spring rain against the windows. The settled hush of normal life lay over the great hall where they had finished dinner, she and Lord and Lady Thornleigh; the chamberlain and steward and their wives who had dined with them as usual had just gone. The maids were clearing away the last of the crockery to the kitchen. Lord Thornleigh was finishing his wine and Lady Thornleigh was dabbing her mouth with a napkin. The fire crackled, and one of the dogs who were stretched out on the hearth, Magnus or Erasmus, snored as he dreamed of rabbits. Justine took a breath, about to broach her news, when the clerk,

Curnutt, came in with an armload of documents for Lord Thornleigh to take on his journey north. Justine watched in frustration at this disruption as Lord Thornleigh got up to examine a scroll that Curnutt spread out on the table. Lady Thornleigh, sitting beside him, leaned over to read it silently, too. Justine got to her feet, determined. Yet she hesitated. Should she interrupt?

"Yes, my dear?" Lady Thornleigh said, looking up at her.

"This one's for Lord Scrope," Lord Thornleigh told Curnutt, rolling up the scroll.

"What is it, child?" The smile in Lady Thornleigh's eyes was teasing. "You look like you're bursting to speak."

"And these, my lord?" the clerk asked, setting down a sheaf of papers.

"I want to marry," Justine said.

That made them all look at her.

Lady Thornleigh seemed amused. "Anyone in particular, or just any individual who can grow a beard?"

"Will Croft. I want Will."

Lady Thornleigh's smile vanished. It was clear she was completely taken aback. She looked up at her husband. Justine caught the look of alarm that passed between them.

Lord Thornleigh said brusquely to his clerk, "That's all for now. I'll look at these later."

Curnutt bobbed a bow of the head to them both, gathered the papers, and padded out.

"I'm sorry to surprise you," Justine said, eager to dispel their obvious concern. "I know it must seem sudden."

"It's not that," Lord Thornleigh said.

They both looked at her with faces so grave, Justine felt a prickle of apprehension. The awful thought struck that they had some other man in mind for her. "I am not free," she said, making it a clear warning. "I love him."

Lady Thornleigh blinked in dismay. "And does he return your feelings?"

"He does," her husband murmured.

She shot him a look. "You *knew* of this?"

"Suspected."

"Good gracious," she said, a mere whisper. They both regarded Justine again in a way that made her very nervous.

"If you were planning a match for me elsewhere, I am sorry to disappoint you. But Will is . . . well, he's wonderful. And we have an understanding. I want to marry him. Please, won't you give us your blessing?"

Lord Thornleigh's grave face softened. "There is no other match in hand. Again, it's not that."

Thank heaven! "Then what? I will do anything to please and obey you, my lord, my lady. Except give up Will. Please understand. I have given him my promise. And my heart."

A gentle smile crept over Lord Thornleigh's features. "So I see."

His wife, though, was not smiling. "Justine, I have only one question. Does Will know who you are?"

Ah, now *this* problem she was prepared for. "No," she said. "Nor do I see why he ever should. He believes what we have told everyone, that I am your distant relation. That's that."

"And when he asks you about your parents? Will you spin some tale?"

"I'll say we lived in the north. They died. That should satisfy him."

"Lived where?"

"York," she invented on the spot.

"How did they die?"

"In a shipwreck."

"Where were they sailing to?"

"Portugal."

"Why?"

"A wedding."

"Of your Portuguese relations?"

She hesitated, realizing how foolish it sounded.

"You see." Lady Thornleigh shook her head. "Lies will not do. Your must tell Will who you really are."

"Tell him . . . ?" The shame roiled up like sickness, a bitterness in her mouth. "About my father?"

"Yes."

They waited for her to answer. She could not. The thought of Will knowing she was the daughter of a traitor made her feel ill. In the silence, rain spattered the windows.

Lord Thornleigh said, as though wanting to ease her pain, "I am happy for you, Justine. Will's a fine young man. And a clever lawyer. As Cecil's protégé he has a promising future ahead of him."

She could have thrown her arms around his neck. "Then you approve!"

"I do. That's not the question here. Her ladyship is right. You have to tell him the truth."

"But why?" It came out like a child wailing, which humiliated her, sharpening her dismay at what they were asking of her.

"Because of who *he* is," Lady Thornleigh said. "If it were any other man you might consider keeping your secret. But not Will. Not the son of Geoffrey Croft."

"Why not?" His father was dead, she knew. What was so special about him? What were they hiding? "Tell me," she demanded.

Again, they exchanged a dark look of complicity. Lady Thornleigh said, "Because our families..." She faltered. "Our two houses, Grenville and Thornleigh. There was once much hatred between us. And bloodshed."

Justine gaped at her. "Do you mean . . . a feud?"

"Yes."

"Why? How? What happened?"

Lady Thornleigh held up her hands. "I have done my best for years to forget it. I don't want to dredge up details. What's past is past."

Anger shot up in Justine. Why had they never told her this?

"The point is that Will, I feel sure, has not forgotten," Lady Thornleigh continued. "The violence between our families led to . . ." Again, she faltered.

Lord Thornleigh said, "It was how he lost his father."

Justine felt a clutch of panic, as though Will stood on heaving earth, reaching out to her but slipping away. "But . . . that was years ago. I was a child. And he is not the kind to hold a grudge."

"No, he has a generous spirit," Lord Thornleigh agreed. "But his love of the law makes him see things in black and white, right and wrong. And one wrong that has marked him is that your family, the house of Grenville, destroyed his family."

"I'm *not* a Grenville. Not in my heart. I'm one of you. Will knows that. He will want to marry me."

"Good," Lady Thornleigh said warmly. "Then tell him the truth. Make it right, my dear. You cannot go into this marriage based on a lie."

"We are with you, Justine," Lord Thornleigh said. "The past died with your father. Tell the truth and claim the future. You and Will."

Lies. They spun like cinders in Justine's head. Shaken, she had come to the long gallery on the third floor to be alone, to think. It was the family's quiet place for games of chess, backgammon, or cards, or a quiet stroll on a rainy day, or an intimate chat. No one was here except two maids strewing herbs on top of freshly laid floor rushes. They bobbed quick curtsies when they saw her, barely pausing as they continued to scatter lavender and rosemary sprigs from the basket each girl balanced on her hip. Concentrating, they backed up with slow steps, moving away from her down the long room. The perfume of the lavender scented the damp air.

Yes, she had obediently told Lord and Lady Thornleigh, *I will tell Will. I promise.* She had lied. She would not tell Will that she had been born a Grenville. The very name made her shiver. She would not tell him—not now, not after they were married, not ever. It horrified her to think what he might have done if she had confessed it to him that night of the fireworks, confessed in all innocence, before she'd known about the feud, the bloodshed. *"It was how he lost his father."* The truth would have killed his love. He would never have proposed. It was impossible even to consider telling him now. To tell him would be to lose him.

She had stopped, waiting for the maids to leave, and looked down at the lavender by her foot to hide the anger that coursed through her again. She had lied to her guardians, but so had they. Was it not a lie to keep the past violence between the two families a secret from her? They should have told her. Should have warned her. Should not have kept her in ignorance like a stupid child.

Well, she would not let her chance at happiness with Will be snatched from her. She was not responsible for bad things other people had done.

She saw no obstacle to keeping her secret. The Thornleighs would not speak of it themselves and would believe what she would tell them in a day or two: that she had told Will the truth and it had made no difference to him. They would gladly let the matter rest there and consent to the marriage, for they had no wish to make it known that they had misled everyone about Justine, about her tainted blood. As for Frances, Justine's aunt, she would not speak up either. Frances had cut all ties to her Grenville kin when she had married Adam Thornleigh. She wanted no stain from her brother's treason.

I can get away with it, Justine thought, her hope crushing any doubt. *And why shouldn't I? Everyone will be happier this way.*

But there was another lie, one lodged deep in her breast like a stone. Eight years ago it had buried itself there. It had burrowed so deep and lay so still, she had given it less and less thought as the months and years passed and eventually had all but forgotten it. Now it shifted, jarred by Lord Thornleigh's words. *"The past died with your father."*

Restless, she went to the window, crushing the lavender under her shoe. She hugged herself as she looked down on Bishopsgate Street where the rain made a muck of mud and horse dung on the cobbles. Merchants, clerks, and servants moved briskly as they came and went from the Merchant Taylors' Hall across the street, their shoulders hunched under the downpour. Pack mules plodded, their drovers stoic in the rain. Farmers' carts clattered.

She had lied from that very first day when Lord Thornleigh had found her hiding in the stone tithe barn at Yeavering Hall. Lied by what she had not told him—not told anyone—about whom she'd seen the night of the fire. She could smell the smoke, remembering. Smoke so acrid it had woken her in her bed at Yeavering Hall, coughing. Servants, woken by it, too, were dashing about in nightdress.

"It's the mill! It's up in flames!"

"The master's there!"

Father! she thought in panic. The household folk rushed down to the river, men and women alike, to see to the blaze. Justine crossed the courtyard in her bare feet, no one stopping her, the last servants dashing past her toward the riverside mill. She could see, over the courtyard wall, the orange glow of the flames, and black smoke billowing against the moon. Cinders, spiraling up . . .

Later, the servants came straggling back, dazed and exhausted from trying to put out the flames. "The master," she heard a footman hoarsely tell a lame kitchen girl who had stayed behind. "Burned alive, he was!" The next day the house was in disorder, the servants at loose ends, many looking at Justine in pity. Then the Queen's men, over a dozen on horseback, thundered into the courtyard, and the servants' talk turned to terrified whisperings. "Treason!" they breathed to one another in fear. "The master plotted against the Queen!" Frightened, Justine ran to the tithe barn to hide. She heard them calling her name, looking for her, but after a couple of days the calling stopped as if they'd given up. She had the stream behind the barn for water, and at nights she crept into the kitchen, took bread and dried apples, then scurried back to her hiding place. She watched the house for days. Some servants fled. The ones who stayed seemed stupefied. Cinders from the mill still drifted over the courtyard.

Hiding was the only way she could deal with her fear at what she had seen when she'd stood barefoot in her nightdress as the household had swarmed down to the mill. All alone in the courtyard, she had heard coughing. She looked around. No one. Down at the mill people were shouting, but around her it was quiet. She heard the coughing again. It came from behind the stable door. The courtyard was dark in the shadow of the great house, but moonlight struck the stable door. Justine went toward it, the cobbles cold on her feet. The door flew open and she lurched back as a horseman bolted out. He swerved to miss her with a jerk of the reins. The horse reared in alarm. Justine gasped at the sight of the man. His clothes were tatters, black with soot. His eyes were white as eggshells, his hair a wild thicket matted with cinders. His mouth opened, a red slash, as he coughed.

She almost fell to her knees in shock. "Father!"

"Hush!"

"They think you're in the mill! Dead!"

"Come here." His voice was dry, sharp. "Justine, come!"

She inched closer. The horse's flesh quivered. Her father's breeches reeked of smoke. "Tell no one you saw me," he said. "You hear me? For my sake, and for yours." He reached down and grabbed the throat of her nightdress. She flinched at his blackened fingers, his frantic grip. "If you tell, they will kill me. And hurt you. Understand? Tell *no one.*"

He tossed at her feet a leather pouch the size of her hand. It clinked as it hit the ground. "Gold," he said in a voice strangled by fury and regret. "It's all I can give you."

He galloped off into the night.

She stood a long time gazing after him at the blackness before she picked up the pouch. She never saw her father again. And never told a soul.

❧ 3 ❧

The Exile's Return

Sir Christopher Grenville, at forty-three, had left his youth behind and for eight years had lived a bitter life abroad, but he was neither too old nor too hardened to appreciate a pretty woman. He was watching her across the market square. Though a servant, and dressed in plain gray, she was a beauty. Christopher's hope was high that she had what he wanted. Information.

Leaning against the wall of the alehouse, he kept his eye on her despite the streams of people eddying between them in this bustling heart of the village of Wooler. Beyond the village was the barren moorland of Northumberland, its population sparse, but people came from miles around for the weekly market. Christopher felt a pang at the sights that had once been so familiar—the farmers plodding on donkeys and on foot; the farmwives carrying baskets of onions, radishes, beans, and wheels of cheeses for sale; the customers haggling, strolling, gossiping. One old crone had a pole yoked across her shoulders with a goose hanging upside down at each end, trussed and squawking. A couple of boys chased an escaping calf. A churchwarden patrolled the crowd, alert for thievery or lewdness. Whiffs of burning charcoal and pork fat drifted from a brazier where a man was cooking bite-sized morsels of the crisped meat and selling them impaled on sticks. It had been eight years, yet Christopher could swear that nothing in the village had changed. What a bittersweet feeling to be home, and far more bitter than sweet. Once, all these common folk would have bowed to him as he passed, the lord of the manor, and scurried to win his favor. Now they looked at him dully, as though he were one of them. He was home, but still in exile.

The beauty he was watching stood talking to a traveling draper at his cart festooned with gaudy scarves. The cart's awning was draped with ribbons, and its open end formed a counter for bolts of broadcloth, worsted, cambric, fustian, dimity, poplin, and taffeta. The girl was dreamily fingering a ribbon of emerald silk as long as her sleeve that fluttered from the awning. Then, businesslike, she set to inspecting a bolt of garnet-red sarcenet. She had good taste, Christopher thought with approval.

He had watched her that morning as she left Yeavering Hall and had followed her here, already guessing where she was headed. He knew the shire: Wooler held a market every Thursday as it had for centuries. Besides, she was not on foot but rode a donkey though the village was less than three miles from Yeavering Hall and the day was fair, the rolling Cheviot Hills basking in the June sunshine. The donkey was meant to carry home her purchases.

Twice he had lost sight of her in the noisy market square where oxen bellowed from the livestock pens, and traders at their stalls shouted "What do ye lack?" to passing customers. Christopher welcomed the clamor and bustle, for he had found that in a crowd he could move about unnoticed. Still, he was taking a risk in coming so close to Yeavering. A risk in coming back to England at all. He accepted the danger. For Mary Stuart he would hazard anything. In France, he had hungrily followed the news about her, rejoicing at the report last month that she had escaped from the heretics who had dethroned her and imprisoned her, then despairing to hear she had been routed on the battlefield, and rejoicing again when he heard she had fled for sanctuary in England. Exhilarated and downcast in turns, his turmoil had been as intense as if he'd been fighting and fleeing at her side. The moment he heard she was safe and settled in Carlisle near the Scottish border, he had set sail from France. He had come home with a mission. He would do anything in his power to restore Mary to her throne. Without Mary, he had nothing.

First, though, he burned with a private need for what this local beauty could give him. He had to get her alone.

She was moving—gathering up her bought bolts of cloth, making for the edge of the square. Christopher pushed off from the alehouse and strode through the crowd to the draper's stall.

"Give me all your ribbons," he ordered the man as he pulled a purse from his doublet.

"*All*, sir?"

"You heard me." He tossed a handful of gold coins on the counter. The draper's eyes went wide at the windfall. Christopher craned to keep his eye on the beautiful girl. "*Move*, man."

He found her beside her donkey, snugging the cloth bolts into panniers slung over the animal's rump.

"Going home so soon?"

Startled, she looked up at him. "God's teeth, you frighted me."

"Fright you? Not I, mistress. I mean to make you smile. Will you share a pot of ale with me?"

She scoffed. "You're a bold one, you are. Out of my way. I must be off."

"Before you've got what you came for?" He slipped the emerald ribbon from his sleeve, the silk cool as it slid past his wrist. "Why leave without what you want?"

She blinked at him. "You were watching me?"

"What man could not?" That was the truth. She had green eyes to match the silk, skin like cream, and a body made for a man's pleasure. "Look, I have more." He opened the satchel slung over his shoulder to let her see the jumble inside of ribbons, scarves, and braided gold cord for trim.

"You're a trader?"

"Not I, fair one. Merely an admirer. And these pretty things, I can tell, are your heart's desire."

She looked wary, one hand still on the donkey's back, but glanced at the colorful silky potpourri with a longing she could not hide. "Not for me, for my lady."

"Ah, but do keep some for yourself."

"I have no coin for *any*. Worsted and cambric are what I came for, and worsted and cambric are what I'll go with."

"No coin needed. These are yours." He lifted her hand off the donkey's back and sank it inside the satchel. Off balance at his abruptness, she stumbled a step closer to him. "Let me go," she said. "I cannot be seen like this. Talking to a strange man."

He held her hand firmly inside the satchel, their fingers together among the ribbons. "It cannot be strange for any man to be smitten by your beauty."

She looked at him in earnest, as though struck by something she saw in his face. She did not try to lift her hand. "You're not from here. Who are you? What's your name?"

"Christophe."

"What kind of name is that?"

"French."

"Aha, I *thought* you seemed different." She pulled her hand out of the satchel. "You're no Englishman, then."

"Oh, but I am. Merely accustomed to what they called me in France. And what do people call you?"

She hesitated, then seemed to decide on taking a chance. "Alice," she said forthrightly. "Alice Boyer."

The name sounded vaguely familiar. At Yeavering Hall he'd once had a gardener called Boyer. He supposed this might be the man's daughter.

"Christophe, eh?" she said. "Is that your first name or last?"

Too many questions. "Both."

She laughed. "Monsoor Christophe Christophe. What cheek." She snugged down the flap of the pannier, preparing to go. "I know a tosser when I see one."

"Not so, fair one. I was once a gentleman."

"Gentleman?" She eyed his doublet of plain brown wool, his dusty breeches. "That's a lark."

"Hard times, sadly, have reduced my state."

"You're a coxcomb, you are. I know your kind."

He took hold of her chin, forcing her to look at him. "Hard

times, I tell you. I now earn my bread as a clerk. Yet I spent my last sovereign on these fine bits of frippery just to talk to you."

She looked him in the eye. "Or you filched them."

"They're yours, if you'll meet me someplace where we can talk."

She looked tempted. Then amused. "Talk, eh? And for *talk,* all this frippery's free?"

"Free as air. Where are you bound?"

"Yeavering Hall. It's on the road to—"

"I know it. Meet me on the way?"

He rode well ahead of her and reached the hamlet of Kirknewton, sleepy at the best of times and almost silent now with most of its inhabitants at the Wooler market. Christopher brought his horse to a halt beside the stone church named for St. Gregory and looked up at its squat Norman tower. From headstones in the graveyard a spray of starlings fanned up into the sky. He took the satchel of ribbons and went inside. The church was deserted. Striding through the cool air of the nave, he remembered attending the wedding of his chamberlain's daughter here and standing nearest the altar, lord of most of the wedding guests. A bitter thought. Now, in the garb of a lowly clerk, dusty from his ride from the coast, his appearance might induce a churchwarden to guard the offering box.

He stopped for a moment in front of the altar and grunted in disgust. Altar? To use the word was sacrilege. It was a mere communion table draped with a plain cloth, the Protestant way. Vile heresy, instituted throughout the country by England's heretic queen, Elizabeth. The drabness looked all the more shocking to him after kneeling for mass at the magnificent jeweled altars of Catholic France in the years he'd been away.

He took the steps to the belfry two at a time, and at the top he went straight for the window. It was unglazed, and the wind moaned past the stone casement. A finger of breeze lifted Christopher's fair hair, which he wore long, chin length, in the French style. He pushed it back from his eyes and gazed across the valley of the River Glen and up the barren mounds of the Cheviot Hills, to the cluster of buildings that hugged the shoulder of a hill, and the grand house at their core: Yeavering Hall. Though small at this distance, the house was a huge and constant presence in his heart. Once it had been his. Now it was in the hands of his enemy, the Thornleighs. Christopher had endured hard years of exile in France, but he prayed to have justice one day. Mary stood next in line for the English throne, since the heretic Elizabeth had no child, and he ached for the day Mary would take her proper place as England's queen. *And when she does I will take back from Thornleigh what is mine.*

A donkey brayed. He looked down. Alice was tying the animal to a beech tree near the church door.

"Up here," he called to her.

Turning from the window, he opened the satchel and worked quickly. He hung the colored ribbons and scarves and braided gold cord from every timber of the bell's casement. A few minutes later, when Alice stepped into the belfry, she beamed at the sight.

"Lord!" she cried with a laugh. "What a show!"

"Not more lovely than you." He draped a crimson silk ribbon as long as his arm around her neck. He stroked her cheek. She pulled back, but only far enough to give the message that she was not so easily had. Not a message that said *stop.* It was all he needed. He slipped her cotton cap off her head. She gave a small gasp at the liberty. "Try the ribbon in your hair," he said, tossing her cap aside. He slid his fingers into her hair and brought the auburn waves tumbling down around her shoulders. She bit her lip, but gave him a smile of adventure, then lifted the ribbon in both hands and wound it around her head. Her eyes half closed as she savored its silken feel.

Christopher glanced at the window, at its view of his property. He had been gone so long, he craved information. "What do you do at Yeavering Hall, enchantress?" He took down a jade-colored scarf and draped it around her shoulders. "You could dance the dance of the seven veils and cast a spell, I warrant."

She smiled at his jest. "I'm my lady's needlewoman."

"And who is your lady? I passed through these parts years ago. The Hall belonged then to the Grenvilles. Does it still?"

"Good Lord, no. Not for many a year. The master was a rank traitor. He's dead. His property was forfeit."

"Who is lord there now?"

"The son-in-law of a baron."

He stared at her, taken aback. Had Thornleigh's wife died and he'd married a peer's daughter? "Which baron is that?"

"Richard, Lord Thornleigh."

So, the man had wangled *himself* a baronetcy. It curdled Christopher's stomach. His enemy had risen to riches. *While I drifted in France, an outcast.* "So, this Lord Thornleigh does not live at the Hall?"

She shook her head as she tugged down another silk ribbon, this one of buttercup yellow. "No, in Hertfordshire." There was pride in her voice. "I just visited them."

That surprised him. "My, you have friends in high places. How so, fair one?"

"I know his lordship's ward."

He was not interested in her acquaintances, only in Thornleigh. "What is his seat?"

"What?"

"His home."

"Who?"

"The baron. In Hertfordshire."

"Oh, it's called Rosethorn House."

"And how does he fare? Is he hale?"

She shrugged. "I suppose."

"And his wife?"

"What a lot of questions. Why do you care about them?"

"It's always good to know who is in favor and who is out."

She left off examining the yellow ribbon to look at him over her shoulder as though touched with suspicion. He could not let that continue. He kissed her neck to distract her. She let him. He felt her small shiver, one of pleasure. "Well," she murmured, her tone of pride returning, "they are very much *in* favor, for they are friends of Her Majesty. That's right, Queen Elizabeth herself! My friend is their ward, and she has been to court, Justine has. Been in the same room as the Queen!"

He froze. "Did you say . . . Justine?"

"Aye. Fancy that, face-to-face with Her Majesty. I'd not be able to get up off my knees for trembling."

He was dumbfounded. Could it be his daughter? He had lost track of her—had hoped and assumed that after he had fled she'd been sent to stay with the wife of his late brother in Essex. He had not dared write to his sister-in-law about Justine, for he needed everyone to believe that he had died in the fire. *No,* he thought now, *this must be another girl.* Yet *Justine* was not a name used in England. It had been his wife's name, French. "This ward of Lord Thornleigh, how came she to befriend you?"

"Oh, we were friends before she went to him." She was winding the yellow ribbon around her wrist, round and round, like a bracelet. "We were girls together here, at the Hall. She was the master's daughter, the traitor I told you of."

He felt a clutch of something like panic. *It is my Justine!* "She . . . lives now with Thornleigh?"

She nodded. "He took her in, and lucky for her, poor girl, for who would want the penniless child of a traitor? She loves his lordship and the baroness his wife. Loves them like she was their own."

Fury flooded him. Damn Thornleigh! The man and his brood had stolen everything from him. Land, property, home. *He stole my life. Even stole my daughter!*

Alice was looking at him with a strange light in her eyes. "It's a funny thing—you'll think me brainsick—but when you first spoke to me at the market you put me in mind of her." She shrugged with a smile and tapped the side of her head as though to say she was a lunatic. "Too much sun, I warrant."

He wasn't listening. He was too filled up with rage. A rage that boiled and blistered. It needed out. He snatched the tail of the yellow ribbon she had wound around her wrist and with it he yanked her to him. She gave a small gasp, but she didn't pull back. He grabbed her other wrist and wrapped the ribbon around it in a flash, then tied the ends together, making silken manacles that bound her hands. She blinked in surprise. And in pleasure? He didn't know, and cared less. He shoved her against the wall, her back by the window so he could see Yeavering Hall. *Mine*, was his thought as he pulled up her skirt, his eyes on his stolen house.

"Hey!" she cried.

Mine, as he fingered her and felt himself stiffen.

"Stop that!"

Mine, as he wrenched his codpiece aside, ready to ram into her as he wanted to ram a blade into Thornleigh's heart.

"Ow! That hurts! *Stop!*"

He covered her mouth with his hand to keep her quiet and to pin her head against the wall. Her tied-together hands were caught between their bodies, and with his knee he forced her legs apart. She squirmed, but he was stronger.

She bit his palm. He flinched at the pain and whipped his hand away.

Breathless, she wrenched her manacled hands up to his face. "Bastard!" Her fingers were rigid to scratch him. He jerked his face aside and she missed. With a grunt of fury she gripped his hair and yanked. His hair came off his head.

She gasped at his shorn scalp. Blinked at the wig in her hand. Then let it go as if it were diseased. It dropped to the floor like a severed head.

Horror filled her eyes as she gaped at him. He knew what she was seeing. The burned side of his head that the wig had covered. The red ear shriveled from the flames. The skin, taut and shiny, over half his scalp where no hair grew.

A breath of shock escaped her. "All your questions . . . about Justine. About the Hall. You're *him*. The master!" She shrank back in fear. "Sir Christopher."

He didn't know what to do. He wanted to push the words back into her mouth, push the discovery back into her head, make it disappear. He could not let a report get out that he was alive, and home. As a traitor, he would hang.

She seemed to realize it at the same moment. She lurched aside, so quickly he was not prepared for it. He lunged for her, but she was already bolting past him, making for the open door. He snatched up his wig from the floor and jammed it back on his head, then grabbed a length of braided gold cord from among the hanging ribbons and went after her, running down the steps. She raced to the bottom, her hair flying.

He caught up to her as she ran down the nave. He snatched the back of her dress and she staggered to a halt. It unbalanced him and they tumbled together.

"Let me go!"

She struggled to her knees, encumbered by her tied-together hands. He got to his feet faster. They were both panting. He whipped the cord around her neck. Her hands flew to the cord to claw it away, but he twisted it tight. She gagged. She flailed at him. Her body thrashed. He twisted the cord tighter. He held it firm, unyielding, as she struggled.

She weakened. Then slumped.

He let go the cord. She fell to the floor with a soft thud. Dead.

Christopher straightened, catching his breath. He forced his mind onto what mattered. His mission to get to Mary. Had he jeopardized it? He cursed himself for his damnable selfish detour. No time to waste, now. *Get to Carlisle*, he told himself. *To Mary.*

He dragged the girl's body behind the altar. No one would find it until Sunday. By then, he'd be seventy miles west of here.

A scrape sounded behind him. He whipped around. No one in the nave. The sound came again, to his right. The vestry door stood ajar. He hurried into the vestry. Across the room the door to the churchyard was open. A figure was running away through the graveyard, round the headstones, running too fast to catch.

Christopher turned back. *Get to Carlisle*, he told himself as he walked down the silent nave. His hand wasn't quite steady as he mounted his horse and turned its head for the western road. He calmed as he trotted on, bending his thoughts to the tasks that lay ahead. He would have justice. For himself. For Mary. For God.

❧ 4 ❧

Will's Gambit

It wasn't the first time that Will Croft, assisting Sir William Cecil, had been in the presence of Queen Elizabeth, but it was definitely the most important. For Will, it was a golden chance to make his mark.

He had been up for hours making sure he had Sir William's papers in order, arranged by date, with the most pertinent on top, and going over once again all his own notes about Mary, Queen of Scots. He had arrived an hour early at Whitehall Palace, and now he stood at the lectern desk in a gilded chamber that was part of Elizabeth's suite, ready to hand Sir William whatever documents, scrolls, letters, or lists he might request. Will was determined to use the crisis with the Scottish queen to prove that he was capable of any commission his patron cared to entrust to him. Sir William was Elizabeth's closest adviser, and the crisis had made him all the more invaluable to her. Will meant to become invaluable to Sir William because the sooner he could distinguish himself and gain advancement, the sooner he could marry. *Justine.* The thought of her sent a ripple of excitement through him. Her eager, glowing eyes that night of the fireworks. Her sweetly crooked smile. Her perfume, a scent that rose from her skin as though she'd been lying in a bed of springtime heather.

He caught his uncle, Baron Thornleigh, looking at him, which snapped Will's thoughts back to the present. Elizabeth had called in his uncle Richard along with Sir William for this private discussion. She stood with her back to the tall oriel windows—voices in the garden had drawn her attention—and both of her advisers stood waiting: the spare-framed Sir William, forty-eight, bearded, professorial, brilliant; Uncle Richard, twenty years older but more erect, more imposing, a veteran of trade missions and the sea. The moment Will had seen his uncle arrive a quarter of an hour ago he had burned to ask him whether Justine had told him yet of their decision to marry. But he could not do so in the presence of the Queen; could not speak at all unless spoken to. His uncle's grave countenance told him nothing: He was here on matters of state. *Patience,* Will told himself. *Talk to him later.*

But it was hard to be patient. Will was itching to be independent. At the moment, his uncle paid for his ongoing law studies at Gray's Inn, and though the law term had ended with the start of summer he faced four more years of attending lectures and sessions of moot court before he could become a barrister and earn a living. Or—and that's why this meeting was so important—he could leap ahead through advancement here at court, win a post with an immediate income. Familiar with the issues around Mary, Queen of Scots after preparing Sir William's papers, Will had a rough mental draft of how he might make the leap. He only needed the right moment.

The men waited in silence as Elizabeth watched whatever was going on in the garden below. The morning sunshine streaming in behind her gilded her slim silhouette. A canary in its cage flitted down from its perch. Across the room two ladies-in-waiting sat in a cushioned alcove silently busy at their tasks, one embroidering a stretched hoop of silk, the other stringing a lute. Will heard, outside, the soft whack of a tennis ball.

The voices in the garden drifted away and Elizabeth turned back, all business. She fixed her dark eyes on Sir William. Her powers of concentration always impressed Will, and especially today with the pressure she was under. The Spanish and French ambassadors, lords of their own hubs of power here at court, pressed her daily to tell them her intentions about Mary, and at this very moment her full council was assembling down the corridor for a meeting with her to decide on her policy. She had asked in Baron Thornleigh and Sir William to lay out the options first.

Elizabeth raised an eyebrow to Sir William, an indication of her desire for him to continue.

"Paramount, Your Majesty, and most alarming," he said, anxious to warn her, "is the Scottish queen's request, repeated in her many letters to you, that you help restore her to her throne, by force if necessary. This is utterly impossible. Any English intervention would antagonize our Scottish allies. And why should we? Having supported the Earl of Moray's government, we have established crucial ties with them. They are England's bulwark against our common nemesis, the French. To provoke Moray would run counter to our interests. Any move to restore the deposed queen could hurl us into war with Scotland."

These were strong words. *War.* Will watched Elizabeth. She betrayed no alarm.

"Indeed," Sir William continued, "even to allow her to come to court as your guest, as she continually petitions you . . ." He held out his hand to Will, who grabbed the sheaf of Mary's letters and handed it to him. Sir William held it up in a theatrical show of its volume, then thudded it back down on the desk. "A flood of entreaties. But to succumb to her would be unwise. If you show her the honor of bringing her to court you would sully your reputation, both at home and abroad, for many would see you as the protector of a murderess and adulteress."

A shadow of distaste flitted over Elizabeth's features, but still she said nothing.

"However," Sir William went on, "there is also a danger, perhaps an equal danger, if you let her roam freely in your realm. Look to the north, Your Majesty. Catholic sympathies there have merely slumbered. Mary's presence could rouse them, rouse some mighty lords to rash passions over religion."

Will knew the likely candidates. The Duke of Norfolk. The Earl of Northumberland. The Earl of Westmorland. Powerful men, all. Norfolk was the richest man in England. The latter two controlled vast territory in the north, far from the reach of the Queen's justice.

"Mary Stuart could inflame these passions," Sir William warned. His provocative use of her common name was intentional, Will knew. Moray's government had forced Mary to abdicate and had taken stewardship of her infant son and crowned him King James. "Indeed, I fear she already has, for my lord Northumberland smarts at your denying him the honor of housing her at his castle. Your command that she be lodged at Carlisle under the care of Lord Scrope was judicious. Scrope is loyal. But the longer Mary remains in England, the greater the danger that Your Majesty's council will break into factions, those lords who champion her religion against those who hold dear the religious settlement that is the hallmark of your reign. We dare not reopen that dark chasm."

He took a moment to let the danger sink in. Then he concluded, "My recommendation, therefore, is twofold. First, keep Mary away from you. Second, keep her in custody."

Elizabeth did not take her eyes from him as she digested this. Will could almost hear her mind at work on the problem, but her expression, though somber, gave no hint of how she rated Sir William's advice. She looked at Will's uncle. "Lord Thornleigh? What say you?"

He did not hesitate. "That Your Majesty has no grounds for keeping the lady in custody. The charges against her have not been proved. She took refuge in your realm in good faith. You would appear a tyrant."

Her chin jerked up a fraction. *Tyrant* was not a word to throw in the face of a queen. There was a chill of silence.

Undeterred, he carried on. "As for her remaining free in your realm, Sir William may have a point about Catholic sympathizers. Mary may attract that kind of high feeling. But what's the alternative? We must not send her back to Scotland. That would put her life in peril. When Moray locked her up, John Knox demanded in his every sermon that she be put to death. And the Scottish people are all for it. That howling mob when Moray brought her into Edinburgh as his prisoner." He shook his head in disgust. "The curses they hurled at her."

Whore, the people had called her. Will had read the reports. The people believed she had colluded in the murder of her husband, Lord Darnley, so she could be united with her lover, the Earl of Bothwell. After less than three months of widowhood, she had married Bothwell. Then, when her army lost to Moray on the battlefield, Bothwell fled to Denmark. Will didn't know if Mary *had* colluded, and in fact he was glad the case was ambiguous. It gave him the opportunity here that he needed. At least, he hoped it would if the stalemate continued.

"I grant," his uncle went on, "there are some in England, especially among these hard new Puritans, who would rejoice at Mary's execution. But I say her death would be bad for us. It would destabilize Your Majesty's realm, for she is your heir presumptive. Sir William warns of factions if Mary remains freely among us, but sending her back to her death could spark a power struggle for supremacy among your lords jockeying to be named your heir, and that could become truly bloody."

Elizabeth was visibly annoyed at this mention of the succession. "Have a care, my lord," she said, "that you do not stray from the issue."

He made a slight bow, deferential enough to acknowledge her command but stiff enough to display his disagreement.

Will was impressed by Elizabeth's forbearance. Her council were unanimous in their anxiety at her unmarried state, and since her coronation nine years ago they had ceaselessly urged her to accept one of her royal suitors, for everyone wanted her to produce an heir lest civil war ensue should she die. An attack of smallpox a few years ago had left her unconscious for days, and the moment she had recovered they had doubled their efforts to persuade her to marry. Will himself had witnessed one of their torrents of advice, which Elizabeth bore with grim tolerance. Actually, she had entertained several candidates, but chosen none. It was unusual, Will granted—all monarchs married. Yet he admired her caution. After all, by marrying she would make some foreign prince the king of England. The thought made him shudder.

His uncle winced slightly as he shifted the foot he had his weight on. Some discomfort there, it seemed. But he pressed on.

"If Your Majesty agrees that Mary cannot be sent back to probable death, nor be kept in custody, yet should not be allowed free rein in England either, there is another alternative. Send her to France. She grew up there. She owns extensive lands there. Let her settle into one of her fine French châteaux and you will be done with this vexing problem."

Sir William's frown showed his strong disagreement. "That would only add fuel to the fire," he said. "Reunite her with her powerful Guise relations who hunger to see her as queen of England? They continually harp on her right, as the great-granddaughter of Your Majesty's grandfather, to be England's monarch. If we oust her from England she would spur on the Duc de Guise's campaign that she claim Your Majesty's throne *now*. And, as we know too well, he is far from alone. Unofficially, France and Spain support Mary. As does the pope."

Will bristled at the stance taken by Europe's two most powerful nations. He was sure all loyal Englishmen felt the outrage he did that Catholics had never recognized as valid the divorce of Elizabeth's father, Henry VIII, from Catherine of Aragon, and therefore the legitimacy of his marriage to Anne Boleyn. In their eyes, Anne's daughter, Elizabeth, was a bastard. Will's feeling was: *Damn* their eyes.

"Mary herself is not innocent in this," Sir William warned. "We know she has sent beseeching letters to every potential ally in Europe. I need not remind Your Majesty that the most dire eventuality for England would be a Catholic League, led by France and Spain, backed by the pope, zealous to put Mary on your throne."

Lord Thornleigh shook his head in opposition. "The French king is too busy hunting down Protestants and massacring them. His country is being torn apart by religious strife. His full attention is there. As for Spain, Philip is basking in his conquest of the Netherlands with its enormously rich trade with England. He will not endanger that trade to help the French press their dubious claim here. No, with all due respect to Sir William, the most dire eventuality for England would be civil war, and Mary's demise could spark it. Like it or not, she is Your Majesty's legitimate heir."

Elizabeth's eyes narrowed as she regarded him. "Thank you for your counsel, my lord. And yours, Sir William." Grave of face, she turned to the canary's golden cage as though for a glimmer of diversion. Will thought, *She's not satisfied with their arguments. They keep going over the same ground. They need to look at the problem another way.* It gave him a jolt of excitement. Did he dare speak up now?

Elizabeth nudged her finger in between the gilded bars, and the bird fluttered down onto her fingertip. It teased a small smile from her. She murmured some affectionate words to the bird, then flicked her finger to send it fluttering back up to its perch. Withdrawing her hand, she turned to the waiting men. "Here is my answer. I will not abandon Mary. She is my cousin, and has sought my protection in good faith. More to the point," she added sternly, "she is a queen. Anointed by God. Subject to none."

Sir William seemed about to interject, but she held up her hand to forestall him. "Make no mistake, sir. By law, she is not bound to answer to her subjects. Much as I value our good relations with Moray's government, he crossed a dangerous line when he imprisoned Mary. God's wounds, we set an evil precedent if we countenance rebels threatening their monarch's life! Furthermore, I would have the ambassadors *know* that I stand by Mary. Philip of Spain and Charles of France shall not call me derelict in defending a fellow sovereign." She let out a tight sigh, then said in a new tone, wryly aware, "However, neither will I send her to France to stir up trouble in those parts."

Will noted Sir William's relief at the last point. Will felt the same, and was again impressed by Elizabeth's unsentimental pragmatism.

"Your fellow councilors are expecting us," she said. "Let them wait." She added pointedly to both men, "Devise a way for me to deal with Mary honorably."

She moved to a sideboard near her ladies' alcove where a decanter and goblets stood ready. The two ladies instantly left their tasks and went to serve her. Will watched his uncle and his patron exchange a tense look. His uncle rubbed the back of his neck, deep in thought. Sir William clasped his hands behind his back and began to pace.

Excitement coursed through Will. *Do it now.*

"Sir William," he said quietly, moving to him. "May I have a word?"

He looked annoyed at having his thoughts interrupted. "What is it?"

Will kept his voice low. "Her Majesty needs more time."

"Obviously."

"No, I mean she is under too much pressure. All attention is concentrated on her, on what action she will take. That's what we should look to change."

"Change? The privy council expects to be told her policy today. So do the ambassadors."

"And so they shall. But what if the policy we announce is one that shifts people's focus away from Her Majesty and onto Mary."

"I don't see it. How?"

"By feeding their curiosity. Mary is notorious throughout Europe. Everyone wants to know, did she collude in her husband's murder or not? Did she have him killed so she could marry her lover? Bring *that* to light and we make this case turn not on Her Majesty but on Mary. On her innocence or guilt."

"A trial?" Sir William looked interested, but skeptical. "English courts have no jurisdiction over foreign monarchs."

"I would call it an examination into the facts, sir, born of Her Majesty's desire to restore stability in Scotland. It would give her more time. Perhaps more important, at its conclusion it would yield straightforward grounds for her to act, because whatever decision she takes then could not be seen as arbitrary."

Sir William seemed tempted. "I doubt she would agree to it. She is much troubled by any appearance of dishonoring her fellow queen."

"But, sir, by launching such an inquiry she would display her heartfelt *support* for her fellow monarch. She could officially declare that she intends to help restore Mary to her throne just as soon as it is established that Mary is innocent. How could Mary or her supporters gainsay that?"

Sir William was now paying keen attention. "Nor could they hold the high ground if she were found guilty."

Will nodded. "Her Majesty, of course, is correct that by law

Mary is not bound to answer to her subjects, but that argument serves us ill, for it casts Mary as the party with rights superior to those of the Earl of Moray. Not so if the case turns on murder. After all, sir, there is a higher law—Thou shalt not kill. From it even crowned heads are not exempt."

Dusk was gathering when Will hopped out of the wherry onto London's Queenhithe wharf where fishing smacks, tilt boats, and wherries crowded the water stairs. He tossed the wherryman an extra tip for bringing him down the Thames from Whitehall Palace and made his way past fishwives' stalls and city men beckoning the wherries with calls of "Oars!" Will felt so buoyed up he began whistling. Hard to maintain the tune, though, because a smile kept twitching his mouth. Not only had Sir William taken his idea to Elizabeth in his presence and given him full credit for it, the Queen herself had considered the proposal then and there. Never one to be rash, she had mulled it, sipping her wine and strolling to the window as her two advisers waited and Will tried to keep his racing heartbeat under control. Then she had turned, flicked a glance at Will, and told Sir William, "I like it. It gives me breathing room, and with no loss of honor."

Striding across Thames Street, Will abandoned the tune he was whistling—the grin had won.

In the fading daylight food vendors were packing into baskets their unsold eel pies and rabbit pastries, muskmelons and fragrant strawberries. Apprentices trudged home, weary from their day's labor. Will's own afternoon had been a marathon of work with Sir William, who had immediately begun to formulate the parameters of the official inquiry about Mary, but Will didn't feel tired, just invigorated. A cart clattered by with hogsheads of ale and he gave a thought to how satisfying it would be to relax in a tavern with a foaming tankard, but he strode on, for he was on his way to visit his mother. He hadn't seen her for several weeks. In term he lodged at Gray's Inn, and lately Sir William had given him a room at Whitehall to have him close at hand. Will was looking forward to giving his mother the happy news. Today, he had made his mark.

The thought of what that promised expanded the very breath

inside him. A secure income. Justine! His every sense felt sharpened to the city's sights and sounds and smells. The church bell clanging near the Glaziers Hall. The bawling of sheep, faint at this distance, as they were herded across London Bridge where the first lanterns would soon be lit in the houses that crammed both sides. Across the river, flags snapped in the evening breeze atop the bear gardens of Southwark. Dart-shaped swallows swooped overhead for insects. In the air there was a scent of fresh sawdust and the river's ever-present seaweedy tang. And what was that other smell? Gingerbread?

"Wait," he called to a little girl wrapping the last of her gingerbread babies into burlap. He bought two of the treats and gave the girl an extra penny. His mother liked gingerbread.

Crossing the busy thoroughfare of Cheapside, Will zigzagged through the traffic. Gentlemen on horseback trotted by. Ladies' maids ambled home with baskets of produce. Merchants and traders, clerks and lawyers marched to and from the imposing edifice of the Mercers' Hall. He sidestepped a couple of grimy boys scurrying to snatch some cabbages that had tumbled off the back of a wagon. Voices rose from St. Paul's Cathedral to the west. Its yard was always bustling with booksellers' stalls—one of Will's favorite haunts. St. Paul's interior was the city's busiest meeting place, where people came to transact business, exchange news and gossip, or hire a serving man or a scrivener. The cathedral's roof looked naked to Will since its steeple, once the tallest in Europe, had been lost seven years ago in a fire from a lightning strike. Would it ever be rebuilt? he wondered. The city aldermen kept haggling about the expense, and everyone knew that competing guildsmen had come to blows over it more than once. What an exasperating, brawling, magnificent city, Will thought. He loved London.

He looked east along Cheapside. That's where Justine was, across the city at Uncle Richard's fine house on Bishopsgate Street. He wished he'd been able to speak to his uncle in private at the palace to ask whether Justine had told him about their decision to marry, but as soon as the Queen authorized the inquiry his uncle had left. Not before voicing his agreement with the plan, though. "Cautiously pleased with the idea," he had told Elizabeth. As he took his leave from her and Sir William he had murmured, in passing Will at his desk, "Well done, lad."

From Cheapside, the V made by Milk Street and Wood Street ran north. Will took Wood Street, its traffic and commerce thinner, its noise more subdued. The light, too, was dimming, and birds were settling in to roost for the night in the eaves of the Bowyers' Hall and the Brewers' Hall. He was approaching the compact graveyard of St. Olave's, where ancient yew trees stood sentinel. Their shaggy branches drooped over his father's grave. Will never passed the spot without feeling a needle of the terror ten years ago when he had seen his father stagger and fall, bristling with Grenville arrows.

"Buy a posy, sir?"

"What?" He turned away from the tombstones. A scrawny woman was offering him a clutch of violets.

"For the grave, sir. Your loved one?"

"Ah. No, thank you."

He strode on, glad to be near his destination. This neck of Wood Street was his mother's neighborhood, Cripplegate Ward. He passed the Castle Inn where the smell of manure wafted from the expansive innyard. The inn offered bed and board and stabling for travelers, and its yard was a hub for porters riding with deliveries to and from the city. Among the people passing by outside it were a couple of faces Will knew. He nodded a greeting to Henry Pierson, his mother's neighbor, a goldsmith and moneylender, who absently nodded back, in conversation with a fancifully dressed fellow, a tout that Pierson employed to wind in young gents in need of cash. *Money*, Will thought. *Who* isn't *in need of it?* Two blocks ahead lay Cripplegate which led through the city wall out into Moorfields with its market gardens, public archery butts, hedgerows where laundresses spread out sheets, and tenting yards where apprentices stretched wool cloth on tenterhooks, while beyond them creaked the windmills of Finsbury Fields. All those folk would be heading for home now, Will reckoned. His own path did not lead through Cripplegate. Dusk was deepening as he turned west onto his mother's street.

Silver Street was a quiet byway one block long. It lay in a pocket of houses tucked into the northwest angle of the city's wall. In former times it had been home to silversmiths, but now its denizens included a catchpenny printer, a needlemaker, a pewterer, a jeweler, a scrivener, a porter, a clothworker, and a saddler, as well as the goldsmith Will had passed. Their shops took up the street level of their houses, the families living on the second floor, and servants and apprentices in the small rooms of the attics. The upper stories jutted out into the narrow street, cutting out what little twilight was left. Will passed a link boy with a glowing lantern heading for Wood Street to make a penny or two by lighting the way of gentlemen going out to sup. Otherwise, the street was deserted.

His mother's house stood at the crooked intersection with Monkwell Street. Bits of chaff, disturbed by the faint breeze, scurried past the doorstep of the printer's shop next door. Three hens pecked at spilled grain. Behind a shuttered window, a baby cried. In the lane between the houses, the Parkers' cow in their back garden stood scratching its shoulder against a post.

Will found his mother in the parlor sitting in darkness before the cold hearth. She looked like a ghost, a shadowy silhouette in the twilight. Eyes closed, head up, her back as straight as an arrow, she wore a cloak over her gray dress. Was she preparing to go out?

"It's dark as a tunnel in here, Mother," he said pleasantly. "Light the candles, why don't you?"

Startled, she twisted to look at him, peering through the gloom as though she didn't recognize him. Then, in a heartbeat, a look of bittersweet surprise washed over her face. "Will! You remembered."

"Remembered?" he asked, coming to her. It saddened him how the ghostly light deepened the lines around her sunken eyes and hollowed out her cheeks. She was much younger than her brother, Uncle Richard, but had none of his vigor.

"Ten years, Will. Ten years to the day."

It shook him as he realized. *Father*. June. The thunder of horses' hooves that day. The swords, the arrows. The blood.

"I've just come from his resting place." She sprang to her feet, agile in her fervor. "Would you like to go and talk to him? Come, we'll go together."

"You've just got back."

"I don't mind. It's where I feel closest to him."

"No. Let's stay. It's almost dark." He hated reliving the horror. Unlike his mother. She visited the grave every day. She had made it her mission to never forget. "Come, take off your cloak and let's have some light," he said. "Where's Susan?" He'd seen no sign of the maid.

She shrugged. "Getting supper."

Will was eager to dispel her melancholy. "Here," he said, presenting the burlap square. "For a sweet."

She mustered a smile. "I can smell it. Gingerbread." She kissed his cheek, her touch as dry as a winter leaf. "Such a good boy," she murmured.

They looked at each other for a quiet moment, she gazing at him with that sad smile he knew so well. She would try to be merry for his sake. He was grateful. He felt too happy today to pretend otherwise.

"Off with this," he said, whirling off her cloak. He took it to the passage and hung it up. The house smelled faintly of apples. A single stubby candle of tallow guttered on the table by the door to the kitchen. He carried it back to the parlor. "Let there be light," he said, heading to the cold hearth. With the flame he lit the tall wax candles on either end of the mantel, then went about the room lighting every other candle, one on the desk, one on the windowsill, one on the small table with its scatter of books.

"Can you stay?" she asked.

"With pleasure. I could eat an ox." He was lighting the lantern that hung over the desk. "What's the fare?"

"Leg of mutton. Richard sent it."

Will was glad, and not surprised. Uncle Richard was generous to his sister in actions large and small. He had offered to buy her a grander house across town, but she would not leave Will's father, buried in St. Olave's down the street.

"There, that's better," he said, his task of lighting the room done. He rubbed his hands together briskly. "Now, have you a bottle of claret? We'll drink to the health of Sir William."

"Oh, dear, I hope he is not ill."

"Far from it. He is prodigiously delighted with the prodigious talents of your prodigious son."

"As well he should be," she said with a smile of pride in her voice. It did Will's heart good to hear the smile.

"And he has made it known to same prodigious son that a sinecure will soon be his. Mine, that is. Indeed, the gentleman is so pleased with me, I daresay he would have given me the post of principal secretary to the Queen if he did not already fill it himself."

She was astonished. "What?"

"Ah yes, vast riches await us, Mother." He chuckled at his own nonsense. "Well, riches enough to buy your own leg of mutton and a bottle of claret whenever you fancy. Sir William has promised me a reward at court. I shall be the Royal Holder of the Royal Mop and gather in the gold that every man must pay me for a license to sell mop heads." He saw her bewilderment and reined in his high spirits. "Jesting aside, Mother, he has given me a secretarial post that brings a modest income, and for his faith in me I am heartily grateful."

Now she understood. "Oh, Will, this *is* good news."

He couldn't resist. "Only a beginning." He winked at her. "I'll be holder of some fat royal patent yet."

She smiled. "Yes, yes, I am sure you shall. Now, sit you down and tell me more." She settled herself on the cushioned oak bench and patted the spot beside her. "How has this come about?"

He didn't want to sit. He was too keyed up. "Indeed, I *shall* tell you more." Though not about the meeting, of course; the Queen's deliberations were confidential. "You know what this means? This income?"

"That it has made you brainsick?"

He laughed. "Besides that. It means I can take a wife."

Her eyes widened. "Have you someone in mind?"

"I do." He saw that he had surprised her. "I've been meaning to tell you, but I wanted Uncle Richard's consent first."

"Of course. Richard is the head of our family." She didn't look displeased, just keen to know. "Is it the Hargrave girl? I saw you speaking to her at church."

He shook his head, amused. Mary Hargrave was a timid little mouse, nothing like his quicksilver Justine. "No. Someone else." He sat down beside her after all and took her hand. She looked all interest, waiting. "I'm going to marry Uncle Richard's ward. Justine Thornleigh."

Her eyes did not leave his. There was an odd stillness about her.

She gave a small, strange laugh. "I am not sure marriage is right for you just now."

"Oh," he said heartily, "I'm quite sure it is."

"Come, come, Will, it really is too soon. You're too young."

"I'm not, actually."

"You're not thinking clearly. A pretty face will do that to a man. Truly, son, you have not thought this through. You have your way to make in the world."

"I am. It's happening." He got to his feet. "I told you, Sir William—"

"Promises are not gold pieces. Let's wait and see what comes of it. Besides, your law term resumes at Michaelmas."

"Great heaven, I won't wait for September. Anyway, I'm done with all that. I'm leaving Gray's Inn. My future is at court."

She looked so flustered he realized he really should have prepared her for this change. "All right, at court," she said. "Then you need to concentrate on *that*, don't you. You can't be tied down by . . . a wife . . . children."

He almost laughed. "Children? We haven't even posted the banns yet."

She flashed angry eyes at him. "Marriage is serious. It can take a bitter turn. Look at Adam. He had to escape."

Her anger took him aback. He didn't follow. His cousin Adam was away on a trade voyage. In any case, what did Adam's sour marriage have to do with *him?* She seemed to be getting things mixed up. He said to her clearly, distinctly, to get her back on track, "Mother, I am going to marry Justine Thornleigh. I wish you'd give me your blessing."

Abruptly, she stood. "You don't know who she is. Where she comes from."

Was *that* her objection? Only that Justine had been left orphaned by some distant Thornleigh relation? "My uncle knows. Ask him for the family tree specifics if it means that much to you. I assure you, it doesn't to me. I love her and she loves me and we want to marry."

She gaped at him. She seemed to be trembling. It astonished Will. Was she frightened at the prospect of him leaving her? "Mother, I'll still be in London," he assured her. "You can live with me and Justine, if you like. We'd be happy to—"

"Never! I won't allow this. *Richard* won't allow it. You, entrapped by that . . . devil's spawn!"

❧ 5 ❧

A Mission
for the Queen

"I visited my mother last night," Will said. "And what she told me . . ." He didn't finish.

At his hesitation Justine felt a chill. She had noticed his worried face the moment she saw him. *Meet me at St. Paul's,* his note had said. It reached her at breakfast and she had hurried to the rendezvous spot, the outdoor bookstalls tucked between the cathedral's buttresses. People milled around them, browsing, chattering, haggling with booksellers. Justine suddenly felt too hot, the sun so strong. All she could think was, *His mother is Lord Thornleigh's sister. If she knows who I really am . . . did she tell him?*

Will plowed a hand through his hair. He looked more troubled than Justine had ever seen him. "I told her we wanted to marry. What she told *me* was . . . well, it was so extreme I still can't believe it."

Her heart kicked in her chest. *She told him I'm a Grenville.* The feud between the families . . . It's how his father died. *Now he hates me!*

He said, his voice tight, "She was quite distraught."

She looked away, feeling close to panic. Her thoughts tripped over themselves as she tried to think what to say to bring him back to her. *I was a child when it happened, Will. It has nothing to do with us!*

"Justine, it was rash of me, I know. I sprang the news on her

with no preparation. Pure selfishness. I wanted her blessing because I don't want to wait. I want us to be together, forever." He
grabbed her hand. "Forgive me?"

She blinked at him, stunned. It didn't matter to him, after all,
that she was born a Grenville? She dared to hope. "Forgive . . . ?"

"For bringing on my mother's antagonism. I have no idea what
spurred it. Maybe just because I bungled the news so badly, or
maybe it's some irrational fear she has of losing me. Whatever the
cause, she was so upset she refused to explain or even to speak
about it further. I wanted to stay with her in the hope of winning
her over, but a message came from Sir William calling me back to
court. I couldn't even stay to sup with her. I worked late at the
palace and spent the night there." He shook his head with a look
of exasperation at his own failure. "I'm afraid I left her in an awful
state."

"I'm . . . so sorry," Justine managed to say, squeezing his hand,
quickly collecting herself. So his mother had *not* told him! It sent a
surge of relief through her that left her almost dizzy. *He doesn't
know.*

"I have just one question," he said.

She held her breath. Did he suspect? "Oh?"

"Have you spoken to my uncle? Did you get *his* blessing?"

She quickly said, "Yes." It wasn't exactly a lie. Both Lord and
Lady Thornleigh had been warm in their approval of Will. She
kept to herself the fact that they had also made her promise to tell
him the truth.

He was clearly relieved. "Good. Because I'm afraid my mother
may urge him to forbid our marriage."

Justine flinched. "Would she do that?"

"It doesn't matter. My uncle is the head of our house. Don't
mistake me, I love and honor my mother, but if she takes such an
action against us . . . well, I would no longer feel constrained by fil-
ial duty. Because nothing has changed, Justine. With or without
my mother's blessing, as long as you are steadfast of heart, mine is
yours forever. We shall be wed." He still held her hand, and now
he pressed it to his chest. "I wish it could be today. But I have no
living yet. I hope to very soon—Sir William has all but promised it

to me. But for now . . ." He looked almost as agitated as before, but this time excitement shone in his eyes. "For now, my darling Justine, will you seal my happiness by betrothal?"

Her heart leapt. Betrothal! It was almost like being married. "Oh, Will. Yes! When?"

"Right now." He grinned. "Right here." He beckoned to a stocky young man who was watching them surreptitiously across a table laden with books. He wore the black garb of a vicar. "A friend of mine in holy orders," Will told Justine, then winked at her. "I hoped, you see."

She laughed in delight. "I do, indeed."

The young churchman joined them, a shy smile on his round face. Will introduced him . "The Reverend John Stubbs. We studied together at Gray's Inn."

Stubbs corrected him. "I studied, mistress. Will did nothing but talk of you."

She laughed and told him she was very pleased to make his acquaintance, and indeed she felt so happy she could have hugged the fellow. "Oh," she said in sudden dismay, turning to Will, "but I have no ring to give you." The one she always used to wear, a favorite of lapis lazuli, she had given to Alice on the night of the fireworks.

"No matter," Will said, digging in his doublet pocket, "I have brought two."

She grinned. "You are thorough, Will Croft."

"The lawyer's mind," he said, tapping his temple. He displayed the rings on his palm—two identical, thin, unadorned silver bands. Plain though they were, Justine knew the cost would have eaten into Will's slight stock of cash. She loved the rings. Loved him.

"And now," he said, "we must make haste before Sir William realizes I have not yet returned from the palace library with the documents he requested."

"Then why are we still talking?" she said gaily and plucked up one of the rings. "This will be mine to you."

"Shall we begin, then?" the vicar asked. He and Will ushered Justine into the bay formed by a huge buttress jutting from the cathedral. Here they were out of the throng and in shade from the bright sun. The grass, untrammeled by passersby, was springy underfoot. The cool, high stone buttress rose around them like a protective arm.

A soberness fell over them as the vicar began the ceremony. He took his office seriously. The ritual was brief, but every word of it thrilled Justine. She and Will both, in turn, affirmed and declared that they were free to marry. They both, in turn, pledged their troth and slid a ring onto the finger of the other. It constituted a solemn vow that they would marry one another sometime in the future, a vow that the church and everyone in Christendom accepted as a legal and binding contract.

The vicar intoned, "I bear witness of your solemn proposal, and I declare you betrothed. In the name of the Father, and of the Son, and of the Holy Spirit. Amen."

It was done. Justine and Will looked into each other's eyes and she saw herself in the warm brown depths of his. He kissed her. Their first kiss. A chaste one to mark so pious a ceremony, but the touch of his lips on hers sent a tingle through her all the way to her toes.

On her walk back to Bishopsgate Street, Justine felt she could have danced. She almost collided with a fat woman carrying a basket of turnips, for Justine's whole attention was on the band of silver on her finger, which she could not stop touching. True, it was a trifle large and slipped too easily over her knuckle, but that was not an insurmountable problem; she would get a silversmith to correct it.

Yet as she turned north, getting closer to the Thornleighs' house, the problem she still faced loomed through her euphoria. Before leaving her to hail a wherry to take him back to the palace, Will had said happily, "Now we can tell the whole world we are betrothed." Caution had pricked her. Did his mother have the power to ruin everything? Did she know that Justine had been born a Grenville? Perhaps not—perhaps Lord and Lady Thornleigh had never told her. Justine had to find out. "Not yet," she had said to Will. "Let's give your mother some time to be calmed. For now, let's keep our betrothal a secret."

He was reluctant at first, but then agreed that, for the moment, he was too busy with Sir William's urgent business with the Queen to take time to deal with his mother. "You may be right. A little time may soothe her. For now, my love, this shall be known by only us two." He had kissed her again, and then he was gone.

Justine slipped the ring off her finger as she entered the Thornleighs' house. She went straight up to her bedchamber, intent on hiding it in her jewelry box. When she opened the door she was surprised to see Lady Thornleigh laying out a gown on the bed where several others were piled. Justine quickly tucked the ring into her pocket as her ladyship turned, saying, "Ah, my dear, I was looking for you. There is no time to waste. We must get you packed. I have news."

Packed? Justine saw that her maid, Ann, was on her knees beside an open trunk, folding a linen chemise to go in amongst others. The wardrobe doors stood open, the wardrobe half-emptied of gowns. "Are we returning to Hertfordshire?" she asked.

Lady Thornleigh held up a hand in a subtle gesture that said, *Wait until we're alone.* She lifted a cloak of garnet satin from the pile on the bed. "Ann, take this to Margaret and have her mend the hem. Tell her it must be done by dinner."

"Aye, my lady." The maid took it and left.

Lady Thornleigh came to Justine and went on briskly, lowering her voice, "I have just come from Her Majesty. I proposed a plan and she has endorsed it." She noticed that the door remained open, and went and closed it. "My dear, you have an important task before you. Urgent business of state. You have been chosen to carry out a mission for Her Majesty."

Business of state? Justine thought she must have misheard. "Pardon?"

"You will go with Lord Thornleigh. He leaves tomorrow for the north as Elizabeth's emissary to the Queen of Scots. Mary is lodged in Carlisle Castle, and Elizabeth has provided her with a small retinue consistent with her royal status. Two ladies chosen from northern high-ranking families now attend her. You are to join them as a third. You leave in the morning with Richard."

Justine gaped at her. "I?"

Lady Thornleigh patted her cheek like a proud parent. "You. However, your duties as a lady-in-waiting will be a façade." She lowered her voice even more. "Your real mission goes much deeper. You are to closely observe Mary. Her visitors, her conversations, what letters she receives, and from whom. All this you will regularly report to Her Majesty's agent in the town. Do you understand?"

Justine was stunned. "Be a spy?"

A flicker of annoyance tugged her ladyship's brow. "A guardian of Her Majesty's interests."

"But . . . why *me?* Surely there are others in the north who—"

"Ah, you are better suited than you realize. Mary Stuart grew up in France and speaks little English. You speak fluent French. It will give you an opportunity to get close to her as few others could." She went to a bookcase and glanced over the volumes. "And thanks to your education here, you have another skill that will serve you well." She slipped out two books and took them to the trunk, adding them to its contents. "Few other young ladies could read Marcus Aurelius and Terence in Latin to entertain a queen."

Justine was dumfounded. Carlisle was hundreds of miles from London. From Will.

Her ladyship's tone turned somber. "Another thing, and perhaps the most important. The other young ladies attending Mary come from stoutly Protestant families. Your early upbringing was Catholic." She took Justine's hands in hers. "Of course we never held that against you, a mere child at the time. And now it can be turned to good use. Mary's Catholicism is another potential bond between you and her, a powerful one. Do you see? You have all the tools to befriend the Queen of Scots."

Justine jerked her hands free. "I am not Catholic. I have no desire to know the Queen of Scots."

Lady Thornleigh looked taken aback. She collected herself and said evenly, "Then modify what you desire, my dear. For this is Her Majesty's wish."

Justine instantly regretted her outburst. It was childish. And she knew she should feel tremendously honored to be chosen to do a service for the Queen. For England. Still, it appalled her to think of leaving Will when his mother might have the power to tear him from her, and she felt frantic to find a way out. "I . . . could fail."

"You shall not fail. You are clever. You know you can manage this."

"I know no such thing. I am not trained at subterfuge."

"I trust you to find your way. More important, Elizabeth trusts you."

"Because you persuaded her. Pardon, my lady, but it's *you* she trusts. She does not even know me." She slipped her hand into her pocket and clutched the ring. "It's just . . . so hard to leave London right now. Leave Will."

"Will?"

"I told you and his lordship. We want to marry."

"Ah, yes. But that can wait. You have a higher duty."

"To stay in the north for how long?" Weeks? Months?

"For as long as you are required."

A year? she thought wildly. *Will's mother will surely tell him the truth.* "Please, my lady, can you not find someone else?"

"Justine, stop this." She took her by the shoulders and said sternly, "Our family owes everything to Elizabeth. You understand? Everything. All our fortune, all we have, is due to her. So *your* good fortune, in being one of us, is due to her as well. And now, when she needs you to make this small effort on her behalf, I will not have you let her down over a trifling matter of—"

"Trifling? Will is my life!"

Anger flashed in her ladyship's eyes. She murmured crossly, "Love. How blindly it governs us." She turned away as though too upset with Justine to stay face-to-face with her. Voices sounded in the garden below. She went to the window and laid her palm on the glass as thought in an effort to compose herself. Justine watched her, waiting in agony. She loved Lady Thornleigh and it made her sick to cross her, but what she was asking was too much. Justine sank onto the edge of the bed, waiting for she knew not what.

"Fair weather for traveling," her ladyship said, looking out at the garden. "Yet the long journey north will be hard on Lord Thorn-leigh. There is a problem with his leg. Have you noticed?"

The shift in topic was jarring. "He hasn't said anything lately."

Her ladyship turned abruptly. "He spoke about it to you?"

Justine saw her blunder. "Only once." This sounded worse—like a conspiracy. She hastened to add, "He didn't want to worry you."

Anxiety, like a shadow, fell over Lady Thornleigh's face. "I would be the worst kind of fool to live with a man for over thirty years and not notice he was ailing." Justine felt she was looking at a woman she thought she knew, but didn't—not all of her. Not this deep worry.

Lady Thornleigh seemed to recover herself. She found a smile. Her voice, when she spoke, was strong and warm. "I know what you are feeling, my dear. Believe me, I wish with all my heart to see you wed the man you love. Marry, and be happy, as I have been."

Justine gasped in joy. "God bless you, my lady!" Buoyed with relief, she jumped up and ran to her and embraced her. "You won't be sorry. I'm sure you'll find several young lady candidates eager to go to Carlisle. Her Majesty can have her pick."

"No. It is you we have chosen. You are the ideal candidate. I told you, Will can wait."

She pulled back in dismay. "But—"

"You are one of us, Justine, a Thornleigh. Thornleighs serve Elizabeth. It is our privilege and our duty. You shall not fail at yours." She started for the door. "Be ready to ride north in the morning."

Justine ran down the stairs to the library. Lord Thornleigh would listen to her. He would not let them banish her to Carlisle, cut her off from Will!

She found him standing at the big oak desk with his clerk, both of them sorting papers and packing them into a wooden chest.

"My lord," she blurted, "I must speak to you."

He looked up. "And I to you." He turned to his clerk. "I'll fin-ish this, Curnutt. See about getting the letters sent, would you?"

"Certainly, my lord." The clerk poked through the papers,

gathering letters—an interminable business, it seemed to Justine. Waiting for him to finish and leave, she noticed Lord Thornleigh rubbing his left hand with his right, slowly, methodically. Was his hand numb? It gave her a prickle of alarm. Had his malady spread? He saw her looking and let his hand drop to his side as though unwilling to let her see.

The moment his clerk was gone he said, "So, has her ladyship told you of your mission?"

"Yes, but—"

"Good. We need to discuss the journey. Can your maid have you ready early tomorrow? I'd like to set out right after breakfast."

"Oh, sir, I am loath to go! May I not decline?"

He looked taken aback. "Decline? A request from the Queen? Certainly, if you want to stain the reputation of our house."

"No . . . of course not," she stammered, "but, I mean, could you not intercede for me with Her Majesty? Get this plan changed? *Anyone* could go in my place. I know she relies on your counsel."

"With good reason, that I advise her honestly. You are her choice, and I agree it's an excellent one. Why do you balk?"

She was in turmoil. How much could she tell him? Looking at his weathered face, his worried look as he waited for an explanation for her extraordinary resistance, she knew his concern for her was heartfelt. He had taken her in when she was a terrified, lonely child and had brought her up like a daughter. No father could have been more kind. She owed him the truth. The whole truth.

She took a breath and began to pour out her heart. How, despite her promise, she had not yet told Will her real background. How she had met him that morning at St. Paul's and heard that he'd told his mother of their desire to marry and that his mother had flown into a panic and refused to give her consent.

Listening, Lord Thornleigh let out a groan. He sat down heavily in the chair by the desk. "I was afraid of this."

Justine froze. She was right. "She knows who I am. That's it, isn't it?"

He nodded grimly. "She does. So, now Will knows, too?"

"No. He has no idea about it, I'm sure. But he said his mother may come to *you* and demand that you refuse your consent."

"Poor Joan. Don't worry, I'll talk to her."

"And you won't listen to her, will you? If she demands that you to forbid us to marry?"

"I told you, I'm pleased about this marriage."

"But if she insists—"

"Justine, don't worry. I'm sorry Joan has reacted so badly, but it changes nothing. You have my consent and my blessing. That's all you and Will need."

She was so grateful she did not trust her voice to be steady. She whispered, "Thank you."

"I feel I should thank *you*," he said with feeling. "This means a lot to me. A new beginning. The hatred between the houses of Thornleigh and Grenville has festered too long, like some witch's spell. You and Will, with your union, are going to break it." He glanced at his hand hanging limply at his side. "I want peace. That's the legacy I intend to leave my family."

"Leave?" She felt a clutch of alarm. "Is your malady so dire?"

He chuckled. "Don't bury me yet, girl. I mean to dance and eat plums at your wedding."

She had to smile. This day, so overwrought, was making her imagine things.

"You and Will have already made peace," he said, "and that's what's so heartening. Now the rest of us need to do the same. I'll talk to Joan." He got to his feet. "And you need to go and get packed. Your first duty is to Elizabeth."

She did not move. Gathering her courage, she swallowed and said, "Sir, there is more." She confessed that this very morning she and Will had become betrothed.

"What?" His extreme displeasure was plain. "That was ill done, Justine. Betrothal is serious. It should be an open, public ceremony, not this hole-in-corner sneaking."

"When I went to meet him, sir, I did not know it would happen. He asked, and I was so happy I said yes. He had brought a friend, a vicar, and the ceremony was done then and there."

"And you never thought to wait until the thing could be properly done? You should have had your family with you. *Me*." He looked almost hurt.

Justine loved him for his concern. But she could not pretend to regret her vow to Will. "I hope you will forgive me, my lord. It was done for love."

He gave her a piercing look as if to warn her that she could not be so easily mollify him. But a ghost of a smile played on his lips. "Love above all, eh?"

It moved her. He understood. He was only putting on a show of anger now. Yet her fears leapt up again. "Sir, I persuaded Will that our betrothal should be a secret for now." His angry frown returned and she hastened to add, "Because I am so afraid his mother will tell him about me."

Wearily, he shook his head. "She won't. When we took you in she gave me her solemn promise never to speak of it."

Ah, that explained so much! Yet, was it enough? "But now that Will has told her about us? What if she breaks her promise and hurls the truth at him? Especially if I am sent north and am not even here to defend myself?"

"Then tell him now. Get it over with. Tell him today."

"He'll hate me."

"Nonsense. You are an innocent in this miserable feud. He'll understand that. And it's clear that he loves you. Trust in that."

She felt a shiver. "But *can* I trust? Won't he see in me his enemies, my kinsmen? Can he really forget how his father was killed and his mother left widowed? Besides, our family and his are so staunchly Protestant, and he'll realize that as a Grenville I was born a Catholic. For all these reasons . . . oh, my lord, I have seen with my own eyes the loathing he bears my aunt."

"Frances? Ah, well, she is a hard woman to warm to."

"It's not that. Will hates her. For her Grenville blood. *My* blood."

That gave him pause, she saw. Made him quiet. She felt a shudder, seeing how truly she had hit the mark.

"Look," he said, "this can't go on. You have to be honest with Will. You cannot build a marriage on a lie."

Anger swelled in her, born of desperation. "Lies are what we've *all* been living with, ever since I came among you."

"I thought it best for you. I would have done you no favor to have people know you're the daughter of a traitor." He heaved a troubled sigh. "However, that may have been a mistake. Your father's sins died with him in the flames, and maybe that wiped the slate clean for you. This damned secrecy. I never thought it would grow into such a problem."

She had to look away. Could not let him see that she held back a deeper lie. Her father had not perished in the fire. Where he had gone, she had no idea, but he was alive, somewhere, and she alone knew it.

"Justine."

She turned back, hearing the new note in his voice. A hopeful note, as though he had discovered something. "This mission you've been chosen for," he said, "to attend Mary, Queen of Scots. It could be the very thing to help you win Will over."

She stared at him, baffled. "How can leaving him do that?"

"By your service to Elizabeth. Will is devoted to Her Majesty's cause, as are all our family. Your being part of that cause will strengthen your bond with him. It will prove to him how deeply, how thoroughly, you are one of us. A Thornleigh."

A glimmer of light broke through her fears. "Think you so?"

"I do. Show Will your loyalty, by your actions. Then nothing can shake him. Not even when you tell him your past."

She clutched at what he had just implied. "*When* I tell him? You mean, not yet?"

He seemed to realize the contradiction: A moment ago he had said she should tell Will today. "You won't be with Mary for long. A couple of months at most, and meanwhile I'll deal with Joan. Once you're back home, that's the time to tell him. You will have proved yourself. I dare say your service to Elizabeth will even boost his prospects with Sir William."

Justine felt a jolt of excitement. The picture he painted was so bright, so beautiful, it made tears spring to her eyes. She *was* part of his family, and she would prove this truth to Will! She would show herself to be such an essential member of the house of Thornleigh and be so valiant in her service to Elizabeth, nothing could shake his love, not even her Grenville blood.

"Oh, sir!" she said through her tears, and flung her arms around his neck. "I will excel in the mission. And when I return to Will, nothing will ever come between us again!"

He chuckled. "I do not doubt it."

"Pardon, your lordship." Timothy, the footman, had come into the room. "A letter."

Justine pulled away, embarrassed at her outburst of affection, but feeling so happy she didn't really care who saw it.

"It is for Mistress Justine," he said, offering her the letter.

"Ah, Will is eager," said Lord Thornleigh with a wry smile.

But Justine saw the handwriting. Not Will's.

"No, I'm wrong," he added, eying the inscription. "That looks like my daughter's hand."

And so it was, she saw as she opened the letter and looked at the signature. Isabel had written from Yeavering Hall. Justine's first thought was of Alice. She'd had a letter from her only last week, Alice saying how happy she was to be working for Lady Isabel, and thanking Justine for her help, and sharing a jest from the servants' hall. Isabel's note was brief, only a few lines. Justine read them quickly.

Her heart juddered. *So very sorry . . . found dead . . .*

"Justine?" Lord Thornleigh said.

She stared at the words that, even now, she knew would burn in her mind for as long as she lived . . . *strangled . . . by whom we know not . . . no trace of the villain.*

The room around her blurred. Inside her, a stillness like stone.

"Justine? What's wrong?"

She looked up. Tried to speak, but horror clogged her throat. *Alice . . . Alice . . . Alice.*

❧ 6 ❧

In the Presence of
the Scottish Queen

Covering the three hundred miles from London to Carlisle in
England's north had taken Justine and Lord Thornleigh and
their party three weeks. They had journeyed hard, for Queen Elizabeth's business required haste, and Justine felt the miles in every
stiff muscle of her legs and back. The reins she held, brittle from
her dried sweat, chafed her newly calloused palms. Her soul felt
no less battered. Three weeks had not been enough to dim the
horror of Alice's death. Murdered. *Strangled*. What kind of devil
would do that to lovely Alice? And why? Every mile Justine had
ridden beat the merciless questions, like nails, deeper into her.
She had no answers, only numbed disbelief.

It was a harsh land she and Lord Thornleigh had come into with
their train of six men-at-arms, five servants, and the luggage packhorses. Carlisle lay in the rugged county of Cumbria at one of the
most dangerous places in England: the border with Scotland. Centuries of intermittent warfare between the two countries had condemned the local people to endless poverty, misery, hunger, and
death, and although there was now peace, tribal hatreds forged
from time immemorial ensured that clans on both sides of the border continued to raid each other with great brutality. Thankfully,
Justine's party had completed their journey unmolested through
this land of brigands. The weather had been fair, the roads and

bridges clear, the inns, though often dirty, were welcome rest stops to such weary travelers, and they were now nearing their destination, Carlisle Castle. It was the seat of Henry, Lord Scrope, Warden of the West March, the Queen's lieutenant in these parts. Lodged at his castle was his charge, Mary, Queen of Scots.

Justine gazed eastward across the stark moors toward Yeavering Hall, a hard day's ride away. Yeavering Hall, once her home, where she and Alice had been such close friends as girls. It was near Yeavering that Alice had met her unspeakably violent death. Had she been the victim of a robber's assault turned deadly? But what did poor Alice have worth stealing? Or had the killer been someone Alice knew? But Isabel had said in her letter that no one among the stunned household, when questioned, had any idea of who could have done such an evil thing. The murderer, they agreed, must have been a stranger, and after killing Alice had taken flight. Justine imagined the servants, Alice's friends, grieving for her. She had always made friends easily. And what about her ailing parents? Their grief, Justine felt, could not be worse than her own. She had loved Alice. *And I sent her there, to Yeavering Hall. Sent her to her death.*

She dragged her thoughts back to her mission, for her party had reached Carlisle. The town hugged its castle, the bastion of English forces through centuries of war, whose primary defenses were its massive thirteenth-century walls enclosing the town. An artillery platform squatted on the roof of the keep, and three fortified watchtowers rose from the citadel. Justine anxiously eyed the watchtowers as she rode across the drawbridge that spanned the moat. The hooves of her weary horse clopped with an eerie echo as she passed under the ancient arched gatehouse.

"Where do we find Lord Scrope?" the captain of Lord Thornleigh's guard was asking the soldier at the gatehouse.

"He is with the Queen of Scots, sir," the soldier said with a bow to Lord Thornleigh. Though his lordship was a stranger in these parts, any man richly dressed, mounted on a fine horse, and followed by a retinue merited deference. "In the Warden's Tower." He pointed down a narrow street. "Southeast corner of the inner ward, sir. You'll find stabling there."

The party carried on down the street, and Justine, rousing herself from her sorrow over Alice, took comfort in seeing people going about their workaday business. Hammers clanged at a smithy. Pigs grunted from a pen by the castle wall. Laundry, strung on a clothesline between the crowded houses, fluttered in the warm afternoon breeze. A rank smell rose from a small window, unglazed and barred, at the base of the castle wall. The lockup, no doubt. Justine had heard from a traveler at their last inn stop that whenever Scottish border raiders were captured, they were held in the castle jail. A fierce desire for vengeance stabbed her: if only Alice's murderer could be manacled and thrown into this lock-up to suffer for his sin. But he was likely far away by now.

Or was he? What if he had not fled but was hiding? Or even going about his business, undetected by the community? She felt an overwhelming urge to investigate the matter on her own. Alice, a poor servant, had no powerful kin to press for a thorough inquiry, so pertinent details could have been overlooked. Justine judged she would be with Mary for some weeks at the very least, and Yeavering was not far. A chilly excitement rushed over her. Yes, she would make her own inquiries there. Someone might have information, might even have seen the killer with Alice. If she could track him down, she would see justice done.

The resolution cleared her mind like a bracing spring breeze. She shook off her sorrow. She would do her duty here with Mary and find out what she could about how Alice had died.

Her duty here. She meant to succeed in this mission. For Elizabeth, for the Thornleighs, and most of all, for Will. To make things right with him, she was ready to do her all. And now that she had finally arrived, she had to admit she felt a deep curiosity. What would the Queen of Scots be like? Justine had learned the basic facts about her, but mystique swirled around this woman three times married and only twenty-five. Crowned queen of Scotland as a baby. Sent to France at five to grow up in pampered splendor at the French court. Married at sixteen to the adolescent French king. Widowed a year later and brought back to Scotland as its queen where she married the young English nobleman Lord Darnley. Widowed again by his murder. Carried off by the violent

Lord Bothwell—a staged incident, people said, for he was her lover; raped by him, Mary claimed—but three months after her husband's murder she married Bothwell. *If the accusations are true*, Justine thought, *Mary is cunning. And wanton. And profane. Cunning enough to see through my posting here?*

She felt a nip of panic. She had no training at being a spy. Lady Thornleigh had assured her that she needed none beyond her quick wits and her loyalty to Elizabeth. Justine wasn't sure about the first, but had no doubt about the second. *So loyalty must be my guide*, she told herself. Yet her heartbeat quickened, for she was very nervous. Once Lord Thornleigh left to return to London she would have no ally here. Perhaps for months. The responsibility was daunting, knowing that, in some part at least, Elizabeth's security rested on her shoulders. The Thornleighs' honor certainly did. And, perhaps, her whole future with Will.

She took a deep breath to ready herself as her party reached the square stone tower that housed the Queen of Scots. Two steel-helmeted soldiers flanked its arched wooden doors. A half dozen soldiers patrolled each alley that ran alongside it. Three alert archers stood on the roof. Lord Scrope's guest was well guarded. Justine was aware of the dual reasons: this level of security was normal to protect a royal personage—but also to contain a threat to England's queen.

The comfortably furnished chamber into which Justine and Lord Thornleigh were ushered was large, lavishly hung with tapestries, quiet, and dimly lit. At the windows heavy gold brocade curtains were drawn against the sun. A hanging candelabra's dozen small golden flames gave the only light. Justine caught the faint scent of a spicy perfume. It reminded her of incense. In fact, the atmosphere of the whole room put her in mind of a church, the old kind she had known as a child, a hushed dim place rich with Catholic splendor.

Their host, Lord Scrope, had brought them to this second floor suite of the tower, and he whispered, gesturing to the drawn window curtains, "Her Majesty suffers from headache."

Justine was surprised by his solicitous tone. A large, fleshy man in his thirties, he was a powerful magnate with authority over the two thousand inhabitants of this town and other towns, and had command of hundreds of soldiers who would butcher and pillage at his order and had done so in the past, but his hushed voice and eager eyes were those of a suitor as he looked expectantly toward the narrow stone staircase curving to the upper floor, Mary's private suite. The stairs were dark except for a wall-mounted rushlight flickering at the turning. Scrope beckoned the visitors to stand still, as though for an audience.

Lord Thornleigh frowned, looking impatient. "Has she been told we're here?"

"Shh." Scrope held a finger to his lips. "Loud noises," he whispered, tapping the side of his head. "She cannot abide them."

Footsteps sounded on the narrow staircase. Two well-dressed young ladies, treading lightly as they came down, emerged from its gloom. After a curtsy to the gentlemen, one went to the window to tug the edge of the curtains more tightly together, cutting out a stray beam of sunlight. The other, carrying a wine decanter, set it down on the gleaming oak sideboard where goblets stood. She did so gingerly, as though not to make a clatter.

Justine eyed the young ladies. She did not know them personally, but knew who they were. Margaret Currier, big-boned and broad-faced, and Jane de Vere, petite, with a washed-out pale complexion but bright eyes. They would be her sister ladies-in-waiting. In silent deference, they took up places at the far end of the room and stood still, waiting. As did the two lords. As did Justine, beside her guardian.

More footsteps sounded, descending the stairs, a heavier tread. Two men strode down, one gray-haired but erect as a soldier, the other younger, frailer of body, but with an arrogant aspect that branded him a noble. Scrope, indicating Lord Thornleigh, made introductions in a low voice. The men were Scots. The elder was John Maxwell, Lord Herries. The younger was William Livingston. Justine had been briefed about them. Loyal to Mary, they had fought for her in her battle against the Earl of Moray, her half brother, who had usurped her. When her forces were routed, these nobles rode with her for England. They, too, now looked toward the staircase.

Everyone waited. Outside, in the inner ward below, the voices and casual clatter of Scrope's soldiers made a muffled hum.

A glitter at the turning of the stairs. Soft-slippered footfalls. In the stairwell's gloom, Mary emerged. Gold embroidery on her black dress was the glitter, caught by the rushlight. Her face was still in shadow.

She was very tall. That was Justine's first, startled thought. Taller than most men. As she reached the last step and moved toward the visitors, the light of the candelabra finally illumined her face. The candles' golden glow showed skin as flawless as a child's. A heart-shaped frame of pearls held back her smoothly coiffed, dark hair. There was a slight slope to her eyes; together with their alert gleam they put Justine in mind of a cat. Mary came straight toward Lord Thornleigh, her face alight with anticipation, and she caught up his hand and held it in both of hers. Justine almost gasped, so astonishingly intimate was the action.

He looked overwhelmed. He cleared his throat. He bowed.

Mary laughed lightly as though to excuse her impulsive action, and then let go his hand. *"Ah, mon seigneur, pardonnez-moi. Votre visite me remplit de joie."* She added haltingly, "I . . . thank you . . . for to come."

"Her Majesty says your visit fills her with joy, my lord," said Lord Herries, stepping forward. "She has requested that I translate." He added with a smile that softened his crusty, military bearing, "My father despaired of my wild youth in Paris, but my years there were worth something." His English, though tinged with a Scots burr, was as elegant as any Whitehall courtier's. "I hope you will accept this service?"

"Gladly, sir." Lord Thornleigh looked relieved. "My French is but a poor relation to yours."

Herries translated this for Mary and she laughed again, a soft, gentle laugh. Herries grinned. Lord Livingston smiled aristocratic approval. The beefy Scrope gazed at Mary, in thrall.

They are all so earnestly pleasant, Justine thought. Even Lord

Thornleigh, who moments ago had been soberly set on his duty here, looked lighter of heart. Mary had done it, she realized in awe. She had heard of the famous remark made by the Venetian ambassador in London, that Mary was the most beautiful woman in Europe, and now she saw why. She was as lovely of form as of face, but it was more than beauty that made people brighten in her presence. Liveliness sparkled in her eyes. Sensuality flowed in her every movement. Justine had a sense that Mary was wholly caught up with whomever she spoke to. At the moment, that person was Lord Thornleigh.

He said, "I hope, Your Grace, that your headache has cleared?"

When Herries translated this, irritation flickered on Mary's face. Justine guessed it was because Lord Thornleigh had not addressed her specifically as a queen; *Your Grace* could apply to lesser royalty or a duchess. Though Mary had abdicated her throne over a year ago, she later declared that she had done so under threat of death and renounced the abdication.

She smiled, as though bent on ignoring such irritations, then charmingly brushed aside his concern for her health with a wave of her slender hand. *"Il va et vient; ce n'est rien."* It comes and goes; it is nothing.

She gestured to Jane de Vere, who took up a lute and began to play soft chords, soothing and sweet. Mary then gestured to Margaret Currier, talking as she did so, and Herries told the visitors, "Her Majesty wishes you to refresh yourselves with wine after your long journey."

Lord Thornleigh declined. He was ready for business.

"Pas de vin?" No wine? Mary asked, her hand on her heart in mock dismay. She went on, casting a disarming glance at Scrope, and Herries translated, "Not even the finest Burgundy from the cellar of our noble host?"

Scrope grinned and bowed, preening at Mary's notice.

"I thank Your Grace," Lord Thornleigh said, "but the best refreshment will be your satisfied acceptance of my news."

"News?" she cried in delight. This English word she knew. She clapped her hands with the eagerness of a child. *"De ma cousine?"* From my cousin?

"From Her Majesty Queen Elizabeth, yes."

"Ah! I have . . . waited . . . hoped!" Keyed up, Mary went on hurriedly in French, and Herries translated, "Her Majesty longs to look on her dear cousin's face. They have never met, she says, but she knows that when they do they will be as sisters. She says she longs to embrace her sister queen."

"Sister!" Mary crooned. "Yes!"

"I assure you that Her Majesty feels no less love for Your Grace," said Lord Thornleigh. "And to show you her love she has sent gifts." He strode to the door and beckoned his two servingmen, who came in with a carved cedar chest heavy enough to require both of them to carry it. They set it down near Mary, bowing, and then, eyes down, retreated backward.

She looked excited and gestured for Margaret Currier to open the chest.

Before Margaret could move Justine said quickly, *"Permettez-moi, votre majesté."* She made a deep curtsy, then went down on her knees beside the large chest.

Mary blinked at her. Justine's heart was beating hard—she should not have spoken until spoken to—but Mary seemed more intrigued than annoyed, though whether by Justine's French or her forwardness, she could not tell. Quickly, she opened the chest, releasing a scent of cedar, to show Mary the contents: several folded, sumptuous gowns.

"Her Majesty," Lord Thornleigh said, looking pleased with Justine's quick action, "sympathizes with the unfortunate loss of your wardrobe." It was common gossip that the Queen of Scots had arrived in England with nothing but the clothes she stood up in. The black dress she wore now was likely the best that Scrope's wife could lend her, and though of fine wool and enlivened with gold embroidery it had no regal splendor. "She hopes these poor offerings will bring you some comfort until you may again wear the raiment befitting your state."

The gowns were anything but poor. Mary scooped up one of emerald satin, the bodice encrusted with seed pearls. She pressed it to her body as lovingly as a mother would a child. Tears gleamed in her eyes as she answered him, and Herries translated, "Unfortunate in circumstance I am indeed, my lord. But blessed in the love of my dear sister-cousin."

"To be sure. Furthermore, Her Majesty sends you my ward here, Mistress Justine Thornleigh, to remain in attendance upon you. If the girl has acted out of turn, do forgive her—it is only because she is eager to serve you."

"Aha." Mary beamed at Justine. *"Très jolie."* Very pretty. *"Mon seigneur,* I . . . thank . . . you."

He gave a courtly bow. "The honor is mine, Your Grace."

Still on her knees, Justine looked up at Mary, who was close enough to touch. Mary winked at her, smiling, which brought amused murmurs of approval from Scrope and the two Scots and gave Justine an unexpected thrill. Jane's sweet lute music lilted on. Justine stood and curtsied again to Mary, and as she resumed her position beside Lord Thornleigh she caught the two young ladies looking at her with friendly curiosity. At such affable goodwill from everyone, especially Mary, she felt a flush of confidence. This would not be so hard a posting after all.

Mary's exchange with Lord Thornleigh carried on, and Herries continued to translate, but Justine easily followed Mary's French, despite her quickness of speech spurred by her excitement.

"Shall I see my dear sister-cousin soon, my lord? I am ready to travel at a moment's notice. Are you to escort me to her court? To London?"

"Not yet, Your Grace. First, there is some business to settle."

"Business?"

He explained that Elizabeth was grieved by the accusations that had been cast upon Mary. He assured her that Elizabeth was determined to end this purgatory of Mary's, and that her ultimate desire was to restore Mary to her throne.

Mary's intense interest was obvious. "Restore me? She said that?"

"She did."

"It is all I want! All I desire!"

"And what she wishes. But she feels unable to do so while these accusations encumber you." To that end, he explained, Elizabeth had authorized an inquiry into the causes of the rift between Mary and the government in Edinburgh.

She blanched. "An inquiry? What does that mean, inquiry?"

"Her Majesty has appointed commissioners to examine the matter. She has also asked the lords in Edinburgh to send their commissioners to account for their actions against you. Working together, along with you of course, a way ahead will be found."

Mary looked horrified. "To defame me!" she cried. "To ruin me!"

At her outburst the Scottish lords tensed. The lute music stopped. Lord Thornleigh said with careful precision, "The aim, Your Grace, is merely to clear the air."

"Defend myself to disobedient subjects? Never! I will not be judged! I will not be put on trial!"

"I assure you this is not a trial. Her Majesty seeks only peace and harmony in Scotland."

She came close to him, so close that Justine, astounded, thought she might actually lay hold of him, but instead she clasped her hands and lifted them in supplication. "Oh, let me *see* my cousin. To her will I state my case. To my fellow queen. But *only* to her. Take me to her. I *demand* that you take me to her!"

He stiffened. "Please understand. Her Majesty cannot receive you at court while these serious charges hang over you. She has already compromised herself by standing by you. Now she asks that you stand by her and agree to this inquiry."

Fury flashed in Mary's eyes. She swooped toward Herries and snatched the dagger at his belt. Everyone gasped.

Mary thrust the blade out, clutched in both her hands, backing away from them all as if from attackers. "By God," she cried in enraged French, "I will kill any man who would drag me off to be tried! Tried by the very villains who usurped my throne!"

Herries stood mute in shock. Justine, dumbfounded, had understood Mary's French, and Lord Thornleigh, it was clear, understood her action.

"Madam!" Livingston lurched forward, consternation on his face, as though to disarm her for her own good.

She gave a menacing jab with the dagger. Livingston halted. Everyone froze.

Mary flipped the blade tip toward her own throat. Her eyes blazed fury at Lord Thornleigh. She spat in French, "Elizabeth will cancel this order, or I will kill *myself*."

Scrope cried out in alarm, "No!" The two Scots looked deathly afraid. Mary suddenly swayed on her feet. Her face was white. Her arm with the dagger drooped. The blade clattered to the floor. Scrope rushed to pull a chair toward her and she sank into it, moaning. Herries and Livingston hurried to her side. Scrope, too. He was bending to take her hand to comfort her when Lord Thornleigh grunted a stern warning to him. "My lord!"

Scrope straightened, stiff, aware that, as Elizabeth's lieutenant, he had gone too far. He stepped away from Mary.

Tears sprang to her eyes. She rolled her head in misery. "A trial . . . never." Tears ran down her cheeks. Her breaths were shudders as she wept. "Only God can judge me!" Herries pulled himself together to translate this.

Lord Thornleigh, alone among the men, seemed unmoved. "As He shall judge us all, madam."

She shot him a sharp look. Ignoring her two loyal lords who hovered by her side, she kept her eyes locked on Lord Thornleigh as she wiped tears from her cheeks and went on in French. Herries translated. "Her Majesty meant, sir, that no man stands between a sovereign and God."

"Be that as it may, madam, the inquiry convenes at York as soon as the Scottish commissioners arrive. You are requested to appear."

Mary was utterly still. Justine marveled at her instant composure. When Mary spoke, her voice was steel. In English, Herries repeated her words. "Tell my cousin this. I will never plead my cause against the usurpers unless they stand before me in chains."

She got to her feet. Herries stood by her and translated. "Go, sir. Return to your royal mistress." She threw Justine a glance of scorn. Her next French words stunned Justine. "And take this girl back with you. I require no such gift."

* * *

Justine paced on the sunlit terrace beneath Mary's tower. Dismissed before she had even begun! Indignation coursed through her. To be treated so disdainfully by Mary was not just a slap to her, it was a gross insult to Lord Thornleigh—to Elizabeth! It sparked in Justine a sharp, fresh desire to fulfill her mission. Yet what was she to do? Mary had retired in anger to her private suite. Lord Thornleigh was in Scrope's rooms in conference with Herries and Livingston, trying to beat out a settlement. Justine was alone on the terrace with her fear that this venture was stillborn, that she would be riding back to London to face Will with no evidence to prove herself a loyal Thornleigh, only a stark confession of her Grenville blood.

Pacing, she reached the waist-high terrace wall and pressed her hands against it to steady her rising alarm. She *had* to stay. Had to somehow make them let her stay. But how? The men would be discussing only the inquiry, Lord Thornleigh urging his queen's agenda while Herries pressed that of *his* queen. Perhaps, after long negotiation, they might come to terms, but what difference does it make to me? she thought anxiously. They won't even be discussing me. She was a minor cog in these wheels of diplomacy, and much as Lord Thornleigh wanted her to stay and wait on Mary for any information she could supply to Elizabeth, he would almost surely sacrifice that point if he could get Mary to accept the far more urgent one of appearing before the inquiry. That was what he had been sent to do, if he could.

Well, I've been sent to do something, too, she thought. *And I will do it.*

The terrace overlooked the slope of the hill the castle stood on, and she gazed across the moors toward Yeavering Hall. It lay miles away, too far to see, but a memory surged back of that night she had seen her father for the last time.

Excitement shot through her. Is *that* the way to stay? My Grenville blood?

She hurried to the chamber she had been given, a small but cheerful room over the castle's chapel. She found her maid, Ann, dozing on a chair by the open window, snoring softly in the afternoon heat. Justine passed her as quietly as she could so as not to wake her. She pulled a key from her underskirt pocket as she reached the cherrywood jewel case on the table. She unlocked it. Her necklaces and earrings, nestling in blue velvet, sparkled. Dumping them on the bed, with a glance at Ann to be sure she dozed on, she righted the casket and with her fingernail pried loose the velvet false bottom. Beneath it lay a hand-sized red leather pouch. She lifted it, its supple leather as soft as skin, and felt a shiver. It had been years since she had looked at it. The leather was pocked with black pinpricks, burned by cinders. Remembering, she could almost smell the smoke on her father's breeches as he tossed this pouch to her from his horse. The day after he vanished she had looked inside the pouch—it held twenty-three coins, all gold sovereigns, and a jeweled pendant— then she had tugged tight its satin drawstring and never looked inside it again. Taken into Lord Thornleigh's family, she had never needed the coins. She had buried the memory of her traitorous father and put aside the pouch. She wanted no part of his gift.

Until now. Not the coins. The pendant.

"Oui?" Mary half turned her head as she sat writing at her desk. *"Qui est là?"*

"C'est moi, votre majesté. Justine."

Mary quickly turned. *"Comment êtes-vous entré ici?"* How did you get in here?

Justine curtsied, her heart pounding. *"L'escalier de terrace."* The terrace stairway.

They continued in French. "Well?" Mary asked, the quill pen stilled in her hand. "What do you want?" She looked irritated, as if she felt a lowly servant had interrupted her though she knew she had to be civil to this relation of an English baron.

"Only to be of assistance to you, Your Majesty."

"Oh?" Her tone was mildly sarcastic. "Not to your guardian?"

"Yes, of course. My attending you is his lordship's wish."

"Because it is his royal mistress's wish?"

"Yes, exactly."

Mary gave her a hard look. "Yes, exactly." She winced, as though her headache had returned, and rubbed her brow, murmuring, "I would I knew Elizabeth's mind."

"Your Majesty, if I have offended you in some way I entreat you to forgive me. I would not distress you for the world."

Mary cocked her head, vaguely intrigued. "Your French is excellent."

"Thank you. My mother was French. From Lille."

"But your father English?"

"Yes. I was born not sixty miles from here."

Mary, losing interest, was tapping the feather end of her quill against the desk. "If you have been sent with instructions to pacify me, save your breath." She turned back to her writing. "You may go."

"I have no such instructions. I have come on my own. Your Majesty, I hope you will accept a gift."

Mary turned. She eyed the red leather pouch that Justine held up. "A trinket from your guardian?"

"No, Your Majesty. From me. And it is no trinket."

She came close and kneeled in front of Mary. Tugging loose the pouch's satin drawstring, she slipped her fingers inside and slid out the pendant. It was a crucifix, two inches of pure gold. The cross had been wrought by a master craftsman to seem like rough, splintered wood, while the skin of the Christ, slumping in agony upon it, was as smooth as water. The wounds in his nailed, bleeding palms and at his nailed, crossed ankles were rubies.

Justine looked up. Mary's face had utterly changed. Boredom and irritation had fled. She looked enthralled. "Beautiful," she whispered, and reached out to touch it.

Justine whispered, too. "The people in these parts hid many such sacred objects. They are keeping them safe, waiting for the day when the one true church is reborn in England."

She waited, holding her breath, watching Mary. What she had just said was near blasphemy in Elizabeth's Protestant realm. Enough to warrant a complaint against her in the church courts, if anyone cared to make it, and certainly enough to compromise Lord Thornleigh.

Mary gave her a searching look. "Is that your wish?"

Justine was committed now. "It is. And the wish of thousands of good people here in the north. But most of all, Your Majesty . . ." Her mouth was so dry she had to swallow to go on. "Most of all, my wish is to serve you. I hope you understand how these two wishes are one and the same." She held out the pendant crucifix as an offering.

Mary held her gaze for a long moment, her face grave, as though weighing a hard decision. Then she took the gift.

Justine let out a puff of breath, too relieved to hide it. And encouraged. Now she dared go on. "Let me stay, Your Majesty? Please. Let me stay."

Mary looked mildly taken aback. "Subtlety is not your forte, is it?"

"If you send me back, the Queen will only send someone else in my stead. And you could do worse than me."

"Really?" She seemed almost amused.

"Really. The two young ladies who attend you now, do they speak French?"

"Yes." Her lips curved in a sly smile. "Badly."

Justine returned the smile, exulting.

Abruptly, Mary stood. "Rise. What did you say your name was?"

"Justine, Your Majesty." She got to her feet.

"Justine, fetch Lord Thornleigh. And would you kindly translate for us?"

She hurried to tell him. She would have run along the corridor if servants at their tasks had not been watching. He was startled when she told him that she had managed to speak privately to Mary, had impressed her favorably, and now Mary was asking to see him.

"Lead the way," he said, clearly pleased.

They assembled again in the tapestry-hung chamber, and this time Mary was waiting for them. Justine stood in pride of place beside Mary as her translator, as Herries had done before.

Mary raised her chin proudly before Lord Thornleigh. "My lord, I have revised my decision concerning this inquiry my dear cousin has set in motion."

He bowed with respect. "Then Your Grace will attend?"

"No. It is beneath my honor to do so. However, I shall send commissioners to make my case. I alone, sir, will choose them."

Lord Thornleigh frowned. This was not what he had expected. Nor had Justine. But she felt, and sensed that he did, too, that it was Mary's final answer. Justine hardly cared. She had won what she wanted. She was staying.

He collected himself and gave another bow, stiffer than before. "I shall take this message to Her Majesty."

"Thank you." She glanced at Justine. "And take your ward home, too."

Justine gasped. "But—"

"Tell my cousin," Mary said directly to Lord Thornleigh, "that as soon as she welcomes me to her court, I shall welcome her people to mine."

❧ 7 ❧

The Crucifix

Night was the only safe time for Christopher Grenville to move. Tonight, though, a full moon shone down mercilessly on Carlisle Castle. Christopher backed up against the recessed door of the castle chapel, shrouding himself in deeper shadows as a soldier on horseback trotted past. The clatter of the hooves faded and silence fell over the narrow, moonlit street. An owl hooted from the castle wall. Christopher let out a pent-up breath. He was taking a huge risk in coming here. The incident with the seamstress from Yeavering Hall three weeks ago haunted him like an ill omen. The price on his head for treason now included murder. Curse the girl for recognizing him! He hadn't wanted to kill her, but what choice did he have? He could not let word of his return get out. Even more worrying was that figure he had seen running away through the churchyard. A witness?

He clenched his teeth, cutting off the galling worries. The risks and dangers he faced would all pay off if his plans for Mary bore fruit. And that looked so hopeful now! He was itching to tell her. All evening he had waited in the castle's cellar tavern, alone with his ale, watching the window until he saw the sun set. Earlier he had tethered his horse in the woods and trudged into the castle precincts where his homespun clothes and the satchel of trinkets he had slung over his shoulder gave him a certain invisibility—a harmless peddler, one of many country folk who constantly came and went with their produce and wares. Now, night was his other ally.

He hoped that Mary had not changed her routine. She, too, liked the night.

He slipped inside the chapel, closing the door quietly behind him. The dimly lit space seemed deserted—just five vacant rows of upholstered benches. The altar slumbered under a pale wash of moonlight crimsoned by a stained glass window. A faint light glowed from an alcove behind a pillar. He moved silently past the benches, past the pillar, and reached the alcove. A woman was kneeling in prayer before a bank of votive candles under a wall-mounted cross. Christopher's nerves leapt to life. *Mary.*

She raised her head suddenly at a sound. She looked over her shoulder, saw him, and gasped in fear.

He moved so quickly he was behind her before she could rise. He clamped his hand over her mouth and pressed the back of her head against his thigh, his other hand pushing her shoulder down to force her to stay on her knees. She squirmed. "Be quiet," he whispered in French. "Do not call for help."

He loosened his hold on her enough to let her twist around, still kneeling. She looked up at him and her eyes went wide, not with fear now but with surprise. "You!" she whispered.

Power surged through him as he kept hold of her shoulder to keep her down. To have Mary Stuart on her knees before him. A queen!

"Give me your hand," he said. He felt her slight shiver at his command—a shiver of pleasure, like the old days. It made *him* shiver. Obeying, she offered her hand. He took it and brought it to his lips. "My lady."

Her wide-eyed gaze, and the way she stayed in a pose of submission when she could have risen—it fired his blood, made him bold. He turned her hand and slid his tongue across her palm. She trembled. He thrilled at her salty taste.

A thud at the altar startled them both. Mary jumped to her feet. Christopher gripped the dagger handle at his belt.

A cat leapt down from the altar, streaked across the chapel, and disappeared into the shadows.

They turned to each other and she gave a small laugh of relief. He relaxed, too, letting go the dagger. Face-to-face with her now, she so tall, her regal bearing returning, Christopher felt the intimate spell dissolve. *A good thing,* he thought, getting control. He had been too near forgetting himself. That would be dangerous, for him and for her. He could hope for that reward later, the taste of her skin, as the crowning prize for their success. He wanted even more—she could restore his lands to him, raise him to greatness, even make him an earl. But only if the plan he had set in motion succeeded. For now, he had to keep his distance.

He carried on, still in French, the language they always used. "My lady." He made a courtly bow. "I thank God to find you so hale." Hale, and beautiful. She wore a silver silk gown, its bodice encrusted with seed pearls that shimmered through the gauzy shawl wrapped around her shoulders like a Scottish mist. The last time he had seen her was over a year ago, in Edinburgh. He had taken a letter from her to France, to her uncle the Duc de Guise. Neither could have imagined then that she would soon lose her kingdom.

"You are wrong, sir. I suffer."

That alarmed him. "Do they abuse you?"

"No riding, no hunting, and only a paltry pair of attendants as if I were some petty gentlewoman. That's abuse enough." With a wounded, angry look she smoothed the skirt folds of her gown. "I have had to send Lord Herries to borrow from the local merchants just to hire pantry servants."

He relaxed, glad to see she had not changed. Mary, the haughty, wronged beauty. Almost smiling, he asked, indulging her, "Is Lord Scrope so spiteful?"

"Scrope, no, he was biddable enough, until his handlers brought him to task for it. Now he makes no move without permission from Elizabeth, not so much as allowing me to purchase a pair of shoes. I swear, when I fled my captors I came into England in good faith, trusting in Elizabeth's friendship. And what have I found? Contempt. Hardship. I have exchanged one prison for another."

Her anger was real and raw—and no doubt merited, Christopher thought. Yet there was much of the child in her. Impetuous and angry when she wanted something, but vacillating when political decisions were needed. Passionate about friendships, but disinterested in affairs of state and therefore an easy victim for a cunning, determined adversary like her half brother Moray. As a ruler, Mary was often out of her depth.

Yet she had been kind to him, a man adrift, in exile from his homeland, and he would never forget that. They had met when she was the young Queen of France, just seventeen. He had been drifting on the fringes of the French court, unwilling to draw attention to himself since the English presumed him dead. Then members of Mary's circle had brought him to her attention, for although the rebellion he had planned had not come to pass he had proved himself an enemy of Elizabeth of England. Mary had welcomed him. And what a dazzling young queen she was! Lively, amusing, generous—a blaze of beauty and high spirits and glittering fashion. But when her sickly teenage husband King François died, Mary's status at the court of his brother, the new King Charles, shrank overnight to nothing. Suddenly adrift herself, a dowager queen with little power, she had turned to Christopher for comfort. He saw his opportunity, a nubile widow of eighteen, hungry for a strong man's hand. He took it, and took her.

That single night together had forged a bond that had remained strong through the next six years, though they had spent them mostly apart. She had left France to take up the Scottish crown that was her birthright and had remarried—the wastrel, Lord Darnley—while Christopher had remained in Paris managing some of her property interests. He had traveled often to Edinburgh to carry her messages back to France. Then came the debacle of her downfall, and Christopher had despaired, sure she was lost, and his own prospects, too. But she had escaped, and the moment he heard she had taken sanctuary in England he praised God and pledged himself to her cause. Helping her was the only way he might one day reclaim his *own* birthright, his English property.

Now that seemed thrillingly possible.

"You shall not be a prisoner for long, my lady. I bring news."

She clapped her hands, eager for it. "Ah! Am I to be rescued?"

He glanced around to make absolutely sure they were alone, then gestured for her to take a seat on the nearest chapel bench. They sat down together, close enough that Christopher could keep his voice low. "I have come from Alnwick, and I bring you the pledge of my lord Northumberland." Though he was saddle sore and bone-weary from his journeying, seeing Mary's excitement energized him afresh. Thomas Percy, Earl of Northumberland, thirty-eight, was the most powerful lord in the north and devoutly Catholic. Christopher had met with him at Alnwick Castle, the ancient seat of the Percy family, where they were joined by the Earl of Westmorland. It was a secret meeting behind closed doors in a long-unused gatehouse apartment, for they were talking treason. "These lords are with you, my lady. To the ends of the earth."

Her eyes glowed. "Good men, and true!"

Christopher did not tell her how nervous the two nobles had been, at first, to plan sedition with him. Not that they lacked the desire to depose Elizabeth. Eight years ago Northumberland had worked closely with Christopher on the uprising they had eventually been forced to abort. Now, the earl was cautiously eager to try again. Together, both earls could raise several thousand men among their followers. But they lacked the stomach to act on their own. To motivate them, Christopher had told them of the rumor gaining strength in France that the pope, at the urging of the King of Spain, was considering excommunicating Elizabeth and condoning her overthrow. That had fired up Northumberland and Westmorland. If they took action in the name of the pope, God's representative on earth, and successfully overthrew the heretic English queen, they would be cheered by all the Catholics of Europe.

He told Mary the same thing now.

She beamed. "The pope? It is the answer to my prayers!"

"God has not forsaken you, my lady. Though Elizabeth has."

"But, oh, the *waiting*," she groaned. "It will take forever for the pope to act. While I wither here." She grabbed Christopher's elbow with a fierce determination. "Ride back to Northumberland. Now, this very night. Tell him he must gather his men-at-arms immediately and descend on this place and free me!"

He could not hide a disapproving frown. Were they to snatch her like the local border raiders who stole cattle?

"Do you doubt me, sir?" she challenged. "I am ready to hazard all, I swear it. I can ride as hard as any man, and you know it!"

"I do indeed, my lady," he said with genuine admiration. "And your loyal followers would gladly fight for you to the death. But this is no way to proceed. Where would Northumberland take you? To what end? You cannot go back to Scotland to be in Moray's power." No, it served Christopher's purposes far better if she remained Elizabeth's prisoner, making her plight irresistible to her followers: Mary, the innocent victim of her cruel cousin. It would help fire them to action. "I beg you to be patient, my lady. There are plans afoot." He added in a keyed-up whisper, pleased to tantalize her, "When you leave here, it will be to ride to your new capital. London."

She gasped. "London?"

"You know it is yours by right. Elizabeth is a bastard and a heretic. She holds the crown in sin. You are England's rightful monarch."

She stared at him, taking it in, clearly enthralled. Her claim to the English throne was one she had publicly stated for years. "But Elizabeth's hold is strong. Are you saying Northumberland and Westmorland will march against her? When? When will they strike?"

"They stand willing now, but they have sent me to warn you that their strength is not yet sufficient, and I agree. They can raise five thousand men, perhaps six. An impressive army, to be sure, but Elizabeth can best it. Before we can move, we need an ally. One with muscle."

She did not flinch at the idea. It was as though she had been waiting for this opportunity.

"France?" she suggested. "My Guise uncles keep urging Charles to back us, but—"

"No, forget France." King Charles was too beset with strangling the many-headed monster of heresy in his own realm. Huguenot factions kept erupting throughout the country, enlisting thousands of French men and women to their ranks. The King had neither the forces nor the inclination to adventure against England. "The ally we need is Spain."

"Philip? Bah! He is maddening. The most Catholic prince in Christendom they call him, but what good is his pious talk if he will not commit to my cause? They say he believes the slanders against me. Believes the vermin who call me adulteress and murderer." Tears glistened in her eyes. She raised her chin with a look of furious pride.

A fine show, Christopher thought. *Quite convincing.* He did not know if she had been complicit with the Earl of Bothwell in her husband's murder or not. Darnley, an arrogant drunken fool by all accounts, had apparently deserved it. As for adultery with Bothwell, Christopher knew Mary's appetites and knew Bothwell's reputation for womanizing and violence, so he was inclined to believe that the two had been lovers before Darnley's death and had worked together to kill him. But Mary had vehemently denied all of it, and Bothwell, who had fled to Denmark at her downfall, wasn't talking.

None of it mattered to Christopher. "Philip's reluctance," he said dryly, "has more to do with trade between Spain and England. He wants no disruption of it, which Elizabeth might threaten if he were to back you."

"I wish I could turn him! I shall write to his wife. I know her, she is pious. I shall tell her that if I were Queen of England I would restore the one true church in this land."

"Pious she is, but I doubt she has the ear of her husband."

Mary frowned at this, acknowledging the truth of it.

"There is another, though, who does," Christopher said. "Philip's representative in London. Ambassador de Spes is fervent in his faith, and in his support of your rights."

"That is true, he is! And he has sway with Philip."

"Let me go and speak with him, urge him to stiffen the King's backbone."

She seemed moved. "A dangerous venture for you, though. London. If anyone should recognize you . . ."

She did not need to finish. They both knew the terrible consequences. If arrested for treason he would be hanged until almost dead, then disemboweled and quartered. *If I'm not arrested first about that Yeavering girl.* It shook him, remembering the figure running through the churchyard. What had the fellow seen? But he could not let such thoughts distract him now. Mary knew nothing of that misadventure, and he had no intention of telling her. He needed her absolute trust in his ability to succeed for her.

"I will be careful," he assured her. "I'll start for London tomorrow. Will you give me a letter for Ambassador de Spes, proof that I am your emissary?"

"Yes, yes, of course." Her thoughts seemed to have strayed elsewhere. She got to her feet and began to pace, her agitation plain. "There is something else. You may not have heard."

"What is it? What's wrong?"

"Elizabeth. She has ordered an official inquiry. About me."

"What?"

She explained as she paced, and Christopher listened, appalled. Elizabeth's councilors about to make a public spectacle of Mary. The Earl of Moray invited to England to make his case against her. It was horrifying. He jumped up and stopped her in her tracks. "Why in God's name did you agree?"

"It was the condition for her help," she said, as plaintive as a child. "Her emissary came to make the offer."

"Help in what?"

"Restoring me to my throne. And I just received a letter from her that goes even further. She says that if the inquiry finds there is no truth to the charges she will restore me by *force* if necessary. But only if . . ."

"If what?" Dear God, what had Mary given away?

"If I will renounce my claim to the English throne."

He could have slapped her. "Tell me that you have not done so."

"No, never! But, oh, I am beset with enemies." She hugged herself as if her plight had iced the air, and she tugged the gauzy shawl tightly to her. "Cecil, that devil who advises her. Moray, on his way to slander me before all the world. My fate is in Elizabeth's hands. I *must* trust her."

"It is her trap. She is lying. She will never restore you. It would shatter the alliance she and Cecil have created with Moray." Cold sweat chilled Christopher's back. He fought to keep his mind focused, find a way to deal with the crisis. "Oh, she is clever. This inquiry will light a fire under Moray. He will be desperate to prove you guilty, because if they find you innocent his position as Scotland's legitimate authority will be untenable."

"It *is* untenable! And criminal. He ruined me and tried to kill me. Once I am restored he will pay!"

"Don't you see? That is the very reason he will do anything to prove you guilty. Because if you return as queen he knows he will face your vengeance."

"And so he would! I would have his head!" She raised her hand like an axe and chopped.

He caught her wrist. "Stop it. You must keep your heart and mind set on the true goal. Not the throne of Scotland. The throne of *England*."

She blinked at him like a sleepwalker jolted awake. "England. Yes. It is my right."

"The whole world, even the Protestants, acknowledge you as Elizabeth's heir. That is what she is trying to undermine."

"Never. I will never renounce my claim."

Dread slithered into Christopher's heart like a snake. "Even if you don't, she has set this inquiry in motion so that you cannot win. *She* is your true enemy."

He saw in her face that the awful truth of his words was sinking in. She grabbed both his arms as though for support. "You mean . . . they could find me . . . guilty?"

His mind was thrashing through the possibilities. "There is no action she can legitimately take against you. She has no jurisdiction."

"But the blot on my reputation. I would seem a monster. People would hate me!" Tears sprang to her eyes.

He groaned inside. Why could she never see farther than her own emotions! People's smiles or frowns did not matter, only whether they would rally behind her or forsake her. *That* was the crisis here.

She was crying outright now, tears wetting her pale cheeks. Her helplessness stirred him despite himself. For one wild moment he imagined licking those salty tears. She laid her forehead on his shoulder and wept. It was her way to move men to action; always had been. He knew that. And knew he was not immune. But her very need for a strong man to guide her gave him a surging sense of power. His pulse gave a sudden thump as he realized the course that lay ahead. Simple. Bold. Terrifying.

Thrilling.

He slipped his arm around her waist. "They shall not find you guilty. I promise you."

Her head came up. "How can you make such a promise? Elizabeth's commissioners will do what she wants."

"Not if she is dead."

Her body went rigid. Eyes fixed on his, she repeated the word, her voice thrumming with excitement, "Dead?"

"Then you become queen of England. It is your due. No one disputes it."

They stared at one another, and he saw she was as gripped as he was by the terrible splendor of the solution.

She whispered, "You would do this . . . for me?"

"It must be done before they reach a verdict."

"But how? How can you get close enough to her?"

He had no idea. His elation crashed. The challenges were fierce. Even if he could get close enough to Elizabeth and did the deed, the Earl of Northumberland would still have to take London to forestall a rush by force of arms from other ambitious nobles eager to fill the void of power. But Northumberland would not make a move until he knew he had foreign backing as powerful as Spain's, and that required collaborating with the Spanish ambassador, a man Christopher had not yet met. He would have to weave all these strands of the plan, and do so while skulking around with a price on his head. It seemed impossible.

Mary was looking at him, her eyes shining with wonder. "Do

this," she whispered, "and you shall reap a vast reward when I am queen."

Suddenly, the impossibility vanished. He felt he could move mountains.

Smiling, she raised both her hands to caress his face. At the motion, her diaphanous shawl slipped off her shoulders, revealing her white neck. He kissed the smooth skin at her throat. She shivered with pleasure. He pushed the shawl aside, about to kiss the naked half-moon of her breast above her bodice, but halted, seeing a pendant that hung from a gold necklace, hidden before by the gauze. A thick golden crucifix. Christopher stared at it in disbelief. The rough cross. The smooth Christ. Rubies as the blood of His wounds.

It was a bolt to his heart. He lurched back a step. "Where did you get this?"

She shrugged. "A gift."

He gripped the pendant, warm from her body's heat. "Who gave it to you?"

She looked perplexed at his tone. "A girl."

He grabbed her arm. *"Who?"*

"She came with the emissary Elizabeth sent."

"The emissary, who was he?"

"Baron Thornleigh."

Christopher was so shocked, he could hardly find breath. *"Richard* Thornleigh?"

"Yes. Why?"

"The girl . . ." His heart pummeled his chest. "Her name?"

"I told you, Thorn—"

"Her *Christian* name."

"Justine . . . I think. She is his ward. He brought her to attend me as lady-in-waiting."

Christopher twisted around. Justine was *here?* In the castle? He snatched Mary's hand and yanked her, heading for the door. "Take me to her."

"No, stop." She jerked her hand free. "I sent her away, sent her back with him. Anyone could see she was Elizabeth's spy."

Christopher gaped at her. Justine had been here . . . but now was gone! He felt his legs go spongy. He lurched for the bench and thudded down on it.

Mary came to him. "What's wrong? What is this girl to you?"

He looked up at her. "She's . . ." He felt helpless. Naked. Sick. "She is . . . my daughter."

They stared at each other, she uncomprehending, he trying to hold his brain together. My child . . . with Thornleigh!

Mary said, "But she is part of Thornleigh's family. How—?"

"He stole her. Like he stole everything else of mine." *Sweet Justine*, he thought. *My child!* A sudden longing to see her flooded him. What was she like grown up? Gentle? Obstinate? Clever? Then fury came roaring back. Thornleigh had had eight years to mold the girl. *She's not mine anymore. She's one of them.*

He got to his feet. "When did they leave?"

"A few days ago."

"Bring her back."

She looked stunned. "What? Why? I tell you, Elizabeth sent her to watch me."

He bit back a rebuke. Mary could be such a fool. "Then let her watch."

She blinked, bewildered. He gripped her arm and squeezed it so hard she winced. He had to make her understand the golden chance that had fallen in their path. "My daughter is the very link to Elizabeth we need. Bring Justine back. Let her watch. We will show her what we want her to see."

❧ 8 ❧

The Carpenter

Justine had not gone back to London. Mary's refusal to accept her as a lady-in-waiting had so shocked her that when Lord Thornleigh suggested they visit his daughter Isabel at Yeavering Hall before journeying home, she had numbly followed. On the way she could think of nothing but how her mission for Elizabeth had ended before she'd even begun. "Nothing to be done about it," his lordship had said darkly, looking as though he would like to clap manacles on Mary. "A pity, though. Before she turned on us I thought you had charmed her."

Justine had thought so, too. That intimate, risky moment she had shared with Mary in giving her the crucifix. Clearly, the risk had been pointless. Mary had her own agenda.

"She's more minx than monarch," his lordship said gruffly. "Still, she has agreed to send commissioners to the inquiry, and that's what matters most."

Not to Justine. She hated to think of the awful task that lay ahead when she got back to London. She would have to confess her true identity to Will, having accomplished nothing to make herself shine in his eyes. Confess her damnable Grenville blood. That prospect had sunk her so low she had scarcely been able to muster civility to Isabel and her husband Carlos when she had first arrived at Yeavering Hall.

Yeavering. How strange it was to be back in the house she had lived in as a child. Memories were everywhere. In the great hall, the stable courtyard, the kitchen, the garden. Ghostly memories: her mother's scent, a wisp of sandalwood floating over a staircase. Painful ones: her father galloping away the night of the fire to leave her with the disgrace of being a traitor's daughter. Heartbreaking ones: Alice teaching her cat's cradle by the kitchen hearth with a string of raspberry-colored yarn; the two of them dashing in a game of hide-and-seek among the May apple trees; Alice stretching out a hand to entice her to climb out onto the roof.

It was these memories of Alice that finally shamed Justine out of her worries about Will. There *was* something she might accomplish, if not for herself, then for her friend. Justice. Now that she was at Yeavering, she would try to find out who had murdered Alice.

She set to it the day after she arrived. She was told that the day Alice was killed she had gone to the market in nearby Wooler. Justine started there.

The alehouse squatted on the edge of Wooler's sleepy market square. Justine stepped into the low-ceilinged room, dark after the bright sunlight she had closed the door on. It took a moment for her eyes to adjust. The beaten-earth floor smelled dank from decades of spilled beer. Three workmen sat at a table over pots of ale—masons, by the look of the stone dust that whitened their jerkins and hair. The benches at the other tables were empty. In front of the bar a thickset man grunted as he hoisted a full keg to set it on its stand. Hugging the barrel, he looked like a wrestler.

All four men looked at Justine with idle curiosity. What was she doing here, a lady in fine clothes? It made her hesitate, unsure. She had ridden here alone and knew no one in the town; the Hall had enclosed her whole life as a child. What, indeed, was she hoping to find?

"Can I help you, my lady?" the barman asked, dusting off his hands, the keg now in place.

"I hope so." She mentioned Alice and saw the three workmen listening intently. The murder, like all abnormal events in a small community, would have fueled evening chats around many a Wooler hearth.

The barman, however, seemed uninterested. "I told them from the Hall when they came quizzing us—I never laid eyes on the lass." He lifted the lid off a tin pot on the bar and ladled milk from it into a wooden saucer. At the sound, a scrawny gray cat slunk out from the next room and began to weave loving circles around his ankles.

"Did you see any strangers that day she was killed?" Justine asked. The servants at the Hall had sworn that the killer could not be a local man. Most families, whether farmers or town folk, had been settled here for generations. Everyone knew their neighbors.

"Strangers?" His look said he thought her question almost too foolish to answer. "Plenty, my lady. It were market day." He scooped up the cat and set it gently on the bar. It prowled to the saucer and sniffed cautiously as though suspecting the milk might be poisoned. The barman stroked its bony back, and the cat began lapping up the milk, purring. His tenderness to the animal touched Justine. And she felt it told her something: He would have noticed an obvious brute in his tavern.

She noticed a girl watching, leaning out from behind a post near the bar. She was about fourteen, slight of body, and was drying her hands on her dingy apron, her hands as red as if they'd been scalded. A scullery maid, apparently, forever washing up. She had a pinched face, but bright, keen eyes. So keen, in fact, that Justine wondered if her interest sprang from something more than a love of gossip. She beckoned her over. The girl came obediently, as she would to any of her betters, and stood in servile silence, but Justine sensed that she was bursting to speak and she asked her, "Did you see Alice Boyer that day?"

The girl's startled expression gave her a prick of hope. Had no one from the Hall thought to question so lowly a servant? The girl looked to the barman, almost certainly her father. He seemed equally surprised that anyone would want to talk to her, but then shrugged, giving her permission to speak.

"Aye, my lady," the girl answered with spirit, "she were at the stall with all the fancy ribbons." She shot her father a nervous glance at this confession of having abandoned her duties on a market day, surely a busy time at the alehouse.

"Can you show me where?" Justine knew all about the ribbons. At Yeavering Hall Isabel had spoken with a shudder about how Alice's body had been found in the Kirknewton church with a yellow silk ribbon binding her wrists together and the cord of gold braid that the killer had used to strangle her still around her throat.

"Go on, show her," said the barman. "Trade today's as slow as a turtle going backward."

Across the market square they went, Justine following the girl, who almost skipped with pleasure. Her eagerness lifted Justine's hope. Could this chit of a girl have some information that everyone had missed, something that would lead her to Alice's killer?

Market day was Thursday; today was Friday, so the square was quiet. The shop-front stalls displayed a sparse leftover selection of wares: baskets of cabbages, ropes of onions, brooms, pewter bowls, a butter churn. Blood from a vacant butcher's stall had soaked a patch of earth, leaving sticky mud. The square's center was its market cross, a stone crucifix taller than a man, rising from its anchor of three circular stone steps worn smooth by centuries of use. Wrens sat twitching atop the cross. A whiskery old man lounged on the steps peeling an apple with his knife in one long strip. A farmer on a donkey plodded by.

"There," the scullery maid said, pointing. "The ribbon man was right there."

Justine saw only a patch of beaten earth between a barren shop front and the road. "Do you know him?"

The girl looked down and shook her head, deflated, her moment of specialness spent. "A traveler."

Justine chided herself. What had she expected? That this girl would march to the door of the killer and point and cry, "It was him"? No, the Yeavering Hall steward had already questioned the town's shopkeepers and aldermen and they said the draper selling ribbons had been an itinerant, his stall nothing more than his cart. No one knew him. She looked down the road that bent as it left the town, the bend hemmed in by willows. The "ribbon man" had gone on his way down that road. He could be anywhere between York and Edinburgh by now. Had he killed Alice? But what would drive a roving peddler, a stranger to Alice, to commit such a monstrous crime?

She turned back. "Did you speak to Alice?"

"Aye."

"Did she seem upset about anything?"

"Not at all, my lady." The girl seemed again proud to have a bit of unique information. "She were gazing at the fancies, the scarves and ribbons all flapping in the breeze, and I said wouldn't it be grand to own one of those. And she said she'd like a dress all of that green silk—green as a dragonfly wing, it was. She said if she had such a dress she'd never take it off. You'd sleep in it? says I. And she says, Aye, sleep in it and dream in it, and if that were so I'd be a fine lady, so who would dare to wake me? We laughed at that. Daft talk, i' faith."

Justine felt tears sting the back of her eyes. Daft talk—how Alice had liked it. Liked foolery of all kinds.

"Did you see anyone else talking to her? A stranger?"

The girl shook her head. "I had to get back to me washtub." She gazed at the spot where the draper's cart had stood with its fluttering silks. Fluttering fantasies. Her shoulders drooped, her eyes went dull. Time, again, to get back to her washtub.

Justine rode northward, leaving Wooler, and her next stop was even more disturbing—the church at Kirknewton on the road to Yeavering Hall. She climbed the stone stairs up to the tower, following the vicar.

"All bedecked with scarves and trimmings and gewgaws, it was," he said as they reached the belfry. He was a fidgety young man, not much older than Justine herself, she guessed, and schooled in stark Protestantism. He shook his head in disgust. "Frippery hanging hither and yon, all round the bell casement. Looked like some York brothel."

Anger flared in her at his heartlessness, and she almost shot back, You know brothels well? She held her tongue, but it galled her that he seemed to care more about the defilement of the space than the snuffing out of an innocent life. The belfry was now austere enough even for him, the colorful "gewgaws" removed. Downstairs in the nave he had pointed out to her the spot behind the altar where the killer had left Alice's body. She shuddered, imagining her friend's last moments. Had the murderer used the pretty scarves to entice her up here to the belfry first? Had she become afraid of him then and tried to flee? Or had he festooned the belfry but then, before he could lure her here, strangled her in the nave? It was agonizing, not knowing. Perhaps, she thought bleakly, it was unknowable.

"You found no other evidence?" she asked. "No hint left behind to suggest who might have killed her?"

"As I told you, I was away reporting to the bishop. My churchwarden found the body, then this vandalism. There was nothing else."

She went to the unglazed window that overlooked the moors. A dragonfly clung to the edge of the stone casement, its trembling wings iridescent in the sunlight. The scullery maid's words came back, how Alice had longed for a dress of green silk, green as a dragonfly wing. Justine lengthened her gaze across the valley of the River Glen nestled at the foot of the Cheviot Hills, and up a low hill to the cluster of buildings with the grand house at their center: Yeavering Hall. Alice had worked there. It gave Justine a shiver, and not just for her friend. Yeavering Hall now belonged to Lord Thornleigh's daughter and son-in-law. In her heart the Thornleighs were her family, yet their ownership of the Hall felt odd. It was an unsettling jumble in her mind: the home she'd grown up in that wasn't her home. The family she loved that wasn't her flesh and blood.

The vicar cleared his throat. "I must get back to my desk. Sunday's sermon."

Justine turned. "Yes, of course." There was nothing here to help her. This was only a site of sorrow.

Yeavering Hall was three stories of honey-hued stone rising into the blue Northumberland sky. It had seemed immense to Justine when she was a child, an entire world of its own, with its pleasure grounds spreading across acres of gardens, terraces, treed alleys, and orchards; its busy outbuildings of bakery, brewery, dairy house, dovecote, stables, and barns; its views that swept up to the twin-peaked hill of Yeavering Bell and down to the River Glen. Yeavering had always been a beautiful house, one that Justine's mother, with her French taste, had made elegant, but Justine did not remember it as being a particularly cheerful place. Now, thanks to Isabel and Carlos and their three young children, it was.

True, the elegance had been somewhat frayed by the whirlwind of family life for the last eight years. Instead of the graceful tunes of lutes that had once lilted from the musicians' gallery, the great hall rang with the sound of running feet, giggling voices, and the high spirits of boisterous children. The gorgeous stained glass windows, the refined work of master craftsmen, looked down on a blithe clutter: two fishing rods propped against the hearth, a shaggy water spaniel nursing her litter of pups on the hearthstone, a rocking horse that wore, incongruously, a baby's bonnet, and on the floor a heap of plums spread on a tablecloth that the children had used to gather their cache from the orchard. It was certainly a change from the formality Justine had known as a child, but she liked it. Isabel and Carlos had made the stately house a home.

Isabel especially. Since coming into Lord Thornleigh's family eight years ago, Justine had looked up to her like an older sister. She was also fascinated by the conjugal bond between lovely, cultured Isabel and her rugged base-born Spanish husband who had once made his living as a mercenary on the battlefields of Europe. Though it was an unlikely match, Carlos had proved a diligent lord of the manor; lately, he'd been working with the Earl of Northumberland to strengthen the border defenses against the marauding Scottish raiders. And anyone could see the deep affection between him and Isabel. When Justine had first met them they had been married for five years and she had seen looks pass between them hinting at a carnal intimacy that had made young Justine blush with curious fascination. Now their happy marriage made her yearn for Will.

The hall today was quieter than usual, for Carlos had gone

hunting with his father-in-law and they had taken twelve-year-old Nicolas with them. Justine wondered if Lord Thornleigh really was well enough for such hard exercise, but she knew enough of men to know that he would never willingly show himself unable. Andrew, age eight, had been invited to hunt too, but declared that he did not like to kill creatures, and was now in the garden playing commander of a tree fort with his five-year-old sister, Nell. Her chirping voice sounded faintly through one of the open windows.

It left the great hall to Justine and Isabel, just as they planned. They sat together in the middle of the long table as though holding court session. In a way they were; they were calling in all the household people, one by one, to question them about Alice's last days.

"Is it really necessary to put them through all that again?" Isabel had asked at first when Justine proposed it. "Our steward questioned everyone weeks ago, right after the murder. It will only distress everyone to relive it."

"Someone might have forgotten a detail," Justine had insisted. "It can't hurt to offer them another chance to come forward."

Isabel had seemed unconvinced. Though horrified by the murder and saddened by the loss of such a vital young woman, she said that the evil was done and the killer long gone and that Justine should let her friend rest in peace. Justine could not do that. There was no peace for her while a chance remained, however slight, of tracking down the killer. "People," she said with some warmth, "do not vanish. He is *somewhere*."

"All right," Isabel had said with sigh of acceptance. "If we're going to do this, let's do a thorough job."

And so they had cleared the table of books, backgammon board, a rag doll, a basket of string beans, and a toy warship and sent word through the house and round to the outbuildings, from bakehouse and brewhouse, stable and barn, for all the manor folk to appear, one by one. The people had gathered outside, chatting on benches in the shade under the porch vines, their voices low in speaking of Alice, but no one complaining about the respite from their chores.

"We'll see old Liza Gordon next," Isabel said, ticking off the name on her list with a flick of her quill pen.

"The laundress?" Justine asked. "My, she must be getting on." It felt strange seeing servants who had worked in the house when she was a child.

"She's a good soul." Isabel added with a wink, "When she's not downing a tankard of ale."

They shared a smile. It suddenly struck Justine as unseemly, sharing a jest when their business was about Alice, but she was grateful for Isabel's good humor at their unsettling task.

They heard from twenty-one people—housemaids, brewers, milkmaids, butchers, scullery boys, grooms, gardeners, the children's tutor, a teenage carpenter, and the cook—and still Justine had no better picture of Alice's last day on earth than when they had started. Several people had seen her go off to the Wooler market on the mule. Three of them had gone to the market later and assumed that Alice had returned home early. No one had seen her there, let alone seen a stranger accosting her. None had noticed anything strange as they had passed the Kirknewton church.

Now the stooped old laundress shuffled in.

"Kirknewton?" she said in response to Isabel's question, looking confused. "Bless me, Lady Isabel, what business would I be having in Kirknewton?"

"You didn't know Alice Boyer was going there?" Justine asked. The old servant hadn't recognized her as the grown-up daughter of the old master.

"Boyer?"

"Lady Isabel's seamstress?" Isabel prompted.

The old laundress blinked in bewilderment. Justine was losing heart. "There's a gardener name of Boyer. He's a good 'un with roses and irises and gillyflowers, but he don't grow the right lavender for me soap. I tell him again and again, but he just laughs and dances a jig. Why do you ask, my lady? Has he run off?"

It was hopeless. The old woman's mind was trapped in the past. Alice's father hadn't been gardener here for over fifteen years. Visiting the ailing parents in their rough cottage behind the stables had been the hardest thing Justine had ever done. They were numb with grief.

Outside there was a sudden swelling of voices. A child's wail cut through it.

"Mama!" Little Nell burst into the great hall. Grass stains streaked her smock. Her hair was a bird's nest. Tears ran down her cheeks, red from crying. She ran to Isabel. "Mama!"

Isabel stretched out her arms. "What is it, my little? Have you hurt yourself?"

Nell bawled, "Andrew! He fell out of the tree! He's not moving!"

"Lady Isabel," a gardener called, rushing in. "Your lad's fallen. Knocked senseless. You best come see."

Isabel jumped up and hurried out. Justine ran after her. They dashed across the terrace and down the steps. The entrance to the formal garden was shaded by a massive old beech tree, and a dozen anxious servants stood at its base. Two men among them were crouched over Andrew lying on his back in the grass. Above, in a crook of the boughs, the tree fort's raw boards gleamed white as bone. The people made way for Isabel. Justine held back a gasp at the sight of the boy's still body, pale face, closed eyes.

Isabel dropped to her knees at his side. She took his face between her hands, searching for signs of life.

"He's breathing!" someone cried.

Andrew's eyelids trembled. He moaned in pain and his eyes opened.

"It's his hand," Justine said. The left wrist was bent at a disturbing angle.

"Aye," said one of the men. "Wrist is broke, looks like, m'lady."

"Oh, you foolish boy," Isabel scolded her son, which brought smiles, for everyone knew her anger was a whiplash of relief.

"Best we get him inside, m'lady."

"Yes, yes," Isabel said, beckoning them to lift the boy. "Gently, Ralph. Gently."

"No"—Andrew pushed the man's hands away with sudden vigor—"I'm no baby." He was struggling to his feet, a difficult task with only one good hand, and he still looked dizzy.

"Are you sure?" Isabel asked in concern.

He looked mortified. "I am very well, Mother." He swayed on

his feet, in pain, but proud. Everyone's spirits seemed lightened by the young master's pluck.

"Inside with you, then," she said with a grudging smile at his stoicism, "and we'll have Mistress Thwaite bind that wrist." She thanked the men for seeing to her son, then let Andrew walk ahead, keeping a close step behind him should he collapse. The small crowd dispersed, a couple of the men chuckling, the women chattering the details of the mishap, a fireside tale in the making.

Justine noticed a young man hanging back. A thin frame, pale eyes, freckles. He stood in the shadows under the leafy beech tree, but she saw his face clearly enough to read deep distress. She recognized him. Not from when she had lived here, for he was too young, about seventeen she guessed, but from the questioning in the hall. He was a carpenter. A hammer was tucked into a loop in his thick belt from which a nail pouch hung. He had been singularly unforthcoming in the hall. A terribly shy soul, she had judged.

She looked up at the fort in the branches. "Were you helping Master Andrew?"

He toed the grass, looking pained. "Yes, mistress." The words were so faint she could barely hear them. She felt sorry for him.

"You mustn't blame yourself," she said. "The lad's intrepid. I dare say he was climbing too high."

He turned away. But not before Justine noticed the red rims of his eyes. She thought, startled, *He's been crying.*

"Will that be all, mistress?" He stood at the base of the ladder to the tree fort, one foot on the bottom rung, clearly wanting to climb up it and be gone.

"Yes, of course. And thank you again for answering our questions about Alice."

A strangled sound came from him, and he hurried up the ladder. Suddenly, she understood. It wasn't Andrew he was upset about. *He's been crying about Alice.*

She had to talk to him! She called after him, "May I see the children's fort?"

No answer. He had disappeared in the foliage. She climbed the ladder. "I loved hiding in trees when I was little," she said, making her voice cheerful. She didn't dare unsettle him.

The top of the ladder rested on the fort's platform, and as she reached it she saw the most fanciful little dwelling she had ever beheld. Though the underside of the platform was raw lumber, above it was a small, finished wonderland. Before her looped graceful arches of polished wood as balustrades. Willow lattice-work formed three walls, but with spaces through which the leafy branches swept. There was a bench whose legs were carved all over with birds, and a broad beech bough was its back. A bird-house with a roof of tidy rye thatch hung at one end as though in lieu of a chimney. At the other end, three narrow steps rose to a loft wide enough only for a child to lie and dream among the foliage.

"How wonderful," Justine said, stepping off the ladder. It felt like stepping aboard a fairyland ship.

He eyed her, uneasy. She sensed that he didn't like her invading the space, but of course he could not order her out, a member of the Thornleigh family.

"Jeremy's your name, isn't it?" He nodded, looking trapped. "You do beautiful work, Jeremy." She sat down on the platform edge, her legs dangling over the side. Looking out through the branches at the garden, she said, "Alice was beautiful, too." She heard him let out a tight breath. "She was my friend," Justine said. "I used to live here, you know. When Alice and I were children we used to climb out on the roof and lie down on the leads. You could see the river snaking all the way to Kirknewton."

Silence. She could see the stable roof through the leaves. A memory jolted her. Her father on horseback bursting out the stable door that night, his clothes pocked with cinders, the side of his face burned. She closed her eyes tight, shook it off. It was Alice she was here for.

"I want to find the man who killed her." She looked up at Jeremy. "I want justice for her."

He came silently to the edge. She gave him a sad smile. "Sit down, if you like."

He did, slowly, looking torn between a desire to speak and a need to stay silent.

It touched Justine. She said very simply, "I loved Alice."

It broke a dam in him. He lowered his head, and his shoulders shook in silent misery.

"You did, too, didn't you?" she said. It was pitifully clear. "Everyone did."

His head shot up. "And so did one that shouldn't," he said, swiping away his tears. The hostility in his voice startled Justine. The bitterness of jealousy.

"Shouldn't . . . have loved her?"

His face closed, as though anxious he'd said too much. But Justine understood. Men had always been drawn to Alice, and Alice had often reciprocated. "Jeremy, was there a man?"

He let out a sound, half groan, half sigh.

"You saw this man with her? Where? Kirknewton? Wooler?"

"Wooler. Market square." He looked away, reluctant to say more.

"Who was it?" She put authority in her voice, a lady ordering a servant. "Tell me."

Callous though she felt at commanding him, it worked. Commands he understood. He looked at her. "I don't know. I never saw him before. A lord."

Justine could not have been more surprised. She had expected some lowborn wastrel. "Are you sure? You say you'd never seen him before."

"I know a lord when I see one. This one was trying to hide it. Plain garb, he wore, like a clerk, his breeches dust all over from the road, but he had a swagger, like he owned the world."

Maybe it was *just a clerk,* she thought. Clerks were educated, and to a rustic young carpenter all men above his station might look like lords.

He seemed to read her skepticism. "That's not all, mistress. He had gold. He paid the ribbon man with a fistful of coins. Dropped 'em like they meant no more to him than stones."

"The ribbon man! You mean you saw this gentleman buy ribbons?"

"Aye, ribbons and scarves, all the peddler had. He stuffed them in a satchel. I followed him. Saw him stop Alice as she stood sorting goods into her donkey's pack. He chatted her up and took her hand, all smiling like he could do what he wanted."

"And Alice? Did she seem frightened by him?"

Jeremy looked wretched. He shook his head. "Surprised a little, but she was smiling, too. She left the market on her donkey. I watched her go. When I looked back, the lord was gone in the crowd."

It wasn't much to go on. The gentleman and Alice might never have met again. Yet the ribbons had ended up in the belfry of Kirknewton church. Why had Alice gone there? A sick feeling crept over Justine. Something had passed between Alice and the stranger. Jeremy's jealousy had not sprung from nothing.

"What did he look like? His face."

"Couldn't rightly see, mistress, what with his hair to his chin. And so many market folk milling between us."

Justine itched to know more. She resolved to go back to Wooler, and Kirknewton, too, and ask if anyone remembered seeing this elusive gentleman-clerk. It was a start.

"Justine!" Isabel's voice broke into her thoughts. "Justine, are you up there? There's someone to see you."

"Coming," she said. She glanced at the carpenter, the two of them screened from Isabel by the leaves, and said quietly, "I mean to find out who killed her, Jeremy. I swear."

She was halfway down the ladder when Isabel said, with some awe in her voice, "It's Lord Scrope of Carlisle. He's come himself to escort you back."

Justine hopped off the last rung, astonished. "What?"

"He says he's come at the request of the Queen of Scots. She has asked for you to return."

Lord Scrope's soldiers opened the Carlisle Castle gates for him to enter with his men-at-arms. Scrope had insisted that Justine ride in pride of place at his side as though she were a princess he was escorting to a meeting of royalty. Justine found it unnervingly odd. Why had Mary changed her mind and called her back? And why this show of respect for a mere lady-in-waiting?

In the blue sky the sun shone down like part of the courteous welcome for the small procession, and Justine felt nervous excitement rise in her. Perhaps Mary had decided that a lady-in-waiting she could comfortably converse with in French was a good thing after all. Or perhaps it was a gesture to mitigate her previous affront to Lord Thornleigh. Whatever the reason, Justine knew that her mission had now truly begun. It was daunting. She was on her own; Lord Thornleigh was on his way back to London. There would be no one to turn to if she were in difficulty. Or worse, if Mary should suspect her real purpose.

Nevertheless, she felt grateful for this second chance. She was ready to do her very best for Elizabeth's cause. And her own. Will's betrothal ring, snug in her petticoat pocket, was her talisman spurring her to succeed.

Her one regret was that serving Mary was taking her away from Yeavering, from searching for the mysterious gentleman who had talked to Alice, his satchel full of ribbons. But Justine had found a willing helper in Jeremy. She had asked him to make inquiries in Wooler and Kirknewton and send word to her if he discovered anything.

There was a clang behind her and she looked over her shoulder. The gates, closing.

She was in.

PART TWO

The Sword of Spain

❧ 9 ❧

Adam's Ordeal

The news hit England's southwest seaport of Plymouth like a squall. A fast pinnace returning from Ireland reported passing a ship that was on a course for Plymouth but struggling in the foggy ocean swells. When the pinnace docked there, a messenger dashed to London with the news. Sir Adam Thornleigh's ship *Elizabeth* was coming in. Alone.

The moment Frances Thornleigh got the message about her husband she left her London house and traveled as fast as she could. The windless conditions kept the *Elizabeth* wallowing offshore for another two days, and by the time Frances reached Plymouth the ship had just arrived. Now she was hurrying on foot down to the city's seafront to meet it. The streets were gloomy with fog, the air cold, but Frances felt none of its chill, warmed by the joyful thought: Adam was home!

But her joy was shot through with nervousness. She had not seen her husband in over a year. It had been an October morning when she stood on the very quay she was hurrying toward now and waved him off on his voyage to the Indies, heartsick in knowing it would be many months until she laid eyes on him again. How handsome he had looked, how full of vitality. Just past forty, he seemed years younger than the expedition's thirty-eight-year-old leader, John Hawkins. Adam's youthfulness had always given

Frances a double-edged pang. No man had ever stirred her as he did, but she was well aware how far past the bloom of youth she herself had wilted. It had long grieved her, for she believed that if she were not older than her husband, their marriage might have been a sunnier one. Certainly, it had had a rough start since she was a daughter of the house of Grenville; Adam's parents had never warmed to her. And Frances herself suffered a silent hatred for Queen Elizabeth for the hold Elizabeth had on Adam. She sometimes thought their ten years as man and wife had seen as many storms as Adam had weathered at sea. One of the worst had come early: her brother Christopher's treason eight years ago. But Frances had played no part in that debacle, and she was not sorry that it had claimed Christopher's life. Since then she had given Adam a daughter and a son, both of whom he adored, while Elizabeth had found other "favorites" at court, and Frances now hoped the storms were all behind them. Almost two years spent apart from him had left her aching to have him back, and she prayed that the long separation had kindled some of the same feeling in him. To welcome him home she had dressed with as much care and art as possible. This reunion, she vowed, would mark a new beginning.

Her skin was unpleasantly damp from the mist as she reached the foggy harbor. Ships' masts and rigging dripped moisture, and a seaweedy smell hung rankly in the air. Frances found that she was far from alone on the wharf—people seemed to have emerged from every street and alley: shopkeepers shutting the doors of their harborside businesses, apprentices sneaking time away from work, seafaring men coming from the chandleries. There were housewives in aprons, and street urchins with dirty faces, and a few finely dressed aldermen. All had been drawn by the arrival of the *Elizabeth*. On that October day over a year ago seven ships had proudly left Plymouth under Hawkins's command, a small fleet but one with enormous prestige because the expedition was backed by a syndicate of wealthy London merchants as well as some of the Queen's highest-ranking courtiers. The *Elizabeth*, it seemed, was the first vessel back. That did not surprise Frances. Adam had always been an intrepid and impatient adventurer.

Hurrying along the wet wharf in the fog she could not see farther than a few horse lengths, but the chattering crowd was moving toward the wharf's southern end, so she knew the ship had to be there. She nudged past people, trying to get to the front. Excitement coursed through her as she anticipated her first glimpse of Adam standing high on the stern deck. But bodies blocked her view. As she got closer the chatter hushed, became a murmur. Something in the voices chilled her. A tone of horror. And there was a putrid smell. She pressed her sleeve to her nose to block the stench.

When she finally broke through to the wharf edge and looked up at the vessel looming in the mist, she gasped. The once-beautiful *Elizabeth* was a filthy hulk. Her hull planking was gouged by two head-sized holes that were stuffed from inside with sopping canvas sails. Her mainmast was gone, its stump a jagged timber. The bowsprit, once a proud lance that had pointed to the horizon and carried billowing canvas, had been half-eaten by fire; its charred remains looked like a burned amputee. Her rope rigging and the hawsers that townsmen were making fast to the wharf bollards were so shaggy they appeared chewed by rats. Her flags with the cross of St. George and the Queen's colors hung faded and fouled, as bleached as bone. The *Elizabeth* was more carcass than ship.

Frances felt faint. The smell from belowdecks was the stench of death. Where was Adam? *As captain, he should be on deck.*

She saw men moving, but so few! When the *Elizabeth* had sailed off to the New World over seventy men had crammed her decks: mariners, gunners, archers, carpenters, merchants' agents. Now there were a mere handful. They moved like survivors on a battlefield, limping, dazed, some wounded, with dried bloodstains on their filthy shirts and breeches, and so thin they looked like clothed skeletons. *They're starving,* she realized. One stood at the railing and stared down at the hushed crowd. Eyes hollow, he was as still as a cadaver.

Frances could scarcely breathe. *Where is Adam?*

Men from the town began marching up the gangplank to assist, and the quiet crowd on shore suddenly came alive. Men of authority among them shouted orders. Other people ran to fetch water.

Others pushed through with boards to carry off the casualties. Frances forced her way past jostling people to the gangplank. A couple of burly guards stood holding back mariners' wives who were clamoring for word about their men. Frances gripped a guard's arm.

"My husband is Sir Adam Thornleigh. Has he come ashore?"

"I know not, my lady."

"Let me pass. I must go aboard and see."

He barred her way. "No one goes on board but those to carry off the sick and the dead."

Frances had to step aside as two men carrying a corpse between them lumbered down the gangplank. The smell was so foul, again she pressed her sleeve to her nose. "The sick. Where are they being taken?"

"Sign of the Trident." He pointed to a harborfront tavern, then turned back to block a housewife who had clawed past the other anxious women. "Back now, you lot," he told them. "Plenty of time. Dead men don't scamper."

Frances hastened across the harbor to the tavern. Its door stood open, awaiting more sick men to be brought from the ship, and inside the tables had been cleared as makeshift beds to receive them. The room was far from crowded. Only five men lay on the tables, and although a few looked barely conscious, their wounds had been dressed already by women who now stood grim-faced with towels and buckets of water, ready to nurse more of the ailing as soon as they should arrive. A scatter of other survivors, seven or eight, sat hunkered along the walls, a few on stools but most on the floor as though too weak to sit on a chair without falling. All were filthy. All, emaciated. None spoke. Cups of water and trenchers with bread and sausage lay beside them. One man was vomiting into a bucket after gorging on the food.

Frances scanned the faces, terrified of seeing Adam among these deathly ill wretches, yet more terrified of *not* finding him. If he wasn't on the ship's deck as captain, and wasn't among the sick, was he among the dead?

Then she saw a face she knew. "John Bingham?" she cried.

She rushed to him. He sat on the bottom step of a staircase and looked up as she reached him. He had sat in her parlor discussing the expedition with Adam, and the man she remembered had been a ruddy-cheeked, clean-shaven, tidy fellow. Now a wiry black beard engulfed half his face, and matted hair hung in ropes from his head. His cheeks were concave, the skin sallow and pocked with sores. A grimy sling held his left wrist, and the linen sleeve was stiff with blackened blood. The shirt hung from his bony shoulders as from a board.

He blinked up at her. "Lady Frances?"

She winced at the sight of his mouth. Gray teeth, some missing. Scabbed lips. He was the son of a wealthy wool merchant and, like Adam, a member of the Company of Merchant Adventurers. He tried to struggle to his feet in courtesy.

"Sit, please sit. Oh, Master Bingham, where is my husband?"

He hung his head. "Adam . . ."

"Dear God, tell me he is not—"

"I saw him . . ." He looked up, desolation in his eyes. "Was it yesterday?"

"Where?"

"Bowsprit. Cutting a man from the nets."

The anti-boarding netting. "Then he's alive?"

"The poor wretch had lost a leg," Bingham muttered. "Cannon-ball. Months ago. Don't know how he lasted. Crawled to the nets to die." His head lolled against the banister. "Shark food now."

"But Adam? Where is *Adam?*"

He fought to focus on her. He licked his parched lips. She grabbed a wooden cup of watered ale from a nearby table and held it out to him. He took it in his good hand, the fingers grimy, and drank slowly, as though it hurt his throat. He looked at her. "God's truth, Lady Frances, I do not know."

She looked across the room and out the open door at the activity around the misty ship. She didn't know what to do. They wouldn't let her aboard to search, so all she could do was wait and hope to see him brought here, alive.

She sank down on the step beside Bingham. "What happened? Was it a storm?"

He grunted, a sound like a snarl. "A storm of Spaniards."

"Pirates?"

He shook his head. "The viceroy himself. Mexico."

She was shocked. "They attacked you?"

He drank more ale and seemed to take a little strength from it. Lowering the cup, he stared into its darkness. "We'd finished our trading south of their territory, all seven vessels. Took on victuals at Curaçao and were about to head home. When we entered the Florida Channel, one of the old salts told me he could smell the hurricane. It hit our fleet like the devil's own hammer. The *Jesus of Lubeck* began to break up, her planks gaping. Fishes swam among her ballast as if in the sea. The *William and John* disappeared. The storm died, but it had blown the rest of us off course. We were lost. Then we realized we were in the Gulf of Mexico, drifting toward reefs off the Yucatán. Spanish territory. With leaking ships we had to make for harbor in Veracruz. San Juan de Ulúa—that's what they call their God-cursed port. We were making our repairs there when we got word that the *flota* was expected any day."

She knew about the *flota*. Everyone did. The fleet that Spain sent out twice yearly to carry back the immense riches of gold, silver, and precious gems from Mexico and Peru across the Atlantic to the coffers of King Philip.

"Thirteen ships, they were, bristling with cannon. And on board their flagship was Mexico's new viceroy. We were anchored in their roadstead, and were well armed ourselves, but we wanted no fight. Nor did they, we thought, for they had to dock, load, and get back to Spain before the weather worsened. So Hawkins and their commander struck a bargain. They would let us finish our repairs and in return we'd let them into port. Then we'd be on our way.

"Liars. When we were lulled by the truce, they attacked. Three hundred Spaniards tried to board the *Jesus*. Many leapt across from the *Jesus* to the *Elizabeth* and grappled us in hand-to-hand fighting. Adam ordered our gunners to open fire and we struck the mainmast of their flagship. We cut our cables and turned to fight, trading cannon fire with cannon fire. But Spanish reinforcements swarmed from ashore. They sank the *Angel*. Overran the *Swallow*. The *Jesus*, with Hawkins aboard, was listing badly. Under heavy fire he ordered Adam and Drake, captain of the *Judith*, to take on men. Then Hawkins gave the order to abandon ship. He was the last to climb aboard the *Minion*."

She listened, appalled. "Adam . . . was Adam wounded?"

He seemed not to hear her, trapped in recalling the horror. "We watched the *Jesus* sink with all our treasure. The Spanish sent fire ships among our midst, separating us. The *Judith* had vanished. We on the *Elizabeth* were alone." He shuddered, as though speaking so much had drained the last of his strength. "We beat homeward . . . northern gales ripping at us. Low on food, water . . . ate every dog aboard . . . every parrot and monkey. When they were gone, we ate the rats."

Frances glimpsed through the open door a man starting down the ship's gangplank. She jumped to her feet. "It's him!"

She dashed out of the tavern. Pushed through the crowd. By the time she reached the wharf edge her heart was pounding from her haste. Adam! Her breath caught at the sight of him. Unkempt beard, gashed cheek, soiled shirt, ripped doublet. He was carrying a boy of ten or eleven who lay in his arms as still as a rag doll. "Adam!" she called.

He looked up. Confusion clouded his face as he scanned the crowd. "Over here!" Frances called. He spotted her, and his confusion slowly cleared into a smile of wonder. The smile made Frances weak-kneed with joy.

The boy he was carrying struggled to look too, and Adam staggered on down to the end of the gangplank as Frances, rushing forward, met him amid dockworkers, barrels, and barking dogs.

"Oh, Adam," she murmured, aghast at how thin he was, how pale. She imagined him giving the last rations of dog meat to his starving men, going hungry himself.

"Frances," he said, his voice a rasp, "we must see Sparling's taken care of."

She flinched. The boy stank, and pus oozed from sores around his mouth. Thankfully, a sturdy dockworker reached them, saying, "I'll take him, sir." Adam looked shaky with exhaustion as he transferred his burden into the arms of the worker. "Lord," said the man, "the boy's in a bad way."

On death's door, it seemed to Frances. If only they would take him away so she could embrace Adam.

"Did we make it, sir?" the boy whispered, blinking at Adam with milky eyes.

"We did, lad." Adam tousled the boy's matted hair. "We did."

The boy slumped in the worker's arms as though the relief was a blow.

"Here's water," a woman said, bringing a bucket. She handed Adam a ladle of water, and he took it in both hands and gulped it down, fingers trembling, then scooped another ladleful and held it to the boy's lips. Much of the water dribbled around his scabby mouth. "But you don't get off that easy, Sparling," Adam said. "Where's my sovereign?"

"Sovereign?"

"A bet is a bet." Adam's voice was still raspy, but Frances recognized his jesting tone. "We made it home alive. I win."

The boy's eyes watered. His mouth opened, but he was too overcome with feeling to speak.

"I'll come round to collect it when you're better," Adam said gently. "No shirking, you hear?"

"Aye, sir . . . a sovereign, sir," the boy murmured. "Thank you, sir."

"Off with you, now."

The dock worker carrying the lad started for the tavern. Frances had held back as long as she could. "Adam," she burst out, "welcome home!"

He looked suddenly rocky and gripped the edge of a barrel for support. He seemed dazed, almost faint.

"You are ill!" she cried.

He shook his head, struggling to gain control. "Sick at heart . . . so many dead. Young Sparling won't make it."

"Come away to the inn," she urged, taking his arm to support him. "You need a doctor. Food. Rest."

He resisted. "Must see to the men." He looked around. "Where's Curry?" His longtime first mate. "His arm's broken."

"Never mind the men, half the town have come out to help

them. You can do no more, Adam. You're sick yourself. Come away."

"Any word of the others? Hawkins on the *Minion*? Drake on the *Judith*?"

"No. You are the first back." She felt almost cheated. Adam would not embrace her in front of so many people even if he had the strength. "Please, come away to the inn. I'll take care of you there and we—"

Her words were cut off by the voices of townsmen who had pushed through the crowd to him, three of them. The chains of office around their necks proclaimed them aldermen. "Sir Adam! Great God in heaven, what hell you have been through!" They barraged him with questions, and as he told them of the Spanish attack, of the loss of ships and hundreds of men, of his own crippled ship, there was cold steel in his eyes, a quiet fury that Frances had not seen in him for years, not since . . . since that day they'd stood together at the altar. No, she would not think about that now, that unhappy past. He was home, his life spared by God, she was sure. God had given her a new chance to make their future happy.

"Gentlemen," she said sternly, coming between the men and Adam, "my husband needs food and rest, and I am taking him to the Green Glass Inn. Visit him there, later. Now I entreat you, let us *pass*." They demurred, acknowledging the need for Adam to recuperate, and stepped aside.

Adam, looking dazed again, muttered with a hollow chuckle, "Yes . . . a wash would be good."

Frances took charge, guiding him through the crowd. People parted to make way, whispering in awe about him, the captain who had escaped the devil Spaniards. She longed to get him quickly to the inn where they could be alone, but he was limping slightly, some weakness in his knee, and she had to keep the pace slow.

"Frances," he said with an anxious look, "how are the children?"

"They are well. Katherine has prayed for you every night."

"Ah, my Kate." He smiled a truly warm smile for the first time. "And Robert, is he grown?"

"Past my waist. He'll be overjoyed to see you."

"My father? Lady Thornleigh?"

"Your parents are hale."

"Look," he said, blinking up at the sky. "The sun's coming out." He looked at her, and his voice gentled. "It's good to be home."

She could have cried for happiness.

At the inn the landlord and his excited wife and customers made a fuss about the "hero," and it was all Frances could do to get Adam up the stairs without being mobbed, and into the room. She closed the door. Alone, finally. Adam sank onto the bed with a groan. Head hitting the pillow, booted feet barely off the floor, he was asleep by the time Frances reached the bedside.

He slept for thirteen hours. She sat in a chair by the bed, watching him, taking breaks to eat quick meals brought to her, to nap, and to send the mayor's messenger away with her own message that no one was to disturb her husband yet. She washed the scabbed gash on Adam's cheek with a damp towel, careful not to wake him, through it would have taken a lightning strike to do so, she thought with tender amusement. She inspected his body as best she could and was satisfied he had no crucial wounds, though his hands were lacerated with tiny cuts and his neck was sunburned to leather and his beard held trapped dirt she didn't even want to imagine. She was content to just be alone with him. She planned how, once he awoke, she would bathe him, cut that beard and shave him, then feed him, just a slice of bread and a little lean meat at first, maybe a baked apple; if he gorged he would be sick.

He awoke with a hoarse shout. "All hands to pumps!"

"Shh," Frances said, moving to his side.

He sat up with a start, looking around with haggard eyes, struggling to recall where he was.

"It's all right, you're off the ship," she assured him.

He stared at her as at a stranger, then seemed to remember. "Is there water?" he asked, licking his parched lips.

She hastened to pour a cup for him from the pitcher. He gulped it down. He rubbed his face with vigor, as though to ready himself for battle. "My boots," he said, swinging his legs over the bed side.

He scanned the satchels of his belongings that Frances had had delivered from the ship. "Where are my boots?"

She smiled. "No need for boots." She had tugged them off him as he slept.

He looked at her. "Get them, please."

She didn't want an argument to be their first conversation, so she fetched the boots. Perhaps they made him feel more like himself. "I'll have the landlord bring you food," she said as Adam pulled on the boots. "You must eat sparingly at first, you know."

"I will." He stood, sucking in a deep breath to steady himself. "Have them pack something for me to take, too."

"Take?"

He raked his fingers into his beard. "And tell them I need scissors. And a razor." He patted his shirt. "And clean clothes." He looked around as though impatient. "Then, time to go."

Home! She could not hide her delight. He wanted to be home! "Why not take a day or two here to get back your strength?" *Just the two of us*, she thought happily. "The children can wait."

He didn't seem to be listening. He was pouring water from the pitcher into a washbasin. "Where is Elizabeth? At Whitehall? Richmond? Or on progress somewhere?"

She stiffened. Elizabeth. The name always made her cringe. "Why?"

He was pulling off his shirt to wash. "If you don't know where she is, find someone who does, would you? One of the aldermen, perhaps. Or the mayor—he may know something of her schedule."

She stared at him as he splashed water on his chest and arms. Though thin, his body was still strong looking. A body that Elizabeth coveted. Frances forced her voice to stay calm. "If your intention is to send the Queen a message, I shall call for paper and pen."

He turned, drying his face and chest with a towel. "Message?" His tone was stern. "Good God, no. I'm going."

It stung her. "You are not well."

"Well enough."

"But why to *her?*"

He tossed the towel aside with a sigh. "Frances, don't do this."

"If you are well enough to ride to her, you're well enough to ride home."

He stared at her with such obvious disdain she felt it like a slap. "Over fifty of my crew lie at the bottom of the sea, limbs ripped off by Spanish cannon. Dozens from our other ships were taken prisoner and will by now have been mutilated under the torture of the Mexican Inquisition. Dozens more, sailing home, starved to death before my eyes. It is my duty, madam, to report these atrocities to our queen. Even *you* should see that."

She said nothing, too hurt.

He let out a tight sigh, his look contrite. "Forgive me, Frances. I know you mean well. But I must, in all haste, make to Elizabeth." He moved past her, impatient to get to his satchels. She saw the steel of hate flash in his eyes as he muttered, "And as God is my witness, I shall make the Spaniards pay."

Not an hour later she stood in the inn's stable yard watching him ride off for London. She had seen his hatred, his fury at Spain, and she understood it. But it could not match her own hatred for Elizabeth. She felt it like a stranglehold, a force so powerful that if she could be in Elizabeth's presence and turn the hatred physically against her, Elizabeth would fall dead at her feet. She watched Adam become a speck swallowed up by the road. She choked back a wail. After almost two years at sea, he was going to her rival.

❧ 10 ❧

The Brawl

Adam reached London after a punishing, fast ride. It was dark when he arrived, bone weary and aching, at Baynard's Castle on the River Thames. Baynard's was the Earl of Pembroke's London house, massive and magnificent, and tonight the earl was hosting a dinner for Elizabeth. Adam rode in through the gates on the Strand and drew rein in the torchlit courtyard. Dismounting, saddle sore, he handed his horse to a groom and looked up at the castle. The windows were alive with candlelight. *Like Elizabeth herself*, he thought. To him, she always moved in a nimbus of light. He heard music. Knowing her, there would be dancing.

Inside, as he climbed the staircase lined with torches that led to the long gallery, the thought of her warmed him like an inner flame. He needed its warmth, for he felt he was still struggling through a cold fog of death. His massacred crew. His maimed ship. It seemed that the torch flames he passed twisted like men writhing, and his every footfall up the steps sent a shudder that brought back torturing images. Howlett's head torn off by a cannonball. Payne with a Spanish axe in his gut. The spurting red stump where Poole's arm had been. The starved cabin boy Adam had carried down the gangplank, Sparling, who'd felt like a bag of bones in his arms. He had come to Elizabeth to do more than report the atrocity. She alone could give him what he wanted. He would make the Spaniards pay in gold and blood.

Going up the stairs he followed servingmen carrying up silver dishes of food. The rich smells made him faintly nauseous; he had eaten a little on the way and his stomach, jolted from near starvation, was still at war with the beef and bread. After so long aboard the spare *Elizabeth* these lavish surroundings, too, felt disorienting—the gilt and marble, the music and laughter. He tried to muster the proper frame of mind to go in among merrymaking courtiers. He had little heart for it, with Frances's plaintive voice— "Why go to *her?*"—still ringing in his ears. He hadn't told his wife that the Spanish attack had all but ruined him. Fitting and arming the *Elizabeth* for the Indies had put him heavily in debt. The expedition had made a huge profit in the trading, but his share of that gold had been stowed in Hawkins's ship, *Jesus of Lubeck*, which had sunk in the sea battle. It made Adam sick with rage. His fortune lay at the bottom of the ocean.

A couple of lords going up the stairs ahead of him were laughing at some private jest. They weren't English; the few words of Spanish he caught were barbs in his brain. He eyed the men with loathing, their black satin finery, their arrogant swagger. What were Spaniards doing here with Elizabeth? Visiting grandees, perhaps. Or part of the Spanish ambassador's entourage. Adam's fingers tightened around the hilt of his sword. He would cut down any man who threatened Elizabeth. An unwarranted response, he realized—she was among friends. But he couldn't help it. Never again would he trust a Spaniard.

He reached the gallery crowded with lords and ladies, and their chatter hit him like a barrage. Their perfume made his stomach rocky. Faces turned to him, and the chatter became an excited buzz. He heard "Spanish Main" . . . "sunk ships" . . . "hero" . . . and realized they were talking about him. He scanned the faces, looking for Elizabeth, but saw only courtiers' jowly cheeks and goggle eyes. He set a course through this shoal of strangers, but after so long at sea he had not yet got his land legs and knew his stride down the gallery must look as deliberate as a drunkard's. People made way for him, stepping back as though from a barnyard animal. *Do I stink so badly?* he thought, almost amused. "I washed," he blurted. *Too loud,* he realized. Their startled looks seemed comical and tugged a hoarse laugh from him. That made them goggle even more.

The roar of the room, the gawping faces, the unsteady floor . . . Adam felt half on land, half at sea. A man's gravelly voice grated on him like keel scraping rock. Viols spun music like the keening of wind in the rigging. He focused on the glow of candlelight at the far end. Elizabeth must be there. Yes! Through the surf of strangers he spotted her bright face! She had not seen him yet; she was doing a lively dance step, head high, a smile on her lips. She was his beacon through this disorienting fog. If he could just make it to her he'd be all right.

"Thornleigh!" a man shouted.

Adam spun around. Anthony Porteous was pushing past people to get to him. Bald as an egg, lean but muscular, he was Adam's chief investor in the Hawkins expedition, and he began firing questions even as he pushed through. Was it true he had sailed into Plymouth alone? Where was Hawkins? Where was Drake? Adam barely got out an answer to the first question when men suddenly closed in around him hurling more questions. Robert Dudley, the Earl of Leicester, swarthy and fit. White-haired, paunchy William Herbert, Earl of Pembroke. Dudley's austere brother Ambrose, Earl of Warwick. All had invested in Hawkins's venture.

"Thornleigh, come sit down, man," said Pembroke. "You look like a ghost."

Adam shook his head, looking again for Elizabeth. "I'll see Her Majesty first, my lord."

"You'll have some wine first, before you fall down." Pembroke flicked his hand to summon a servant.

"Have mine," said Leicester, handing Adam a goblet. He added with admiration, "You've made the devil's own time racing from Plymouth."

"The *Elizabeth*," Porteous demanded, "is she salvageable?"

"Yes," Adam said. "With work."

"The bullion?"

He shook his head, holding back his fury at remembering. "Went down with the *Jesus of Lubeck*."

Porteous winced. His profit, gone. The others kept battering Adam with questions and he gulped wine, knocking back the whole goblet full, more to keep them at bay than because he wanted it.

"Where *is* Hawkins?" Leicester demanded.

"Don't know."

Someone groaned, "At the bottom of the sea, I warrant."

A man looking over Leicester's shoulder muttered sourly, "As he deserves."

Adam stiffened at the accent. Spanish. "What did you say?" he challenged. The man, sunken-cheeked, with a sleek goatee like chiseled black marble, gave no reply, only sneered. In the din the others hadn't heard his comment about Hawkins. Pembroke was shouting at the crowd to stop pressing Thornleigh: "Let him be!" Adam locked eyes with the Spaniard. He was dressed in the finest black satin, one of the grandees he'd seen on the staircase. Amid the hubbub the Spaniard snaked through the circle of men until he stood face-to-face with Adam. "God sees what you are," he said with quiet venom. "A common pirate." He turned and pushed his way out of the circle.

Rage boiled up in Adam. It squeezed his vision into a red haze, blotting out everything but the man strutting away. In that shimmer of black satin he saw carrion hovering over his dead crew, saw beating black wings as the birds settled on corpses to feed.

He rammed through the circle, grabbed two fistfuls of the black satin, and wrenched the Spaniard around. That sneering face! He raised his fist and hammered it. The man staggered back from the blow, blood spurting from his nose. A woman screamed. Adam lunged again and punched the Spaniard's jaw. The man toppled and sprawled on the floor.

Cries went up. Men swarmed Adam in a blur. He saw only the Spaniard flailing on the floor in a furious effort to get up. *No, you don't get up. My slaughtered crew will never get up again.* But the Spaniard made it onto his hands and knees, blood dripping from his nose, spattering the floor. He looked up at Adam and hissed, *"Bastardo!"*

Adam kicked him in the ribs. The Spaniard sprawled onto his back, coughing blood.

"Thornleigh! Stop!" Hands grabbed him from behind, fingernails scraping his neck. Wrenched from his prey, he fought to lunge again. The Spaniard looked up at him, blood smearing his face. "God curse you, pirate." He spat blood at him. "May your children sicken and die!"

It made Adam wild. He broke free and leapt onto the man and straddled him, dropping to his knees. He snatched the satin doublet at the throat and made a rock of his other fist and smashed the bloodied face. Bone cracked. Pain seared his hand. He welcomed the pain, a spur to give this devil some of the agony his men had suffered. He punched the Spaniard's face again, splitting the skin of his knuckles, then again and again until his hand was slippery with blood.

An octopus of men's arms grappled him, fists seizing him. They hauled him off the Spaniard. Adam kicked and writhed to get free, but they were all around him, dragging him away.

"For God's sake, Thornleigh!"

"The man's a lunatic!"

"Don't let Thornleigh go! Hold him!"

They wrestled him to his knees, hands pushing down on his shoulders, gripping his elbows, his neck, his hair. With his head forced down, he saw nothing but the floor. He fought to catch his breath. Voices ranted at him: Porteous's, Leicester's. There were Spanish voices, too, frantic with fury about the man he had beaten.

Suddenly the roar hushed to a murmur. "Her Majesty!"

"Stand back!"

"The Queen!"

Some of the hands holding Adam let go. He rocked on his knees at the sudden freedom. Men around him were bowing, women curtsying, everyone shuffling back to make way. Adam shrugged off the last hand restraining him and shot to his feet. The suddenness of the move made him dizzy. The liquor he had gulped swam in his head. He blinked at his glistening red hand, not sure what he'd done. Spaniards on his ship's deck? He had fought one of them. But all these people . . . *Where am I?*

He turned, swaying. Elizabeth stood before him. His breath caught at the dazzle of her. She wore crimson silk spangled all over with golden suns, and a rainbow of gems gleamed in her red-gold hair. People had ebbed back, and Adam saw the Spaniard on the floor, bleeding, moaning. Men were on their knees beside the fallen man, shouting in outraged Spanish. Adam recognized the crane-like figure of the Spanish ambassador, Guerau de Spes. He was gibbering in fury, pointing at Adam. Feeling confused, Adam looked back at Elizabeth. Had the Spaniard on the floor attacked her? *Have I saved her?* Unsteady on his feet, his bloody hand throbbing, he bowed his head to her. "Your Majesty."

Silence. He raised his eyes to hers. Her face was a storm. She said with quiet fury, her dark eyes on Adam, "My lord Pembroke, take charge of this miserable brawler."

"Yes, Your Majesty." The old man gestured to Leicester for help and the two of them grabbed Adam's arms. He stood still, in shock, as reason flooded back. *Brawler?* Was that what he had done?

"Señor de Spes," Elizabeth said gently to the livid ambassador, "your noble kinsman has suffered an unconscionable attack and I offer my deepest apology. Do not stand on ceremony, but go, see to his injuries, you and your people. I will send my physicians to wait on you."

But the ambassador, white-faced in his struggle to remain diplomatic, demanded immediate retribution against Adam. "This very night!"

All faces turned to Elizabeth.

"My lord," she said, "you have good cause for anger. I value our friendship with Spain above all things, and I swear to you that this wretched troublemaker will be punished. But now, go, see to your noble cousin's welfare. My lord Warwick, go with him, help our Spanish friends."

De Spes made a stiff bow to her, barely civil, then whipped a gesture of command to the Spaniards who surrounded the fallen man. They lifted him in a hubbub of indignation and carried him away, de Spes stalking out after them.

Pembroke said to Elizabeth, "Your Majesty, I shall send Sir Adam under guard to my lockup."

"No," she said. "The wretch must be interrogated. To the barge."

Adam was marched out the gate to the river surrounded by four of Pembroke's men-at-arms. He did his best to walk confidently, proudly, not let them see how unsteady he was on his feet, how painful his hand, wrapped with a kerchief that wept blood, his own mixed with the Spaniard's. He was furious at himself for botching his audience with Elizabeth. The Spaniard could go hang, but Elizabeth . . . he had to make her understand.

The guards took him across a short bridge and down a flight of steps to the earl's private wharf. Visiting lords' boats lay alongside, bobbing around the tethered royal barge that rose above the smaller craft with the splendor of Elizabeth herself. Its golden prow glimmered under the wharf torches, and its banners of green silk rippled in the night breeze. Candlelight flickered between curtains inside the glass-windowed stern cabin under a gold-embossed roof. Two steel-helmeted guards stood sentry, at bow and stern. Ten oarsmen sat in the bow, five on each side, hands on oars. Adam eyed the cabin. Was the royal marshal in there, waiting to question him? He felt shaky, humiliated by the weakness in his legs, enraged at his own stupidity. Get through this interrogation, he told himself, then send word to Elizabeth that he *must* see her, to report, to explain. But that could take hours. He didn't know if he had the strength. The breeze felt cold. The water was black.

Pembroke's men marched him on board. The captain knocked on the cabin's mahogany door. It opened and the captain turned to Adam and jerked his chin, a command to enter. The moment Adam was across the threshold, the door closed behind him. He was alone. The cabin was luxurious, an oasis of golden candlelight cocooned by red brocade curtains and tentlike hangings of red silk above a divan plump with gold silk cushions. There was no sound but the faintest lapping of water on the hull.

He heard a rustling and turned.

Elizabeth! It was she who'd closed the door. She pressed her back against it, still gripping the handle as though she needed it to support herself as she gazed at him. In that gaze Adam saw a tortured mix of misery and joy. She took a step closer to him and raised her hand and caressed his cheek. He shivered at the sweet touch of her slim, white fingers. She whispered, "All these months. I thought you were dead."

Everything in him yearned for her. He reached out and pulled her to him. She wrapped her arms around him and pressed her cheek against his shoulder. The scent of warm skin rose from her bare neck and he kissed it. He held her tightly, hungry for more of her, wanting her, body and soul, as he had wanted her for ten years. Ten long years of feasting on the memory of one night, a snowy night in a farmer's hut, an incandescent memory that still held heat for him. Ten years of cold nights with Frances, and never again with this woman he loved. He moaned her name, "Elizabeth . . . Elizabeth," holding her tightly against him, her warmth a balm to his aching body. Suddenly he remembered the bloody cloth wound around his hand. He must not leave the stain of blood on her. He pulled away, indicating his hand.

She looked at the blood. Then up at him. A darkness swept over her face and her dark eyes flashed. She raised her hand and slapped him. "How dare you brawl in my presence!"

The slap was like icy sea spray knocking him back to reality. She was a queen, the monarch of a great realm, and he could never have her. He had always known that. He didn't even belong in her world, a place of courtiers and politics, of talk and show. He belonged on board a ship. There, he was in command. He took command now. "Very well. Next time I'll hit him outside your presence."

"What did he *do* to you?"

"He was born."

"This is no answer! Do you even know who he is?"

"Spanish, and therefore cursed."

"A cousin of Ambassador de Spes. A count! A relation of King Philip's *wife*. Bah, I should have let de Spes take you away. He would teach you a lesson about brawling that you would not soon forget."

"But you didn't. And you know why. Because you stand for Englishmen."

He saw how it startled her. And moved her. He knew her well: England's heartbeat was her heartbeat. He had seen her mobbed on her progresses, people crowding round her, shopkeepers, housewives, servants. She enjoyed it, often stopping to talk to them. Adam doubted that any other monarch in Europe took such a warm interest in her people. They loved her for it.

"I brought you something," he said, digging inside a pocket in his doublet. "They sank our treasure, but not all of it." He pulled out a wad of paper the size of an egg, the paper grimy with gun grease. He unwrapped it and held it out to show her. A flawless pearl, big as an eye, tear shaped, tinged with pink like a girl's blush. Candlelight burnished its smoothness like skin aglow.

She looked at him with wonder. "You starved . . . but saved this treasure for me?"

"It kept me alive, dreaming of this moment." Lifting the pearl, he crumpled the grimy paper, about to toss it away.

She caught his hand and took the paper. "This is just as precious." Lovingly, she rewrapped the pearl and tucked it away in a small gold satin pouch at her waist. Tears glinted in her eyes. She ran a fingertip over Adam's lips. The softness of her touch aroused a fierce desire in him to kiss her. He fought it. "How thin you are," she murmured. "You have suffered."

"Not as much as my men."

"What happened? Is it true the Spaniards attacked you with no provocation? Is Hawkins dead?"

Before he could answer, a hubbub sounded on the wharf. Feet pounding, men shouting. Adam looked through a crack between the curtains. Courtiers were running to their boats, jumping into them while calling orders to their oarsmen. He knew why—they were all keen to stay close to Elizabeth, to be *seen* close to her. He felt the barge slide away from the wharf, saw the wharf torches recede as the barge surged into the river's chop. Elizabeth's oarsmen were expert, and the barge glided like a blade through a mill pond. The raucous din of the lords in their boats followed them abeam and astern, while ahead music struck up. The royal musicians in a boat ahead of Elizabeth, Adam realized. The little flotilla was heading upriver. To Hampton Court? He needed time to get what he wanted from her. "Where are we bound?" he asked.

"Whitehall. Where a hill of paperwork awaits me." She gave him a cross look. "I haven't yet decided what awaits you. The ambassador wants to eat your liver."

Not if I rip out his first, Adam thought grimly. So, to Whitehall. It didn't give him much time. "Elizabeth, I have much to report."

"Yes," she said, ringing a little silver bell. Her steward opened the door and she asked for a basin of water. "Sit down," she told Adam, pointing to the canopied divan. "I want to hear it all."

He sat, and when the steward brought the water she took it and dismissed him and sat down on a cushioned stool in front of Adam, the basin on her lap. She took his hand and unwound the bloodied kerchief. He took in a breath of surprise. She was going to clean his hand? "You don't need to do that."

She ignored him, examining his raw knuckles. She pulled from her sleeve a white silk square embroidered with flowers—Adam caught its rosemary scent—and dipped it in the water. It was wonderful to feel her long smooth fingers slip over his wrist, feel her pat the cool water on his burning knuckles. He felt the thrill of being alone with her, their knees touching, while outside a jovial din came from the boats of the court hangers-on around them, and shouts came from on shore of Londoners cheering the barge as it passed, and strains of music from the boat ahead rolled back like the barge's bow wave. Elizabeth ignored it all as she dripped water on his hand. "Tell me everything."

He did. How the hurricane had damaged the *Jesus of Lubeck,* forcing Hawkins to order their fleet of seven into San Juan de Ulúa for repairs. How the Spanish *flota* arrived, thirteen ships with the new Mexican governor aboard. How Hawkins met with the governor, who agreed to let the English complete their repairs and then get under way. How they had traded gentlemen hostages as insurance that neither side would fire their cannon. Elizabeth listened intently as she worked at cleaning his hand.

"They lied," he said. "We sent them gentlemen—Richard

Temple, John Varney, Thomas Fowler—but they sent us sailors got up in gentlemen's clothes. Then they sent fire ships to burn us as we stood at anchor." He told her about the battle. The blood and fire and smoke. The dying. The sunk *Angel* and *Swallow* and *Jesus*, going down with all the expedition's treasure and most of their victuals. The vanished *Judith*. Told her how the Spanish had captured scores of men who by now would have been tortured by the Mexican Inquisition. How he had taken on survivors from the crippled English ships. How, in escaping, he was separated from Hawkins on the *Minion*. How, aboard the *Elizabeth* as he sailed her home with only the mizzenmast and ruptured canvas, his men had suffered famine and thirst and festering wounds, and had died in the dozens.

When he was finished, he saw horror in her eyes. And something harder. Steelier. It fired him with fresh energy. This was why he had come. "Elizabeth, you hate them as much as I do."

She let out a scoffing breath. "Much good that does us." She squeezed blood-tinged water out of the white silk, which she then wrapped loosely around his palm, finished.

"I know you," he said. "You won't let them get away with this."

She raised an eyebrow coolly. "Will I not?" Getting up, she took the bowl of water and set it on a table and picked up a towel to dry her hands. "Much happened while you were in the Indies. You do not know how badly things stand between us and Philip."

"Why? What's happened?"

"It started in Spain, with the people at my embassy. Over religion—always religion," she said with wearily. "It was one of the church processions through the streets that Spaniards are so obsessively fond of. My people, being Protestant, refused to doff their caps as the religious relics passed. They were arrested. I objected, pointing out to Philip that I allow the people of *his* embassy to celebrate mass. He answered that it was the Inquisition who arrested my people, so there was nothing he could do." She tossed the towel on the table in disgust. "Then my foolish ambassador, Dr. Man, made matters worse when he was heard grumbling an insult about the pope, called him a canting little monk. Philip put him under house arrest."

"I heard about this. You brought Man home, and quite rightly, and you've sent no replacement."

Her look was pained. "My claws are as a mouse's against the beast of the Inquisition. And in the Netherlands things are even more dire since Philip invaded. He has given the Duke of Alva a free hand over the Dutch, and a cruel hand it is. He is butchering Protestants. That so infuriated some of my councilors they raised money to send arms to the Dutch rebels. Philip was apoplectic, and de Spes even more so. I tried to calm the waters, made a proclamation that no munitions could be shipped to the rebels."

"Ah, but I heard you held off announcing it for several days, giving Leicester time to ship the arms before your proclamation came into force. I have kept myself informed, Elizabeth. And I know your ways. You've done your sly best to stand up to Philip, just as you should. And now it's time to do more."

"You know nothing of what I should do," she snapped. "I need Spain. *England* needs Spain. Our lifeblood is trade with the Netherlands, and if Philip cuts that he can strangle England. And Spain isn't the only danger, Adam. There's France. Charles massacring Protestants, calling me a heretic." She rubbed her temples as if the worry made her head ache. "The Catholic realms aligning against me . . . that's my worst fear. A Catholic League sending troops across the Narrow Sea to turn our green pastures red with English blood. So no, do not vex me with foolish talk about standing up to Philip. I dare not openly defy him."

It sent a knife of dread into him. Had he misjudged her? He got up and came to her. "The Spaniards have *already* massacred Englishmen. *My* men. Being timid with them just invites more assault. Philip responds only to strength. Show him you are a force to be reckoned with."

"Don't talk nonsense. I have no such force."

"You do. You have me. Let me go after them."

"Go after—?"

"Attack them, as they did us. Hit their next treasure fleet bound from the Indies for Spain."

She stared at him in disbelief. "The *flota?* They sail with enough cannon to blast apart a mountain. An attack would be lunacy."

"Not if you supply me well. I'd need fast ships, seasoned men, and plenty of gun power. I can do it, Elizabeth. You know I can."

A door seemed to close in her eyes. "I know this much—the Spanish call you a pirate. You were in their territory. You had no right to be there."

"I told you, the hurricane blew us off course."

"Hawkins knew the risk of encroaching on Spain's New World territory. So did you. It's a criminal trespass in Philip's eyes."

"Philip is not God. He made a law, that's all. You can make laws, too. Let's make these devils pay. Give me justice."

"No. He is already furious about English piracy in the Channel. If I were to condone it in his New World possessions, it could push us to the brink of war."

"We're already at war. Elizabeth, they slaughtered my men, sank our treasure. If that's not an act of war, what is?"

She glared at him. "Attacking Philip's kinsman tonight, that's what. They tell me the count has a broken nose and three broken ribs, and his heart is weak. If he dies, Adam, God knows what price I'll have to pay."

"Pay nothing. It's *Spain* who must pay. Let me take their treasure fleet and I'll fill your coffers with gold and silver, enough to buy an army to match his and to build the finest navy in the world."

"Stop! You are fevered. Or drunk. Or just mad for revenge. Whatever, this scheme is not rational. A rupture with Philip would be disastrous for England. I will not give you license to ruin my realm!"

She turned her back on him, leaving him smarting at her rebuke. She heaved a troubled sigh and muttered, "Mad for revenge, like Mary. You're as irrational as she is."

"Who?"

She threw him a wry look. "You have been away too long." She sat down wearily on the divan and rattled off a tale about the Scottish queen: her imprisonment, escape, defeat on the battlefield by the Earl of Moray, her flight into England. "She has asked me to raise an army for her. Great heaven, she actually expected I would let her lead English troops against her enemies. Revenge, that's what drives Mary."

Adam was only half listening. Scotland meant nothing to him, but he saw Elizabeth's deep concern, which worried him. Caught in a web of Scottish politics, she would not focus on the *real* enemy. "The Scots are an inconsequential nation and their queen is a froth-headed fool. Dispatch her back to her own land and turn to face the true threat. The guns of Spain."

"Mary has more power than you know. A power that swords and cannonballs cannot match."

"What power?"

"The succession."

The pain in her voice caught him off guard. He knew about this burr in her heart. Childless, she had no heir. After her coronation nine years ago she had told him she would never marry, because her choice would have to be a foreign prince, and such a king-consort would draw power to himself, eclipsing hers. Adam had heartily approved her decision, glad that if he could not have her, no other man would either. Gossip abounded, of course, mostly about her and the Earl of Leicester. Some said they were lovers. Adam didn't believe it. He bridled at the lurid court whisperings, but he knew Elizabeth's heart was his.

But the succession was a matter he knew she took very seriously. He sat down beside her. "Mary Stuart is nothing but a French marionette. A woman with so sense."

"She stands next in line to my throne, that I cannot dispute. And who else can I name?" She gave him a sad smile. "I envy you your family. You have a wife, children—" She held up a hand to stop him interrupting, a gesture that acknowledged she understood how joyless his marriage was. "The children are worth it all, Adam. And your splendid parents—you know the love I bear Lord and Lady Thornleigh. I have lost father and mother, sister and brother. I shall never have a husband. Nor children." There was a catch in her voice. She got control of it. "The people of England are my family. I ask for nothing more. Shall I endanger them by leaving no one to guide and protect them? Shall I invite civil war? Already the succession has dangerously split my council. Half of them hound me to name Mary my heir, the other half to marry and *produce* one."

"She is not a tenth the ruler you are."

"But more a woman. She has a bonny baby son." Tears glinted in her eyes. "While I am barren stock."

He saw her anguish. He took her hand and kissed it gently, wishing with all his heart that he could comfort her. She pressed his hand to her cheek and looked into his eyes and whispered, "I thank God for bringing you home."

He pulled her to him to kiss her, but before their lips touched cheers burst from the shore. Elizabeth flinched and pulled back. Through the crack in the curtains Adam saw that they were approaching Whitehall Palace and people were jostling on the wharves for a chance to see Elizabeth. He cursed them. They had snapped his bond of intimacy with her.

She stood up with sudden vigor, banishing self-pity. She smoothed her skirt, her hair, preparing to disembark. Adam saw his chance to convince her slipping away. In a moment she would become the public person, no more the private woman. He jumped up. "What are you going to do about my murdered men?"

She turned slowly. "*Your* men? Were they not my subjects?"

There was a knock on the door. "Your Majesty?"

"I'm coming."

Adam said, "They were indeed. Loyal Englishmen, butchered by Spain. It's time to take action."

She gave him a cool look. "Vengeance is not wise politics."

It grated him. He was not a politician. "I tell you, I cannot let them get away with this."

"We are done here," she said dismissively. "For your misbehavior tonight with my foreign guest, my decision is that you shall bide in quiet seclusion at your house outside London until the Spaniards' fury cools." She swept past him to the door.

Their fury? "Good God, Elizabeth, their foul attack on us cannot stand. I am going after their fleet, with or without your help. They are a menace to you, to all of us. I am going to stop them."

She turned at the door. Her voice was steel. "Don't. I have saved your skin tonight, Adam. Disobey me on this, and I promise I will have you dragged to the Tower in chains."

❧ 11 ❧

Mary's Tale

The noonday sun was hot, the road dusty, and Justine was thirsty, her hands damp with sweat inside her riding gloves. Yet she felt a fresh, exciting sense of accomplishment as she rode with Mary across a bridge over the River Swale in the Yorkshire Dales. They trotted side by side behind Lord Scrope and his ten outriders, while his thirty men-at-arms followed as Mary's guard. The household carts brought up the rear. Mary was being moved south, deeper into England, and Justine was responsible for the move.

Mary did not know of her involvement, of course, which made Justine cautiously proud of having managed it. At Carlisle Castle she had paid a laundress, a woman whose husband was the barman at the village tavern, to report to her any local talk about Mary, and the woman passed along what her husband had heard: that there were northern gentlemen so zealous to protect Mary and support her claim to the English throne they were murmuring about descending in force on Carlisle Castle to carry her away. Alarmed, Justine had asked for names, but the laundress had said, "I know not, mistress, and my man knows no more." Then she had whispered with some awe, "But round here everyone knows the Scottish queen's champion is the great earl himself." Justine was amazed. The Earl of Northumberland! She wrote to warn Lord

Thornleigh, making it clear that she had no evidence, was only doing her duty in conveying the rumor, but he had obviously thought it important enough to tell Elizabeth, because Elizabeth's command quickly reached Lord Scrope: Mary must be moved.

Mary had not made it easy for Scrope. Justine knew how infatuated he was with his royal guest, and it was with much anxious bowing that he had informed her that his orders were to escort her to his seat of Bolton Castle eighty miles southeast. Mary had burst into tears, wailing that she did not deserve such mistrust and disrespect, that she loved Elizabeth, who should love her in return. She had flung herself down on the window seat and wept. Lord Scrope had looked almost as upset himself, and for a moment Justine thought he might capitulate to Mary. But he was no fool; despite his infatuation he was Elizabeth's man, immovable about her command. Justine had seen Mary's tears harden into a cold glare at him. Icily, she had agreed to the move. Justine felt a small thrill at this early measure of success in her mission.

The entourage traversed the bridge, the horses' hooves clanking on the stone, and Justine welcomed the cool air on her face from the gurgling river. She breathed in the subtle scents of the wildflowers scattered along the green riverbanks—water violets and wood sorrel, yellow pimpernel and marsh hawk's-beard, bluebells and bog myrtle. There was something achingly beautiful about high summer; August would soon slip into autumn, and here in the north autumn was but a short prelude to winter. Though she had lived for eight years in England's cultivated south she had to admit that something of this wild moorland country was in her blood. It gave her a pang, a reminder of her one deep regret about the move: Bolton, though still in Yorkshire, was farther from Yeavering Hall and therefore she would be farther away from a chance to uncover information about Alice's killer. The longer she stayed with Mary, the colder the killer's trail would become. It grieved her. But she was committed to the mission. Doing her duty with Mary was paramount, for Elizabeth and for herself.

She glanced back at Jane de Vere and Margaret Currier, her fellow ladies-in-waiting, their horses' flanks almost touching as the girls leaned close to talk. *About me?* Justine wondered as she caught

Jane's inquisitive glance. She was aware of the honor of riding in pride of place beside Mary. She had settled well into Mary's household, though she'd been careful not to fall into gossiping with Jane and Margaret. Her sole aim had been to get Mary's trust, and happily she had succeeded beyond her highest expectations. Whether it was because of her fluency in French, which was clearly a comfort to Mary, or the unstated bond of Catholicism between them, Mary was treating her as the most favored of her ladies, almost a confidante. Justine was thankful—and quite prepared to exploit the situation. *If Mary wants a friend, I'll be that friend.* Recently, she had begun to teach Mary English. In Scotland Mary had dealt with her educated nobles in French; she had only a rudimentary knowledge of the Scots language. Her letters to Elizabeth were in French.

"River valley," Justine said, gesturing at the lush greenery that crowded the riverbanks. *"Vallée de la rivière."* Continuing the lessons on the journey had helped to pass the time.

"River valley," Mary repeated, concentrating on the hard Anglo-Saxon *R* . She looked up at a scatter of swallows on the wing. *"Et comment dit-on oiseaux?"*

"Birds, my lady. Swallows."

Mary's brow furrowed in confusion. She pointed to her neck. "Swallow? As, to drink?"

"Ah, no, that is a different swallow."

Mary shook her head, frowning in frustration. "English."

"I know," Justine said, amused. "A baffling tongue."

They shared a smile. They reached the other side of the bridge, the river burbling behind them, and trotted up to the crest of the riverbank. A deer ambled out from the woods ahead, froze at the sight of Scrope's outriders, then bolted across the road, disappearing into the trees.

"C'est arbre, que'est-ce que c'est?" Mary asked. What tree is that?

"An oak tree, my lady. A tough hardwood. The oak is the symbol of England."

"England," Mary mused, scanning the moorland that stretched before them, a rolling expanse of woodlands, grasslands, and open heath. "It is very . . . green."

Justine heard her admiration. Was she coveting this realm, wanting to be queen of it? "You must miss your own land, my lady. Are you homesick for Scotland?"

The word was new to Mary. "Homesick?"

"*Nostalgique.*"

"Ah. No, I am thinking this is green like France."

It made sense. Mary had lived in France for most of her life, hadn't come to rule Scotland until she was eighteen. It struck Justine with a small shock that they had this experience in common: Both had been transplanted far away from the place of their upbringing.

"Either way, my lady," she said, slowly so that the English words were clear, "you are far from home."

Mary gave her a warm smile. "You teach well, cherie. It remembers me that I—"

"Reminds me," Justine gently corrected.

"Ah, *oui, reminds* me to write letters to my English friends. You will help me with the words, *non?*"

Justine felt a pinch of excitement. What friends? About what? A plan to escape Lord Scrope's custody? She said diplomatically, "You honor me, my lady."

Mary looked up at the birds and melancholy stole over her face. "I would wish to be like them. To fly."

I warrant you would, Justine thought. *But not if I can help it.* She decided to make a bold try. "Is one of your friends the Earl of Northumberland?"

Mary gave her a sharp look. "Why should you think so?"

"He sent you that haunch of venison last week," she said innocently. "It was delicious."

"So he did. Yes, he has showed me kindness. Other gentlemen, too. Sir George Bowes sent a Turkey carpet." She added bitterly, "This place where I am going, I do not know the people."

Justine switched to French to stress her sympathy. "Bolton will not be your home for long, my lady. The inquiry commissioners will quickly dispatch this matter." Mary herself had told Justine that the inquiry was about to begin. Not in London, but York, just fifty miles from Bolton. Elizabeth had sent a dozen commissioners to hear the case the Scots would make against Mary. The Scots, led by Mary's half brother, the Earl of Moray, had arrived with their retinue of lawyers, while Mary had sent her loyal men Lord Herries and Bishop Leslie to lead her team. "Their findings," Justine assured her now, "will end your purgatory in this country."

Mary gave a mirthless laugh. "Will they, indeed?" Now that they were speaking French, her tone was both more relaxed and more pointed. She was at home in this language.

"Of course. Her Majesty's purpose is to compel the Scottish lords to account for their conduct against you, their sovereign. I am no lawyer, but how can their actions be called anything but treasonable?"

Mary turned on her with sudden sharpness. "Do not pretend with me."

Justine's skin prickled with caution. "Pretend, my lady?"

"You know the purpose of this inquiry as well as I. So does all of Europe. Calling Moray to account is just the official reason. The *real* reason is to debate what everyone wants to know. Did I abet the killing of my husband."

Justine was stunned. No one in Mary's retinue ever mentioned the murder of Lord Darnley to her face. But what an opportunity! She quickly gathered her wits. "That tragedy is past, my lady. I know the talk continues, but Her Majesty's intention is to put an end to it."

"Bah. It has just begun."

"Then you shall stop it. With the truth."

Mary looked her dead in the eye. "Will I? Do you know the truth?" Her tone was a challenge, almost a taunt. "Go ahead. Ask me."

Justine was itching to do it. *Did you order your husband's death?* She opened her mouth to say the words.

"Dinner, my lady," a man's voice rang out.

Startled, both women turned. Lord Scrope was trotting back to them. "We'll set the tables under those trees," he said, pointing to a shady copse of holly and hazel. Justine could have screamed at him for interrupting. Mary had been so close to answering! Now the moment was lost. Already, Scrope's men of the vanguard were turning their horses off the road.

"Thank you, my lord, you are kind," said Mary, suddenly all charming complaisance. The instant change in her unnerved Justine. It was as though their dangerous talk of murder had not happened.

Scrope wiped sweat off his upper lip with the back of his gloved hand. "I warrant you are saddle weary, my lady, so rest as long as you like." *What a fool he is,* thought Justine. Mary was an excellent horsewoman, known to love hunting and hawking, and her smooth face bore not a trace of fatigue. She could probably outride Scrope. Justine glanced nervously at the woods that flanked the road ahead. If Mary's supporters intended an ambush, they would find their prize ready and willing to ride.

Bolton Castle, a fortress staked on the moors, was a quadrangle of four gray stone ranges around a central courtyard, with bulky rectangular towers rising at each corner. The entourage rode in before nightfall. No ambush. No mishap. Nothing but tired ladies and bored men-at-arms looking forward to a tasty supper and soft feather beds in the comfortable chambers of Lord Scrope's castle.

Justine helped Jane and Margaret unpack Mary's wardrobe as maidservants bustled to lay fresh linen sheets on the royal guest's bed, tack up the final tapestry on the wall, scatter sweet herbs among the floor rushes, and light candles in the deepening dusk. Mary lounged in a bath.

It was dark by the time she and her ladies finished a light but succulent meal of roast capon and fig tart. During it, Mary had given an audience to Scrope's chamberlain and the captain of his castle guard, both of whom seemed in awe of her poise and beauty. Justine was used to seeing men gaze slack-jawed at the Queen of Scots. Women, too. *How little it takes to impress people,* she thought. Surface glitter. Yet she had to admire Mary's gentle way with inferiors. Haughty she was, always the queen, but with a mildness of manner, never raising her voice to servants, that seemed to make maids and footmen stand taller in her presence.

"Stay with me, cherie," she murmured to Justine as Margaret and Jane moved to the door, dismissed for the night.

"Of course, my lady." Justine hid her surprise and delight. Hop-

ing to resume their conversation cut short on the road, she had
been about to ask if Mary wanted her to stay and read to her.
"Shall we continue with Sir Thomas Wyatt's sonnets?"

"No, no," Mary said with a sigh, "enough of English." She
strolled to the casement where the window stood open letting in
the evening breeze, earthy with the smells of cut hay and ripening
fruit. Torchlight winked in the distance across the fields. "We'll sit
here, cherie. And sew."

Justine fetched her embroidery hoop and basket of silk yarns
and Mary's cherrywood box of beads. She had seen Mary at work
on bracelets for friends, male and female, eye-catching creations
that were her own design. Justine pulled their chairs to the window and they sat side by side, rummaging through the yarn and
beads, discussing which colors to choose. Justine settled back to
ply her needle through the stretched linen while Mary worked at
stringing a bracelet of garnet beads and tiny glass pearls. Justine
was all thumbs at embroidery; she had no knack. Mary's needlework was superb, as was her skill with these bracelets, and Justine
told her so.

Mary's smile was rueful. "A skill I honed in the long days at
Loch Leven." Justine understood: her eleven months as a prisoner
in a tower on an island in Loch Leven. Mary added bitterly, "As
Moray's guest."

She always called her half brother "Moray," which sounded odd
to Justine, as though the two were not kin. They had had the same
royal father, James V, but while Mary's mother had been his wife
and queen, he had sired this son between adulterous sheets. The
boy had been raised almost on an equal footing with Mary, though,
and given the best education, and they had once been close; in the
early days of her reign she had ennobled him as the Earl of Moray.
Then rivalry for power had shattered their friendship. Each was
now the other's mortal enemy.

Mary said, while slipping a shiny pearl onto the silver wire,
"He'll be as eager as a new-trained hawk now that Elizabeth has
cut him loose from her jesses. This inquiry is his grand chance to
ruin me."

Justine held her breath, trying not to show her eagerness to hear more. She concentrated on poking her needle in and out of the linen. "He has tried to before and failed."

"Ah, but this time the hawk has been starved and will go for the kill. He *must* win, you see, by proving my guilt. If he does not, and I am restored to my throne, he fears I'll have my revenge on him."

Justine dared to look up. "Would you?"

Mary's eyes locked on hers. "Wouldn't *you?*"

In the silence, a dog howled far across the fields.

An apologetic smile softened Mary's face. "Forgive me, cherie, I should not burden you with my worries."

"It is no burden, my lady. I am your friend. I hope you know that."

"I do." She leaned closer and whispered conspiratorially, as though aware of Lord Scrope's spies at her door, "The sacred object you gave me? It is safe in my keeping."

Justine felt a rush of victory she could not hide. But she made her smile one of reassurance. "As your secrets are safe in mine, my lady. You can tell me anything. I am your servant."

Mary's look was intense, as though to examine her. Then, grave of face, she went back to stringing her beads. Justine's hope plunged. Had she gone too far? She went back to plying her needle, but her mind was far from the stupid task. She had bungled this chance to get Mary to talk. She was a fool to have pushed.

The candle flames jerked in the window breeze. Someone in a far room was plucking a lute idly, tunelessly. Justine struggled to decide what to do next.

Then Mary said, very quietly, her eyes on her task, "It wasn't my husband they came to murder. Their target was me."

Justine tried to stay still, to lure her to go on, but she was too surprised. "You?"

"It was the coldest night that winter. February. Henry and I were traveling to Edinburgh." Justine was so surprised to hear this intimate use of the Christian name it took a moment to realize: Henry Lennox, Lord Darnley, Mary's husband. "We stopped for the night just outside the city at Kirk o' Field, at the old priory, where we settled into the provost's lodging. We had stayed there before in the happy days when we were first married. How I loved

Henry. He was so dashing, so . . . manly." She glanced up with clear eyes. "Have you ever loved a man?"

Justine felt a blush heat her face. *Will.* "Yes," she said, perhaps too quickly.

Mary's smile was tender. "Then you know what I mean. What woman ever forgets that feeling? Henry gave me my baby boy, James." Her smile faded. "I have not seen my son for over a year. Moray keeps him under his thumb in Edinburgh." Her eyes stayed on her bracelet as she worked on it. "Henry and I had our disagreements. What married couple does not? Gradually, he drew away from me. We spent more time apart. I don't know why. Perhaps it was my fault. He was a proud man, and maybe in my efforts to rule my realm I did not pay him enough attention. Whatever the reason, I deeply regretted the bad feeling between us and I wanted to repair it. So I invited him to join me at Glasgow. He came, and we had friendly words, which heartened me, and then we set off for Edinburgh to see our son at Holyrood Palace. But that February night was so cold, so bitter, we stopped at Kirk o' Field, at the old priory, the provost's lodging. That's where Moray's killers struck."

Moray's? Justine blurted in surprise, "Your brother?"

"Not in person. He is clever, he stayed far distant from the vile deed itself. But he had done his work, inciting his fellow Protestant lords against me. Morton, Lindsay, Ruthven, and more. Their henchmen set gunpowder in the basement of the priory. Many barrels, packed with gunpowder. I went out that evening to pay a brief visit I had promised to two faithful servants who were getting married. The murderers hadn't expected that. While Henry slept, they struck. The explosion was so huge, so monstrous, people in Edinburgh felt the ground tremble. They found my poor husband's body in the garden, in the snow, the blast so powerful it had thrown him there, all mangled. When I returned and was told I almost collapsed in shock and grief."

Tears sprang to her eyes. Impulsively, she reached for Justine's hand and squeezed. "It is such a relief to have someone to talk to. A friend. I have been so alone."

Justine saw her raw loneliness, and it moved her. "Oh, my lady. How terrible for you."

Mary nodded, then drew back, clearly struggling to regain her composure. "After, the lords who had done the foul deed, and who held sway in my fractured government, quickly laid the blame on a man they loathed for his ambition, the Earl of Bothwell, James Hepburn, the captain of my guard, a hard, experienced soldier. Long before this tragedy he had done good service to me and I had rewarded him by making him an earl. That had angered many nobles who felt they were his betters. So they tried him for the murder of my poor husband."

"But Lord Bothwell was acquitted, was he not?" That much was common knowledge.

"Yes, but the lords had created a monster. Bothwell hated them for trying to bring him to the executioner's block. He decided to strike for power—the power that lay in me. He proposed marriage to me. You can imagine my revulsion—poor Henry's body was scarcely three months in the ground! That did not daunt Bothwell. He came at me in the countryside. I had left Edinburgh to visit my baby son at Stirling Castle, where I had moved him for his safety, and was returning to the capital accompanied by a small escort of thirty men. Five miles from the city, near the bridge over the River Almond at Cramond, Bothwell intercepted us with a force of over four hundred men, all with swords drawn. We anxiously drew to a halt, and Bothwell took hold of my horse's bridle as though I were his captive. He told me I was in danger from a brewing insurrection in Edinburgh and he was taking me for my own safety to his castle at Dunbar. My men did not believe him and were about to defend me, but I was appalled. Stalwart they were, but so vastly outnumbered. How could I let them be slaughtered for my sake? So I stopped them, and I went with Bothwell." She shook her head in bitterness. "There was no insurrection, of course. It was Bothwell's ruse to lay hold of me, to control me and thus control the crown."

Her voice became tight and thin. "And lay hold of me he did. It was a forty-mile ride to Dunbar. We arrived at his castle at midnight, and after we entered, all the gates were shut. He took me to his chamber and boasted he would marry me. I refused. But I was so weakened by these terrible events—Henry's murder, this violent abduction—and felt so alone I was near to breaking. I knew I was completely in Bothwell's power. He forced me into his bed and . . ." She shrank back into her chair, as though cringing at the memory. "He is not a gentle man." Tears choked her words.

Justine was horrified. *Rape.*

Mary swallowed hard, raised her head, and went on. "With me so weakened, Moray and his band of murderers saw their chance. Ascendant in the government, they sharpened their knives for Bothwell. They declared publicly that they would liberate me from his tyranny and thralldom, protect the Prince, my son, and bring Bothwell to justice, as they said, for my husband's murder. And I?" She lowered her eyes, "By then I knew the worst. I was with child by Bothwell."

Justine gasped. She pressed her hand to her mouth, wishing she had not made the sound which seemed coarse, a further insult to Mary, who had suffered so much. But she was mesmerized by the tale and could not help hungering to hear more.

"Yes," Mary said, "he had won. What could I do but marry him?" She took a breath before going on. "But our marriage was the end for Bothwell. With his enemies so strengthened, he knew he had gone too far—he could not fight them all. He fled to Denmark, and is there still." Mary seemed to take no joy in relating his downfall. "That's when Moray and his fellows finally came after *me.* They publicly accused me of having masterminded my husband's death, using Bothwell as my creature. They took me to Loch Leven, to a lonely tower on the island. They took my son away . . . my baby boy. I have not seen him since . . ." Her voice faltered. She closed her eyes. "Forgive me." After a steadying breath, she went on, "At Loch Leven they came to me with papers of abdication, Lord Lindsay and Robert Melville and more, the cowards. They crowded into my small room and shouted at me, demanding that I sign. I refused. Lindsay held his knife to my throat and told me if I did not sign he would slit my throat. I was weak with fear. I signed their miserable paper, silently vowing to have it overturned when I was free. Every court in Christendom rules that an enforced abdication is void. Their paper was worth as much as Lindsay's spittle."

The desolation on her tearstained face was awful to behold. Justine had seen her tears before when Mary had been crossed, tears of anger and frustration, but this was something else. No one with a heart could behold this woman's pain and not feel pity. Justine felt close to tears herself. It startled her, unnerved her. Was she being disloyal to Elizabeth by pitying Mary?

Mary shook her head at the misery of remembering. Her face was pale, her mouth trembling. "At Loch Leven I was so distraught I became ill. And in that weakened state of abject wretchedness, I miscarried. Twins. Born dead. Dear God . . ." A groan escaped her and her eyes closed and she slumped forward.

"My lady!" Justine lurched to break Mary's fall, taking her by the shoulders. Mary felt limp in her arms. In pity Justine went down on her knees and wrapped her arms around her to hold her upright in the chair. "My lady, you are ill!"

Mary jerked, resorted to consciousness, though her face was drained of color. "No . . . no, I am fine . . . though sick at heart!" She smiled faintly through her tears. "God bless you, cherie." She stroked Justine's cheek. "God bless you."

That night, sleep was impossible for Justine. She lay on her bed, her body as still as if hands pinned her there, but her mind awhirl with all that Mary had told her, all that Mary had suffered. To find her husband's mangled body in the snow . . . the horror of it. To be raped . . . the degradation! To be made pregnant and then bear dead infant twins . . . how pitiful. To be kept apart from the baby son she loved . . . how did any woman bear that sorrow? Justine thought of Will, of the happy future she hoped to share with him, and of one day having his child. It made her feel all the sorrier for Mary.

Of course, there had to be another side to Mary's story, Justine knew that. The Earl of Moray would no doubt air it at the inquiry, and Elizabeth's commissioners would listen gravely and come to a conclusion. But they were men, their world a regimented place of facts and politics, and none of them would ever see what Justine had seen tonight. The private, woman's hell that Mary had been dragged through by forces more powerful than she was.

Justine stared out the window at the stars, and under their cold glitter a thought stole over her that shook her. Her own private hell—the chasm that threatened to open between her and Will—was one she had had no part in making. It was a legacy of the feud between the Thornleighs and Grenvilles. Like Mary, she was in chains forged by forces beyond her.

She and Mary, she realized, had much in common.

Again, she felt a pinch of guilt. Was the sympathy she felt for Mary a disloyalty to Elizabeth? No, she told herself, feeling quite clear-eyed. She was sworn to do her duty—she *wanted* to do her duty—and nothing would change that.

Yet, which of these queens had the more urgent cause? Elizabeth, who had good reason to fear the men who wanted Mary in her place? Or Mary, who had been so cruelly wronged?

Who was right?

In the dark garden below Mary's suite, Christopher Grenville wolfed down meat on a leg of cold roasted capon, his eyes never leaving the open window above. Its rectangle of candlelight was a maddening blank: He could see no one. From it came the murmur of women's voices, and the lilt of it told him they were speaking French, but the sound was so faint he could not decipher a single word. Justine? Mary? Both? He dared not go any closer. He had watched from the shadows of the rose trellis as a kitchen maid had brought out a plate of meat scraps and bones, apparently for the water spaniels in the kennel beyond the garden. At the smell they had barked and jumped in their chains. Christopher felt no less ravenous, famished from his ride from London. The maid had set down the plate on a stone ledge just outside the kitchen door and gone back inside as though she'd forgotten something. Water for the dogs? A cloak for herself? Watching, Christopher didn't know and didn't care. He had snatched the capon leg and gone back into the shadows. He felt the humiliation more sharply than the hunger. As lord of Yeavering Hall he had been served succulent dishes morning, noon, and night. Now his life was skulking and hiding, eating cookhouse food in corners, forever on the move to avoid suspicion, forever a-horse in Mary's service. He'd had his bitter fill of being a fugitive. But he ordered himself to swallow his impatience. Once Mary was on the throne his fortune would be restored; God would smile on him again. Yet there was much to do to bring that about, he thought as he wolfed the meat, watching her window. Had she got the note he'd paid the scullery boy to take up to her? He had to talk to her.

And he hungered to know about Justine. It wracked him that his daughter was so near, yet he still had not seen her. She might as well still be locked in Thornleigh's house, ignorant that her father was even in England, let alone a stone's throw away. He was so on edge he tasted nothing of the meat as he tore off another bite with his teeth while the dogs barked on.

Hinges creaked. He tensed, eyes darting to a narrow wooden door at the base of the round tower. A woman emerged into the darkness, tall, hurrying toward him with a rustling of silk. Mary. Christopher tossed away the stripped capon bone. "Over here," he said, glad of the dogs' barking that masked his voice.

"What news?" she said the moment she reached him.

All he could think of was Justine. "Where's my daughter?"

"Upstairs. I've just sent her to bed."

Disappointment crashed over him. Ridiculous, he realized. What had he expected? Mary would hardly bring the girl to this fraught rendezvous. Yet he could not keep from asking, "How is she?"

"She is well," she said crossly. "I wish I could say the same for myself."

That shook him back to reality. "Are you sick?"

"Sick to death of being Elizabeth's captive." She shivered and hugged herself, though the night was balmy. "As for your daughter, I wish I could send her away. This is not working."

"Why not? Have you not befriended her as I said?"

"I have done my best, but . . ."

"But what? What's gone wrong?"

"I'm not sure. I fear she is clever. She keeps asking questions.

Today, about Northumberland. Is he one of my friends? she asked. Dear God, if she discovers his plan to help me and tells Elizabeth, I am doomed."

Caution prickled him. It was true, they could not afford to have Elizabeth find out about Northumberland. Yet he doubted they were in danger from his daughter. "How could Justine know anything about that? She has been with you night and day. She sees no one. No, you are imagining things. What have you gotten from *her?* Anything of Elizabeth's intentions?"

"Nothing. I tell you, the girl is clever. She guards herself carefully. If we want to make use of her you must step in. You must make yourself known to her. Beat down her defenses. Bring her to our cause."

Should he? Part of him longed to see his daughter, to embrace her and reclaim her from Thornleigh's indoctrination. But was it safe to do so? Reluctantly, he said, "Not yet. Not until—"

The kitchen door swung open and the kitchen maid stepped out. Christopher yanked Mary back with him into the shadows. She gasped and stiffened. To keep her quiet he whipped his arm around her waist, her back to him, and pulled her close. He held her tightly, willing her to be guided by him. She gave a slight sigh and leaned back against him and he felt her muscles soften. He knew that she had always taken comfort in having a strong man act for her. Christopher was more than ready to be that man now. He would not let on how anxious he was about his chances of killing Elizabeth before the inquiry could ruin Mary and blast his future. He still had no idea how to get close enough to Elizabeth to do it. Even if he could, would Northumberland be ready with enough force to back up Mary's push for the crown?

They stood together, their body heat merging, and watched as the maid took the kitchen scraps to the dogs. The barking ceased as the animals fell on the meat. Humming a tune, the maid padded back into the kitchen. The door closed. There was no sound but the faint rustling of leaves in the night breeze.

The interruption spurred Christopher to shake off his problems. Somehow he would find a way to reach Elizabeth, and as for Northumberland, Christopher now had reason to hope they would get the foreign backing they needed. It was why he was here. He turned Mary around. "I've come to give you some good cheer. We are a step closer to bringing the ally we need to our cause, to bolster Northumberland. Spain."

Her face lit up. "Spain? How so?"

"I've been with Ambassador de Spes in London. He is in a rage about English piracy."

She frowned, disappointed. "What do common cutthroats on the seas have to do with me?"

"Not common—Sir Adam Thornleigh. And not on the seas, but at the Earl of Pembroke's home in the presence of the Queen. It seems that, unprovoked, Sir Adam attacked de Spes's cousin and beat him senseless. Thornleigh was like a mad dog, de Spes told me. The next day, still coughing blood, his cousin died."

Christopher had felt sheer glee when the Spaniard had given him the account. The brawl was the kind of flashpoint that could push two countries, already snarling at each other, into raging armed hostility. The fact that Richard Thornleigh's son had been the berserk fool who had fomented the standoff made it all the sweeter. As was Elizabeth's quandary because of it. Christopher had heard that she had been outraged at the Spanish attack on Hawkins's ships in the Indies, but she could make no complaint because Hawkins had had no right to be in Spanish waters. Now, after Thornleigh's violence, she had been forced to publicly apologize to de Spes, and to Spain. She was seething. De Spes was seething. All of it was fertile ground, Christopher hoped, to sow seeds of upheaval. Indeed, if he could assassinate Elizabeth, Spain would smile.

Mary still looked doubtful. "But is it really enough to push Philip to join us? He is no hothead."

"No, it's not enough. But a step in the right direction. I'm on my way to Alnwick to ask Northumberland to come and meet with de Spes. My lady, it is time to bring together our allies, English and Spanish. Time to show Philip our home-grown strength."

She seemed to take heart. "Do it. Elizabeth has no right to hold me captive. Do it, and quickly. Set me free."

* * *

"A visitor?" Justine asked the next morning. She stopped pouring water into a basin. It was for Mary to wash her hands before breakfast, though Mary had not yet left her bedchamber. She set down the ewer and looked at Jane de Vere, who had come in with the news. "For me?"

"For you," Jane confirmed. "A dirty-looking young fellow. He came in by the kitchen and frighted the cook. I've left him there."

Justine hurried down the stairs and along a corridor, then down another flight to the castle kitchens. A kitchen maid was talking to a young man whose back was turned to Justine. Seeing her, the maid curtsied. The man turned, and Justine took in a breath of surprise. It was the young carpenter from Yeavering Hall. Jeremy.

He tugged off his cap in deference to her. "Pardon me, mistress." His face was dusty from the road and his clothes were chalky with dried mud. An icy excitement shot up in Justine. He could only have come with news about Alice.

"Lady Isabel sent me," he said as though fearing she might suspect him of running off without leave. "I went to her with a thing I'd heard and asked would she send word to you. She said it was important to you, so she gave me leave to come and tell you myself."

Justine sensed an eagerness in him, and she was itching for him to go on, but first she guided him out into the passageway where they could speak in private. A footman trudged past them carrying a coal scuttle. The moment they were alone she asked, "What have you heard?"

"I did what you said. Asked around in Kirknewton about what people might have seen the day Alice was killed. I asked the folk that get passed over by the high and mighty . . . begging your pardon, mistress, I know they're me betters."

"Never mind that, I'm glad you did. And?"

"Well, across from the east end of the churchyard is the stable that's back of the butcher shop. The ostler told me a farrier had been shoeing an old mare that day. So I goes to the farrier in his cottage, edge of the village. And what the farrier told me was, as he was shoeing that mare he glanced out the open stable door and what he did see but a man running through the churchyard."

She felt a tingle at the back of her neck. "Running?" Jeremy's eyes narrowed. "And that's not all the farrier said. He *knew* that man. Not knew him like he was from the village or even the county, but he'd seen him in the village before. Selling wine, he was. And he said that wine man was running like a felon from the law."

Justine found she was holding her breath. Was the running man Alice's killer?

❧ 12 ❧

Spanish Gold

"We'll step her foremast more forward, do you see?"
Adam tapped the spot on the charcoal drawing of the ship,
showing his eight-year-old daughter Katherine his new design,
a small, three-hundred-ton galleon. They were in the parlor of his
Chelsea home, Kilburn Manor, five miles west of London. The
riverside hamlet of Chelsea was a quiet backwater, but the house
itself was far from quiet. Across the courtyard Frances had a clanging crew of masons and carpenters and plasterers and glaziers at
work building a new three-story wing onto the house. When Adam
had arrived home last night he'd been appalled to see the scope of
the construction. Appalled at the expense. He didn't begrudge his
wife her diversions, but this grandiose project would sink him. He
would have to break the news to her. The building had to stop.

At the moment, though, he was taking pleasure in explaining
the exciting new ship design to Katherine. How the length-to-
beam ratio of three to one made the hull form below the waterline
more like a galleass, but with a deeper draft. How he'd kept the
superstructure low, sweeping upward from waist to stern. Most important, how she would carry a powerful armament for her size,
twenty-eight guns. Altogether, she was leaner, faster, deadlier.
Good for killing Spaniards. He didn't tell her that last thought.

"And the rakish stem, here, will give the helmsman better handling in rough seas." He swept his hand across the paper with such gusto he knocked the apple he'd placed as a paperweight and it rolled toward the table edge. Katherine lurched from his side and grabbed it before it fell.

He smiled and squeezed her shoulder. "Good catch, Kate."

She beamed up at him. Adam looked across the parlor at his six-year-old son Robert who stood just inside the doorway, his hands behind his back pressed against the door jamb. The boy was pale and quiet. And small. Adam had expected him to have grown more in the year and a half he'd been away. He took the apple from Kate and held it up to Robert, coaxing. "Want a bite?"

Robert shook his head. Not a word. He'd barely spoken a sentence since Adam had arrived home yesterday. He had watched, though, staring at his father with intense gray eyes, more like a worldly-wise man than a child. Adam found it unnerving. But he thought he understood: It was shyness. Robert had been four when his father had sailed away, and Adam knew that despite his few days of rest at the palace he still looked gaunt and haggard—perhaps, to a child, even frightening. *The lad hardly knows who I am.*

He felt like a stranger himself here at home after so long at sea. It did his heart good to see his children—Kate so tall, and so clever—but it unsettled him that there was so little for him to do. He was no gentleman farmer, had no interest in hunting and hawking and no patience for dinners with bores. He wanted to get to work on repairs to the *Elizabeth* and longed to start building this new galleon he had on paper, but all of that would have to wait. God only knew how long. He was home on orders from Elizabeth—temporarily dry-docked. It galled him. How was he to know the Spaniard he'd struck had a weak heart and would die? He got word that Elizabeth had done her best to defend him to the livid ambassador, de Spes, telling him that Adam was deranged by his ordeal in the Indies, which only infuriated Adam when he heard it. Afterward, she'd made a great show of appeasing the Spanish delegation, ordering Adam to pay them an enormous fine of five hundred pounds. Five hundred pounds that he didn't have! He'd had to go cap in hand to his investor, Anthony Porteous. Elizabeth was so angry at the whole affair she had ordered him to go home to

Chelsea and stay there until de Spes's blood cooled. Adam had itched to suggest that his sword would cool the man's blood, in fact turn it stone cold. But he had held his tongue.

"What will you call her?" Kate asked.

Her voice snapped him out of his dark mood. It was a treat to see how the new ship design enthralled her. "What name would you like?"

"*Zephyr.*"

"Not bad."

"So she'll always take you into fair winds, and never a hurricane." She spread her smooth small hands on the map that lay beside the design. Adam had been showing the children the waters he had sailed—well, showing Kate, who was full of questions. He had hoped to draw Robert's interest, too, but so far had failed. He'd never seen a child so shy. An unwelcome thought stole over him, that Frances kept the boy too close to her.

"Was this where the storm caught you, Father?" Kate was pointing to the Florida Strait.

Clever girl, he thought with a swell of pride. Even as a baby she had liked to sit on his knee, imitating his pensive face as he'd pored over nautical charts. She had perused the markings of landfalls and soundings, none of which she could read, with the solemnity of a scholar. "That's right. And caught we were. Top-heavy, you see, not like"—he smiled at her—"like *Zephyr.*"

Hammers clanged. Adam shot an anxious glance out the window at the gang of workmen busy at Frances's grandiose project. He didn't know how he would pay even half the debts she had incurred. The battle off San Juan de Ulúa rushed back at him, and he saw again the coffers that held his expedition profits sinking beneath the waves. The brutal truth was, he didn't have enough money even to repair the *Elizabeth,* let alone build *Zephyr.* His throat tightened at the prospect before him. Bankruptcy. A kind of panic jumped him. He felt caught, a vessel snagged on a reef.

"Did it hurt?" Kate asked.

"Did what hurt?"

"The hurricane."

He looked at her serious face. He hadn't told his children about the Spaniards' murderous attack. They thought the worst he'd been through was rough seas. It was better that way. How do you tell a child about a cannonball splattering a friend's brains on your boots?

"Look here," he said, pointing to Florida to change the subject. "That's where *Zephyr* wants to go."

"Doesn't Florida belong to Spain?"

"Not all of it. It's a huge land, nobody even knows *how* huge. That's where England needs to be. Other nations got a head start. We have to catch up." He tapped Brazil on the map. "Who owns this?"

"Portugal."

"Right. And over here how much is Spain's?"

Eagerly, she leaned close and with her finger traced the enormous scythe-shaped bite of world that was the Spanish Main running from Florida through Mexico and Central America to the north coast of South America, gateway to the vast riches of Peru. Adam thought how his daughter's small finger made Spain's immense New World empire look even bigger. For over fifty years Spain had held dominion over half the globe, and from Mexico and Peru a constant river of gold and silver flowed across the Atlantic and into the Spanish King's treasury. For even longer, on the other side of the world, Portugal had held a monopoly on the trade routes that connected Africa, India, and the Spice Islands, becoming rich from the traffic in spices, ivory, silks, and precious gems. It had left the English nowhere to go but north. Frobisher had sailed to Newfoundland, and Chancellor and Willoughby to Moscow, but those expeditions were commercial failures, no gold, no spices, nothing but hunger, disease, and death in the icy, heaving wastes. Ten years ago Adam had sailed as a common seaman on one of the Moscow voyages and seen dozens of his shipmates perish.

Now, at San Juan de Ulúa, he'd seen more good men die. *His* men.

He didn't shrug off the dark memories; he hoarded them, as fuel. Somehow, he would make the Spaniards pay. But that was not for his daughter to see. "England lags behind," he told her. "It's like a race. What do you do in a race, to win?"

"Go fast," said Kate.

He nodded. "And that's what *Zephyr* will do. Go very fast."

Robert's voice piped up, "Why?"

Adam looked at him in surprise. He was pleased. Finally, the boy was taking an interest. "Because of her shape."

"No. Why *do* it?"

Adam didn't know how to answer. Seafaring was his life. The boy had never seen blue water, of course. No water at all but the River Thames outside his door. "Robin, come over here."

The boy didn't move.

"Come." Adam stretched out his arms, fists balled. "There's something in one of my hands that will *show* you why." He put both hands behind his back. "It's yours if you guess which hand."

Curiosity sparked in the boy's grave eyes. He crossed the room slowly, still on guard. He stood before Adam, looking up at him, his eyes darting from one of his father's bent arms to the other. He pointed to the right arm. Adam brought his right hand around and opened it. Nothing in his palm.

Disappointment flicked over Robert's face. He pointed to the other arm, determined to know.

Adam brought around his left hand and opened it. Nothing. Both children looked confused and let down. Adam reached for the side of his son's head, and with the flourish of a magician displayed the prize he had apparently snatched from behind Robert's ear. A bright silver coin, a Spanish piece of eight. The boy's eyes widened in astonishment. Kate laughed at the trick and clapped her hands. "You're rich, Robin!"

Adam grinned. "Why a fast ship, you ask? *That's* why."

Robert regarded the coin, his interest waning. "Just money."

Just? Adam blinked at him. Where was the boy's delight?

His son looked up, wariness in his eyes. "Did you steal it?"

Adam was shaken. And angry. He said sternly, "You'll speak with respect to your father."

The boy flinched. He piped in a small voice, "Yes, sir."

It made Adam feel a tyrant. Did his son think he was going to have him lashed? Regret surged through him. He hated being put so off balance. "Well," he said, briskly rolling up the drawing to get his bearings, "we'll talk later. Off with you two, now. Master Rowan has set lessons for you, I warrant."

They went upstairs to their tutor and Adam set out across the courtyard, maneuvering past workmen's carts and apprentices hoisting shovels and picks, barrels and ladders. Kilburn Manor was a hive, the activity centered on the new wing, which stood parallel to the old manor house, the two connected by a new roofed passageway so that together with the waterfront gates, the buildings formed a square around the courtyard. Beyond them lay drowsing orchards and gardens. Beyond that, farmer's fields.

Adam strode through the shadows of Frances's topiary works that were a feature of the courtyard, two lines of tall yew shrubbery clipped into shapes of columns, pyramids, vases, and globes that her gardeners maintained as stiff as statues. The light west wind barely ruffled their leaves. It did, though, carry a scent of watery plant life from the River Westbourne as it made its way down from Hampstead to the Thames, which fronted the old manor. Adam had never warmed to being in Chelsea; it made his trip upriver from the Thames estuary longer than when they'd lived in London. But seven years ago Frances had set her mind on moving to this sleepy spot. Said she wanted to bring up the children far from the noisome city. Adam knew what she'd really meant: far from court.

Into the new wing he went and up the stairs and into the long gallery, dodging workmen and tramping over sawdust that floured the floor. The air was dry with plaster dust. The hammering never stopped. The place was cavernous. Canvas sheets were tacked up to cover the long, empty expanse of wall where, at one end, glaziers were fitting new windows that soared two stories high. The canvas hung limp in the still afternoon, like sails becalmed. Adam shook his head at the folly of the project. Above this gallery were two more ostentatious floors. Frances was building a palace.

She stood at the far end, gesturing to a burly stonecutter in a scarred leather apron who listened intently to her instructions. The fellow knows who's captain, Adam thought wryly. He had never discounted his wife's skills as a manager. She took pleasure in running a large household, and was good at it.

She noticed him coming her way and hurried to greet him. "My lord and master," she said gaily, making a mock curtsy. "Come."

She beckoned him with happy urgency. "I must have your word on a matter of vital importance."

She hooked her arm around his and led him down the length of the gallery, chattering about the marbled pattern underfoot beneath the sawdust, the columns the masons were installing by the stairs, the gilt plasterwork for the ceiling, the cherrywood linen-fold paneling she had ordered. The gleam in her eyes told him how much she was enjoying the project. He was sorry to have to frustrate her.

"There." She stopped him and pointed at the far wall. "Should the portrait go above the door, or nearer the windows? Above the door would catch the viewer's eye best, but that spot won't get the splendid light from the windows, so I can't decide. What do you think?"

Adam looked at her. "Portrait?"

"Of us. I've commissioned Hans Eworth. Lady Fanshaw says he did an excellent job on her." She added with hushed reverence, "He painted the late Queen Mary, you know."

And charges a princely sum, Adam thought. "Frances, that's impossible."

"No, don't worry, he has worked us into his schedule," she said reassuringly. "It's all arranged. He starts next week. It takes a month or so, and he'll stay with us." She added happily, patting his arm, "It will let you rest and get back your strength. You'll have nothing to do but sit for Master Eworth."

Sit for a month? What a god-awful thought. "Cancel the arrangement. There will be no portrait."

"Cancel it? But why?"

"I can't afford it." He had raised his voice in exasperation, but thankfully the workmen hadn't heard him above the din they were making. Saws kept sawing, hammers kept banging. Adam suddenly saw them as leeches on his life. "And cancel all of this." He swept his arm to take in the whole huge wing.

Frances was staring at him as if he were speaking a foreign language. He remembered how his son had looked at him like a stranger. Neither of them saw *him.* "You heard me," he said. "Send these people home. Today." He turned to go.

She caught his arm. Her voice was a tight whisper. "You cannot. Your reputation will be ruined."

"I'm already ruined. Frances, *there is no money.*" A plasterer's apprentice glanced up from stirring paste. Adam looked away, irritation biting him. And something sharper—a gnawing sense of failure. He said to Frances, forcing himself to speak more gently, "I told you, it all went down with the *Jesus.* I'm sorry." He noticed two more workmen looking at him. It was humiliating. "No more of this in public," he said to his wife, and headed for the stairs. He felt he couldn't get out fast enough.

Frances caught up with him as he walked away from the wing. "But . . . there's the income from your lands. The rents. The revenues."

He kept walking. "And most of it will go to cover what I owe Porteous."

"Well then, there's your father. He has—"

"No." He would not ask his father to pay for his wife's folly. Hot bitterness surged through him. He'd *had* all the money they needed and more! He had sailed off on a great venture and made a great profit, but the Spaniards had sent it to the bottom of the sea.

"Adam, stop. Please!"

He halted, hearing her distress. She was out of breath. They were in her topiary row, and the foliage shadows cast an unforgiving mottle over her distraught face. Adam heaved a tight sigh. He wanted no more wrangling. "I'm sorry. I know you want this grand place. But it's impossible."

"Me?" She looked hurt. Redness sprang to her eyes. "I haven't built this for me. It's for *you.* A haven from the dangers of the sea. A shelter. A sanctuary."

A mausoleum, he thought. He couldn't stifle a shudder. *Dear God, give me an ocean.*

She saw it, and stiffened. "For you, yes. And for the children. Even if all my efforts mean nothing to you, think of your children. They must have a legacy."

"A legacy of debt?" He looked at her, baffled. Was she *willfully* blind to the facts? It irked him, too, the way she wielded the mention of the children like a weapon. He remembered his son's probing look of suspicion. "The boy called me a thief. How did he get that notion?"

"Robert? I don't know. I had to tell him why you didn't come home, since he knew you'd landed. I told him of the Spanish count insulting you and how, to clear it up, they kept you at the palace."

"That's how you put it to him? That I was kept there?"

"Isn't that what Her Majesty did? *Keep* you?"

The double meaning was too clear. Adam's anger boiled, but he held his tongue. He would not take her taunt. "That's no way to talk to the boy. You should have explained I was reporting to the Queen about my trading mission. A mission to enhance the power of England and the glory of Her Majesty."

"Not to provide for your family?"

"My family prospers only when Her Majesty's interests prosper. Why can you not see that they are one and the same?"

"Yet you do not. You esteem her *above* us."

"Good God, she is our queen."

"And nothing more? To you? Can you swear that?"

He was fed up. "You talk rot." He turned and strode on.

She shouted after him, "I say no more than what half of London is saying. How she entertained you alone on her barge. How she took your part after you attacked the count. How even when the man died and the Spaniards called for justice, she gave you her protection."

He turned, appalled at the loudness of her voice. No one was near, but anyone could be beyond the yew trees. He went back to her. "Frances, whose side are you on? I roughed up a Spaniard and I regret his death. But he is just one man. We English lost over three hundred!"

"She kept you in her private rooms! Like some male whore!"

He raised his hand in fury. Then froze, rocked by how near he had come to striking her.

She was trembling. "It's revolting," she croaked. "The show between the two of you. You love her! Do not deny it."

"You are mad."

"Swear it, then. Swear that she is no more to you than your queen. Swear it on the souls of your children."

He seethed in silence.

"You see?" she cried. Red anger splotched her face. Tears brimmed in her reddened eyes. "You make our marriage a mockery!"

His anger suddenly drained. He could not even muster that much passion. All he felt was dull, cold revulsion. This moment had been long coming. "Our marriage was a mockery from the moment we said our vows. No, before. From the moment you threatened my father's wife."

"Lady Thornleigh has done very well for herself, so do not blame—"

"You would have informed on her. Marry me, you said, or see her burned at the stake. That was your ultimatum. Till death do us part. Well, I've kept my end of the God-cursed bargain. So keep yours, madam, and spare me your prattle about love."

She was weeping now. Uncontrolled, racking sobs. Adam turned and walked away.

"Where are you going?" she shouted.

"The *Elizabeth*," he shouted back, no longer caring who heard.

Her voice was a wail behind him. "She robbed me of my husband!"

I was never yours to lose.

Portsmouth harbor lay rosy under a blood-red sunset. The water, calm as dimpled glass, radiated pink tints back to the sky. The tightness in Adam's chest eased as he walked up the gangplank, taking in the familiar shipboard smells and sounds: the air's salty tang, the haylike smell of the canvas, the water lapping gently at the hull, the rhythmic creak of rope against wood. His anxiety drifted away. A ship beneath him soothed him the way a tankard of ale before a hearth soothed other men. He was home.

Some work had been done to clean up the *Elizabeth* when she'd been brought here to Portsmouth, but there was still much to do. He felt bad about how he had galloped off to London and left his ship with her topsides filthy, mainmast a giant jagged stub, spars splintered, canvas in tatters, lower decks reeking of sickness. He had ordered a cleanup and basic repairs, and these had been done, and now the ship dozed at rest like the patched-up veteran she was, wounds bandaged, body bathed, but still a long way from fighting form. Ah, but what a campaigner she had proved, baring her teeth against the Spaniards in the skirmish! And how faithfully she had brought them home, the handful who'd survived, though she had been limping from her own injuries. She had slogged on as a veteran carries a wounded comrade off the battlefield. Adam crossed her bare, beaten deck and went down the worn companionway stairs. He felt he owed his ship more.

How much would it cost to refit her? he wondered as he opened the door of the stern cabin. He unbuckled his sword and hung it on the bulkhead hook, then flopped down on his berth on his back with a weary, grateful thud. Rose-tinted light from the stern window warmed the dark wood paneling that cocooned him. With the slow gentle rocking of the hull, the ropes that were the sinews of the vessel carried on their whispering creaks. His compass on the table clinked softly against a pewter plate. His eyes drifted closed. Refit her? As impossible as Frances's foolish palace. Bitterness was a worm in his heart. He didn't have enough money even to replace the bowsprit.

"Had enough of home life?"

Adam's eyes sprang open. Anthony Porteous sat on the edge of the table. With arms folded over his broad chest, his bald head agleam in the rosy light, and a satisfied aura of omnipotence, he put Adam in mind of a genie from a fable. But a genie, he suspected, who wanted to be paid.

"Couldn't stay home," he replied. "There's work to be done." He sat up and threw his legs over the side of the berth to show he meant business.

"Tonight?" Porteous smiled like a man at cards calling a bluff.

"A candle will do."

"For what task?"

"My log, for one. Accounts, for another."

"Accounts? What, will your pen conjure profit from disaster?"

Adam slumped. "No." He ran a frustrated hand through his hair. "Look, if you're here about what I owe you—"

"I am."

"Porteous, you know I have nothing. Once I get the ship refitted I'll do whatever it takes to pay you back. I'll slog to Flanders
with tin and hides and slog back with pots and boots. It will take a
few years, but I swear you'll get your money back."

"Years? No, no, my friend, that will not do." He toyed with the
compass. "I want it all repaid by Michaelmas."

Adam stared at him. Next month? The demand was insane. Unnerved, he tried to make a jest of it. "Then tell me where I can
conjure a chest full of gold."

"I shall. It's scheduled to leave Seville, bound for Flanders. I'll
give you a ship to intercept it."

A shiver scurried up Adam's back. Piracy? He remembered his
son's words, *"Did you steal it?"* The thought revolted him. He
glared at Porteous. "I'm no thief."

"You haven't heard whose gold it is."

"A rich Castilian merchant's? A fat Dutch burgher's? I'm not interested, I tell you. I am no pirate."

"No, you are a man who's been wronged. By Spain. A man who
wants revenge. On Spain." He set down the compass and spoke in
earnest. "The ship I speak of sails for Philip of Spain."

Adam's breath caught. "What?"

"That's right, the king himself. Next week that ship will be
bound for the Spanish-occupied Netherlands. It will carry a hoard
of gold destined to hire more troops in Philip's murderous oppres-
sion of the Dutch. This is your chance, Thornleigh. The King's
gold will not bring back your men, but it will give us back what the
Spaniards stole from us in the Indies." Porteous crossed his arms
with a satisfied smile. "Interested now?"

Adam made no effort to hide it. Excitement coursed through
him as sharp as hunger. He wanted this! It was a huge risk. He
would be going alone against Spanish guns. And there was Elizabeth. Would she stand by him again or have him arrested? This
raid, he saw, would either make him very rich or get him hanged.
He stood up with fresh vigor. Either way, he was going send a pack
of Spaniards to the bottom of the Channel.

❧ 13 ❧

The Casket Letters

Early to work as always, Will strode down a crowded corridor of the Council of the North in York on his way to the chamber where the inquiry about Mary, Queen of Scots, in its third day, was about to resume. He had been here from the start acting as Sir William Cecil's representative, a position that put him in daily company with Elizabeth's three commissioners hearing the arguments, and he didn't intend to miss a word.

"Master Croft, beg your pardon, sir," a young page said as he caught up to him. "You asked me to tell you when Lord Thornleigh arrived."

"He's here?"

"Yes, sir." The boy pointed past the milling crowd. "North entrance, sir."

Will turned on his heel and set out in the direction he'd just come from. This day had already begun well with a letter from Sir William praising his diligence and entrusting him with more responsibility in liaising with the commissioners. Now Uncle Richard's arrival made it even better. He had come as Elizabeth's personal envoy to the proceedings, a hugely prestigious position, and Will was not above basking in his uncle's glory.

And he in mine just a little, he thought with a tickle of pride. After all, the inquiry had been Will's idea. Now in full swing, it was mak-

ing history and Will was making a name for himself. That promised quicker advancement through Sir William at court, and *that*
meant he would soon be in a position to marry Justine. He had got
her note that she had been sent to attend Mary and he'd decided
that as soon as they were both back in London they would wed.
He was grinning as he reached his uncle.

His lordship was shrugging off his cape to a footman, and Will
greeted him with a respectful but cheerful bow. "My lord, welcome. Will you take some refreshment after your journey? I'll alert
the commissioners that you're here."

His uncle's look was almost a scowl. "I'm fine. Let's get to
work."

Will took no offense. The journey from London was wearying,
and his uncle was not a young man. In the saddle for weeks, no
wonder he was testy.

They moved through the crowd of men who parted, murmuring
and watching Lord Thornleigh as he passed. There were clusters
of the Scottish delegation, huddles of English lawyers, knots of
York aldermen, and Will knew they were all hungry for clues from
his uncle about Elizabeth's position in the matter of Mary.

"How they study you, sir," he said quietly as they walked. "I
warrant they'll be noting every twitch of your eyebrow, every frown,
every sigh." It made him smile. "Puts one in mind of Romans
reading entrails."

A cool glance from his uncle, and a gruff grunt.

He's in no mood for jests, Will thought. It sobered him. *Down to
business, then.* "You know Sir Ralph Sadler, of course," he said, indicating one of the commissioners they were passing who stood conferring with his clerks. Sadler, sixty-one, was an old hand at
Scottish politics. Lord Thornleigh nodded to him and Sadler gave
a courtly bow of his head in return. Farther down the corridor a
swarm of underlings buzzed like bees following another commis-
sioner as he strolled into the inquiry chamber, the mustachioed
Earl of Sussex, a highly influential man as Lord President of the
North.

Will quietly told his uncle, pleased to be in the know, "His
Grace the Duke usually arrives late." The Duke of Norfolk, thirty-

two and immensely wealthy, was the highest-ranking nobleman in England and presided over the inquiry as the foremost of Elizabeth's three commissioners. Will could not suppress a chuckle, "Perhaps thanks to the night's libations. He brought half his wine cellar with him."

His uncle rounded on him with a scowl and halted. "This is no good. Where can we talk alone?"

Will was taken aback. Had some problem arisen at court? He indicated a spot under a staircase out of the flow of men. The moment they were alone his uncle said with severe, clipped anger, "Betrothed. In *secret!* What in God's name were you thinking?"

The bubble of good cheer in Will burst. He saw in an instant how he had misjudged his uncle's mood. "Sir, let me explain—"

"Oh, Justine explained. *Love,*" he said in a withering tone. "Damn it, is this your character? I expected better from you. A betrothal should be public, a family ceremony. You did wrong, Will."

He smarted at the rebuke. "I believe it was right, sir."

"It was plain skulduggery. And there was no *need.* I told Justine you had my blessing. Nothing was blocking your way."

"With respect, sir, there was a need. I had told my mother my intention to marry Justine, and her reaction was . . . well, a violent hostility. It was unnerving, as though she'd gone slightly mad. She has taken a notion to hate Justine. I have no idea why."

His uncle looked away with a groan. "This is what comes of secrecy."

"Sir, she threatened to ask you to forbid our marriage. I wanted to assure Justine that nothing my mother might say or do would change anything, so I asked her to become betrothed. I take full responsibility, I persuaded her." Wounded through he was at his uncle's anger, he could not pretend to be contrite. "I did force the issue, but I'm not sorry that she and I exchanged vows. We love—"

"You love each other, I know. But that's not enough. You've cast a blot on our whole family. Her majesty takes a personal interest in approving marriages within great houses, and she would heartily disapprove of what you've done. As do I. A mother's bitter words are not reason enough for a man to act so dishonorably."

It cut Will so deeply he stood mute.

His uncle let out a breath of angry impatience. "I gather you haven't told Joan that you two are betrothed?"

"No. Given her hostility, I was afraid it might make her ill. And I thought if she had some time to—"

"Time. Bah, this is ill done. Ill done." He glared at Will. "I can still forbid the marriage."

It was a blow Will had not seen coming. A future without Justine was a future he did not want to imagine. "Don't, sir. Please. Give me a chance to make good this blunder. To prove myself to you."

"Oh, you shall. Believe me, you shall." He shook his head, heaving a sigh, as though attempting to get past their wrangling. "The fact is, I have a job for you."

Will grabbed the opportunity. "Gladly, sir. What is it?"

"Later. This is not the time or place to talk." He looked out at the crowd. "We have business here. Come, let's go in. I want you to tell me what's happened so far. Everything."

"Of course." Will pulled himself together. This was a chance to make a good impression. He meant to use it.

They made their way into the inquiry chamber packed with men, the session not yet under way. The leaders of the various parties stood in animated talk with their respective supporters and clerks: the three English commissioners, the Scottish delegation of the confederate lords who had usurped Mary, and the commissioners she had sent. Will was aware of all eyes on his uncle as they headed toward the English commissioners' table.

"So," his uncle asked quietly, "is this exercise giving us any joy?"

"If the purpose is to find a *modus vivendi* between Her Majesty and the confederate lords, and between the Scottish queen and them—"

"And it is."

"Then I'd say we have not found it yet." He knew by now the many strands of religious factions, family betrayals, and vendettas that were the tangled web of Scottish political life. It made the central issue of the inquiry—Mary's alleged complicity in her husband's murder—far from clear.

His uncle nodded. "I'm not surprised. Bring me up to date."

"Yes, sir. On the first day Mary's commissioners were called, she having refused to attend in person. Lord Herries presented her case."

"Point him out."

"There, by the window." He nodded toward the Scottish noble, a gray-haired soldierly man, one of the dwindling cadre of Scottish peers who had remained loyal to Mary. "He laid out what he called the crimes of the confederate lords. That they took up arms against their lawful sovereign and deposed her. That they incarcerated her at Loch Leven. That they violently forced her abdication—meaningless in law, of course, since it was coerced—and usurped her throne. That they took control of her infant son, James, and crowned him king to give their offenses a sheen of legitimacy while the Earl of Moray took de facto power as regent. That they besmirched her reputation with slanders. These crimes, Herries concluded, had compelled Mary to seek justice from her royal cousin, Elizabeth."

"And Moray? Has he spoken?"

"Yes, yesterday he presented the confederate lords' case. And a compelling one it was." They both glanced across the room at the Earl of Moray, Mary's half brother, who stood talking with his colleagues amid a cluster of lawyers. Moray was thirty-seven, tall, fit, and fair-haired as they said his father, King James, had been. He had a reputation as a fierce fighter in battle eight years ago against the French and, last year, against Mary. As leader of the lords who had usurped her, Moray now ruled Scotland, and he moved among his delegation with the aura of a sovereign, one with an iron resolve. Will had never seen a man so single-minded in his purpose, so bent on winning.

"His claim is that Mary, as queen, planned the murder of her husband, Lord Darnley, in collusion with the Earl of Bothwell, her lover, so that she would be free to marry Bothwell. Moray presented depositions from Bothwell's servant William Powrie confessing that he laid gunpowder in the cellar of the provost's lodging at Kirk o' Field where Mary had brought Darnley for the purpose of having him killed. After the explosion, which threw Darnley clear into the garden, Mary did nothing to investigate the murder, and it was left to the lords to indict Bothwell. Moray says that Mary then colluded with Bothwell to stage her own abduction by him, a ruse which allowed her to be with him while avoiding the lords' opprobrium of her. But when the lords threatened to take up arms against Bothwell for wresting control of their queen, she abandoned the charade of being Bothwell's unwilling captive, and married him."

"What's your opinion on all this?"

The question caught Will off guard. "Opinion, sir?" He was trained to examine only facts.

"Is she guilty?"

"That has yet to be determined. And this is not a trial."

"Don't talk like a lawyer. Come, come, let's hear your thoughts. It will help my report to Her Majesty."

Given this license to speak, Will took it. "I'd say she has proved herself an inept ruler, one with catastrophically poor political judgment. I've talked to a lot of people here and everyone agrees that from the beginning of her reign she showed little interest in governing. She attended few meetings of her council, and when she did she spent the time sewing. She married Lord Darnley, her personal choice, in haste and against the advice of her council." He felt a nervous stab, realizing how this mirrored his own hasty betrothal. His uncle, thankfully, did not seem to make the same connection, his eye on Moray across the room, so Will carried on steadily, "Once married, however, she and her husband fell into violent arguments and eventually were estranged. When crises befell her, she seemed prone to weeping and fainting, leaving control to some strong man. She enraged the lords by making Bothwell her chief adviser, cutting them out of all decision making—"

"But the murder, Will, the murder. Do you think she was behind it? Elizabeth will not let this case turn on the justification of rebellion against a sovereign. It has to be about Mary's innocence or guilt. What have you learned?"

"No facts, sir, I'm sorry." He saw his uncle's disappointment, and knew that did his own cause no good. It made him bold to delve further into speculation. "But her actions do invite deep suspicion. Though estranged from Darnley, she suddenly told him she wanted a reconciliation and invited him to join her in traveling to Edinburgh. They stopped outside the city at the Old Provost's house, at Kirk o' Field, and around midnight she slipped out to visit friends. While she was gone the house exploded. She displayed shock, but the very next day, when she should have been in the seclusion of mourning, she put aside her mourning clothes to go and make merry at a retainer's wedding. She gave Darnley a mere private burial, not the state ceremony his rank deserved, which fueled people's suspicions. Despite widespread belief that the Earl of Bothwell was the chief murderer, she stood by him, defying public opinion. She seems to have submitted herself totally to him, and he, seizing the opportunity, gathered a great force around him. When the lords finally indicted him for the murder, Mary allowed him to bring four thousand armed men to Edinburgh to harass the witnesses and jurors, and after a trial that lasted just a few hours he was let go, a free man. She says he then abducted her, yet when she was at his castle of Dunbar, not one of her supporters made a move to rescue her, an indication of how generally it was felt that she had connived at her own abduction. Finally, she committed political suicide by marrying him. In allowing Bothwell to rule her, and therefore the country, the lords declared she was not fit to reign, and deposed her. By her own conduct, she lost her realm."

Lord Thornleigh's expression was grave. "Yet Moray does not look happy." Will followed his uncle's gaze. Moray was haranguing one of the lawyers clustered around him, poking the man's chest with his finger to make a point. "Certainly, he has cause to be nervous," Lord Thornleigh went on. "If Mary returns home in triumph, Moray will lose everything in Scotland. Even, perhaps, his head."

Will conceded that Mary's restoration to her throne seemed a possible outcome.

His uncle turned to him, keenly interested. "Think you so?"

"I do. Because of my lord of Norfolk." They both looked at the duke, pale-eyed, slim, unsmiling, who was settling himself at the head of the table, arranging his gold velvet robes, preparing to open the session. Norfolk had not impressed Will. Though born into a family of great power, the Howards, he seemed vacillating and vain, an unstable combination. "He has a personal interest, sir, in not antagonizing Mary."

"The succession?"

Will nodded. If Elizabeth should die childless, Mary would inherit the throne as her legitimate heir, and she would not forgive Norfolk for publicly branding her a murderer and an adulteress.

Lord Thornleigh said coolly, firmly, "Never mind Norfolk. He will not decide this. Elizabeth will."

They ate supper that evening in the Duke of Norfolk's private suite. Only the English contingent were present: Norfolk, the Earl of Sussex, Sir Ralph Sadler, Lord Thornleigh, Will representing Cecil, and the commissioners' secretaries. The day's session had been uneventful, with erratic depositions from a page at Holyrood Palace, an Edinburgh porter, the Earl of Bothwell's cook, the Earl of Moray's master of horse, and Mary's childhood tutor. Much hearsay, few facts. Will had stayed at his uncle's side through the session, explaining details, hoping his diligence would win back his uncle's good regard.

The supper was very fine. As England's sole duke, Norfolk's rank was only slightly less exalted than a prince, and it seemed to Will that even in this temporary lodging the man held a court as if he were, indeed, royalty. He sat at the center of the table and throughout the meal people flitted around him—richly dressed kinsmen, armed retainers, fawning supporters—one delivering a note, one bending to place a word in his ear, one fetching him a fresh napkin, another a ewer of water to wash his hands between courses. Servants came and went with steaming dishes of poached bream with fennel, stewed rabbit with onions and sage, apricots in cinnamon syrup, and many decanters of claret and Burgundy. Beyond the mullioned window made fast against the chilly evening, a dog in the street barked and barked in hoarse monotony.

The commissioners' mood was relaxed and fraternal, and now with the meal finished they sat at ease, chairs pushed back, Sussex prodding his gum with a silver toothpick, Norfolk treating a terrier at his knee to a scrap from his plate, Sadler and his secretary chuckling about a peer whose wife was famously unfaithful. A fire rippled in the hearth, one log sparking and spitting, too green. Will stood behind the table discussing a deposition with Norfolk's secretary, but his eye was on Lord Thornleigh, who had got up and was moving toward the window. He gave Will a jerk of his chin to indicate he wanted a word with him alone. Will quickly excused himself and joined his uncle at the window.

"Keep on the good side of Norfolk and watch him," his uncle said very quietly. "He feels underrated at court. A mighty peer feeling slighted is a headache that Elizabeth does not need." They both looked at the duke, who was teasing his terrier with a rabbit bone dangled too high and laughing at the dog's ineffective jumps. The trio of retainers standing behind him laughed, too. "Remember, with him, smooth words go far."

Will felt of surge of pride at this confidence. "Good advice, sir. Thank you."

His uncle said wryly, "Keep your flattery for Norfolk."

Will had to smile. "Sir, about my vows with Justine, I promise you—"

"I know." His tone softened. "Will, I'm not against this marriage. I told Justine I'm for it. As for Joan, I'll talk to her. Maybe I can bring her round."

Will's hope shot up. "Thank you, sir. She'll listen to you."

His uncle's look turned sober. "Now, I told you I had a job for you."

Before Will could respond the door suddenly swung open. Everyone in the room looked in surprise as the Earl of Moray strode in.

"Sir?" said Norfolk, looking flustered.

Will was astonished. What did Moray mean by barging in like this?

"Your Grace." Moray bowed to Norfolk. Behind him two of his fellow Scots trooped in, the Earl of Morton and Sir William Maitland. They both made respectful bows to Norfolk, Sussex, and Lord Thornleigh. They stayed behind Moray, the clear leader. "Pardon this interruption, Your Grace," he said. "I would not so roughly intrude on your well-earned leisure if the matter were not of crucial importance. My poor apology cannot make amends, but I believe that what I bring you will."

"Oh? What have you brought?"

Moray beckoned to Maitland, who came forward with a box about a foot long. He moved to set it down on the table before the four lords, but the surface was crowded with gravy-puddled serving platters, salvers with fish bones, a dish of almonds, and two tall candles. Morton came forward and pushed aside a platter and a candle. Maitland set down the box. Under the candle flame its features glinted clearly. It was a small coffer of silver and gilt, and its dome and sides were embossed with the letter *F* set under a royal crown.

"A pretty casket, sir." Norfolk sounded annoyed. "What does it do? Play a tune?"

"If it did, Your Grace, the tune would be French. This casket once belonged to King Francis. You see his crest, there, and there." He pointed to the embossed crowns. "His wife brought it back to Scotland with her." Now Will was interested. The late King Francis had been Mary's first husband.

Sussex said gruffly, "Come, my lord, what cares His Grace for such trifles?"

"Hold on," said Sadler. "Of what *consequence* is this object?"

"None, sir," replied Moray. "It is a mere receptacle. For evidence."

"Evidence?" Sadler leaned forward on his elbows, peering at the casket. "Of what?"

"Sin."

Norfolk blinked at the word.

Lord Thornleigh said instantly, "Mary's?"

"Yes, my lord."

"Then let's see."

Moray placed his hand on the lid. "There was no key, so we had to force the lock." He lifted the lid. Everyone leaned closer to see inside. Will saw papers. Folded, fine grained, a pale color like flesh.

"These, my lords, are letters. Eight of them. All written in her hand. All written to Bothwell. They tell of gross adultery and pre-meditated murder. Her sins, my lords. Her foul sins." Moray lifted the casket and dumped out the papers. They slewed across the gravy-splotched cloth. The three astonished commissioners gaped at them, then at one another, then at Moray.

Lord Thornleigh was the first to move. He picked up a letter and unfolded it.

"Yes, my lord, do read," Moray encouraged him. "All of you, read her own words and judge for yourselves."

With a unanimous motion Norfolk, Sussex, and Sadler each grabbed a letter. There was a hush as they read. The green log hissed in the hearth. Will was on edge with curiosity.

Sussex said, excited, his eyes on the page, "She says here, 'I bring the man Monday to Craigmillar.' " He looked up. "That's Kirk o' Field."

"And here," Sadler said, "she writes 'Cursed be this pocky fellow that troubles me. I thought I should have been killed with his breath.' " He looked disturbed by this contempt of a wife for her husband.

Moray said, "As you heard in yesterday's depositions, my lords, she had broken off carnal relations with him many months before. Then, suddenly, she offered to resume conjugal relations. That was why he joined her on the way to Edinburgh. She ordered that they stop at Kirk o' Field, and there Darnley was murdered on the very night he was to have her again in his bed."

Lord Thornleigh muttered, scanning the page he held, "Here she tells Bothwell she is making a bracelet for him and warns him not to let anyone see it." He read aloud from the letter, " 'God knit us together forever for the most faithful couple that ever He did knit together. This is my faith. I will die in it.' " His face showed distaste for the florid sentiment.

Sussex and Sadler clearly felt no such compunction. They went on quoting aloud with obvious relish. Sussex read, " 'I remit myself wholly to your will. Send me word what I shall do. Whatever happens to me, I will obey you.' "

He and Sadler continued reading passages aloud, alternating, one after the other.

Sadler: " 'I am ill at ease and glad to write to you when other folks are asleep, seeing that I cannot sleep according to my desire, which is between your arms.' "

Sussex: " 'I am so far made yours that that which pleases you is acceptable to me, and my thoughts are so willingly subdued unto yours.' "

Sadler: " 'The most faithful lover that ever you had or shall have.' "

Sussex: " 'I end, after kissing your hands. Love me always, as I shall love you.' "

Sadler: " 'Your humble and faithful lover, who hopes shortly to be another thing unto you for the reward of my pains. Burn this letter, for it is too dangerous.' "

They both looked up, shocked.

Moray said darkly, victoriously, "Three months later she married him."

They all stared at him. "Great God in Heaven, so she did," Norfolk whispered.

Will felt such tension in the room it prickled the skin at the back of his neck. What an amazing development this evidence was! *It's only circumstantial,* he reminded himself, trying to keep the proper perspective. Nevertheless, he could see the enormous impact it had on the commissioners.

"But, wait," Norfolk said. He seemed to be in a battle with himself, and Will knew why. Norfolk was wary of taking a stand against Mary that might come back to haunt him. "These letters are written in English. It is a tongue the lady speaks little of."

"We had them translated, Your Grace. The originals are in French."

"Where are they?"

"Safe in my care. You shall have them whenever you wish."

Lord Thornleigh said, "Her Majesty must see them."

Moray bowed. "Of course, my lord."

Sadler narrowed his eyes at Moray. "Translated, you say? How long have you had them?"

"Since the traitor Bothwell fled to Denmark. Our forces captured some of his men, among them his tailor. Under questioning the tailor led us to this casket under a bed. It held these letters."

"That was over a year ago," Norfolk said. "Why did you not produce this evidence until now?"

"There seemed no need, Your Grace, since Mary had abdicated. We were loath to tarnish the reputation of Scotland by making public the foul doings of its queen."

"Foul, indeed," Sussex said. "The cunning strumpet."

"Come, come, sir," Norfolk protested. "We speak of a queen, anointed by God—"

"A queen who conceived after her husband was dead and before she remarried," Moray cut in, dropping all deference. His eyes were fierce with resolve. "The twins she miscarried were Bothwell's bastards."

∽ 14 ∽

Loyalty Tested

The ride from Bolton Castle to the village of Bedale was just sixteen miles, but the frigid bite of the wind gusting across the moors made Justine glad her mission took her no farther. It was only early November but already so cold. Her instructions were to rendezvous with Elizabeth's agent and make her report, and she was waiting for him to arrive, feeling colder by the minute as she paced the wagon track that was a spine along the low hill above the village. Whoever the agent was, he could not fail to see her; she was alone on the barren hill.

The wind flapped her cloak and lashed strands of hair that had escaped her hood, and she hugged herself for warmth, treading wheel ruts made iron-hard by frost. Where was the man? She could not wait long. The reason she had given for leaving the castle had been legitimate—a wealthy local gentleman, the owner of many sheep, had sent Mary three beautifully embroidered lambswool shawls and Justine had taken him Mary's note of thanks—but she had gone there right after breakfast and was quickly done. This rendezvous at Bedale was keeping her away. She would have to hasten through her report to the agent to get back in time to attend Mary in her suite for dinner at midday.

The sun was a misty smudge behind a moving veil of clouds. Justine's breath as she puffed out her impatience made more mist, snatched by the wind. Her mare, tethered to a stone cairn, stomped like a signal that she, too, wanted to be gone. Justine looked down at the village that hugged the foot of the hill as though for protection. St. Gregory's Church, with its squat Norman tower, stood like a shepherd to its flock of cottages. Smoke rising from the cottage chimneys was instantly shredded by the wind. A few people straggled along the muddy main street. A pig trotted forlornly past the churchyard wall, looking lost.

The church doors opened and a cluster of people came out. Laborers, by the look of their bulky workaday clothes in colors of straw and clay. An extended family, apparently, ranging from an old man hobbling with a cane, a half dozen middle-aged folk, and three small children. A young couple was at the family's core, a moon-faced man and a sturdy, short woman cradling a baby bundled against the cold. Must be a christening, Justine thought. The children romped ahead, shouting with such exuberance their voices reached her like tiny bells. She had to smile. Cold didn't bother little ones absorbed with the wonder of the world. It gave her a pang of homesickness. She had been with Mary for almost three months, doing her duty for Elizabeth, away from everyone she loved. She missed the Thornleighs' lively household, always achatter with family, friends, visitors. Most of all she missed Will.

Faces I love, she thought. *Alice*. Looking at St. Gregory's tower she thought of the church belfry at Kirknewton where Alice had died so horribly. She pictured its interior that day, the shadowed space eerily festooned with bright ribbons and scarves. Who was the man who had bought all those scarves? A gentleman, Jeremy had claimed. Was he the killer? Or could it be the man the farrier had seen running through the churchyard—a London wine merchant's agent, according to the farrier who had recognized him, saying the agent came north once or twice a year to sell to the local gentry. Was *he* the killer? Justine realized bleakly that both suspects were beyond her reach. The mysterious gentleman had disappeared, and the traveling ribbon seller who might have been able to identify him had drifted like smoke into the hills and dales of the moors. As for the wine seller, he had likely gone back to London. Even if she could get a description from one of his local gentry clients, she could not get to London to try to trace him, not while she was tied to Mary. It galled her. Her inept investigation had stopped cold. She had vowed to see justice done for Alice, but justice seemed as dead as the shriveled yellow leaves on St. Gregory's churchyard elms.

A hollow sound rose behind her, the thud of cantering hooves. She turned. A cloaked horseman pulled his mount to a halt and swung down from the saddle. Justine's breath caught in surprise. It was Will!

He didn't stop to tether his horse, just strode to her still holding the reins in his gauntleted hands. "You are patience itself, and I am late," he said with a grin.

"Will! What are you doing here?"

"Making everything right with the world, my love." He wrapped an arm around her waist and pulled her to him and kissed her.

She returned the kiss with dazed excitement. How had he found her? It didn't matter—he was here! Her heart skipping, she pressed against his body, so welcoming, so warm! His horse nosed his shoulder with a sudden push that made Will stumble and break off the kiss with a laugh. He jammed the reins into his belt and made up for the lost kiss by taking Justine's face in his hands and brushing quick kisses over her cheeks, her forehead, her mouth. Dazzled, she gave herself to the heat that pulsed from her lips down to her belly. Then rational thought surged back. *Elizabeth's agent could arrive at any moment!* She pulled away, anxiously looking around. "Oh, Will, it's wonderful to see you, but I'm waiting for someone, and he . . . he mustn't see you."

"Have I a rival?" His eyes had a mischievous sparkle that confused her.

"No, of course not. But I—"

"Good," he said with a laugh. "*Two* agents would muddy the waters."

"Two?" She gasped. "*You?*"

"None other." Enjoying her shock, he took the moment to lead his horse to the cairn and tether it beside her mare. He pulled off his gauntlets and tucked them in his belt, his eyes twinkling as he watched Justine.

"Good heavens!" she said following him. "My instructions came from Lord Thornleigh's clerk. I had no idea!"

"And to his lordship I am forever indebted, for this was his idea." His expression became serious. "Justine, he told me about your *real* mission with Mary, how you are pledged to help Her Majesty. I'm so proud of you. And now, thanks to him, I am part of that mission. That's right, we are working together, you and I. You report to me, then I to him. He wants it, and I . . . God knows I could not want you more." He took her in his arms again, this time with a grave expression that made his eyes shine as they had at their betrothal. His kiss was earnest, sober, making it all the more passionate. Justine held him tightly, losing herself in the kiss. The love in their embrace was so powerful it seemed to tame the very elements, for she felt the wind encircling them like protective arms.

"Tell me everything," she said, hungry to know. "I thought you were at York, at the inquiry. When did you see your uncle?"

"He's there, arrived yesterday as Elizabeth's envoy. At first he railed at me for our betrothal, but only because we did it in secret. He's on our side, Justine. That's why he recruited me to meet you."

Her heart swelled with love for her guardian. Clever Lord Thornleigh! Her last meeting with him rushed back to her mind and she remembered his words: *"Tell Will the truth. You cannot build a marriage on a lie."* She caressed Will's cheek, his skin chilly but the warmth of his kiss still tingling her lips. A new realization tingled her, too. If ever there was a perfect time to tell him about her blood family, this was it. He loved her, and he was seeing in her words and deeds what a loyal servant of Elizabeth she was. Had that been his uncle's goal in throwing them together on this hill? She felt sure it was, and it was exhilarating. Her *real* family was Lord Thornleigh's family, a kinship knit by cords of love, and Will was part of it. Lord Thornleigh knew that, knew her bond with his house was unshakable. Will would feel it, too. *Tell him*, she thought. *Tell him now.*

"All right," said Will, rubbing his hands together with sudden gusto, "let's get the business out of the way. Then, my love, we can walk at our leisure and talk of *us*. Or not talk at all, just let me kiss you until it's time for you to go back."

Business. Mary. She had almost forgotten. Her longing to share the secret of her life was so overpowering, she felt her heart would burst with the need to have the truth out in the open, to dissolve the fence between them, invisible to him, but a barricade she ached to tear down. "Will, there's something I have to tell you."

"Yes, your report. Come, let's have it. I'll file your words up here," he said, tapping a finger at his temple, "and tell Uncle Richard the moment I'm back at York."

There was a new tone in his voice, the lawyer, efficient and objective, able to stand back from personal matters and briskly deal with the business at hand. Justine hesitated and felt the moment to speak her heart slipping away.

"You're shivering," he said, the tenderness in his voice rushing back. "Come, out of the wind." He slipped his arm around her shoulder and guided her into the narrow space between the two horses who stood side by side munching the scrubby grass, oblivious to their owners. The bulk of Will's horse blocked the wind, and the bellies of both beasts, heaving breaths like shaggy bellows, gave off a comforting, humid heat. Face-to-face with Will, Justine had the sensation of being children happily huddled in a makeshift fort. The conspiratorial friendliness gave her courage. *I'll get the moment back*, she told herself. *Business first, then tell him.*

"There's not a great deal to report," she began, smiling as Will extended an arm on either side of her head to grip the saddle ends so that his cloak enveloped her, warming her even more. "Mary has received several of the local gentry, but it's all been open and aboveboard. Lord Scrope is always in attendance."

"Names?"

She rattled off the brief list. It felt vaguely distasteful, like spreading unkind gossip about a friend. Mary *had* befriended her, had taken her into her confidence, and Justine pitied the lady for the hardships she had endured. But, as Will said, this was business. *I'm doing my duty for Her Majesty,* she told herself. And, after all, she had nothing to say about Mary that was damaging.

"All are Catholic families," Will said, mulling the names, apparently not surprised.

"Yes. They bring her gifts. She entertains them with wine and music, then they go. They seem bewitched by her—I've seen that happen over and over—but they are meek withal. None has made a comment remotely seditious."

"At least not in your presence."

"But I am almost always with her. She has been gracious in singling me out for favor."

"Who would not?" he murmured with feeling.

That gave her a happy rush. He admired what she was doing. He loved her. It prodded her to go on. "A Master Ligon has visited her four times, another admirer bringing gifts. A brace of partridges once, and another time a tapestry. He is a servant of the Duke of Norfolk. I'm not sure if that's of any significance."

Will frowned. "It may be. At the inquiry Norfolk seems unwilling to tarnish Mary's reputation."

"Which reminds me, she has become quite friendly with Lord Scrope's wife. That may be more noteworthy than I'd thought, since Lady Scrope is Norfolk's sister."

"My uncle will certainly take note. Anything else?"

"Only idle talk. Don't you lawyers call it hearsay?"

"Depends on the talk. Anything treasonable?"

"Hardly. Just prattle in the village by the castle. Loose talk about local gentlemen who love the old church and are planning to attack and rescue Mary, but the gentlemen spoken of are always nameless. I have heard not one fact. It's all tavern talk."

Will pondered this. "Does Scrope let her go out?"

"A few times, riding and hawking, which she loves, but his armed retainers are always with her. Thirty or forty of them. It would take a considerable force to overcome them." She added wryly, "A force of nameless gentlemen."

Will smiled at her jest, relaxing. "Scrope knows his duty. Anything else?" He asked the question with a new warmth, his voice low and intimate, as if to signal that their business was almost finished. He moved a step closer so their bodies touched. His mind was clearly no longer on Mary.

Justine's mind was equally wayward. "No . . . she lives quietly," she said, but all she could think of was the nearness of him. He smelled of leather and freshly laundered linen, and of horse. He bent his head and nuzzled her neck. It sent a thrilling shiver down her spine. She managed to add, "I've seen no threat from her to Her Majesty." Will's lips on her throat made her shudder with pleasure. She ran her fingers into his wind-matted hair and took a handful of it and pulled his head up, and her mouth found his. Their kiss was long and sweet and made her ache for more of him. Love dazzled her. She was so sure of *his* love. *Do it now*, she thought in exultation. *Tear down the barricade.* "Will," she said, catching her breath as he kissed her throat. "I said I have something to tell you. It's important."

He straightened up, his eyes alight. "And I have something to tell you. I promised you in London that the moment the inquiry was over we would get married. Well, it's going to be over very soon. Something's happened."

She saw that the something must be momentous. It gave her a quiver of excitement. "What? Is Her Majesty going to restore Mary to her Scottish throne?"

"The opposite. We have heard evidence that shatters Mary's case."

Justine felt an unpleasant jolt. This was the last thing she had expected. "What evidence?"

He hesitated, as though aware that he had gone as far as he should.

"Will, tell me. You said it yourself, we're working together."

He smiled. "So we are, my love. Well, it's this. The commissioners have been presented with letters, eight of them, all written by Mary to Bothwell when she was queen and married to Lord Darnley. They contain damning statements of her contempt for Darnley, her adulterous passion for Bothwell, and a homicidal pact between the two of them."

Justine took a shocked step back, up against her mare. The cold metal stirrup dug into the small of her back. "No." The word jumped out of her mouth before she could think. "I don't believe it."

"It's astounding to get this break, I know, but I assure you it's true."

"You've read these letters?"

"Ad nauseam. I was up most the night making copies of them for Sir William and my uncle." He rattled off key phrases, quoting Mary. "I cannot sleep according to my desire, which is between your arms. . . . Whatever happens to me I will obey you. . . . I am so far made yours that my thoughts are willingly subdued unto yours. . . . I end, after kissing your hands, your humble and faithful lover, who hopes shortly to be another thing unto you for the reward of my pains. . . . Burn this letter, for it is too dangerous."

She stared at him, struggling to find words, a sense of dread stealing over her. These lurid lines apparently written by Mary contradicted everything Mary had told her. But it was Mary she believed. Mary she pitied. Mary, who had been wronged by powerful men using her to further their ends. "You say the commissioners were presented with the letters. Who presented them?"

"The Earl of Moray himself."

"How did her spokesmen respond? Lord Herries and Lord Livingston and the Bishop of Ross. What did they say on her behalf?"

"They weren't there. Moray brought the letters to the commissioners in private."

"What? Mary's representatives had no chance to defend her?" Outrage welled up in Justine. "How did this happen? Were you there?"

He said that he was, and his uncle, too, and told her that they were supping with the Duke of Norfolk when Moray and the other Scottish lords came in, Maitland bearing a silver casket. He described how dirty dishes were moved aside for Maitland to deposit the letters on the table and how the commissioners had snatched them and read them aloud. Justine was appalled, imagining it, the letters dumped out helter-skelter like a catch of mackerel, and Norfolk and Sussex and Sadler pawing over them, passing them around, commenting and opining like tittle-tattle fishwives. It was grotesque. And Lord Thornleigh! How could he have taken part in such a travesty? "Did Lord Thornleigh do nothing?" she asked.

"Of course he did. The moment I finished copying the letters, he sent them under guard to Her Majesty."

They were talking at maddening cross purposes. "Will, I'm saying this is not *right*. I don't know the law as you do, but I know there are rules of procedure. Rules of evidence. No court in England would allow such a trampling of proper process."

"This is not a trial, Justine. The purpose of the inquiry is to supply Her Majesty with information. She alone will decide on the evidence."

"It has all the marks of a trial," she snapped, "except justice." He looked taken aback at her outburst. She reined in her indignation. "The commissioners may have barred Mary's spokesmen, but Mary herself will have plenty to say."

"No, she won't. The matter is confidential. She will not see the letters."

Justine gaped at him. "Not be shown this evidence used against her? You mean the commissioners will carry on without even *hearing* from her?"

"For that she has no one to blame but herself. She refused to attend."

Justine winced, knowing this was true. Mary had locked the door on her own confinement. But that was no reason to unjustly condemn her.

Will was looking at her with worried eyes. "Why this tender feeling for Mary? Justine, has she bewitched you, too?"

The idea was preposterous. And insulting. "Duty to Her Majesty does not mean willfully ignoring the truth." Something in Will's account was nagging at her. "How did the Earl of Moray come by these letters?"

He told her how Moray's men, victorious over Bothwell, who fled to Denmark, had captured of one of Bothwell's servants, who led them to a casket in his master's house. "They found it under a bed."

"How convenient."

Will's eyes went wide. "Do you doubt that the letters are genuine?"

She remembered Mary's harrowing tale of rape at the rough hands of Lord Bothwell. She lifted her chin, ready to stand by her defiance. "I do."

He shook his head. "No. Moray would never have brought the

letters to light if he were not positive about them. The risk to himself would be too great in the event that Mary is restored to her throne. He knows she would have his head. In any case, the point is moot. Her Majesty knows her cousin's handwriting. Elizabeth will decide this." He took Justine gently by the shoulders. "You have a kind heart, Justine, but do not let that blind you." He added soberly, "Or sway you from your task. We are loyal to Elizabeth, you and I. And to my uncle. Remember, we owe him much."

"I owe him everything," she said with feeling. "But, Will, I have come to know Mary. She is a victim of violent men. Scheming men. And with these letters they are out to ruin her."

His face clouded over. "She has done plenty of scheming herself. She encourages disaffected Catholics who hate Elizabeth for suppressing their religion. You *know* that's why they visit her and pay court to her. The ones you saw may seem tame, but there are fiercer lords who would love to see Mary on Elizabeth's throne. And never doubt that if she sat there she would bring back all the horrors of Catholic tyranny. Inquisitions. Burnings. Terror."

His bitter tone made Justine shudder. She had been raised a Catholic. "Those horrors are long past," she said. "Her Majesty began her reign by proclaiming tolerance in religion. She does not despise Catholics."

"And I honor her, a wise and dedicated ruler. But I cannot extend my own tolerance to vicious Catholics. They killed my father."

She froze at the words. It was a new Will she was seeing. Harsh. Unforgiving.

"Grenvilles," he said. "They were the bloodiest papists in our county." His face was hard with hate. "They murdered him."

She pretended amazed ignorance, wielding it as a shield. "Grenvilles?" She forced out the name like a stone from her throat. "You mean Frances's family?"

"The same. God only knows what witchcraft she used to snare my cousin Adam into marriage. To this day I cannot look at her without choking."

"But surely she was not responsible for—"

"She is a *Grenville*. Justine, I saw them slaughter my father. I was twelve. We were at my uncle's Essex manor, Speedwell House. John Grenville, may he burn in hell, came thundering in with his henchmen. My father rushed out of the house. Their arrows felled him. I saw through the window. Three arrows in his chest and neck. I watched him drown in his own blood."

She was shivering. The wind had thrust into their hiding place and whipped icy fingers around her throat. The truth she had been ready to confess for love of Will was strangled mute in the face of his hate.

At the Bolton Castle stables Justine left her horse with the groom and hurried across the courtyard. The gusting wind rattled a loose door and whistled over the steel helmets of soldiers coming out of the mess. It snapped Lord Scrope's flag atop the southwest tower, sounding like cracks of a whip, and it plastered Justine's skirt against her thighs as she made for the southern range. She was late for the noonday meal in Mary's suite. She couldn't eat a bite, but she wanted out of this wind. Wanted refuge from her wretchedness. She had left Will like a nervous thief, with no kiss of good-bye, no smile, only a few abrupt few words about how she had to get back.

Margaret Currier caught up to her. "Dear me, I nodded off in the solar," she said. Wearing no cloak, she was hugging herself as she fell in beside Justine. "We'd better run. Cook will be in a fume if we miss her roast partridge. Where were you?"

"Master Tudholm's. Delivering my lady's note."

"Ah, that man can talk your head off. No wonder you're late. Come!" She hooked her arm around Justine's to urge her on, and together they hurried to the arched door that led into the southern range. Inside, blessedly out of the wind, they hastened along the corridor, tidying their hair, making for the staircase that led up to Mary's rooms. A door opened ahead, and a young man came out, tugging his cap into place. Justine knew him, a gentlemen usher from Aberdeen, one of the handful of Scottish servants Mary had been allowed to admit to her small court here. He gave her and Margaret a casual nod and carried on past them. Justine halted. He had left the door open and she looked in at the candlelit room. The chapel. A wisp of incense reached her. It tugged a thread of memory, a thread of promised comfort.

"Come *on*," Margaret urged.

"You go ahead, Margaret. I see Master Forbes in there, and I need a word with him about repairing my lady's desk."

Margaret frowned with disapproval. The chapel, with its ornate Catholic trappings, was an indulgence that Elizabeth accorded to Mary out of respect to her foreignness and her rank. English men and women were officially Protestant, and none more so than Margaret. "I'll tell my lady you're on your way, shall I?"

"Thank you. I won't be a moment."

Margaret hurried on up the stairs. Justine stepped into the chapel. Forbes was not there—she had said so only to give credence to her detour—but a few of Mary's small entourage were. A master clerk from Fife kneeled at the rood screen before the altar. The pretty Paris-born lady's maid who dressed Mary's hair stood at an alcove lighting a votive candle. A jowly Edinburgh chaplain sat with the white-haired priest at the end of the last row of padded benches, chatting in hushed tones, two old friends. Justine hung back, wary of the impulse that had drawn her here, not sure why she had come, but savoring a deeper breath of the fragrant incense. Savoring the comforting opulence. Protestant churches were stark, devoid of so-called idolatry: no paintings, no carvings, no statues, no incense. The mass, with all its grand mystery, was banned; Protestants merely took communion, and their altar was a plain wooden table.

This sumptuous space was an enchantment for all the senses, and it left Justine at once awed and soothed. Light filtering through the stained glass window crimsoned the floor's ivory-colored tiles. Silken banners and tapestries glimmered. With the doors closed against the household noises, the only sound was the whisper of the worshippers' feet. A rood screen of carved cherrywood segregated the nave from the altar, the screen crowned with a shining cross of gold. On the marble altar, candlelight glinted off child-high silver candlesticks. The chapel was dedicated to St. Anne, mother of the Virgin Mary, and a life-sized statue of the matriarch holding the Christ child, painted in bright hues of azure and gold, stood watch over all who came to her for succor.

Justine raised her eyes above St. Anne. A wide arch formed a gallery on the second story. The light up there was dim, but she could make out the wooden railing that fronted it, the wood carved with crosses and with crowns of thorns. Justine remembered the same kind of gallery in the chapel at Yeavering Hall, an elevated place where her family could observe the mass privately. Here, above St. Anne, generations of the Scrope family would have done the same. The arch's gold brocade curtain was closed. The Scropes were Protestant now.

The murmuring of the two churchmen drew her gaze back down to them. Sitting in genial conversation with his friend, the priest wore gorgeously embroidered vestments. *He's just concluded a mass,* Justine realized. A memory rushed over her, indistinct but as powerful as an ocean wave—phrases of the ceremony, fragments of the ritual. She saw in her mind's eye the solemn faces of adults around her, their eyes closed in prayer. Saw the sheen of candle-light on her father's smooth blond hair, his eyes opening before the prayer ended and glinting at her like a cat's eyes. She smelled the spicy incense. Heard the tinkle of the sacring bell. Felt a warm hand, her mother's, gently enfold her small one. She strained to re-call her mother's face, heart-shaped, and to feel again the skin of her cheek, petal soft against Justine's, but the image was already lost, like a blossom borne out by the tide.

She tried to call back the dissolving memory, but instead Will's bitter words rushed back, swamping her: *"The Grenvilles . . . the bloodiest papists."* His raw hatred for her family chilled her. Sick at heart, she sank down on the rearmost bench, longing for sanctuary from the tumult of her thoughts. The churchmen at the opposite end ignored her, engrossed in their talk. Justine fidgeted with the folds of her skirt, her hands feeling bereft having no rosary to slip through her fingers with soothing soft clicks. She felt so alone, cut off from Will. Their meeting should have bound them more lovingly together, but instead they had parted in strained silence. Her sympathy for Mary had baffled him, and her abrupt good-bye had startled him. But *she* had the greater pain to bear, and the unjustness of it made her seethe. *I had no part in our families' quarrel!* She had been prepared to tell him the truth about herself, to bravely trust in his love, but now? After what he had said? Tell him that she had been born into the family who had murdered his father? No, she could never tell him now.

She lowered her head and closed her eyes, willing her misery to vanish, but her problems swarmed in her head. What was she to do about Mary now that letters had been brought forward to blacken her name? Letters brought forward in secret. Was she to say nothing and go on spying on Mary? But how could she possibly report to Will again? It wasn't just his hatred of her family that dismayed her—it was also his callous disregard for this injustice to Mary. She suddenly realized that she had hoped Elizabeth would restore Mary to some position of rank in Scotland—not as monarch, because Moray's government would not accept that, but perhaps as the respected mother of the infant King James, a retired but honored dowager queen. Now she saw that men on both sides of the border intended to ruin Mary and leave her with nothing. Will was *abetting* her ruin. So was Lord Thornleigh. Justine felt hot anger flare in her, and it struck her again how much she and Mary had in common. Both had been uprooted. Both had been born in the Catholic faith and found themselves in a Protestant society. Both had been made powerless by the crimes of men around them, Mary by her ambitious brother and his fellow ruthless lords, Justine by her traitor father and his murderous kin. A voice inside her wailed, *It is not fair.*

An air current touched her neck. She shivered and caught a lemony scent and opened her eyes. Mary's French maid was slipping past her, on her way out. Justine straightened, trying to order the wildness in her heart. A wink of light jerked her gaze to the gallery above St. Anne. The dimness made the light all the more brilliant as it glinted again. It was the flash of a belt buckle. A man stood looking down, looking straight at Justine. His arm was raised, holding back the gold curtain, and his lean body dressed all in black was utterly still as if frozen at the sight of her. Justine's heart stopped. That long, pale face. Those eyes aglint like a cat's. She jumped to her feet. "Father!"

Gasps rose at her outburst. The priest and chaplain stared at her and the clerk kneeling at the rood screen gaped at her over his shoulder. She looked back up at the gallery. The man was gone. The curtain swayed. She blinked, disoriented by a burst of crimson sun through the stained glass. Had she imagined the man? The one word torn from her throat left it sore, as if from long shouting. The faces around her eyed her with alarm. She could not afford suspicion. They all knew that she, Lord Thornleigh's ward, was no Catholic. She said to the priest with forced calm, "Father," hoping he would think she had meant him before, and continued in a loud tone as though having scant respect for her surroundings, "My lady sends her thanks for your sermon last Sunday. That is all. Good day."

She hardly knew how she made it out of the chapel with her head high, her heart was pounding so painfully. The moment she was through the doors she looked around quickly in all directions. No one. Nothing stirred along the stone corridor. She went up the staircase, trying not to hurry and draw attention to herself. At the top, the corridor led to the left where Mary's suite was, and to the right where the gallery overlooked the chapel. From Mary's rooms she could hear snatches of soft women's voices and the faint clatter of cutlery. She turned right and reached the door to the gallery. It was closed. She grabbed the handle. It would not budge, rusted or stuck. A motion beyond her shoulder made her turn with a gasp. Down a corridor a black-clothed figure was hurrying up the narrow staircase to the fourth floor. She dashed after him. He glanced over his shoulder, that pale face, and in a moment disappeared around the bend in the stairs.

Justine followed, her pace so rapid up the steps she bunched her skirts in both hands to keep from tripping. She heard a creak ahead, then a thud, like a door closing. She carried on up another flight, her hands trembling. She reached a landing, a cramped space so dark she could scarcely see. A smell of dust and mice. A scarred wooden door. She put her hand on the metal latch. Without her pushing it, the door creaked open the width of a hand. Then, caught by the wind, it suddenly flew wide open and banged against the outer wall. Sunlight flooded Justine's vision. She was on the rooftop battlements.

There was no one. Nothing but the crenellated battlements rising all around her like giant teeth and beyond them the moors stretching to the horizon. In the blue sky ragged gray clouds sailed past the sun so fast they dappled the moorland with ever-shifting shadows, giving Justine the sensation that the tower she stood on was moving. The wind snatched her skirt, tugged at her hair. Her heart was banging so hard she thought it might crack her ribs. Was she chasing a ghost?

The door clicked behind her. She twisted around.

He stood with his back against the closed door. There were tears in his eyes. He stretched out his arms to her. "My child . . . my child."

᪥ 15 ᪥

On the Battlements

The joy at seeing his daughter face-to-face choked Christopher Grenville. He had not expected this clutch of emotion, this grip on his heart. What a beauty she was! He had left a gangly child of ten and she had grown into a woman, lovely of form and face. But how startled she looked, eyes wide like a hunted doe backed up to a cliff edge. The wind gusting over the battlements flapped her skirt wildly as though alive with her distress. How could he calm her? Words crammed up in his brain. He took clumsy strides toward her and enfolded her in his arms. "My child . . . my child," he moaned. "My darling girl." The threat of tears constricted his throat. His voice came out rough and raw. "I could die happy . . . now that I have seen you."

She stood rigid in his embrace. He heard her catch shallow breaths of near panic. He wanted to hold her until she calmed, but he sensed that it would frighten her even more. With a pang of regret he let her go. She staggered back a step at the sudden freedom, as though her legs had suddenly gone weak. He reached for her arm to steady her. She stared at him, dazed.

"Forgive me," he stammered. "I didn't mean to so alarm you. I simply . . . had to see you."

"What are you—" She fumbled the words. She swallowed. Tried again. "How can you be . . . *here?*"

"I have been watching you." He reached out to touch her cheek. She flinched. It cut him deeply. "Are you not even a little pleased to see your father?"

"Pleased . . . ?" Her mouth suddenly trembled. Her chest heaved with the indignation of an aggrieved child. "You *left* me!"

"Justine—"

"All alone! I had no one."

"You had kin in Essex. I thought they—"

"They did not come for me. They wanted no child of a *traitor*."

The word stung. From his own daughter! It was a bitter thing to bear. She was breathing hard now, nostrils flaring, a redness in her eyes, her hair disheveled by the wind, and he realized with a shock, *She hates me.* Fury swept him. Not at her—she was an innocent. His fury was for the man who had turned her against him. Richard Thornleigh. He wanted to roar out his grievances to his daughter. But something cautioned him not to. He had to tread carefully. She was not ready to hear about Thornleigh. Not yet. He said, "If I had not fled they would have hanged me." He managed a bittersweet smile. "Would that have made you happy?"

Her face crumpled in confusion. "No . . . but—"

"Ah, Justine, I am more sorry than I can say if you suffered for my sake. Believe me, I have suffered, too. I have been well punished. I lost everything. Lands. Home. *You.* I have struggled as an outcast all these years. Hanging me would have been more kind."

"Outcast . . . where? Where have you *been?*"

"France. Exiled from all that I knew and loved. Can you imagine what it is to wander foreign streets, penniless, friendless? Believing I would never see you again?"

"Is that why you've come back?" Bewilderment swam in her eyes, yet he thought he saw there a flicker of hope. "To see me?"

Here was the challenge! He took a breath to steady himself, to be absolutely sure. Then he answered quietly, firmly, "No."

She blinked in surprise at the stark confession. Christopher knew he was taking a terrible chance. He had already hazarded so much by making contact with her. But he needed her help. She alone could pass along what he wanted Richard Thornleigh to believe about Mary—what he wanted Elizabeth to believe. But his heart was thudding at the risk. His daughter, so hostile thanks to Thornleigh, could instead have him arrested and sent to prison in chains. This time he would not escape the noose.

He pressed on. The truth was his best hope. "I have come to see the Queen of Scots."

A breath of astonishment escaped her. "Ha. You lie."

"It is true. In France, when she was queen there, she was kind to me."

He saw in an instant that he had misjudged. She didn't believe a word. "You're mad," she said, backing away as though from a dangerous animal. She shot a look behind him at the door. It was the only way down from the battlements. She bolted toward it.

Christopher caught her arm, halting her. In turning, he now faced the wind and it swept back his hair, the wig he wore to cover his disfigurement. She froze, and he knew what she was staring at: his scarred, burned, shriveled ear and the patch of raw scalp behind it. He pawed the hair back in place. Still holding her arm, he dug inside his shirt beneath his doublet and lifted out a chain. Dangling from the chain was the crucifix he had given her eight years ago as he fled—the smooth gold Christ on a rough gold cross, rubies His wounds. Christopher held it up for her to see. It was his proof.

Her eyes went wide with shock. "I gave that to Mary." She blurted in suspicion, "You stole it from her."

"She gave it to me. Just as you gave it to her, as a surety of the faith that binds us, we three." Justine's body was rigid, but he held her arm tightly. The wind flailed her skirt, wrapping it around Christopher's leg.

"Let me go."

"Justine, when Mary told me you were serving her I had to see you. Hear me out, that's all I ask. Then send me to the gallows if you must." He managed a tortured smile. "It is worth it, to have seen you one last time."

Her arm in his grip was trembling. Weakening? He jerked his chin toward a wooden hut a few steps away, a crude, low square built in a more violent time to shelter the rooftop guards during blizzards and storms. It had no door, just a narrow entrance where a canvas flap rippled. "Come, out of this wind," he said, tugging her gently.

She shrugged off his grip, her head high. "I am not your prisoner."

"Heaven forbid." He lifted the canvas flap. "You are my guest." He beckoned her in with a wry, hopeful smile. When she still hesitated, he added, with a glance at the moors that stretched around them like the sea, "Please. Any rider out there might spot us. It's dangerous for you to be seen with me."

That reasoning seemed to hit home with her. Accepting, but still wary, she crossed the threshold into the hut. He followed her in, ducking his head through the low doorway.

The space was gloomy and stank of wet rotted wood, and the wind whistled shrilly through cracks. Christopher feared she might bolt out and try again to run. But he sensed the burning curiosity that held her in place. He motioned to the bench against the wall. "Come, sit." He sat down. "Please," he urged, patting the spot beside him on the bench.

She resisted, shaking her head. "What have you to do with Mary?"

"I'll get to that. First, tell me this, have they mistreated you, Richard Thornleigh and his wife?"

The question seemed to startle her. "You knew I was his ward?"

"I have been attentive, from afar."

"No, they have treated me gently. With love." She said it almost like an accusation.

Christopher accepted her barb with a tender smile. "No more than you deserve."

"You are wrong. It is their way. They are kindness itself."

"You don't know them as I do." He put steel in his voice. "They took everything I had. Yeavering Hall is theirs now."

"No, you forfeited it by your treason. Your property became Her Majesty's. She bestowed it on Lord Thornleigh's son-in-law for his brave service to her."

"It amounts to the same thing. Their family enjoys riches and rank. We have nothing."

"Nothing but infamy."

"Justine, it was eight years ago. I have repented most heartily, and paid for my error. Can you not forget and forgive?"

"Forgive treason? No loyal English subject can."

"And yet, you did not tell Richard Thornleigh that you knew I was alive."

She stiffened. His challenge hung in the air. "How do you know I haven't?"

A dangerous silence pulsed between them.

"Have you?"

He saw her defiance waver. She said quietly, almost a whisper, "No."

He exulted in her confession. He could scarcely keep seated. But he must not startle her. "There is nothing wrong with a secret, Justine, when it is done for love."

"It was not from love—from fear. I was a child and you commanded my silence. What did I know but obedience to you?"

Their eyes locked in the dim light. Christopher forced himself to hold the challenge. "Well, you are free to tell him now."

She looked down. "No." It was a grudging, rancorous surrender. "I will not be your executioner."

Relief flooded him, as great as his exultation. "Call it what you will, I call it love."

"You said you would tell me why you're here," she said curtly. "I'm listening."

He noticed a broken arrow on the floor at his foot. He picked it up. The fletched end was gone, an arrowhead on a jagged stick, lacking guidance. He rested his back against the wall, watching his daughter, turning the arrow in his hands.

"I arrived in Calais eight years ago, very ill. From this." He pointed the arrowhead at his ear where his hair, his wig, hid the burned flesh. "It was festering. Gradually it healed and my strength returned, but every now and then, when I was exhausted from tramping the roads, or from hunger, the skin broke out again in festering sores. I tried herbs, special waters, apothecaries' concoctions—nothing helped. I lived with the affliction. After a miserable year my wandering led me to an old friend at an abbey in Montreuil. I had studied with him many years before when I was a green student at the University of Paris, and now he was the abbot. He had friends at court. He introduced me to some gentlemen there, and I joined a group that met to study the lives of the saints. One day, Mary stopped in for a word with one of these gentlemen and deigned to sit with us for a half hour. To my mortification, my friend the abbot mentioned my affliction. The next day, Mary sent me a salve. I was astonished. But I used it and the effect was miraculous. The festering sores never returned. It is something I shall never forget, not just the healing salve, but that this tender young queen should care. I sent her a message, vowing to serve her. And I have done so, sometimes carrying letters, sometimes small gifts that she would send to friends. When the young king, her husband, died she sailed back to the land of her birth to be its queen. I visited her there and continued my services."

"You've been in Scotland?"

"Coming and going, yes, between France and Edinburgh." He added with a sigh, "Nearer to you, yet still in exile. Then, last year, Mary's brother usurped her and imprisoned her. She escaped, thank God, and she was grateful to reach the haven of England. But, Justine, she cannot stay. Her cousin Elizabeth is a jealous queen, a dangerous queen when crossed. And she feels crossed by Mary because of the love so many people have for her. Mary needs help. That is why I am here."

"What help can you give her?" Her wariness had vanished. Christopher saw that his tale had transfixed her. His success surprised him; he had thought it would take longer to disarm her of that shield of duty and doubt.

"I have brought her assurances from her French friends that a home awaits her in France, and security, and all the respect that is her due. They want her there. I brought Mary this news, and I am pleased to say she is considering it—an honorable retirement in France—if only Elizabeth would let her go." He paused to let the import of his words sink into his daughter. *That's right, my girl, report this straight to Richard Thornleigh.* "That's when I saw that Mary had the crucifix I gave you. I remarked on it in wonder, and she told me you were here, serving her, and had given it to her. She told me to show it to you as proof of her trust in me." A nervous look flickered over Justine's face. He understood and was quick to reassure her. "Child, I vow to you, no one else will ever know you gave Mary the crucifix."

She said very softly, "Thank you."

"No, thank you. For caring for Mary. And for preserving your faith despite the heresy all around you."

She still stood before him. He lifted the chain over his head and leaned toward her and took her hand. She did not flinch. He placed the crucifix in her palm. "It is yours. It has come home."

Did he see a glimmer of tears in her eyes? When her fingers curled around the crucifix, it moved him so deeply he felt a hot tightness in his throat. "Justine, I cannot stay in England long. I am a hunted man. Soon I will return to France and never trouble you again. My exile will keep me from you to my last hour on this earth. Please, won't you sit with me for just a moment? Our last time together?"

Shyly, she sat down beside him. "It is so strange . . . to see you, yet now you will be gone again."

"A day has not passed in these eight years that I have not thought of you. And I will do so until the day I die."

She looked at him as though searching his soul. "Father, will you—" She stopped, looking struck by her own word. *Father.*

Christopher said with affectionate encouragement, "Go on, child."

"Will you . . . answer a question?"

"If I can."

"Did you take any part in killing Geoffrey Croft?"

It startled him. "Who?"

"Lord Thornleigh's kin. The husband of his sister."

"I've never heard of the man."

"Don't pretend you know nothing of the feud between the Grenvilles and Thornleighs."

"Know it? I *lived* it. The Thornleighs spilled so much Grenville blood."

She frowned, disbelieving. "It is Lord Thornleigh's brother-in-law whose blood was spilled. Three arrows in his chest. An attack on the Thornleighs' home in Essex."

"Speedwell House?"

"Yes."

"I had no part in that. My brother John was overzealous. But he had cause, Justine. We *all* had cause, we Grenvilles. And do not think the Thornleighs suffered like saints in that day's violence. They used their weapons with a vengeance. We lost good men too."

"So it's true. Geoffrey Croft died at our hands."

He did not like the horrified note in her voice. "Justine, that unfortunate event was our family's only transgression. If John went too far, it was because the Thornleighs drove him to it. They are murderers."

She looked at him fiercely. "You lie."

"No. I never told you about it. You were a mere child. And when we moved north to Yeavering Hall, we were so far away from them I thought we were safe from their butchery. That *you* were safe."

She recoiled at the word. "Butchery? How can you say such a thing?"

"What else would you call it? Richard Thornleigh beat my father to death. He did it with a fire iron. Beat him, a frail old man, until his face was bloody pulp. Ask Thornleigh yourself. He cannot deny it—he went to prison for it. Ask Isabel, his daughter. She was there, watching, as Thornleigh struck my father again and again with that poker until he crumpled and lay bleeding and dying at Thornleigh's feet."

She gaped at him, her breath stilled.

"His wife, that heretic, is a murderer just as vicious. She came into my brother John's house when he was at supper with his family and she attacked him with a knife."

"What? Lady Thornleigh?"

"She fell on John in front of his children. Stabbed him sixteen times. You don't believe me? It's all there in the public record of her trial. Over a dozen witnesses testified against her. Honor Thornleigh was convicted and she was sentenced to hang. But her bosom friend, the new queen Elizabeth, pardoned her. And then ennobled her husband. Richard Thornleigh, the murderer, was made Baron Thornleigh. Those devils took my father's life and my brother's life. They took Yeavering Hall. They took *you*. Justine, the blood spilled is all Grenville blood, and it is on Richard Thornleigh's hands."

"But they never . . . spoke a word of this."

He took her hand that held the crucifix and held it between his hands. "It is you who have been wronged the most. My property should have been your inheritance. Instead, Thornleigh doles out largesse to you as if you are his poor relation. It grieves me, daughter. Grieves me to my soul. A father longs to provide for his child. Thornleigh robbed me even of that."

Her hand lay motionless in his. He could see how rocked she was, how defenseless. He sensed that he no longer needed the cudgel of facts to bring her over to his side; his best weapon now was a feather. "My darling girl," he said, slipping his arm around her shoulders. "Forgive me for troubling you with these old woes. Eight years is a long time to let fury fester. Too long, I think. It has drained me. And after all, I can do nothing to change the past. I want peace. For your sake. There is nothing in England for me, but your future lies here. I want that future to be unclouded and free, as open as your sweet face."

He snugged her closer to him, and she, looking pale and confused, leaned against him. Luxuriating in her trust, Christopher almost did not dare move.

"I feel so . . . lost." Her voice was as thin as a reed.

"No, my dear, you are found. Nothing can sever a father's love, and it will be with you always, even if I cannot. Remember our happier days at Yeavering Hall? Think on that, and know that you are loved."

She looked up at him. "Father, I was there. Not a month ago."

"At Yeavering Hall?"

She nodded. "It felt strange . . . worse than strange." Her voice became hushed, stricken. "My friend Alice . . . do you remember Alice Boyer?"

A shiver of caution touched his scalp. Where had this question come from? "The gardener's daughter, wasn't she? Didn't you two romp together as children?"

"Yes." Her eyes on him were troubled pools. "She was murdered. In Kirknewton. In the church."

He forced himself to keep his arm calmly around her shoulders. "How terrible. Who could have done such a thing?"

"I don't know. No one knows. But I have made a vow to find out. Because . . . it was my fault."

"What? How?"

"I sent Alice there . . . arranged work for her at Yeavering Hall. If I hadn't, she might still be alive." She looked down at the crucifix in her lap. "Maybe it's hopeless. All I've found out is that a man was seen running away from the church. I don't know if he witnessed the murder or committed it. Or neither. They say he's gone to London."

The man in the churchyard! Christopher asked as calmly as he could, "But you don't know this man's name?"

She shook her head. "But I have to try to find him, because . . ." Her voice wavered. "I feel as though everyone is turning into . . . someone else. As though . . . I don't know who I am." She took a breath. "Alice was my friend. That is one thing that will not change. I will keep my vow. If I don't . . . I'll have turned into someone else, too."

❧ 16 ❧

Justine's Gamble

Justine reached the stables, her thoughts as chaotic as the wind-wild shreds of straw swirling at her feet. She made her way to the mews, the falconer's domain tucked into an elbow of the stables where a double-door system kept the birds from escaping. She opened the first door, and once it had closed behind her she crossed the dim narrow space to the next one. As she reached for the latch she felt shaky. A door seemed to be closing on her whole world, on everything she had thought was fixed and unchanging. The kind Thornleighs . . . her lost father . . . her duty to Elizabeth . . . her future with Will. She gripped the latch hard, needing its metal coldness to ground herself. She took a steadying breath and pulled open the door to the mews.

Mary stood near the birds' perches, and at the sound of the door she looked over her shoulder. A peregrine falcon sat on her thickly gloved hand and it jerked its head at Justine, nervous at seeing the stranger. Two freelofted birds, a gyrfalcon and a goshawk, also peered at her from their perches. Sunlight fell in stripes between the slatted partition that separated the mews from the outdoor weathering yard, and through the slats Justine saw the falconer, a grizzled old greybeard, tossing pea gravel in handfuls around the weathering yard like a farmer sowing seed.

"We missed you at dinner, cherie," Mary said pleasantly. Using her knuckle, she stroked the falcon's slate-gray back to soothe it. "Especially your skill on the lute," she added with a smile in her voice. "Margaret performs an unpleasing solo."

"Forgive me, my lady. I had cause. I have been speaking with . . . my father."

Mary's head jerked up. She cast a nervous glance at the weathering yard. They were speaking French, a language Justine doubted the old falconer understood. Even if he could, he was too far away to hear. Nevertheless, she kept her voice low.

"I do not mean to alarm you, my lady. Only to thank you for your trust." She lifted the pendant crucifix from under her bodice to show her, then let it fall back inside.

Mary's lips curved in a slow smile. "Ah."

"My lady, may I . . . ask a question?"

"Of course."

"How long have you known I was Christopher Grenville's daughter?"

"Not long. Days."

"But why did—" She stopped. It was not her place to interrogate a queen.

"Go on, cherie. You have leave."

"Why did you not tell me he was serving you?"

"Because he is not safe in England. He has taken a great risk to come to me."

"He is not at risk from *me*."

A nod and a smile. "I told him so."

Justine heard the warmth in Mary's assurance and was moved. Again, she stammered, "Thank you."

"Poor Justine. Was it a shock, seeing him?"

She looked down. There were no words for the tumult in her heart.

"It must have been hard for you," Mary said, "living all these years as someone else."

Justine had no answer. She still felt more Lord Thornleigh's daughter than her father's. Her father had deserted her. Lord Thornleigh had raised her, cared for her, counseled her, championed her union with Will. Yet her father's accusations chilled her. When she pictured Lord Thornleigh beating her grandfather to death . . . Lady Thornleigh stabbing her uncle John . . . horror stalled her mind. She felt like a rider halted by fog, unsure of what lay ahead or behind. She didn't know the truth of anything. All she knew for certain was that she could not betray her father. She would not send him to the gallows.

"We all have our crosses to bear, cherie," Mary murmured. She turned her attention to the peregrine falcon whose yellow claws were clamped on her wrist. From one of its legs a thin leather cord looped, tethering the bird to its perch, a square of wood on a post. "This poor fellow has hurt his wing." She gently stroked its neck. "I know how he feels. When Scrope allows me to go hawking, I am hemmed in by his men-at-arms so that I cannot fly."

"If you could, my father says your friends in France would welcome you."

Mary heaved a sigh, preening the bird. "So he tells me."

Justine took a deep breath. This was why she had come. "My lady, can I help you fly there?" She had bent her troubled mind to the problem as soon as she had left her father on the battlements. If nothing else seemed clear, this solution did. If Mary went to France, then Justine's burdensome mission to spy on her would end and a political crisis in Scotland would be averted, all with no harm done to Elizabeth. Her father, too, could slip back to France and live out his days there, out of harm's way, serving Mary. Clearly, having Mary out of England would be best for everyone, so Justine had decided it was up to her to make it happen. "If you will let me," she urged, "I shall devise a ruse to get you out. A disguise, perhaps. You escaped Loch Leven dressed as a countrywoman, did you not? I know people in the village who would assist us, for gold. With a fast horse you could reach the coast overnight. My father would secure a boat to take you across the Narrow Sea. I would ride with you and stay by your side until you sail."

A probing look from Mary. "Would you, indeed?"

"It would be an honor."

Mary shook her head. An injured tone hardened her voice. "No. I will not sneak away like a thief in the night. Oh, I know my enemies would love to see me reduced to such meekness, bundled off to some crumbling rural château where they can shut the gate on me and have the world forget me." She lifted her chin. "I am a queen. The inquiry's findings will make that clear to all. I am a *queen*. Elizabeth must respect it, and my vile brother must acknowledge it."

Her self-delusion was jarring. There was courage and dignity, too, which Justine admired, but those qualities would not help Mary in the face of what was happening at the inquiry. "My lady, are you sure? You could make a contented life for yourself in honorable seclusion in France."

"Contented as a cow?" Mary's look was frosty. "I have told you, no. That is my answer. Do not mention this again."

Justine sadly realized that she should not be surprised. Mary had never once deviated from absolute insistence on her royal rights. Nonetheless, her refusal was a blow because it now forced Justine to make a decision she had been avoiding. Did her loyalty to Lord Thornleigh and to Elizabeth leave her duty-bound to watch in silence as the inquiry shredded Mary's reputation, making her a monster in the eyes of all Europe? It was not fair, not right, and Justine could not do it.

"In that case, my lady, there is something you should know." The sharp eyes of the falcon glared at her as if in warning. She knew the risk, and she cleared her throat and went on. "In Bedale this morning on my errand for you, I chanced to meet an acquaintance visiting from York. He is a clerk at the inquiry, and I asked him how things are proceeding." She felt a guilty blush warm her cheeks at the lie. Will was far more than a clerk; he was Sir William Cecil's eyes and ears, and Lord Thornleigh's.

Mary's interest was keen. "Ah, there is news?"

"None to cheer you, I fear. The commissioners are in possession of some new evidence. Letters you wrote to Lord Bothwell."

Mary frowned. "Why have I heard nothing of this? Herries or Ross should have told me."

"Your representatives were not told. The Earl of Moray showed the letters only to the Duke of Norfolk and his fellow commissioners. Over a private dinner." She added to maintain her story about her source, "A few of their clerks were present."

A fierceness gleamed in Mary's eyes. "What is Moray scheming now?"

She does not deny the letters, Justine thought with a stab of dismay. She had to be sure. "My lady, *did* you write to Lord Bothwell?"

"Of course. He was a member of my royal council. I communicated thus with all my councilors."

"But the letters speak of a relationship far more . . . intimate." She hesitated. This was dangerous ground.

"Tell me." An icy command.

Justine steeled herself. She explained what Will had said, that the letters were those of a woman to her lover. That details in them identified dates, making it clear they were written while Mary was married to Lord Darnley. That the writer had coldly discussed with Bothwell a wish to murder Darnley. She plowed on, quoting a few phrases she remembered Will quoting. "I cannot sleep according to my desire, which is between your arms. . . . I am so far made yours that my thoughts are willingly subdued unto yours. . . . I am your faithful lover, who hopes shortly to be another thing to you for the reward of my pains—"

"Lies!" The shout from Mary sent the falcon on her wrist into a panic. Wings flapping, it beat into the air, but the tether on its foot snapped taut, forcing the bird down. It made another wild attempt to fly and Justine lurched back from its flailing claws. The cord snapped it back again and it collapsed on the perch, fighting for balance. Its thrashing frightened the freelofted gyrfalcon and goshawk, and they flew in crazed circles.

"Filthy lies!" Mary paced, oblivious to the birds. "Moray forged these writings. He will stop at nothing to destroy me." She turned on Justine. "They *all* read these lies, you say?"

"The letters were passed around, yes, and each man read parts aloud. So I was told."

"Villains!" She yanked off her glove and hurled it. It slapped the far wall. The gyrfalcon flapped and shrieked, "Kak! Kak! Kak!"

"What's amiss?" the old falconer cried, hobbling in from the weathering yard. His rheumy eyes took in the birds' distress. "Your Grace, be you hurt?" He looked terrified that her wrath would fall on him.

"Get out," she said.

"No hurt has come to my lady," Justine assured him. "Please, go. She and I must speak in private."

He shuffled out, bewildered, bowing abjectly. Mary continued to pace in furious indignation. "Moray is out to make me look a fiend. So are they all!" The falcon she had been stroking thrashed feebly on its perch, in pain from its injured wing. Mary walked past it. The other two alarmed birds sought perches farther away. "No doubt they will send these letters to Elizabeth."

"So I was told."

She suddenly halted. "Wait." She seemed afire with fresh energy. "This may not be so bad, then. Once I have seen the forgeries I will rip Moray's so-called evidence to shreds. I will make him tremble at his perjury. Yes! Elizabeth will be honor-bound to give me justice."

"My lady, it pains me to tell you this. You are not to be shown the letters."

Mary looked stricken. "Not . . . ? But how can I fight something I cannot even *see?* What kind of justice is that?"

Justine parroted Will's words, ashamed of them. "They say the rules of evidence do not apply because this is not a trial."

Mary's face was pale. "Done in secret, then? I see now . . . a conspiracy to ruin me." She covered her face with her hands. Her shoulders heaved. "Dear God in heaven." She was sobbing. "These men have sealed my doom."

Justine watched, pity reaming her heart, hating that she had no comfort to offer. She wrapped her arm around Mary. It was a liberty, embracing this royal person like a close friend, but Mary's plight touched a chord in her that sadly sang of Alice. "Would it make a difference if you *could* see the letters?"

The pale face lifted. "Of course. All the difference."

"You could prove they are forgeries?"

"I am sure I could. The counterfeiters will have made mistakes.

Details of phrasing, or names, or places . . . something. I would
root out the errors and prove that I am innocent."

Innocent. Thank goodness. "Then, my lady, there may be a way."
Justine's heart beat wildly at the offer she was about to make. *Does
this make me a traitor?* With a pang she thought of her father fleeing
Yeavering Hall eight year ago. *Is treason in my blood?* But Mary's
tearstained face was answer enough. Giving her a chance to fight
the inquiry's secret dealings was the opposite of treason. It was
mere justice.

"Take heart," she said. "If you need the letters, I will get them
for you."

Christopher slipped into the Bolton Castle chapel at midnight.
He had come silently through the priest's darkened room and the
first thing he saw was Mary kneeling before the altar. Head bowed,
she had not seen him. He glanced around to make sure they were
alone. He could not afford to have anyone see him here. Especially
Justine.

In the gloom a few votive candles flickered. The chapel was
silent. Outside, the wind had died. He and Mary were alone. *Let
her finish her prayer,* he thought. He had news for her, but he still
felt shaken by his talk with Justine. He had arrived back from
London this morning and had waited for nightfall to meet Mary
here, but any hope of a quiet few hours of rest had been blasted by
seeing his daughter. What a wondrous and disturbing reunion!
Wondrous because he felt sure he had begun to win her over, win
her back from Thornleigh's thrall. But disturbing because of what
she had said about Alice Boyer. About the man seen running away.
A witness—that's what Christopher dreaded. How much had the
man seen? Who was he? He had apparently disappeared, but could
Justine track him? She did not know his name, and if he had gone
to London, as she said, he would be next to impossible to trace, especially since she was hundreds of miles away, here with Mary.
Mary—all Christopher's hopes returned to her, as always. If she
became queen of England his guilt would be moot. She could pardon any crime. Ennoble him to be a peer of the realm. His past
subsumed in a glorious future.

"My lady," he said eagerly as he saw her get to her feet.

She whirled around. Her face looked drawn, fretful. "Where have you been? I've been *waiting*."

"I have been busy in London on your behalf. There are developments."

"You don't know what's happened *here*. The inquiry—"

"It has begun, I know. I'm working as fast as I can. I have been with Ambassador de Spes. He informed King Philip about Adam Thornleigh's murderous attack on his kinsman and urged immediate retaliation, as I hoped."

"Ah! This will push Philip to my cause."

"Not quite yet. He is no doubt mulling the cost of taking on England."

"Bah! His armies are invincible, they could smash Elizabeth's paltry force. She has no standing army. She relies on the musters of her lords."

"It is not a question of might but of desire. An English adventure may not yet be to Philip's taste given Spain's trade ties with England. And unfortunately Northumberland will not make a move to rise up against Elizabeth until he is sure of a commitment of Spanish troops. But do not fear, I will continue to urge de Spes to urge the King."

She wrung her hands. "But if I have neither Philip or Northumberland, what am I to do? Who else will come to my aid? Oh, I am undone! The letters . . . the letters!"

Christopher was used to her emotional outbursts, but he had rarely seen her so anxious. "Letters? What are you talking about?"

"Moray. He has given Elizabeth's commissioners letters they say I wrote to Bothwell. Forgeries!" She threw up her hands in supplication to God, crying out for justice. Christopher took her firmly by the elbow and demanded that she explain. She told him. Eight letters. Written while she was married to Darnley. Professing love for Bothwell and hatred for her husband and tacit approval of removing him. "He gave them to the English in private. I am not allowed to even see them!"

Christopher was appalled. "You wrote to Bothwell?"

"Of course, he was on my council."

"But *these* letters."

She held her head high. "How can I answer for contents I am not allowed to see?"

Christopher didn't know what to believe. Everyone close to her knew she had been Bothwell's lover. She had once told Sir William Maitland that she would follow Bothwell to the ends of the earth in her petticoat. Whether she had conspired with him to kill the idiot Darnley, Christopher did not know and did not care, but he knew that written evidence of it in the hands of the English commissioners was a catastrophe. He turned away from Mary, feeling a needle of panic. This damning evidence changed everything. It could so befoul her reputation, their allies would back away from her. It could turn Northumberland against her. Turn Spain against her.

"But Moray has not beaten me yet," Mary declared. "I shall fight back."

He rubbed the back of his neck, trying to think. "How?"

"Your daughter. She is going to get me the letters."

Christopher spun around. "What? How?"

"She has a friend at the inquiry. A clerk. It's how she heard about the letters."

He stared at her. "*She* brought you this news?"

"Yes. You did well, my friend, in bringing her to our side. I did my part, too. We have won her over to my cause. She is on her way to York to get copies of the letters."

Justine had turned against Elizabeth? Against Thornleigh? It was too wonderful! "To York? You asked this of her?"

"She offered."

Joy rushed over him. How brave his daughter was! She was truly his flesh and blood. It moved him to his soul.

"With the letters in hand," Mary said, "I will crush Moray's conspiracy."

Christopher collected himself. This was no time to savor his personal triumph with Justine. The crisis was still upon them. "We cannot rely on that," he said. "If word of these letters reaches Northumberland and Philip of Spain, you will lose the battle. We must strike before the news gets out." It was up to him to remove Elizabeth, and now even sooner than he had expected. He had to find a way. "I will do my all for you, you know that. But there is something you must do as well. It's what I came to tell you. Northumberland might be spurred to move if we can enlist a powerful ally in England."

"Who? Even those with good Catholic hearts dare not cross Elizabeth. Northumberland is merely the least timid of a timid lot. She keeps all her lords on short tethers."

"Not the Duke of Norfolk."

She gave a slight gasp. "The mightiest of them. What have you heard?"

"I too have ears at the inquiry. Norfolk seems loath to condemn you. I warrant he is thinking that one day he may have to bow to you as queen of England, as Elizabeth's natural successor. Then you would not look kindly on him having branded you a harlot and a murderess."

She flinched at the offensive words. But Christopher noted that she did not refute them. "So he is neutral in my cause," she said.

"Neutrality is cheap. To take up arms is another thing entirely. After all, he is Elizabeth's cousin."

"But he grumbles at how his greatness goes unrewarded. *You* could reward him."

"I? How?"

"Marriage."

She looked appalled. "What?"

"Think of it as he would. If Elizabeth dies childless then you, her heir, ascend to her throne. Offer Norfolk marriage and you'll have him feverishly dreaming of being King of England."

"Need I remind you that I am already married? Bothwell may have gone to ground in Denmark, but he is still my husband."

"So rid yourself of him. Have the marriage annulled."

"On what grounds?"

"Anything. That his own marriage was not yet annulled when he married you. Just get this in motion. All that matters is that Norfolk knows you are proceeding toward annulment. We must give him hope of marrying you himself. We need Norfolk with us."

She hesitated, but only for a moment. "All right. Can you get word to him to broach the union?"

He was relieved at how easily she was abandoning Bothwell. "Yes. Leave it to me." It was bracing how alliances were shifting all around him. Mary cutting herself loose from Bothwell. Norfolk ripe for plucking away from Elizabeth. Most wonderful, Justine taking Mary's part, no longer under Thornleigh's thumb . . .

Justine. A sudden fear gnawed him. "You say my daughter has gone to York?"

"Yes, she left this afternoon."

"As soon as she returns, do not let her out again. And watch her closely for who she speaks to."

"Why? Don't you trust her?"

How much should he tell her? Everything, he decided. Otherwise she might not keep a watch on Justine. "There is a problem." He told her about his visit four months ago to the town near his former property of Yeavering Hall. About his meeting a servant from the Hall. "The girl recognized me. I could not let her babble that she had seen her former lord. Everyone thinks I'm dead. So I silenced her."

Mary asked, unblinking, "She is dead?"

He nodded. "The trouble is, she was my daughter's friend. Justine has vowed to find the killer. She told me she has questioned people and unearthed what may be a witness. He has disappeared, but if she keeps searching . . ." He could not suppress a shiver. He had brought his daughter back to his side, but how strong was her bond with him, really?

Mary's eyes flashed in alarm. "You fool!" She slapped him.

Stunned, his hand flew up to strike her back. He stopped just in time. He glared at her, breathing hard. Any other woman would now be on the floor, bleeding.

"How could you be so stupid?" she cried. "What if she finds this man? Dear God, they will arrest you. They'll discover your treason of years ago. They will put you on the rack to question you. And you will tell them everything!"

"No, I promise you—"

"What good is a promise when they are tearing your limbs from your body?" Her eyes had the wild look of a cat cornered by dogs.

"You will tell them I'm plotting to kill Elizabeth. And then she will cut off my head!"

He took her by the shoulders. She was rigid with fear. "It will not come to that. Trust me. Before Justine can find the witness, you will be queen of England."

"You do not know that!" She shook her head with such a fearful look she seemed beyond reasoning. "No, no, we cannot let her find him. If she does you will have to silence her."

He was stunned. "Silence . . . my own daughter?"

"If they capture you, *I am dead!*" She shook off his hands. "Give me your word. If it comes to choosing your daughter or your queen, swear that you will choose your queen." She jabbed a finger toward the floor. "Swear on your knees, before God."

He could not move. Yet, without Mary, he had no future. No life.

"Swear it!"

Stiffly, he sank to his knees. He swore what she asked. And silently prayed that he would never have to make such a choice.

❧ 17 ❧

The King's Gold

Adam Thornleigh was sure he was going to die. Either today on the sea with his throat slit by a Spanish blade, or later on Tower Green, condemned by Elizabeth, his head hacked off by the executioner's axe. Alone at the helm of his pinnace, *Curlew*, he chased the big Spanish carrack *Nuestra Señora* through low chop fifteen miles off the Dutch coast, his mouth as dry as canvas as he thought of his chances. He told himself that if he was going to die over this he would rather it came on the water; here, he'd always felt most alive. The sun was shining, the waves were dancing, and the fresh breeze blowing steady from the west made his lively boat with its single sail fairly sing. It was the kind of day he had loved as a boy larking on the estuary in his father's skiff.

This enterprise, though, was no lark. The *Nuestra Señora* carried a hoard of gold bullion to pay King Philip's troops stationed in the Netherlands. The modest merchant vessel was a mask for transporting the gold, and Adam was desperate to capture it. Otherwise, bankruptcy would drown him. But there was maybe one chance in fifty he would succeed. Then, if he survived, maybe one chance in a hundred of success with the second part of his plan: convincing Elizabeth to be his accomplice. If he couldn't do that—if she took Spain's part against him—she might not even grant him the dignity of the axe but would have him swing like a common pirate from gallows in the riverbank mud of Wapping's Execution Dock. That made him shudder. They used a short rope for pirates. It didn't snap the neck, so the condemned died by slow, agonizing strangulation.

He set his mind to the wind to shake off his fear. *If death is coming, let it be here. Give me at least the satisfaction of taking some Godcursed Spaniards to Hell with me.*

The big merchant carrack was lumbering at a lazy pace, bellying in the wind, and Adam's nimble boat soon closed on her. He skimmed alongside the tall hull and eased the sheets to slow his way and keep pace with the ship. Her fresh paintwork of gold stars and green chevrons gleaming in the sun was a pretty sight, but a false front; he knew that behind the closed gun ports level with his head lurked three demi-cannons and two culverins, with the same array on the starboard side. The guns weren't much compared to the armaments on a man-of-war, but they were enough to make any would-be attacker think twice. The culverin amidships would blast straight into Adam's face.

He cast a nervous look at the sea behind him. The big brigantine that bristled on the horizon was the *White Boar*, the only insurance for his plan to work. But she was so far away he could not even make out her flags. He needed her near, or else he'd be stranded. He squelched his fear and took courage from the strong, steady wind. If it remained constant, with the *White Boar* running fast before it, he had a chance.

Up on the *Nuestra Señora*'s deck three seamen had come to the port rail to look down at him. Adam held up a hand to shade his eyes from the sun behind the men. The glare made them black, featureless forms. He grinned, then hailed them with friendly words in Spanish. "I am Sir Adam Thornleigh. Is your captain Miguel Fuentes of Seville?"

"*Inglés*"—Englishman—one said to the others with a chuckle at Adam's clumsy, accented speech. He called down in Spanish, "Yes, sir. Señor Fuentes. You know him?"

"I do. What luck to sight you. Where are you bound?"

"Rotterdam."

"I am for Amsterdam." Adam was lashing his boat's line to the ship's chain plate. "I'll come aboard and say hello to my old friend." They dropped the ladder for him and he climbed up, leaving *Curlew* nudging the big ship as if for company as the two vessels carved through the waves together. On deck he forced himself to keep his fighting hand at his side, not lay it on his sword hilt. A friendly visit, that's what he had to make them believe.

A couple of curious passengers, merchants by the look of their rich doublets and capes, sauntered closer for a look at him. They didn't interest Adam, but the five men across the deck did, steel-helmeted Spanish soldiers with pikes. They were aboard to protect the cargo of gold destined for King Philip's troops. He hired mercenaries by the thousands to fight his wars and quell the peoples he had conquered. Adam did his best to hide his churning hatred. Spanish soldiers like these had butchered his crew at St. Juan de Ulúa.

The merchants made way for the captain striding forward from the sterncastle, a squat, square-shouldered man with a bulbous nose and weary eyes. "Greetings, Miguel," Adam said.

The captain looked mildly baffled. "I do not recall our acquaintance, sir. Have we met?"

"We have not." Adam kept his tone breezy. "But what better time than the present to make new friends?"

The seamen around them frowned, puzzled. Fuentes shot a glance down at the pinnace alongside. Harmless, no one aboard. "Do you require assistance, sir? Is your boat in difficulty?"

"None whatsoever." He stepped close to the captain and said very quietly, "But your ship will be if you don't listen carefully. Where can we talk alone?"

Fuentes looked anxious. "What's the danger? Have you seen pirates?" He motioned brusquely to the seamen to move on. They obeyed him, walking away. The merchants, too, drifted off to leave the captain to his private business.

"I'm here for the King's gold," Adam said. Surprise flickered in the captain's eyes. The special cargo was a carefully kept secret.

Adam blessed Anthony Porteous for his uncanny access to information. "I want it transferred to my boat. Now."

Fuentes's eyes widened, incredulous. He let out a bark of a laugh. "You are mad." He cast a glance at the soldiers.

"Pikes won't stop cannonballs," Adam said. "See that brigantine?" He jerked his chin astern to indicate the *White Boar* bearing down on them, running fast before the wind. Her English flags were plain now, fluttering above the hull whose gun ports yawned open, ready for action. The ship belonged to Porteous, who had armed her well. Adam had commissioned his longtime first mate, James Curry, to captain her and they had culled a crew of hard men from Portsmouth's taverns to sign on for the spoils. "She's mine, Fuentes, and she's coming for you. She'll blow holes in you unless you give me the gold."

Now the captain understood. His eyes flicked nervously between the oncoming ship, Adam, and the soldiers.

"Her cannon will start firing," Adam warned, "unless my mate sees my signal."

Fuentes unsheathed the dagger at his hip and growled, "You cannot signal if you're dead."

"Kill me and you'll have a war on your hands." Adam pulled folded papers from inside his jerkin. "These are letters of marque from the English Admiralty, signed by Her Royal Highness, Elizabeth, Queen of England and Ireland by the grace of God."

Every seafaring man knew the significance of letters of marque issued by whatever country. They allowed a victim of piracy, if he could not get justice in a foreign court, to mount an attack on a vessel of the offending country to recoup his losses. Adam jabbed the tightly folded papers close to the captain's face like a knife. "Ever hear of San Juan de Ulúa?" He prayed the man would not demand to see the writing, but was ready to unsheathe his sword if he did. The papers were drawings by his daughter for his new ship's figurehead. Drawings of her cat, Gilly.

He stuffed them back in his jerkin and put steel in his voice. "Do as I say and no one gets hurt. Or be blasted by my ship's guns and die. Either way, I'll get the gold."

The Spanish captain's look was fiercely unrelenting. He swatted the document aside with contempt. Paper was only paper. Gunpowder and swords settled matters at sea.

A knife-tip of panic pricked Adam. He was alone. Curry in the *White Boar* was not bearing down fast enough. *Come on, Curry!* he yelled in his head. *Don't make this my day to die.*

A few snowflakes drifted from the pewter-colored sky over London's Cripplegate Ward as Richard Thornleigh and his wife reached his sister's house on Silver Street. Honor knocked. The door opened and the servant girl curtsied and told them the mistress was not home. Richard felt a tinge of relief. He wouldn't have to tell Joan yet about Will and Justine's betrothal. He felt a coward, since he had known about it for months. He had wanted to spare his sister the blow. But he also wanted to protect Justine. Joan's grief ran so deep it had long ago hardened into hate.

"But she's just up the street, your lordship," the girl added helpfully. "At St. Olave's churchyard."

Richard and Honor shared a look. They understood. Joan was making her afternoon visit to Geoffrey's grave. Richard groaned inside. He feared that no good could come of this visit. However, he was here to try.

"Another time?" Honor suggested to him. "Leave her in peace today?"

"No, I cannot put this off any longer. Come, let's get it done."

They set off walking eastward, and as they turned the corner onto Wood Street Honor gave him a sly look. "I'm not sure I would visit *your* grave twice a day."

"Good Lord, not even once, I beg you. Bury me at sea."

"Gladly, my love, if I'm alive to do it. But if I'm not, the churchwarden will have his way, so be prepared for worms."

He looked at her, glad she could turn a jest to try to lighten his mood. Snowflakes touched her cheek and instantly melted at the warmth of her skin. It stirred a memory in him. He was a lad, dashing outside with his little sister Joan into the white-speckled field by their house—the first snowfall of the season. She was laughing as she turned her face upward, mouth open to catch the flakes on her tongue. Poor Joan. It seemed to Richard ages since he had heard her laugh.

"Maybe she won't take it so badly," he said, forcing hope. "After all, it's been ten years."

"I would not forget it if they murdered you. Whether ten years ago or twenty."

"But you would not brood like Joan does, surely."

"Would I not? Do you imagine me dancing?"

"Look out." He gripped her elbow to tug her out of the path of a fat porter on a winded horse trotting into the Castle Inn's yard. "That fellow's half-asleep."

He'd used his left arm to pull her, though it was nearly numb again. The clumsy maneuver was not lost on Honor. He saw concern flicker over her face, but she said nothing and looked away. Keeping her promise. He knew what it was costing her to bottle up her worries. Weeks ago she had questioned him about his malady—it was hard to conceal a dragging leg, though the leg was fine now; it was his arm giving him grief—and he had finally told her about the ongoing numbness. She had taken immediate action, calling in one doctor after another to ply their cures. Richard had acquiesced for her sake, though in his estimation they were charlatans and mountebanks, the lot of them. He had swallowed their herbal potions that tasted like horse piss and worn amulets around his neck that smelled like dead rat. He had let them bleed him and bind him and chant over him, until finally he'd had enough and sternly told Honor no more doctors. Told her to promise him she would give up searching for some miracle cure and accept the truth, that his body was failing and there was nothing they could do. His words brought her to the brink of tears, and she silently shook her head, refusing. She rushed out to her garden and fussed with her flowers for a while, and when she came back in it was with clear eyes and a small, brave smile. "Once the inquiry is over and Elizabeth can spare you, let's visit Isabel and Carlos. I long to see the children, and some hunting would do you good." She had kissed him and promised to say no more about his malady. Nevertheless, at moments like this with his clumsy movements, he saw her struggle to keep her promise.

"There she is," Honor said. They had reached St. Olave's churchyard shadowed by shaggy ancient yew trees, and Richard saw Joan kneeling on the grass by Geoffrey's headstone, a garden trowel in hand. She was digging weeds from a small square of autumn flowers. Even on her knees, his sister's back was straight as a board.

"Richard, are you sure this is a good idea? She looks so lonely." He almost changed his mind. His wife had a tender spot in her heart for Joan. He, too, would always be grateful to his sister for nursing Honor after her ordeal in the Tower. But that was the past. He was thinking now of the future. "It's time."

Joan looked up as they approached. Her smile was small but genuine. "Well, this is a surprise."

"Susan told us you were here," Honor said. "My, don't these purple asters make a brave showing, even with frost threatening. And your Michaelmas daisies, too."

Joan set down her trowel with a satisfied look at her handiwork. Richard regarded the pitiful tiny garden. Either the women deluded themselves or else he couldn't see what they saw. A few hardy bright blossoms stood erect, but the rest was a choke of drooping, haggard summer blooms with withering yellow leaves. The thinness of his sister's face struck him. Didn't she eat?

"Richard," she said, getting to her feet, "you have made Susan and old Joseph very happy with your gift. A whole side of venison. They'll be enjoying it until spring."

"You too, I hope. Your servants have plenty of meat on them."

She gave him a tolerant smile. "I devoured the honey cakes Honor sent." She added warmly to her sister-in-law, "Thank you, my dear. So kind." She rubbed her gloved hands together briskly to loosen the dirt. "What news of Adam?"

"Marooned at his house in Chelsea," Honor said.

Richard said, "He chafes and grumbles, but it's no more than he deserves." He spoke roughly, for his son was in disgrace with Elizabeth for his lethal assault on the Spanish ambassador's cousin. Secretly, though, he sympathized with Adam lashing out after Spain's perfidious attack on him and Hawkins at San Juan de Ulúa. The terrible loss of English lives and treasure. When he heard of Adam's safe return from the Indies, Richard had felt deep relief.

"He has survived tempests at sea, so I dare say he'll survive Her Majesty's anger," Joan offered kindly. She added with obvious pleasure, "I've heard from Will. He is making his way with some distinction in York. I owe you thanks for that, too, Richard, bringing him to Sir William Cecil's notice. Will writes that he is mightily busy at the inquiry."

Richard studied the sky. "He is, indeed. I've just been there." How best to break the betrothal news?

"Were you? Ah, then you saw him. Good. I confess, I was laid quite low before he left. He told me a terrible thing, Richard. He said . . ." She paused with a glance at Honor.

"Go ahead and talk, you two," Honor said, waving them away. "I'll finish taming these weeds." She kneeled and took up the trowel and set to work, digging around the daisies.

Richard guided his sister away from the grave. He knew what the "terrible" thing was, but he would let her have her say. "Go on."

"Before he left, Will told me he wanted to marry the Grenville girl. Can you imagine? It turned my stomach." With a worried look at her husband's grave she lowered her voice as though he might overhear. "I said nothing to you because I hoped this monstrous fancy of Will's would pass, especially when Sir William sent him to York." She lifted her chin with a look of satisfaction. "I was right. It was a fleeting infatuation. In all his letters there is not a word about the girl. Wonderful, isn't it, how a few hundred miles of separation can sober a young man and bend him to his work."

Her blindness astonished Richard. "Joan, you made such an outburst he feared you were ill. He hasn't written you about her because he didn't want to upset you more."

"What? You *knew?*"

"Yes, Justine told me they had an understanding. It was to be a secret." He shook his head. "Like many secrets, a bad business."

"Bad? It's revolting. Unthinkable."

"No, I meant—"

"That's why I told Will my heart, and I am very glad I did. It stopped him from getting further entangled. He has escaped the girl's snare. And now, with time, he will put this behind him. Time and work, that's all he needs. He will forget all about her."

Pure self-delusion, Richard thought with a pang. He looked back at Honor as she leaned to tug a stubborn weed. He remembered the first fire of loving her, thirty-five years ago. He had tried to forget her. He was married, his sickly wife dependent on him, and he had his way to make in the world. He had tried to bend himself to fidelity and work, but there was no forgetting Honor Larke.

He turned back to his sister. "Joan, your son is in love. And Justine returns his love. They have gotten betrothed. That's what I came to tell you."

She gaped at him. "Betrothed? No, that's . . . impossible."

"I know it's hard to swallow, this hole-in-corner secrecy. They pledged their troth in private before he left. A secret. Justine told me only afterward. When I saw Will in York I told him it was ill done. But the fact is, it *is* done. They are eager to be married as soon as this business with the Queen of Scots is over."

She blanched. "You must forbid it. Forbid the marriage."

"On the contrary, I have given them my blessing. I urge you to do the same."

She looked so stricken he was afraid she might faint. He took her arm, wanting to guide her to a bench.

She shook off his hand, red blotches of anger firing her cheeks. "How can you even consider it after your own son's experience? Adam married a Grenville. He married misery."

"Nonsense, Joan. There is no comparison."

"No, this is far worse! Don't you see? Will doesn't know the truth about this one. He would never even consider marrying her if he knew what she really was."

"What is she but an ardent and innocent girl?"

"She's a God-cursed Grenville whelp!"

The harsh words brought Honor to her feet in alarm. Richard shook his head at her, a signal that he would handle this.

"Will's wife? Never!" There was a wildness in Joan's eyes. "Every time I looked at her I would feel sick. Every time I saw their children I would see Grenville arrows ripping Geoffrey's flesh. No, no, it is time Will knew the truth. Past time, that is plain. He needs to know how abominable such a union would be."

"I warn you, Joan, let them work this out between them."

"Eight years ago you told me to keep quiet about the girl, about who her family was. I have kept that promise. But it was a bad decision you made, Richard. It was wrong, and now look where it's led us. You must forbid the marriage."

"What makes you think that would stop them?"

She gave a strangled gasp. Clearly she had not considered this. "If you won't lift a finger, I'll do it. I'll bring him here, to his father's grave. I'll make him remember Geoffrey's agony."

Her reaction was so extreme, Richard had no words. Honor came to them and touched her sister-in-law's arm in sympathy. "Joan, accept this marriage," she said. "It's for the best."

"I would rather die!" She pushed Honor aside, grabbing the trowel from her. "Leave me! Both of you. Leave me and Geoffrey alone!" She went to the grave and fell to her knees and hacked the soil, severing flowers and weeds alike.

Richard had had enough. "I remind you that I pay for your house, your servants, your table. Give Will and Justine your blessing, or don't expect any more money from me."

"He'll soon have plenty of his own. He'll have a position at court."

"And you think he'll want to support you when you say you hate his wife?"

"He will hate her, too, when he knows! She will not become his wife!"

Richard groaned, angry with himself. Her perverseness had led him to make a threat he didn't mean. He crouched beside her and said as gently as he could manage, "Open your eyes, Joan. Be part of something good. Will loves the girl. Nothing can change that."

She stopped her digging and searched his eyes. Hers looked haggard. She asked in wounded bewilderment, "Why do you care so much about her?"

"I want peace. The feud has caused enough suffering. I want the rancor done with. I want things *settled*." He caught Honor's expression, her pained recognition that he might not have many more years. It filled him with a longing to finish this battle with his sister. He had been on the road in Elizabeth's business with Mary, back and forth, and he was tired out from it. He wanted to be home with his wife.

"Peace?" Joan moaned. "Geoffrey's soul will never have peace. I have no peace. Why should you?"

Richard got to his feet, done with her. "I head this family and I will have an end to this discord. My nephew will marry my ward as soon as they return to London. Get your thoughts in order and be ready to smile at their wedding. Order a new gown for it. Geoffrey always liked you in blue."

There had been no bloodshed. It was dark but nearing dawn when Adam, alone at the helm, brought his pinnace *Curlew* alongside London's Billingsgate Wharf. He still could not quite believe how his gambit on the water had worked.

It hadn't at first. Fuentes, the Spanish captain, had sneered at his demand to hand over the King's gold. His job was to defend it with his life. Sick with dread, Adam waved a red kerchief, the signal for Curry on the approaching *White Boar* to fire his cannon. Flame erupted from the big gun's mouth and the iron ball flew, moaning in the wind. It crossed the stern quarter of the *Nuestra Señora*, splitting its Bonadventure mizzen mast, sending splinters flying, then plowing into the sea. The mizzen toppled in a crash of canvas and tackle and rigging that sent the Spanish crew scurrying and Adam and Fuentes flinching. That single cannon blast turned Fuentes into a rational man. That and the fierce-looking boarding gang lined up along the *White Boar*'s rail with raised swords, axes, and knives. With the *White Boar* on his heels, her fired cannon smoking like a dragon's mouth, Fuentes had ordered the transfer of the nine chests of gold onto Adam's small boat. Adam had paid off the *White Boar* crew with a bucket of the King's gold and the brigantine had sailed off into the North Sea. It wasn't until he was on his way back to London on a swift beam reach that he noticed a slender wooden shard embedded in his wrist. Had to be a piece of the blown Spanish mizzen. So, a little bloodshed after all, just enough to redden the cuff of his sleeve. With a weary smile he tugged out the splinter, feeling very lucky indeed.

Not for long. The sea had kicked up nastily as he neared the English coast, and a new anxiety kicked up in his heart. Getting the gold had been easy. The next step—pursuading Elizabeth— would be far harder. As he brought his boat alongside Billingsgate Wharf, the city lay quiet in the darkness, and not far from Billingsgate the Tower rose into the moonlit sky. Behind its walls lay Tower Green. Would that execution platform be his final destination?

Not if he could convince Elizabeth. And he had to do that before the Spanish clamored for his head.

He hopped onto the wharf and made fast the *Curlew*'s lines. The King's gold lay below deck, snug under tarpaulins. A rat scurried by him. Watching it disappear among a jumble of empty crates, he remembered offering his son a Spanish piece of eight and the boy peering at him with suspicion and asking, "Did you steal it?" Later, Adam had told Porteous, "I'm no pirate." Now he was.

So be it.

Billingsgate was known for its market where vendors sold fish, fruit, grain from Essex, and salt from France, but mostly fish, and the residue smells from the fishmongers' vacant stalls hung thick in the misty air. The city slept, but the smell of wood smoke and yeast told him that some baker's apprentice nearby had already lit an oven. On the ships moored in the Pool, lantern lights hooked on spars swayed in the breeze, and faint sounds echoed across the water of men waking, coughing, clanking breakfast pots in galleys. A horse and wagon clattered by on the wharf's cobbles. Adam walked west on Thames Street, his way lighted by the first pearly flush of dawn. To convince Elizabeth, he needed a banker.

He reached Lombard Street where the grand houses of foreign merchants stood cheek by jowl with narrow shops. He knocked on the massive door of the dark-timbered, three-story mansion of the Genoese merchant banker, Benedict Spinola.

A footman opened the door, stifling a yawn and a look of annoyance. He lifted his lantern to inspect the too-early caller and frowned at the dried blood on Adam's sleeve. Warily, he asked him to return in two hours because his master was still abed. Adam pushed past the fellow. He climbed the broad staircase where a lavish chandelier, its candles out, hovered in gloom.

Adam pushed open the bedchamber door. "Signore Spinola?"

The sleep-rumpled man, startled from slumber, struggled to his elbow. "Who's there?"

"Sir Adam Thornleigh. I have a catch at Billingsgate that you'll want to see."

❧ 18 ❧

Evidence

York was a maze of crowded streets and footpath byways, but Justine had no trouble finding Monk Bar, the imposing four-story arched gatehouse in the city's Roman wall. Her destination was the narrow brick house that stood directly across from it. Rented for the clerks of the inquiry, this house was Will's lodging. The early-morning sun winking through Monk Bar brightened his front door, which Justine took as an encouraging sign. She needed one. She had come to find the letters being used in evidence against Mary. Will had said his job was to make copies of them. Of course, there was no guarantee that he kept any copies in his lodging—he might keep them, if there were any, at the hall where the inquiry was taking place. But if they were here, she meant to get them.

Evidence, she thought uneasily as she crossed the street to the house. Leaving Bolton Castle, she had been given a scrap of evidence about Alice's killer. She'd been about to mount her horse, the groom snugging the cinch under the horse's belly for her, when a footman delivered a message from Yeavering Hall. A shabby paper with three lines of writing as wobbly as a child's:

Dear Mistress Thornleigh,
The wine man that was running is called Rigaud. Ask
at the French Church, London.
Yr servant,
Jeremy Roper

A name! *Rigaud.* She felt a jolt of exhilaration. Evidence, finally. But . . . of what? Her spirits plunged again, for the carpenter's note gave her no better sense of whether this man Rigaud was a witness to the murder or the murderer himself. Or maybe neither, just someone innocently hurrying through the churchyard. And since she could not get to London to find him, the scrap of information did nothing but torment her. The powerless feeling was maddening.

A little servant girl let her into the house, and Justine went up the stairs and stopped outside Will's door. About to knock, she took a steadying breath. Getting the letters, if she could, meant deceiving Will, which she would rather not do. But did it really matter, since he would never know? She almost wished she *could* tell him. *Then, once everything has come right, he'd be proud of how I managed things.* But she knew the deception was necessary.

She knocked.

The door opened instantly and Will took both her hands and pulled her into the room and closed the door. "What's happened? I hardly slept after getting your message last night. Are you all right?"

The loving concern on his face made her want to throw her arms around him and blurt out everything. But she quickly gathered her wits. She smiled. "I'm fine."

"Thank God. You didn't say *why* you were coming. I was afraid you'd been found out by Mary and needed sanctuary."

"No, no, nothing's changed." She spouted the lie too brightly. Could he see through her false smile?

"So what brings you to York?" His concern for her had turned to puzzlement. "That's a long, cold journey." Still holding her hands, he rubbed them between his to warm them.

"It was, yes. I arrived last night."

"Where are you staying?"

"With a friend of Lord Thornleigh. An agent from his wool trade days. On George Street."

"Ah, near the castle. How did you get leave from Mary?"

"She offered to buy me a new lute, and it gave me the perfect chance to say the best lute maker was here. She sent me to choose an instrument, with a servant as escort. He's at my lodging."

He was clearly waiting for her to explain her visit. "Do you have something urgent to report to me?"

"Well . . . yes. Two Catholic churchmen from Scotland have joined Mary's entourage. An Aberdeen priest named Rowland Baines, and a chaplain from Edinburgh, Archibald Sinclair."

"Ah, good. We actually knew about the priest. I'll ask around about Sinclair. Have you noted any suspicious activity between either of them and Mary?"

"No."

"I see." His puzzled look returned.

"The truth is, Will, I just wanted to see you. I felt terrible about the way we parted on that bleak hillside. It was the shock of hearing you quote Mary's letters. She's been kind to me, you see, and it made me defensive about her. But as soon as I left you I realized I'd been foolish. I came to say I'm sorry."

His smile was so warm, so loving, she hated having to deceive him. "I said some thoughtless things, too," he owned. "I should never have suggested that Mary has bewitched you. You're far too clever for that."

"Clever?" she said with a laugh. "I don't know about that, but I do know my duty to Her Majesty."

"Of course you do." His pride in her shone in his eyes.

It moved her, but flustered her too, because of what she was keeping from him. "I'm sorry if I've startled you, turning up out of the blue."

He grinned. "Best thing that's happened since . . . well, since I saw you last." The warmth in his voice told her he was remembering their kisses on the hillside. She had to turn away.

"So, this is where you live." The room, though small, was pleasant with pale morning sunshine filtering through a mullioned window that overlooked the back garden. Birds chittered in a big beech tree whose bare branches snugged against the window as if for companionship. Justine took note of the desk littered with papers, scrolls, and books. Noted the closed trunk in the corner and the luggage tucked beneath the bed, including what looked like a strongbox. Were the letters inside it?

"I suppose I'm keeping you," she said. "You must have to get to the inquiry."

"I was about to leave when you came."

"Oh, don't let me stop you." She did her best to hide her satisfaction. She had timed her visit perfectly. "I should have waited until the end of the day. I don't want to make you late."

"I'll gladly risk it for a few moments with you. Come, sit down." He was lifting a stack of books off a chair to clear it for her. Justine saw that the two other chairs were also doing double duty as bookshelves, stacked with thick volumes that looked like law books.

"Do your duties here require your *whole* library?" she asked with a smile. She reached the desk and flipped open a volume of Julius Caesar's *The Gallic Wars*. Beside it lay a dog-eared volume of Marcus Aurelius's *Meditations*. "Are you planning an invasion?"

"They are old friends. I hate to travel without them." He looked around for a bare surface on which to put down the books. There was none. Catching Justine's enjoyment at his predicament, he set the books on the floor and added with a grin, "You see how I need Marcus Aurelius's advice on equanimity in the midst of conflict."

It made her smile—Will's orderly mind, his unfailing good humor. Looking into his amused eyes, she almost relaxed. But she did not sit. She hadn't even taken off her cloak. She had come with a square leather satchel whose strap she had slung across her chest like a schoolboy, and she slipped it over her head. "I've brought you something." Lifting the flap, she took out a hand-sized framed square of embroidery depicting a leafy tree with red apples and blue birds, a river flowing by it. She was not a skilled needlewoman. The work could have been done better by many a ten-year-old.

He looked delighted. "Superb."

She laughed. "Mediocre. But all the time I was making it I thought of you, which made me happy. It's the tree of life."

"My love," he said, moved. "I shall hang it by my desk. Right above this." He picked up a black ebony box so small it fit into the palm of his hand. He opened its domed lid to show Justine the contents. A lock of her hair! She had given it to him after pledging their betrothal vows. It lay starkly blond against the ebony black. It almost made her cry.

"I hate this inquiry," she said, unable to hide the tumult in her heart. "It keeps us apart, me with Mary, you here."

"Ah, Justine, it won't last much longer."

"Oh? Has something happened?"

"I feel we're nearing the end. Her Majesty is moving the inquiry to London."

London! For one piercing moment she thought, *I can look for Rigaud.* Then instantly she realized that Mary would stay in Bolton; she had refused to attend any part of the inquiry. Justine would have to stay with her. "But why move the proceedings?" she asked.

"She wants to include her whole council in the deliberations. So, along with the Duke of Norfolk, who will continue to preside, there'll be the Earl of Leicester, Admiral Clinton, the Marquis of Northampton, Sir Nicholas Bacon, and all the rest. Most significantly, she's invited the northern earls, Northumberland and Westmorland. The Catholics, you see? She's heard the rumors about northern gentlemen grumbling at her treatment of Mary, so she's seeking to defuse their discontent." He set the embroidered tree of life beside the locket, propping the frame against a candlestick, and went on with enthusiasm, "It's a fascinating lesson in statecraft and it highlights a difference between the two queens. Elizabeth involves her nobles in decision making, even the dangerous ones, whereas Mary never learned this kind of prudent politicking. By consulting her lords, Elizabeth achieves two things. First, they feel valued and respected. Second," he added with a wink, "it allows her to keep a close eye on them."

Justine felt only indignation at this further affront to Mary. She was sure Mary had not yet been told that the inquiry was moving to the capital, leaving her even more distanced from its doings. They meant to find her guilty, Justine was convinced of it, and equally convinced that a guilty verdict would be the worst outcome. The best for everyone, she was sure, was for Mary to settle in France. Her French friends were offering her a haven where she could live in luxury and ease, her reputation intact, and Elizabeth would no longer be encumbered by her. But if the inquiry branded Mary an adulteress and murderess, her French friends might withdraw their offer. No, Mary needed to fight the accusations and be declared innocent by the inquiry, and then Elizabeth could graciously allow her to retire to France. *Why can no one see this?* Justine thought, her frustration boiling. Well, she meant to hasten the right outcome by getting the letters for Mary. There would be no thanks from Justine's own people, of course; the Thornleighs would never know. Mary alone would be aware of it. *And Father?* she suddenly wondered. *Will Mary tell him?* She was surprised to find that she hoped for it. He, at least, would applaud what she was doing.

"So, Sir William has called me back to London," Will went on. "We'll reconvene at Westminster. I'm glad you came when you did. Two days hence you would have found me gone." He took Justine's hand. Affectionately, he ran the back of his finger gently down her cheek. "It's good news for you and me. I'll be home, and as soon as you're done with Mary, you'll be home, too. Then we can be married."

Home. Jarringly, she thought of Yeavering Hall, her first home. Had Lord Thornleigh stolen it? Had he really murdered her grandfather as her father said? Thornleighs . . . Grenvilles. Would she ever know the truth about the feud? "That's all I want, Will," she managed. "But what about your mother?"

"She'll come round. Uncle Richard convinced me it's best to tell her we're betrothed. He said he'd tell her himself, smooth the way for us. So she'll know by now. Don't worry, Justine, it'll be fine."

She did worry. Will didn't know that her father was Christopher Grenville, but his mother did. Still, his confidence gave her hope. All she could do was take one step at a time.

"What a lot of papers," she said, indicating the stacked documents and books. She forced a laugh. "You'll have a task packing up all this for Westminster. And do the commissioners still have you copying the letters Mary wrote? You said you were sick of reading them."

"Thankfully, that task is over."

"Oh?" He sounded so definitive. Was Mary already doomed? "You mean they've established that the letters are authentic?"

"Not conclusively. The originals are still being examined for the handwriting. There's little doubt, though." He shook his head, muttering, "What a degenerate woman."

The slur on Mary stiffened Justine's determination. "Do you still have copies here? Maybe I can be of help. I've gotten to know Mary quite well—her habits, her ways of thinking. Perhaps I could spot some references in the letters that would establish her guilt."

He stared at her. It made her so nervous her heart thumped.

"A good idea," he said, clearly intrigued. "But unfortunately not feasible. I cannot let anyone see the letters. But thank you for offering." He smiled. "You *are* clever."

She scarcely heard the last words, excited by what he had implied. He *did* have copies. Otherwise, why say he could not show them?

A church bell clanged somewhere across the city. Will heard it and frowned, looking torn. "Justine, forgive me, but I must get to the morning session. I hate to leave you, but—" He shrugged with a stoic look. "Duty calls." He grabbed his cloak off a hook and draped it over his arm, then took her elbow. "Come," he said more cheerfully, "I'll walk you to George Street first. We can talk on the way. And not about dry matters of state. About us."

She didn't move. "Oh, I don't mind staying. They must let you leave at noon for dinner. Come back then and we can eat together." She whirled her cloak off her shoulders and tossed it on the bed.

He frowned. "That's no good. You'd be alone for hours."

"Really, I'll be fine." She added lightly, nodding at the volume of Caesar on his desk, "I'll reacquaint myself with the conquest of Gaul."

He looked uncomfortable. "I mean, it wouldn't *look* good. You staying in my room. There are fellows here who would see it the wrong way."

"They won't know. I'll keep the door closed. And be as quiet as a mouse."

He shook his head. "It's not what I want for you. Nor for me, for that matter, because . . . well, there are documents here that I'm responsible for."

The letters, she was sure! "Come, come, Will, this is *me*."

"I know that. But the other fellows don't. No, come along now and I'll walk you to your lodging."

He sounded adamant, though he was smiling. Justine's thoughts tripped, trying to find a way to stay. Delay him? Keep him here until he was late for the session? Then he would have no time to walk her to George Street. It was her only hope. "Oh, Will, please don't go yet. We've only just said hello."

"Believe me, I don't want to. But I must."

She stepped close to him. "I've missed you so much." It was the truth, and so was the emotion that made her voice waver. "That day we were betrothed we were so happy. But happiness was snatched from us. It's been awful, not seeing you for months." She brought her lips so close to his she could smell a hint of cloves on his breath. "All I want is for us to be together."

His eyes were on her mouth. "So do I," he said with feeling. "And we shall be."

"But when?" She caressed his cheek, the stubble of his beard rough on her fingertips. "We're almost married. Yet so far apart."

"Not for long, I promise you."

"Oh, Will, what I'm trying to tell you is . . ." She looked down, shook her head. "I'm no good at this. I'm no coquette." She looked him in the eye. "I can only show you straight out." She took his cloak from his arm and tossed it on the bed beside hers. She kissed him. A deep, needy kiss. The need was not a lie, for the moment his lips pressed hers, desire sparked through her.

He pulled back his head to look at her in wonder. "I want no coquette. Only you." He kissed her with longing. "You are my love, my life. You know that, don't you?"

"I know I want to be your wife," she whispered. "Isn't that what you want?"

He swallowed hard. "Nothing more."

"I don't want to wait. Do you?"

"I want . . ." He pulled her away to arm's length as though forcing himself. "To get you to your lodging. Come." He made a move for their cloaks.

She stopped him, kissing his cheek, his chin, his throat, his lips. "No. Stay. Please."

He resisted for one moment more, then suddenly wrapped his arms around her and pulled her to him with a groan. His hardness against her made her take a small gasp. The strength in his arms as he held so tightly her made her breathless. She tried to keep her mind detached enough to think ahead to the task she had come to do, but as he held her, pressing her to him, *this* was all she wanted to do. Everything in her yearned for him for his own wonderful self, his warm, hard body.

She caressed his face with both hands. He bent his head and kissed her throat. His hands were on her hips, clasping her close, then sliding up the front of her bodice and over her breasts. He tugged loose the strings of her chemise at her throat, and his lips and tongue slid over the skin of her bosom, making her shiver.

She tugged off the pearled hair band that held back her hair, and he slid his hands through her hair, all the while kissing her mouth. She fumbled to unfasten the lacings of his doublet. He wrenched the doublet off and dropped it, and she opened his shirt and spread her hands on his chest, kissing his warm skin. He unfastened the ties of her bodice and she wriggled out of her heavy garments and let them fall. Standing in her chemise, she tingled at the sudden lightness, the freedom. Her fingers brushed his erection and at her surprise and wonder he gave a quick, excited laugh. She laughed, too, knowing her inexperience made her clumsy, but wanting him so much she didn't care. She opened her mouth to his and grabbed his hair to get more of him, and to steady her weakening legs.

He took her in his arms, lifting her, and carried her to the bed. They lay looking at each other, wide-eyed, hungry to see, to touch, to taste. His kisses were fast on her bare shoulder, her arm, her neck, his hand on her breast. Her nipple under the chemise was hard against his palm. His mouth was hot on her throat. His stubbled chin roughed her cheek. Heat surged through her.

He shoved up her chemise, cool air sweeping her thighs. His hot hand slid up the inside of her thigh. She gasped . . . could not catch her breath. The swirl of heat was all she felt, and the craving for more of him. She wriggled to get his hand higher, get his fingers to her wetness. Her mouth opened and her legs opened, every part of her spreading from the pulsing heat in her belly. She groped for his erection, which strained at his codpiece. He wrenched the codpiece aside and entered her. Fire shot into her and she gave a small cry, a sound that made him stop, his breathing hard, a glassy gleam of mastery in his eyes. At his stopping, fire licked through her, a torture of yearning for his hardness again. He thrust into her. Again and again and again. She arched and wrapped her leg around his to hold him tight, her body beyond her control. With his next thrust, the hot wave inside her crested and she clung to his back as pulses quivered through her.

After, they lay on their backs, dazzled, catching their breath. She felt him turn his head to her and she turned to look at him. Love shone in his eyes. His chest heaved, gradually calming. Justine could not speak for holding on to the thrill, her body atingle, her heart choked with love.

He ran his hand gently over her cheek. "Justine, did I . . . hurt you?"

"No. It was . . . wonderful."

He grinned. "You. *You* are wonderful." His face gentled. He said soberly, quietly, "Now, we are man and wife in the eyes of God."

She could not hold back tears of joy. She had loved Will from the moment she saw him as a child of eight. The truth rose to her lips. "It's all I ever wanted."

He kissed her softly. "My love."

Bells clanged. Will, startled, flopped onto his back. "Oh, Lord," he said with a blink of dismay, "I'm late." He bounded to his feet and turned away, fastening his codpiece, jamming his shirt into his breeches. "Justine, I'm so sorry . . . I must go. The session."

She sat up quickly in her rucked-up chemise, throwing her bare legs over the bed's edge. "Yes, of course you must. I understand."

"Oh, God," he groaned, "it's awful to leave you like this. I'll have to go straight to the hall." He grabbed his doublet from the floor and thrust his arms in, turning back to her. "Can you make your way to George Street?"

"Of course. Don't worry about me."

"I'm sorry. I meant to take you, but—"

"I think, my love, you just did."

He laughed, happily flustered. He bent and kissed her, still tying the last lacing of his doublet. He ran his hand lovingly over her bare knee. "I'll come to your lodging after the session. All right? We can have supper together. Where's the house?"

She told him and gave him the name of her host. The church bells kept clanging. Will grabbed his cloak. Justine felt suddenly shy, sitting in just her chemise. She tugged it down over her knees. "I'll let myself out." She indicated her garments in a heap on the floor. "It will take a little time to make myself presentable."

He looked at her as if his heart was too full to speak. He kissed her again, a lingering kiss that told her everything he could not put into words. "Until this evening," he whispered.

Then he was gone.

Alone in the silence, Justine felt a rush of shame. She had got what she wanted—she was free now to search for the letters—but at what cost? She had used Will. Pretended and contrived and maneuvered so that he would have no choice but to leave her alone here. And she had bargained her maidenhead to do it. Her first union with Will, which should have been a moment of pure and open trust, she had degraded.

She stood up abruptly. What's done was done. And Will, thank God, would never know. She steeled herself for her task. Idiotic not to go through with it after she had paid such a price for it. She made a vow that from that moment on, she would never dissemble to Will again.

She quickly dressed. Smoothing her hair, she looked around the room. Where to start? The desk. Shoving aside the volumes of Caesar and Aurelius, she examined the scatter of papers. Most were in

Will's handwriting. Lists of names, witnesses perhaps. There was a memorandum to himself in the form of questions and answers about the various potential conclusions of the inquiry. Many scrawled notes, apparently about witnesses' depositions. Other papers were letters of instruction from Sir William Cecil. She unfurled a scroll. The cramped handwriting that covered it, neither Will's nor Cecil's, was in Latin, and though she had some knowledge of the language this was legal terminology, all but incomprehensible to her. Another scroll was the same. She opened a ledger. Accounts: money Will had spent on his room, meals, paper and ink, candles, stabling, oats for his horse.

There were two drawers. She pulled open the one on the left. More notes in Will's hand, these in Latin. A small volume of Cicero, bristling with scraps of paper. A broken quill pen. Some walnuts. She suddenly remembered the strongbox under the bed. The most secure place for important documents.

She went down on her knees and dragged out the green leather-clad box bound with bands of iron. It wasn't large, not much bigger than one of Will's law books, but it was heavy. She examined the lock, feeling around it, prodding the lid, thinking there must be a key somewhere, or perhaps she could somehow break it, when the lid lifted. A laugh of surprise escaped her. It hadn't been locked! She raised the top. Inside were three seals of brass, the marks of Cecil's office, each one the size of a goblet's diameter. And there was a leather pouch. She tugged it open. Gold coins. Nothing else lay on the bare base of the box. No documents. No papers of any kind.

She shoved the strongbox back under the bed and pulled out the luggage, two leather satchels, and opened both. Linen shirts, breeches, hose, a pair of boots. It felt distasteful to be rooting around in Will's things. And foolish. He was too orderly to cram important papers in with his shirts and hose.

She tried the trunk in the corner. More books. Would he put the letters inside a book? She opened the top volume and leafed through it. No papers. In any case there were eight letters, so at least that many sheets, probably more, too many to stuff inside a book.

The right-hand drawer in the desk. She had not tried it. She went back to open it and was surprised to find it locked. Excitement jolted through her. Where would he keep the key? She pawed through the items in the other drawer. No key. She looked under every document and book on top of the desk. Did he keep the key with him? She could only hope not. She jiggled the drawer, angry at its immovability, and tried to force it open, jerking it so roughly that her framed embroidery that he had propped against the candle trembled and fell. The tree of life. She felt a dart of shame and set it back in place. Her eyes fell on the little ebony box beside it. Her heartbeat quickened. She lifted the domed lid. With her fingertip she moved aside the thick lock of her hair. A key lay nestled beneath. Excited, she slid the key into the drawer's lock and turned. It clicked. She opened the drawer.

Creamy vellum pages lay in a neat, shallow stack. On the top page, handwriting in sloping, orderly loops. Will's handwriting.

Justine read: *I have not seen him this night for ending your bracelet.* Her heart lurched. Mary made bracelets for people she liked, men as well as women. *Send me word whether your will have it, and more money, and how far I may speak.* She scanned to the end. *Burn this letter, for it is too dangerous.* Hand trembling, she lifted the page and read on the next one, *I remit myself wholly to your will, and send me word what I shall do, and whatsoever happens to me, I will obey you.* Further on, *He has great suspicion, but nevertheless trusts upon my word.*

Justine found she was holding her breath in excitement. She had found what she'd come for. Mary, writing to Bothwell. Was it genuine evidence of her guilt, or forged lies? Justine didn't know, and right now the answer did not matter. Carefully, she scooped up the pages—it felt like about a dozen—and slid them into her schoolboy satchel.

Down the stairs she hurried, then out the front door. She headed for the spiked towers of York Minster. The city was bustling. Carts clattered in and out under the arch of Monk Bar. A farmer shouted to the cattle he walked behind, driving them in to market. Outside an alehouse, apprentices rolled barrels down a slide off a wagon. A gentleman on a tall gray horse walked his mount alongside a churchman all in black, the two of them arguing. Justine turned onto Minster Yard, passing a scatter of people coming to and from the great church. She went inside. The massive vaulted space was purpled by light filtered through the huge stained glass window in the shape of a rose. Like every great church, the Minster's nave was a hub of business. Merchants met to trade information. Servingmen lounged, looking to be hired. Ladies met to gossip. An old woman hawked pastries from the basket on her hip. Justine went to the table where two scriveners available for hire by illiterate townsfolk sat at their portable desks amid their wares of papers, quills, and inkpots. A skinny young man wearing a leather apron crusted with dark dry blood, a butcher apparently, was dictating a letter to his mother.

Justine approached the other scrivener, a stooped man with ink-blacked fingertips and a face lined in furrows. He was sharpening his quill with a penknife. "How quickly can you copy these?" she asked, pulling the letters from her satchel.

He perused her fine clothes, gave a cursory look at the pages, mentioned an inflated price, and waited to see if she would accept.

"I didn't ask the price, only the swiftness of your work. There's half a crown more than you quoted if you can do it in an hour."

His eyebrows shot up at his luck. "An hour it is, mistress."

She didn't want anyone to see her. The inquiry had drawn scores of men, and some might be in the church or its busy yard. Many would know Lord Thornleigh, and some might know her as his ward. It was safest to not loiter. Will's house was near. She left the church feeling a glow of accomplishment and returned to his room to wait.

The room made her feel safe and content, surrounded by his things. She tidied the bed, a flush warming her face at the thought of what they had done. She was Will's true wife now in all but ceremony. They would spend their lives together and would always love each other as they did today. She leaned against the window casement, arms folded, and watched a squirrel scamper along a beech bough. Something about the bare branch, smoke rising behind it from the landlord's kitchen chimney, made her think of the bakehouse at Yeavering Hall. She had looked at it from her window as a child. Home. With a pang, she thought of her father, her meeting with him on the battlements, a meeting so brief she had scarcely had time to catch her breath at seeing him again, let alone sort her jumbled emotions before he had to leave her, hurrying away lest he be seen. Brief though her time with him had been, she had heard eight years' worth of pain in his voice. How hard life must have been for him after he fled Yeavering Hall. Wandering French roads, ill and weak, penniless, cut off from all he had known at home and all he once possessed. And now, back in England, his life was no less hard, for he was a fugitive, risking his life to serve Mary. When he had embraced her Justine had been moved by his affection for her, but she was not sure she felt the same. He had been out of her life for so long, and for years she had thought of him as a traitor. Lord Thornleigh had taken her in and treated her like a fond father, and she loved him. But now her true father was back, and his tales of the Thornleighs' crimes appalled her. She was no longer sure what to think of either of them, or their feud. One aspect of it, though, was clear: their immoveable loyalties. Her father was Mary's champion, Lord Thornleigh was Elizabeth's.

And I? she asked herself. The question bewildered and vexed her, for the choice seemed a false one. By helping Mary she would not be harming Elizabeth. Elizabeth had everything: a throne, faithful subjects, security. Mary had nothing. It gave Justine a chill to realize that the state of the two queens mirrored that of the two men: Lord Thornleigh had everything, her father nothing.

"Justine?"

She whirled around. Will! She hadn't heard the door open. "What's wrong?" she asked, tense as she glanced at the desk drawer, the ebony box. She had put everything back the way it was.

"I forgot the witness list." He frowned. "Are you all right? You look pale."

"I'm fine."

He relaxed. He went to the desk and Justine held her breath. He grabbed a scroll and came to her, grinning. "I blame you. I'll be lucky if can remember my own name today, for thinking about you." He kissed her. Then looked puzzled. "I thought you'd be gone by now."

"I wanted a little while longer here, amongst your things. You're not the only one who can't think of anything else."

They kissed again. Then Will said he had to go, and for good this time, and so should she. There was nothing she could say to resist, so they went down the stairs together arm in arm, she nuzzling close, he murmuring again about meeting her for supper. Outside the front door, they stopped. "Off you go," she said, smiling. "I won't be responsible for making you late twice."

He grinned and took a step to leave, but his eyes were still on her and he stopped and gazed at her as if longing to kiss her right here in the street with people all around.

"Mistress?"

Justine was startled to see the stooped old scrivener bustling toward her.

"I finished *before* an hour," he said proudly. "If you feel you'd like to top up that half crown, I won't complain." He was presenting her the letters in two hands. "Originals," he said lifting one hand. "Copies," lifting the other.

Will stared at the papers. He didn't move. For Justine the noise of the street had been sucked into a tortured silence. Later, she would remember the slowness of Will's motions. His slow look at her. His slow breaths. As if weights in his mind were dragging every thought down to die. As if he didn't *want* to think. Without looking at the scrivener, his eyes on her, he pulled coins from his pocket and offered them to the man. "I will take the papers for this lady." His voice did not sound like Will's. Even the scrivener seemed alarmed by its steeliness, and he handed Will the letters, took the money, and was gone.

"Will, before you—"

"Who are you taking these to? Please, tell me it's my uncle."

There was no point in lying. She had to make him understand. "No. To Mary."

He looked as though she had struck him. "Why, in God's name?"

"So she can fight back. The secrecy of this trial is a mockery of English justice. You should be ashamed to be part of it."

"It is not a trial."

"Mary's *life* is on trial. I told her about the letters and she assured me that they are forgeries, and that if she could see them she could fight them."

He blinked in disbelief. "Assured *you* . . ."

"Will, this is best for everyone. If the inquiry finds Mary innocent, she'll be able to retire to France and live there in honorable privacy, and Her Majesty will never have to bother with her again. You see? It's a conclusion tolerable to both queens. It's best for *everyone*."

He was staring at her as if he had never seen her before. A chill crawled over her skin.

"It's tantamount to treason." Stiffly, he still held the papers exactly as the scrivener had delivered them, in both hands, and Justine saw the pages quivering, his grip so shaky. He looked down at the writing as if hoping some answer lay there. He found none. His voice was raw. "I'll have to tell my uncle. He'll have to tell Elizabeth."

She gasped. "No. I beg you—"

"I have to." Tears glinted in his eyes. "How can I . . . trust you?" He shook his head with an angry jerk to clear the tears.

She gripped his arm. She felt dizzy. "Will, don't talk like that. Of course you can trust me. I love you, I would do anything for you. This is about *other* people."

"My life is with those people. My uncle. Sir William. Elizabeth. Who are *you* with?"

"You! We are one, you and I. You said it yourself, man and wife in the eyes of God."

"So we are. I cannot change that." He shook off her hand. "But I will never trust you again."

The world fractured, the air splintered. Frozen, she watched him turn and walk into the house. When he shut the door, the sound was an axe in her heart.

❧ 19 ❧

Elizabeth's Command

Hoarfrost and cold fog kept the wintery gardens of Hampton Court Palace barren of people, but the palace courtyards, galleries, and public chambers bustled with courtiers, visiting dignitaries, merchants, clerks, pages, and servants. Queen Elizabeth was in residence.

Adam crossed the noisy great hall where people milled around trestle tables laden with food, then marched straight into the great watching chamber where Yeomen of the Guard stood on duty. He gripped a scroll he had brought Elizabeth, his hand around it damp with sweat. Adam had taken many risks in his life, but none as hazardous as this. The chests of gold from the *Nuestra Señora* still lay hidden under tarps on his boat at Billingsgate next to scruffy fishing smacks and wherries. Having stolen a fortune, he now had to convince Elizabeth to take it. If he could not, the scroll he held might be his death warrant.

He found the watching chamber crowded with men and women in showy courtiers' finery, all of them waiting to see Elizabeth. Some lounged on benches, some chatted and laughed by the hearth, some whispered in corners. The door to the presence chamber was closed and guards flanked it, but they had admitted Adam often, as they did all of Elizabeth's councilors and close friends, and he made straight for the door. Nevertheless, a hush

fell as he crossed the room and every face turned to him in astonished curiosity. They knew he had been banished from court in
disgrace. He paid them no mind. But he did note a huddle of
somberly dressed men glaring at him and hissing Spanish. Among
them was Guerau de Spes, the crane-thin Spanish ambassador, his
narrow face tight with resentment. It was Adam's attack on this
man's cousin that had got him banished. De Spes stepped into his
path, forcing him to halt. Their eyes locked. The Spaniard said in
heavily accented English, "The brute returns." His thin lip curled
with contempt. "Like a dog to his vomit."

Adam wanted to cut the man's tongue out. But the guards
would evict any brawler, friend of Elizabeth or not. He mimed a
head butt and flicked his hands in de Spes's face, not touching
him, just looking comically fierce as one would to fright a child in
jest. The Spaniard started, alarmed for a moment. Then his face
flared red at the humiliating insult.

Adam was glad, a cheap satisfaction though it was. He sidestepped de Spes and told the guard at the door, "I come with news
for Her Majesty."

The guard looked unsure, as though worried he had not been
told that Adam's banishment had been lifted. "Sir, Her Majesty is
about to meet with Ambassador de Spes."

"It's urgent." Adam indicated the scroll. "She must hear this
news without delay." He didn't wait for a reply but opened the
door himself. As it closed behind him he heard the voices at his
back crescendo, the courtiers gabbling in excitement at his bold-
ness, the Spaniards protesting in anger. None of them mattered to
Adam. Only the woman before him. Elizabeth.

She stood at the other end of the chamber with three of her
ladies. This high-ceilinged, opulent room was where she gave audience to important persons, but there was no one else at the moment, and Adam felt the empty space between them like a chasm.
She was dressed in a stiff, bejeweled gown of crimson and gold
elaborately embroidered, so unlike the simple black velvet she
often favored when he had seen her alone at her desk over paperwork, her gold-red hair a finer ornament than any jewels. She stood
near the presence chair, her throne, above which hung a golden

cloth of estate. No one but she was allowed to stand under it. Two of her young ladies were preparing her, one holding a jewel-rimmed mirror up to Elizabeth's face while the other primped her rigid lace ruff, though Elizabeth had turned her head to see who had come in prematurely. Her eyes widened in surprise, and Adam read a flicker of joy in them as he crossed the room to her and bowed. But when he straightened, a stormy look swept her face.

"Leave us," she told her ladies.

They curtsied and turned away in a swirl of silks and perfume and disappeared into Elizabeth's private apartments.

"Was I not clear in conveying my pleasure to you, sir?" she asked with quiet iciness. "You were to confine yourself to the delights of your family at Chelsea."

"You always make your pleasure clear," he said, trying a smile, hoping the bond of their past intimacy was strong enough for what he was attempting. "But I could not stay home. I had urgent business to transact on your behalf."

"*My* behalf?" she scoffed. "I sent you on no business."

"No, you were remiss. I went anyway." He handed her the scroll, his heart beating fast. "This will explain why."

She took the scroll but did not look at it. Her dark eyes stayed on him, narrowing dangerously. "You take too much liberty, Adam."

The door opened and Elizabeth's chamberlain stepped in. He bowed, looking flustered. "Pardon, Your Majesty, but Ambassador de Spes is insistent in requesting that you honor his appointment."

"Tell my good friend Señor de Spes that the pleasure of seeing him will be mine in just a moment." She spoke calmly, but Adam knew her well and read the strain she was hiding. A look passed between them, and when the chamberlain left, she allowed Adam a dark half smile. "In truth, I would rather stick pins in my eyes. De Spes is a fanatic." Her face turned sober. "However, some of us know our duty. Mine is to keep peace between our nations. Yours, at the moment, is to stay out of trouble. And you are courting vast trouble by flaunting yourself to that man after you killed his cousin." She jerked the scroll toward him, unread, for him to take back.

He raised his hands. "Just read this and hear me—"

"No, I cannot afford your insolence." She prodded his chest with the scroll, leaving him no choice but to take it. "De Spes is here to vent his outrage, and with cause. The *Nuestra Señora*, a Spanish ship carrying Philip's gold, was attacked by pirates and the gold taken. Eighty-five thousand pounds! De Spes is livid and says the pirates were English. He will demand hard retribution from me, you can be sure." She let out a frustrated puff of breath. "I cannot keep him waiting. Go home, Adam." She let her fingertips brush his sleeve and she added quietly, sadly, "Go back to your wife."

"My place is with you, Elizabeth. Protecting your rights. You need to stand up to these Spanish bastards. That's why I'm here."

She frowned in angry bemusement. "Do you *willfully* misunderstand? Do you really not know how dangerously relations between us and Spain have deteriorated?"

"I cuffed his cousin—whose weak heart killed him, by the way. I can hardly be blamed for that."

"You poured oil on the flames! Which makes you the *last* person I would entrust to put out the fire." She cast a sharp glance at the door behind which de Spes waited, and Adam saw her deep anxiety. "That Spanish bull is snorting to come at me."

"Let him. We can outmaneuver him *and* his master. I have brought—"

"Stop!" She took a breath, collecting herself. "Philip has fifteen thousand battle-hardened soldiers stationed in the Netherlands under the Duke of Alva. That's a mere hundred miles off my coast. They could invade us overnight, and I can raise no such army to defend us. War, Adam, turning our peaceful pastures red with English blood. No, I dare not openly defy Philip."

It sent a stab of dread through him. Had he misjudged her? Had he made a fatal mistake? "Elizabeth, the Spaniards have already massacred Englishmen. *My* men. Being timid with them only invites more assault. Philip responds only to strength. Show him you are a force to be reckoned with."

"But I am not. I am weak. He is strong."

"Not as strong as before his gold was taken from the *Nuestra*

Señora." The words were out, surprising even himself. But it was what he had come for, and he seized the risk. He had to make her see the way to help herself—and him. "Nine chests. Eighty-five thousand pounds' worth of gold in ingots and coin."

"Nine chests . . . ?" The shocked look on her face turned to suspicion. "How do you know that?"

"As I said, I have been seeing to your interests."

She gaped at him. "*You* attacked that ship?"

"For you." He gripped her arm to press upon her the urgency. The opulent fabric was stiff in his hand. "All I ask is a tenth part." He added grimly, "The Spaniards owe it to me."

She shook off his hand, then slapped him. "Damn your eyes! I told you I would send you to the Tower if you did this. Now, by God, I will." She turned and called, "Guards!" She started for the door.

Adam caught her elbow and spun her around. His heart was in his mouth. "You said you'd send me to the Tower if I attacked their New World treasure fleet. I haven't."

Her eyes blazed fury. She said quietly, dangerously, "Do not underestimate me."

The door burst open and four guards pounded in, swords drawn, followed by the chamberlain, who shouted at Adam, "Unhand Her Majesty!"

"Elizabeth," Adam said under his breath to her, pleading, "I am the only one who does *not* underestimate you. Hear me out."

The guards surrounded them and hands yanked Adam away from Elizabeth. They started dragging him away so quickly he could not get his balance, let alone resist. The scroll tumbled from his grip. People had crowded outside the open door to watch. De Spes was pushing through them to see, his face was alight with satisfaction at the guards' rough handling of Adam. Elizabeth was looking straight at the Spaniard and Adam saw her stiffen. The sight of de Spes's malicious joy seemed to send a shiver through her.

"Stop," she commanded the guards. "I have thought better. Leave Sir Adam with me. I will question him."

They halted, and Adam, in a burst of relief, threw off their restraining hands. But the chamberlain looked aghast. "Alone, Your Majesty?"

"Alone, yes. Wait outside."

"At least let me disarm him."

She nodded. Adam winced as his sword was wrenched from its scabbard and the dagger from his boot.

"Now leave us," Elizabeth said, "and shut the door."

As soon as she and Adam were alone, her whole manner changed. Concern flooded her eyes. "We must get you out of here. If de Spes finds out that you are the pirate, he will send someone to cut your throat." She opened the door to her private apartments. "Dorothy," she said in a quiet summons. When a matronly lady appeared in the doorway, Elizabeth said, "Take Sir Adam out through the closet passage to the garden."

She turned back to him and put her hand on his shoulder, urging him to go. "Follow Lady Stafford. She will take you a secret way."

He didn't move. His heart swelled, seeing how she could not hide her love for him. *No more than I can hide how I love her.* He lifted her hand to his mouth and kissed it, then looked her in the eye. "My throat is my business, Elizabeth. And glad I am to risk it for your sake." Her tender smile and the soft gleam of her gaze felt almost reward enough. *Almost.* He said to the waiting gentlewoman, "Thank you, Lady Stafford, but I will leave as I came in."

At his refusal, Elizabeth looked pained, but she nodded a dismissal to the lady, who curtsied, then disappeared back down the corridor. Elizabeth shook her head at Adam with fond exasperation. "What am I to do with you? You have committed monstrous piracy. All the laws of God and man compel me to have you arrested."

He picked up the scroll from the floor. "You are not compelled to do anything. You've always done what you wanted, even in the teeth of your whole council. For years they have harangued you to marry, but you have not taken a husband."

"You are wrong. I am compelled to do whatever it takes to protect my people. *That* is why I have not married, to save them from a king who does not love them as I do. And now, damn you, I must protect them from Philip."

"Elizabeth, hear me. The gold on the *Nuestra Señora* was going to pay Philip's troops in the Netherlands. To pay them now he'll have to tax the Dutch, and they already so hate the Spanish boot on their neck they will turn against him. Philip will have his hands too full to attack you."

"Are you brainsick? You may have started a war. A war that I will lose!" She rubbed her temples, trying to cope with the crisis. "I'll have to apologize to Philip. Where is the gold? I'll have to send a warship to escort it to the Netherlands."

"No, you don't. That's what I came to tell you. You can keep it for yourself."

"Have you lost your wits? Me? Keep Philip's gold?"

"Ah, but it's not his. It's a loan. From the Genoese banker Benedict Spinola. Do you know him? He lives here in London."

"Cecil does business with him. What does this signify?"

"Spinola's agents in Spain were shipping the gold to Philip's troops, but since it didn't reach its destination it's still Spinola's property. He can loan it to someone else if he wants. I talked to him this morning, persuaded him that since the money is now in London, he would do better loaning it to the Queen of England rather than risking it on the seas." He unfurled the scroll. "This is Spinola's offer. The same interest rate he offered Philip, ten percent, payable in Antwerp. He's waiting out there, in the long gallery. Do this, Elizabeth. Take the loan. Philip won't be able to pay his army. And with the gold, you can raise your own."

She stared at him so long, with such a tense face, he was suddenly sure he had misjudged the whole mad enterprise. She would not risk war with Spain. He had been an idiot to think she would. She called back the guards and the chamberlain, and Adam's nerve broke. She was going to arrest him after all. He closed his eyes to summon the strength to bear it. A conviction for piracy. Death by hanging.

"Bring Benedict Spinola to me," Elizabeth told her chamberlain. "You'll find him in the long gallery."

Adam looked at her with a jolt. Was she arresting the banker, too, as his accomplice?

"Return Sir Adam's sword," she told the guard. Her eyes

sparkled at Adam as she added to her chamberlain, "And convey to Ambassador de Spes my sincere regret that our meeting must be postponed until tomorrow."

A thin snow swirled around the battlements of Bolton Castle on the Yorkshire moors. Logs blazed in the hearth in Mary's chamber, but the warmth could not touch the chill in Justine's heart. The thirteen days since she had parted from Will had been a torture of shame and dread. She stood at the sideboard pouring Burgundy wine into goblets for Mary and her visitors from York, Lord Herries and Bishop Leslie. The fire crackled in the silence that had fallen over them. They were Mary's lead commissioners at the inquiry and had brought her a grim report. Justine only half listened, her thoughts mired in her own disaster.

"In short, Your Grace," Herries finished, "though it grieves me to tell you, our strategy is in tatters." Gray-haired, erect as a soldier, he stood with his back to the fire, his eyes sunken from fatigue. "These so-called casket letters spell the ruin of your claim."

Bishop Leslie nodded anxiously from his chair. An injury to his ankle had forced him to sit, though in Mary's presence. Both men were staunch supporters of her royal rights. "Moray has found the weapon to smite you. Your own words."

"Forged," Mary said coldly. "As you well know." She paced at the window, hugging herself as though the snow that fell outside it fell on her.

Justine caught the look that passed between the two men, a glance fraught with meaning. It seemed to her that they accepted the letters as authentic, sight unseen. Still, they remained committed to defending Mary. "Be that as it may," the bishop said, "your options are dwindling."

Justine herself could scarcely bear to look at Mary. When she had returned from her devastating visit to Will, she had told Mary only that she had failed to get the letters. Mary had been greatly downcast but had not blamed her, had even thanked her for trying. Justine had not confessed what really happened—that Will had discovered her in the act of getting the letters copied. For two weeks she had relived the horror of that moment on the street. His trembling hand as he held the pages. His stricken look at her. The waver in his voice as he said he would have to tell his uncle about her deceit and Lord Thornleigh would have to tell Elizabeth. Justine had wished the street would crack open between them and swallow her. How could she live with the shame? And what would happen now? What would they do? How would they punish her?

For two weeks she had dragged around, reeling from the wound in her heart, dazed by her disgrace, plagued by a headache that pounded day and night. Ragged from lack of sleep, she would watch the dawn break, her legs feeling too heavy to get out of bed. Mary had noticed and asked if she was ill, and Justine had not been able to hold back the tears. But she maintained her tale that she wept from her failure to get the letters. She kept secret her own personal calamity. To mention the trail that led from Will to Lord Thornleigh to Elizabeth would be to confess her purpose in being sent here: to spy. In fury, Mary might cast her out on the frigid moor. Yet what *was* her purpose here now? Justine's thoughts stumbled over themselves, and she felt she was half in exile already, adrift on the heath, wandering between the camps of Elizabeth and Mary, belonging to neither.

Yet two weeks had passed and no word had come from London. In her sleepless nights she had wondered over and over why Elizabeth had not recalled her. She imagined all sorts of scenarios: They had decided that recalling her might alert Mary that she was an agent for Elizabeth. Or the opposite: They simply considered her too small a cog in the machinery of state to be a concern. Or might Lord Thornleigh, in his fondness for her, have kept silent? She prayed for that. Even tried to make herself believe that Will might not have told his uncle at all, that he hadn't had the heart. *Because he loves me.*

No, *loved* me, she thought, her hope spiraling into despair for the hundredth time. Never would she forget the way he had looked at her, like she was a stranger, a liar, someone foul. That look had blasted their betrothal vows of loyalty and love. *No, I blasted them.*

It took all her willpower to calmly hand Lord Herries a goblet of wine, and when she went back to the sideboard she gripped its edge to hold herself steady, not let Mary and the men see her misery as they went on talking about the inquiry. She felt sick to death of the inquiry for the wretchedness it had brought her. She wished she might never hear another word about it, wished she could be left alone to weep. All she had ever wanted was to prove to Will that she was a true Thornleigh! Instead, he thought her a traitor. He hated her. She didn't know how she could endure it.

"When we reconvene in London, Your Grace, all of Elizabeth's council will have considered the letters, so there will be little time left," Bishop Leslie was saying. "Once again I urge you to make a defense. Our strategy to hold Moray to account for his treason must be abandoned. Now that he has made these charges against you, you must answer them or else be thought guilty by all the world."

"A queen is not bound to answer to her subjects!" Mary cried. Justine looked at her in weary wonder. Since the beginning of the inquiry Mary had not wavered in holding to this single principle, that her royalty conferred special status. "I will appear before Elizabeth and no one else. I have written her again and again entreating this of her. Let her call me to her, queen to queen, and I shall make my case." Head high, she continued to pace.

The men exchanged a glance that showed their alarm at her self-delusion. "She will not call you," the bishop said. "She has made it clear that she cannot do so in good conscience while you are under suspicion of such . . . crimes."

"And meanwhile our enemies have her ear," Herries said, his voice a growl of disgust. "She has given an audience to Moray."

Mary whirled around in fury. "What?"

"The moment we were adjourned to London, Moray rode there as fast as horse would carry him."

"She has seen *him* but refuses *me?*"

The bishop reminded her, with pain in his voice, "He is not under suspicion."

A wild light leapt in Mary's eyes. "Then change that! Charge *him* with Darnley's death."

They stared at her, astonished. So did Justine. The idea was so rash, so erratic.

"It is the truth, I know it," Mary said. "He snared Bothwell into the plot. Bothwell may have done the deed, but Moray was the mastermind. His whole scheme was to remove Bothwell by getting him charged with the murder. I tell you, call Moray to account for murdering my husband."

Herries found his voice. "Even if it were true, it is too late. To hurl such counter-charges would only weaken your case."

"Why?" she demanded.

The bishop pointed out with great forbearance, "Is there evidence?"

"Find some," she commanded. "As Moray has done. If he can produce letters, so can we."

They gaped at her. Herries cleared his throat and said diplomatically, "Your Grace, you are under a great deal of stress. We understand the frustration you feel. But I entreat you to look rationally at—"

"Do not patronize me, sir. It is not *you* Elizabeth keeps in this prison."

"Please." Bishop Leslie held up his hands in a gesture of appeasement. "There is one more tactic we might try. The English commissioners are deliberating on this evidence given to them in private. To express our outrage at the secrecy, and perhaps knock some shame into them, we could withdraw from the inquiry. Withdraw in protest."

Mary instantly was eager. "And then it would be over?"

He shrugged. "Who knows? It would depend on Elizabeth." He added gloomily, "It always has."

"I will take that chance. The one outcome I will not endure is a verdict of guilt." Her face was alight, keen at taking action. "Do it, my lord bishop. Make my protest."

Herries looked horrified. "If you withdraw, you *proclaim* your guilt. That is how the whole world will see it. I beg you, do not cram yourself into that corner."

"Then what?" she wailed. She threw up her hands, abandoning hope. "They drive stakes through my body and I can do nothing to save myself! Nothing!" She let out a cry of despair and sank down onto her knees, covering her face with both hands. She bent over, her forehead almost touching the floor, and wept.

The bishop jumped up in alarm, wincing at the pain from his ankle. Herries had frozen in dismay. Justine rushed to Mary's side. "My lady!" She threw her arm around her waist in pity. Bending to whisper in her ear, she urged Mary to stand. "Do not let them see you like this, my lady. You were born a queen."

Mary groped for Justine's hand with a whimper of gratitude. She raised her head, still looking stricken, but she nodded, wiping her wet cheeks. With Justine's help she got to her feet. She patted Justine's hand in thanks and as a signal to let her go. Justine curtsied and withdrew to the sideboard, feeling shaky herself. She felt an intense kinship with Mary's plight. They were both powerless against a tide of events rushing to drown them.

"Pardon me, my lords," Mary said, summoning her dignity. "You have served me faithfully and I thank you with all my heart. But I ask you now, can nothing be done to save my reputation?"

Another look passed between the men and the bishop gave Herries a solemn nod. Herries took a tense, formal step toward Mary. Justine sensed that whatever he was about to say, he and the bishop had previously discussed it.

"Your Grace, I know I speak for Bishop Leslie and for all your delegation, and indeed for every one of your loyal supporters in Scotland, when I say that we would go on defending you in this arena, the inquiry, until our dying day if that is what you want. However, the outcome looks bleak. And not only for you. There is your son. A verdict of guilt against you could cast suspicion on his legitimacy. I urge you to consider abandoning the treacherous legal quagmire that awaits your case in London, and to take a different course."

"What course?"

"Abdication."

Mary stiffened like a doe sighting fire. "How dare you—"

"I dare, Your Grace, because of the love I bear you. You cannot win in this English arena. You have already lost in Scotland. Accept the loss—do it *before* the inquiry judges you—and leave for France with your head high."

Justine watched in astonishment. Mary's abdication had not crossed her mind, but she immediately saw it would end the crisis in a stroke. And her going to France with dignity was the outcome Justine had always thought best, for both Mary and Elizabeth.

Mary only sneered. "Never. They made me sign my abdication when they had me in their power, but I rallied and raised an army. I repealed the vile decree."

"Ratify it now, Your Grace," said the bishop sadly. "Do it, for the sake of your son."

"Never." Mary's look was steely, but tears welled up and her voice wavered, and Justine read in her face the agonized knowledge that there was little other option if she was to preserve her reputation. She would no longer be a queen, but neither would she be branded an adulteress and a murderer.

"Leave me," Mary told the men. "We will speak further, but I cannot think of this now."

When they left, Justine stayed with Mary. They sat and sewed, neither speaking, both struggling with their own private pain. The fire crackled and the snow fell and dusk crept across the moors by stealth.

Just as the last of the light faded, visitors were announced.

"Sir Walter Mildmay, my lady," Margaret Currier said as she ushered in the arrivals, a stout man who looked in his late forties, with a bony nose and calm gray eyes, and a plump young woman whose cheeks and hands were chapped from the cold. "Sir Walter brings greetings from Her Majesty Queen Elizabeth," Margaret added.

Mary jumped up in excitement and rushed to Mildmay. She grabbed his hand, which made him start in surprise. "Sir," she said eagerly, "do you bring an invitation from my dear cousin? Am I to see her?"

Sir Walter recovered from her shockingly effusive welcome. He bowed with great respect and smiled, but shook his head. "That is not my mission, Your Grace." He had courteously addressed her in French and spoke with an easy mix of friendliness and formality that indicated much experience in diplomacy. "However, I take much pleasure in the mission I *am* entrusted with. Allow me to present my daughter, Winifred." He beckoned the young woman, who stepped forward, blushing, and curtsied.

Mary barely looked at the girl. "Yes, yes, but what message do you being from Elizabeth?"

Mildmay looked unperturbed, smiling again. "My daughter is the message. Her Majesty sends her as your lady-in-waiting."

"I have three," Mary said, vexed. "I need no more."

"Quite so, Your Grace. My daughter is to replace Mistress Thornleigh."

Justine stiffened. Mary gave her a puzzled look. Dread crawled over Justine. For thirteen days she had agonized over what her fate would be. Now the answer had come. Not in words of forgiveness from Lord Thornleigh, as she had prayed, but a cold, impersonal dismissal.

"This young lady is to leave me?" Mary asked, indicating Justine. "Why?"

"Sheer indulgence on the part of Her Majesty, Your Grace," he answered pleasantly. "Lord Thornleigh is her great friend, as you may know, so Her Majesty kindly accommodates his wishes. His wife plans to visit friends in Venice and Lord Thornleigh's wish is to have his ward home that she may accompany his wife abroad. Mistress Thornleigh is to return to London with me."

Justine found it hard to breathe. Lady Thornleigh had no friends in Venice. This was a fabrication, a film of gauze to cover up the truth.

Mary frowned in a moment of resistance, then gave it up and heaved a sigh. "Cherie, I will be sorry to see you go."

Justine barely heard the words. Mildmay was looking at her with his amiable smile, but deep in his eyes she saw a hard glint. He said to her, "Can you be ready in the morning?"

Was he taking her to prison? Fear shot dizziness into her. The room seemed to sway. Every face was turned to her, but the only one she saw was Mildmay's, stonily waiting for an answer. What choice did she have? She swallowed and said, "Of course, sir."

❦ 20 ❦

Kinship

When Christopher Grenville reached the Spanish embassy in London, he was dismayed to find the place in an uproar. Men packed the corridors, arguing and shouting, many jostling to gain admittance to Ambassador de Spes's private chambers. Secretaries were fending off the barrage of questions and demands. There was some crisis, that was clear from the alarm and anger of the petitioners. Though some of them appeared to be Spaniards, most of the voices were English, but in the din Christopher could not tell what had them so upset. He guessed it was connected to news he had heard on the road, that English pirates had stolen treasure from a Spanish ship. The pushing and shouting frayed his nerves, for he was bone-weary from hard riding on the wintry roads, and constantly on edge lest someone recognize him. Every day he spent in London moving about in public, he risked being discovered by someone who knew of his past. The ordeal left him so drained he could have slept for a week, but there was no chance of even resting until he had seen de Spes. He had brought a letter from Mary that had to go immediately to the King of Spain.

He pushed through the jostling bodies but could not get past a tight cluster of men clamoring to get close to an embassy secretary barring the door to de Spes's rooms. The secretary mopped his brow as he tolerated the verbal abuse of a man shouting in his face. Christopher recognized the secretary from one of his clandestine visits to de Spes. "What's happened?" he asked a scowling Londoner next to him.

"We can't get our goods," the man growled. "Bloody Spanish papists!" His answer explained nothing, but before Christopher could ask for more information the man barged toward the secretary.

A thought struck Christopher with alarm. Had Philip recalled his ambassador to protest the piracy? That would spell disaster for Christopher's plan—Mary's plan—to get Philip to support Northumberland's imminent uprising. De Spes was a fervent defender of the Catholic faith and zealous to have the heretic Elizabeth ousted and Mary installed in her place, and Christopher had been working closely with him to get Philip's commitment of Spanish troops. But if de Spes was leaving, Christopher's link to Philip was broken. A new ambassador would know nothing of the plan, and possibly would be horrified if he did. Without Spanish support Northumberland would not act. Mary would not become queen. Christopher would be thrown into wretched exile again, this time forever.

Desperate to see de Spes, he squeezed through the crowd toward the beleaguered secretary. An elbow jabbed his rib as men pushed around him, and he felt a rising sense of panic. The inquiry was reconvening at Westminster, and with the so-called casket letters in hand, the commissioners would almost certainly find Mary guilty of abetting the murder of her husband by her lover. If that happened, Northumberland and Philip might both abandon her. Christopher had to get Philip's commitment before a verdict came. He prayed that the letter he was bringing from Mary would finally push Philip to act.

Letters . . . letters. The one flicker of light in this blackness was Justine's attempt to get copies of the casket letters. She had failed—Mary had told him—but it gave him profound satisfaction that she had tried. He wished he could tell her how proud he was of her. Richard Thornleigh had stolen her as a child and done his best to make her one of them, but she had proved herself a Grenville, loyal to Mary, and it moved Christopher. Thornleigh now had her under his thumb again, though. Justine had been called home, Mary said. It galled him. *Her home is with me. She is my daughter.* If he could ever get Thornleigh alone he would ram a dagger in the man's heart.

The secretary spotted him. "Sir!" he cried. He beckoned Christopher with an arm raised above the heads of the petitioners. The door to the room behind him was ajar and Christopher glimpsed de Spes moving past the crack. The secretary beckoned Christopher on. He pushed through the shouting men, the secretary opened the door for him, and he shot in and quickly closed the door on the crowd. He was in de Spes's study—a muffled place of crammed bookshelves, a desk heaped with papers, a globe, maps—and they were alone.

"Grenville, finally. I've been waiting." De Spes was clearly agitated, but the expression on his narrow face looked to Christopher like excitement. The ambassador went immediately to his desk. "What kept you?"

"The roads. Ice and snow." He jerked his thumb to indicate the crowd. "What are they howling about? You're not leaving, are you?"

De Spes snorted. "Never." Christopher was relieved. De Spes was pawing through papers on his desk, and when he found the one he wanted he went to the door, opened it a crack, and called over the secretary. "Have this taken to the French embassy," he said quietly. "For Monsieur Fenelon's eyes only, you understand?" He closed the door and turned back to Christopher, rubbing his hands with a restless look. "So much to organize. Where are you staying?"

"The Savoy." The derelict old mansion was a warren of filthy tenements and he could not wait to leave the place, but it was useful for a man who wanted to disappear.

De Spes frowned. Everyone knew the Savoy was a hideout of cutpurses and thieves. "Is it safe? No one must trace you to me."

"It will serve." He had considered contacting his sister, Frances.

Her house was in Chelsea. But she thought he had died years ago, and he didn't know how she would react to him turning up. More to the point, he could not be sure which way her allegiance ran. Frances, the fool, had married the enemy. Adam Thornleigh.

"Messages?" De Spes held out his hand, impatient.

Christopher cast an anxious glance toward the far door, which lay in shadow. It was open, leading into de Spes's private rooms.

"Don't worry, we're alone."

Christopher went and shut the door anyway. The letter was too incriminating for anyone else even to know about. He had helped Mary compose it. He pulled off his hat and slipped the letter out of a hidden pocket in the hat. He handed it to de Spes, who hurriedly read it. Christopher watched him, anxious. Not about de Spes, who was eagerly collaborating with them, but about those Englishmen beyond the door. They would be incensed to violence if they knew that Mary was entreating Philip to send her military aid to overthrow Elizabeth. *With your help*, she had written, *I will be queen of England in three months and mass will once again be celebrated all over this country.* God only knew what would befall Mary if Elizabeth should find out. But there was no question about what they would do to Christopher as her accomplice. English law had a special death for traitors. They would hang him until almost dead, then cut him down and disembowel him. He might still be alive when they hacked off his limbs and then his head would be stuck on a pike on London Bridge.

De Spes let out a short laugh as he finished the letter, which alarmed Christopher. "Is her request so hopeless?" he asked. Without Spain, everything fell apart.

"No, no, my mirth is born of delight, for the lady is bold." De Spes looked exhilarated. "And she need beg no longer. The sleeping giant of Spain has been roused."

"What?" Christopher hardly dared hope. "How so? What's happened?"

"You haven't heard the news?"

"I travel at night, de Spes, and I don't stop for chat."

A fist pounded the door. Someone yelled, "Come out here and give us some answers!" Christopher heard the secretary's muffled stern rebuke, then English voices rising in anger. De Spes ignored the clamor. "English merchants," he said with a snort that spoke of both satisfaction and contempt. He took the letter to his desk. Slipping a key from his pocket he unlocked a drawer, placed the letter inside, and relocked the drawer. "I have told them to press their complaints on their queen, not me. She is the one who brought this calamity on their heads."

"What calamity? What's *happened?*"

"Her pirates attacked a ship of ours carrying the King's gold to pay the Duke of Alva's troops." Fury leapt in de Spes's sunken eyes. "I demanded restitution from Elizabeth, but what did the Jezebel do? She took possession of the gold *herself!* A banker's loan—that's what she has the insolence to call it. No loyal Spaniard can allow such a gross offense to His Majesty. I recommended to him, in the most forceful language possible, that Spain retaliate with drastic action. I thank God my king listened. He acted at once. All English assets in the Netherlands have been seized. Ships, gold bullion, goods and chattels." He shot a look at the closed door and added with righteous excitement, "Let Elizabeth's merchants suffer for her sins. Spain cannot be tricked."

Christopher fairly jumped at the news. What a lightning bolt of luck! Elizabeth herself had pushed Spain into his arms! Into Mary's arms. Fresh energy coursed through him. But then a jolt of caution. Could he trust this sudden turn of fortune? A mercantile confrontation was one thing, military intervention quite another. "Is it provocation enough? Is the King angry enough? Can we hope that he will now commit troops to our cause?"

"He is *eager* to do so. His Netherlands troops can cross to England in a day." De Spes's own eagerness was evident, but he added sternly, "*If,* that is, our English friends can rouse themselves to action. His Majesty will not invade, but he will assist. You understand?"

"Perfectly." Christopher's thoughts were leaping ahead. "We must get this great news to the northern earls as fast as horse can carry it." Northumberland and his friend the Earl of Westmorland had pledged seven thousand men. The time to muster them had come.

"But wait." De Spes looked suddenly concerned. "Everything

has happened so fast, all at once. Elizabeth has called her entire council to attend the reconvened inquiry, and Northumberland and Westmorland are councilors."

"Good God, they've come to London?"

"No, not yet. But will they risk disobeying the royal summons? Elizabeth already mistrusts them for their faith."

Christopher feared the earls would indeed obey. They were disheartened, believing they had no Spanish support, unaware that everything had suddenly changed. "We have to stop them before they leave their northern strongholds. We must tell them the time to strike is now."

De Spes nodded. "So it is. Yes, I'll send word. The Duke of Norfolk's man has a relay of fast riders."

"Norfolk? Is he reliable?" Christopher had brokered a marriage match between Norfolk and Mary, and the two had exchanged letters of intent to wed, Norfolk pledging his love. *Self*-love, of course, for the union could eventually make him king of England without lifting a finger. But that was before the casket letters surfaced.

"The marriage agreement has put backbone into him," de Spes assured him. "I spoke to him this morning. He is with us. He wants to join the earls."

More good fortune! Norfolk could raise thousands of men! Even better, as the country's leading peer he would give the uprising the luster of legitimacy. Christopher felt almost light-headed. Moments ago he had thought that all was lost and he would face exile if he was lucky, a traitor's death if he was not. Now it seemed he had mustered the might of Spain and the home-grown support of the richest nobleman in England. Success was suddenly, thrillingly, possible.

"Grenville." Anxiety crept over the Spaniard's face. He asked gravely, "Can you do the rest?"

Christopher had never felt such a mix of exultation and fear. His action now could mean the difference between immediate, total success and a prolonged war that Mary could lose. Immediate success was possible only if Elizabeth was dead. *Time to do my part.* He nodded: *Yes.*

"Are you sure? What is your plan?"

Christopher had given it long, hard thought. At first the challenge had seemed impossible. How could he get close enough to Elizabeth to do the deed? Then, on the frigid ride to London, he had thought of the cold February night at Kirk o' Field near Edinburgh, and Mary's husband Lord Darnley asleep in his bed, and the explosion that had blown up the house, killing Darnley. As Christopher rode into London he had decided how he could accomplish his mission.

But he would need help. Where was he to get it? De Spes would not risk his own neck, and Mary was a virtual prisoner. As for English friends, Christopher was a stranger in his own country.

Then it struck him: Who did one turn to in times of need? Who were the only people one could ever really trust? Family. He had a daughter. He had a sister. For this crucial enterprise he would need both of them. He did not know if the bonds of kinship would prove strong enough or would snap from the strain. But they were all he had.

"Send Mary's letter to bolster His Majesty," he told de Spes, "and send Norfolk's man to rouse the earls to muster. Leave the rest to me." He went to the desk and opened a drawer and pulled out a pouch of coins. "I'll need more later," he said, pocketing the money.

The ambassador watched him solemnly. "Whatever you want. Beyond that, though, I cannot be involved."

"I need only one more favor. Can you get a message to my sister?"

Frances's hands and nose felt frozen. The boat's canvas canopy kept out the gusting snow, but the air was still frigid. The four miles from Kilburn Manor in Chelsea to London could be covered quickly in fine summer weather, but everything seemed agonizingly slow in winter, her rowers included. Tonight they were sullen, too, at being put to the oars after dark. She might have ridden, but her back was sore from a painful fall on her own icy jetty two days ago and she did not think she could endure even an hour on horseback. Nevertheless, the bubble of excitement she had felt at receiving the note from Ambassador de Spes buoyed her as her boat approached the landing of Durham House, the Spanish embassy. This felt like an adventure. A rather mysterious one, too. The note had asked her to meet him "to help Holy Mother Church," but had given no indication of what that might entail. A gift of money, Frances had assumed, but de Spes hardly needed a clandestine rendezvous to ask her for that. He knew her, and knew she would oblige him as a friend of the true faith.

Whatever the reason, she was not surprised that he had requested the meeting after dark. It was for her own security. She had often attended mass in his embassy's chapel, but always in secret, since it was illegal for English subjects to celebrate mass. The ambassador had been allowed the privilege as a mark of his rank, but only for himself and his embassy people. Frances knew she was taking a risk in attending and was very careful to keep Adam from knowing. Yet she had embraced the risk. It made her feel a kinship of suffering, in her own small way, with the blessed saints who had given their lives for their faith, some in unimaginable agony.

Tonight Frances was especially glad to get out of the house, even in the cold, for it kept her mind off Adam. She had not seen him for almost three weeks, not since he had stormed off after their awful quarrel over the new wing to the house. Worrying about him had kept her awake night after night. She had complied with his wishes, of course, had sent the masons and carpenters away, though it broke her heart to leave the wing half-finished. But when had she ever denied Adam anything he wanted? When had she ever been anything but a dutiful and loving wife? Much good it did her. He never noticed. And this time he hadn't come home.

Where had he spent these last weeks? After their quarrels in the past she knew he often went to his ship, staying aboard for days under the excuse of refitting or repairing things. It hurt her deeply that he preferred those rough, close quarters with smelly seamen to the comforts of home and her company. But at least those separations had lasted only a few days. This time it had been weeks.

Was he with Elizabeth? The thought turned Frances's stomach. She suspected that Elizabeth saw plenty of Adam, whenever and however she wanted him. It made her so sick with anger and frustration she sometimes found it hard to think straight. Some nights, in the dead small hours, she admitted to herself the painful truth: that he came home—when he did come home—only for the children. But she still felt sure that if she could just *keep* him home, could obliterate the lures of the outside world, she could make him happy. Make him, finally, hers. She did not expect a miracle. After ten years of marriage she knew that his habits, and his heart, were not likely to change. But she clung to the possibility. She loved him too much to give up hope.

This time, though, there was another worry to torment her. Had Adam stolen King Philip's gold? All of London had been abuzz at the firecracker of news about the piracy and agog at the report that followed like a cannon broadside: Elizabeth was in possession of the gold and was keeping it as a banker's loan! Londoners had cheered their queen's audacity, for they felt no love for the mighty Philip. Yet Frances had immediately suspected who the truly audacious one was, the man who had delivered the windfall to Elizabeth. Adam had all the seafaring skills. The motivation, too; she had seen his smoldering hatred of Spaniards. Had Elizabeth enticed him into this terrible danger, though he risked paying the price for piracy?

The boat nudged the embassy water stairs under the wharf's torches, and Frances stepped out, wincing at the sharp pain in her back. Composing herself for the meeting, she looked westward. Around the river's bend lay Elizabeth's palace of Whitehall; farther on, Elizabeth's palaces of Hampton Court and Richmond. To the east lay her fortress, the Tower of London, and beyond it her palace of Greenwich. Elizabeth was everywhere, with all the enticements of her court and her person laid out to snare Adam. Frances was near blind with hatred for the woman who had taken his heart. It made her nauseous to think that Elizabeth might one day cost him his life.

Durham House was a riverfront mansion, and its many windows blazed with light. The ambassador and his people were working late. *No wonder,* Frances thought. She had heard her steward and chamberlain heatedly discussing the Spanish seizure of English goods in the Netherlands. "God-cursed papists," the steward had called the Spaniards, which made Frances wince. She endured Elizabeth's regime of heresy because it was the law and she was compliant, but within her own house she did not tolerate blasphemous insults to the true faith. Tomorrow she would sack the steward.

She did not go in by the main riverfront entrance but walked quickly along the gravel path that led around the building to a door that opened to the kitchens. She asked a footman for the secretary, Señor Guzman, as the ambassador's letter had instructed. The footman took her to wait in the butler's pantry. Guzman arrived within minutes. He welcomed Frances and took her, along with a torch, down to the wine cellar.

Frances followed, intrigued by the secrecy. What could be the meaning of it? They passed casks that gave off the damp and musty odor of oak, and shelves stacked with bottles, and reached Ambassador de Spes. He rose to greet her from a table that held the cellar ledgers and a single candle. Guzman went back up the stairs with the torch, plunging the casks into a gloom that the candle's light could not penetrate.

"I thank you for coming, Lady Frances," de Spes said, offering her a dignified bow of the head. "Forgive this rude meeting place. It was necessary."

Still cold from the river, Frances would have preferred his cozy chamber off the great hall with a roaring fire, but curiosity pinched her. "Why, sir? What can I do for you?"

"Ah, not for me, dear lady, for the Church. You have proved your abiding faith by celebrating mass with us despite the danger to yourself. I hope and trust that your devotion will guide you now, in a crucial effort for God."

His hushed words thrilled her. "I am God's servant, sir. But what do you mean? What effort?"

"Nothing less than liberating England. We intend to free this benighted realm from the darkness of heresy and bring a new dawn of truth and faith."

Before she could say another astonished word, he indicated the shadows behind him and a man stepped forth from between the casks.

Frances peered at him. The light was so dim, and his face was further shadowed by hair that reached his shoulders. But in the glint of the candle she could tell that the hair was blond. He lifted his head and the light caught his eyes. Frances gasped. Christopher! She jerked backward a step in shock and her leg hit the table with such force the candle rocked. De Spes snatched it before it fell.

Christopher smiled. "I always could surprise you, Frances."

"You . . . you died," she stammered. Eight years ago she had seen the blazing mill at Yeavering Hall crash down around him. "You burned to death."

He put a hand to the hair beside his cheek and lifted it. "Burned, but still of this world."

She winced at the sight of his ear, the scarred flesh. She realized she was trembling. It wasn't just the shock of seeing him alive, it was the memory of his treason. His terrible threat that she cooperate or else see her baby harmed.

He pulled out a chair by the table. "Sit down, Frances, before you fall."

She spat at him.

"Good God," de Spes whispered.

"That is for my child," Frances said, shaking. She would never forget how her brother had held his hand over Katherine's small mouth and nose, pressing down, stopping the baby's breath. Frances had lunged and stopped him. And then, in terror, obeyed him.

Christopher calmly wiped her spittle from his chin. With his eyes on her he said, "Señor de Spes, would you kindly leave us for a moment?"

"Grenville, are you sure you—"

"Thank you, my lord ambassador, my sister and I have much to discuss."

De Spes gave a grunt of concern, but seemed to accept Christopher's authority in this. He bowed again to Frances, then marched toward the stairs.

Christopher pulled out the chair for Frances. She felt rocky enough to need it. He took her arm and guided her down onto the seat.

"How is she, your daughter? Katherine, that's her name, isn't it?"

"She thrives. No thanks to you."

"Come, come, sister, I would never have let the child perish. You must know that. She is of my blood. We are kin, you and I and she. I simply had to jar you into doing your duty."

"Duty to you?"

"To your country and your faith. I was trying to rid England of our tyrant queen. I still am."

The words sent a shiver through Frances. Rid England of Elizabeth? Eight years ago she had refused to take any part in his treason, quelled by her fear that Adam would be suspected of abetting her brother's crime. But now? She had suffered so long from Elizabeth's hold on Adam. How she would cheer her death. "Why have you brought me here? Where have you been all these years? What do you want?"

"What we all want. The return of the true faith. I have been living in France, and I serve the queen who *should* sit on England's throne. The queen who would reign as a devout Catholic. Mary."

Frances was stunned. "Queen of the Scots? You . . . serve her?"

He bent close to her and rested his hands on the table on either side of her. "Then, Frances, there would be no more skulking into mass here with the ambassador."

She stiffened. It sounded like a threat. She could be arrested for attending mass.

"Just think, you could worship again in the great cathedral of St Paul's," he said soothingly, painting a bright picture of the future. "All of London would worship with you, pious and pure again in their faith."

Frances could not hide her interest. "But . . . how can it be done?"

"We have friends. Powerful nobles in the north where people love the old church. And powerful friends abroad. Spain is keen to wipe out heresy in England, Frances. All of them, these true patriots and foreign friends, are ready to join forces with us."

"An uprising?" she asked in astonishment. Her thoughts were

tumbling wildly trying to take it all in. Christopher alive . . . an uprising . . . backed by Spain. It was all too much to grasp. But one thought pierced through. "Can this truly destroy Elizabeth?"

Christopher's eyes gleamed. "If you will help us."

"I? What can I possibly do?"

"Make your house available to me. That is where I will kill Elizabeth."

❧ 21 ❧

Rigaud's Price

Enough tears. Justine was through with tears. She had cried so much since she had been brought back to London she felt as hollow as a husk. The headache that had pounded for days pounded still, and her stomach was rocky, but she rose from her bed in the Thornleighs' house and went to the window and peered through the frost-blurred glass. Was it safe now to leave? Snow swirled past her, looking as restless as she felt. She itched to get out.

All the way from Bolton Castle, escorted like a prisoner by Sir Ralph Sadler, she had been terrified that he would hand her over to Elizabeth's officers, who would cast her into jail. The journey had taken twenty-two days, yet the details of roads and bridges, inns and meals seemed a blur, so all-consuming was her fear. Sadler had told her nothing of her fate, leaving her to ride in suspense alone behind him as he spent the journey in desultory talk with his men-at-arms while the servants brought up the rear. They had traveled right through Christmas—the most cheerless, cold, and frightening Christmas Justine could have imagined.

But when they reached London she had not been cast in jail. Sadler had delivered her to the Thornleighs' house on Bishopsgate Street. Seeing their stricken faces, Justine had almost wished she *were* in a jail, some place where she could hide away. She had felt Lord Thornleigh's condemnation like a lash. She had abused his trust, he said, and his words had stung more deeply than any whip. Lady Thornleigh's anger was more straightforward, but just as cutting. Defending herself, Justine insisted that her only intention in trying to get the letters had been to speed Mary's going to France, which would be a boon to Elizabeth, but in her turmoil she also blurted that she felt Mary was being treated unjustly. Lady Thornleigh had cut her short. "Affairs of state are not *your* affair."

What was Justine's affair was Will, and the memory of York, of Will's shocked face at realizing how she had deceived him was still the most painful. She had not heard from him since then. Every night the memory pricked fresh tears from her swollen eyes.

Everyone she loved thought she had betrayed them.

She was empty now from crying. Sick of it, too, for she still believed that she had done her duty and that her goodwill efforts had been blocked. She stood at the window, determined to cry no more. Peering though the lace of frost, she was trying to see if Lady Thornleigh's footman still stood waiting in the courtyard. Justine could not see him. She hoped that meant that Lady Thornleigh had finally gone, the footman with her. Justine had overheard her and Lord Thornleigh discuss their plans this morning. He had left for Westminster to attend a meeting about the Spanish trade emergency. Lady Thornleigh was on her way to Hampton Court to see Elizabeth, who, they said, was highly vexed about the situation with Mary.

Justine turned from the window. The time to go was now. She got dressed with a purpose. There was one duty she meant to see to its end. Justice for Alice.

She rummaged in her satchel and found the book in which weeks ago she had slipped the note from Jeremy, the carpenter at Yeavering Hall. She read again the message in his wobbly handwriting:

The wine man that was running is called Rigaud. Ask at the French Church, London.

Justine tucked the paper into her pocket with a shudder. Had Rigaud strangled Alice? If so, why? Who was he, this "wine man"?

When she last talked to Jeremy he said his informant, the farrier, had told him Rigaud might have been in Kirknewton on business. She wanted answers, and now that she was back in London she might get them.

She whirled her cloak around her shoulders. Would the chamberlain stop her? Had Lord Thornleigh left orders that she was not to be allowed to leave the house? His command to Justine herself had been plain: no communication with Mary. Beyond that, she had no real idea where she stood.

She went down the stairs and through the great hall. She had always loved the merry season of Christmas through to Twelfth Night when the Thornleighs' house rang with their grandchildren's voices and the laughter of guests, and the hall was scented with evergreen boughs and the kitchen's aromas of cinnamon, nutmeg, and cloves. The house was not merry now. She saw no guests, only a couple of maids sweeping the floor, a clerk whose pen scratched lazily over a ledger, and the two dogs asleep at the hearth. She did not see the chamberlain. No one stopped her.

It was snowing heavily, and Bishopsgate Street was slick with a treacherous film of ice. As she started south on foot a frigid wind sent snow needling her face. The cold bit her nose even in the short distance she covered to Threadneedle Street. People tramped past her in the grimy slush, their heads down. Men on wagons and those on horseback squinted against the wind-driven snow. Cloud cover blocked the sun that shone feebly between the houses and shops and over barren gardens. Justine passed an old woman whose overturned pushcart had spilled loaves of bread into the slush. The woman shrieked at two dogs fighting over a loaf.

Just before she reached Broad Street, Justine turned into the yard of St. Anthony's Church. Everyone in London called it the French Church because it was the religious center for hundreds of French immigrants, Protestant Huguenots, who had fled the religious wars in their homeland. Justine pushed open the heavy oak door, and snow darted in as if seeking sanctuary. The church, devoid of all its former rich Catholic trappings, was cold and austere. Her footsteps on the stone floor echoed starkly. An inhospitable place, but she hoped that someone here might know of Rigaud. She had heard that the Huguenot elders maintained a strict Calvinist discipline over their congregation.

She passed a black-clothed cleric tramping down the nave, flapping his arms across his chest to get warm. He put her in mind of a crow. And looked just as unapproachable. In the chancel she noticed an older cleric unpacking books from a crate into a bookcase. She reached him and made her inquiry.

"Alphonse Rigaud?" He gave a snort of disapproval. "He has not been to church in over two months." He spoke English with a French accent that sounded like a sneer. "We fined him for nonattendance, but I doubt he will pay. He ignored the fines for lechery."

Justine suppressed a shiver. Had the lecher committed murder, too? "Can you direct me to where he lives?"

He peered at her. "Is this about one of the bastards he has sired on the laundress?"

"I do not know the man, sir," she said, uncomfortable under his scowl. "I must speak with him on a private matter."

He grunted, shrugging off any concern in the matter. "Precinct of St. Martin's le Grand. Parish of St. Anne and St. Agnes." He told her the house, then turned back to unpack more books. "You'd better be quick. We deport those who disobey God's law. That *pécheur* will soon find himself on a boat back to Le Havre."

She took Cheapside, the city's main thoroughfare bustling with people, from hawkers to horsemen, merchants to maids. As she neared St. Paul's Cathedral she passed clergymen ambling to and from its grounds and schoolboys with satchels dashing out from the cathedral school. Ahead to the west lay Newgate, wagons rumbling under its massive arch, a part of Newgate prison, but Justine's route lay north and she turned onto Aldersgate Street. The fine shops of goldsmiths, jewelers, and saddlers soon gave way to more modest tradesmen's shops of tailors, pewterers, cordwainers, and catchpenny printers. This was St. Martin's le Grand, one of the city's "liberties," so called because by an eccentric custom of old monastic rule these pockets of habitation lay beyond the city's jurisdiction. St. Martin's le Grand was an enclave of immigrants, French and Dutch mostly, crammed tightly together, its narrow streets as busy as Cheapside but with a grimmer air. All immigrants were taxed at double the rate of Londoners, and the dwellers of St. Martin's le Grand were scraping by as best they could.

Justine's destination, the parish of St. Anne and St. Agnes, was on the northern edge of St. Martin's le Grand. It lay just outside the city walls in the northeast pocket of Aldersgate Ward, and the moment she passed through Aldersgate she found herself among a gloomy jumble of dilapidated tenements, each shabby house being home to several families, it seemed. The shops were mere rude stalls and were outnumbered by taverns and alehouses. There was a smell of rotting cabbage and the caustic reek of urine. A drunken man mumbling into his long, dirty beard bumped Justine as he passed her. A baby screamed beyond a third-floor shuttered window. A blank-eyed woman bundled in rags stood in a doorway. *Selling herself?* Justine wondered with a shiver. She had to step over a fallen laundry line, its frozen shirts and hose lying on the muddy snow like dismembered corpses.

She found the house across from the sign of the Cobbler's Nail and went up the open staircase of rough-sawn wood. She knocked on the first door. Voices sounded throughout the house, barely muffled by thin walls: bickering, haranguing, shouts of anger. Strangely, a woman somewhere was singing with a lovely voice, a sweet but plaintive tune. The door opened a crack and a man appeared. He was short with a face like a fox: sharp, clever, wary. His thick black hair was swept straight back from his low forehead. He was munching a crust of bread.

"Monsieur Rigaud?"

He took in her fine clothing at a glance, swallowing the last of the crust. "And who might you be, mistress?" His French accent was thick but his English flawless. His voice was a low rumble that seemed to vibrate Justine's bones.

She squared her shoulders with pretended courage. "I come from Kirknewton, in the north. I bring regards from the vicar." She hoped the lie would prod him to talk to her.

"Hobson?" His wary look changed to one of keen interest. "Is he interested in buying after all?"

"It depends what you are selling, monsieur."

Two women tramped up the stairs, their hard eyes on Justine. A man watched her suspiciously from his doorway. Rigaud growled at the man, *"Bâtard,"* then opened the door wide for Justine and jerked his head in a command for her to come in, away from the prying eyes.

"No." She would not walk into a room with a man who might be a murderer. The room breathed out a rank odor of stale sweat and rancid fat. The only furniture seemed to be a makeshift table of a board set across trestles, and two stools. A patched shawl was tacked over the single window and the fabric lifted in the draft, like a ghost. Three small children sat on the floor around a mound of soiled garments, picking out the seams with fingernails and teeth. They watched her with coldly impassive stares that filled her with a mixture of pity and fear. In the far corner a sunken-eyed young woman lay on a straw pallet, propping herself on her elbow to get a look at the stranger at the door.

"No?" Rigaud frowned at Justine's reply. "Then what the devil is your business with me?"

"Come outside." When he scoffed she pulled out her purse from inside her cloak and dug out an angel coin. It was obvious he could use the money. She offered the coin to him.

He took it and offered back a foxy smile, his teeth yellow, a front one chipped. "So, what *am* I selling?"

"Answers."

His eyes were on her purse as it disappeared back inside the folds of her cloak. He gestured toward the stairs. "Lead the way, mistress."

Down they went, and out to the street where they stood under the tenement's overhanging second story. A few paces away, at the street's crooked corner, an old woman with a plump, pinched face like a dried apple crouched over a brazier of coals, roasting chestnuts. She glanced at Justine and then, with weary disinterest, went back to prodding the charred chestnuts. Their earthy aroma tinged the chilly air.

Justine said to Rigaud, "You were in Kirknewton in early June. Why?"

"To see the vicar, Hobson. He was away, off to see the bishop, that's what his churchwarden told me. But I left him a good offer. Better than good—ten casks of Burgundy, half price. That interfering churchwarden said there was no business to be had from Hobson, but I told the fellow to pass along my offer anyway. Has Hobson sent you?"

"Burgundy? You were there to sell wine?"

He looked eager to please. "If he doesn't want Burgundy I can get Malmsey. Claret, too. I can get the best, cheap. For Hobson, half price."

"You are well-connected," she said, almost scoffing. How did a denizen of this wretched neighborhood have access to fine French wines?

Rigaud bristled and said with some defiance, "You don't believe me? I ran a profitable trade for years, before I fell on hard times. Supplied northern gentlemen's cellars from York to Berwick." He raised his chin and added with a snarl of wounded pride, "Twelve, fourteen years ago, at Wooler, I did business with the lord of Yeavering Hall himself."

He knew my father. It made her squirm to think that this man had any connection with her own family. The expression on his face was hard to read. There was pride, and bitterness, too, but something else lurked. Fear? Of being found out? She imagined Alice struggling against his hands squeezing her throat, gasping her last breaths, and in a rush of fury she said, "I have not come on the vicar's business. Not on business at all."

Rigaud's eyes narrowed in mistrust. "Are you from the French Church?"

"No. It's Kirknewton church I want to ask you about. And the murder of Alice Boyer."

He stiffened. "Never heard of her."

"Oh, I think you have. You were there the day she was murdered in the church nave. June fifth. A farrier at the stable across the lane saw you running away through the churchyard."

His scowl was so fierce she was afraid he might strike her. Part of her wanted to run. But she stood her ground, fists bunched at her sides ready to defend herself. "Did you kill Alice?"

"*Me?* Is that what you think?"

"You were there. Then you fled to London."

"I was done with my business so I came home. Where's the crime in that?"

"You were seen running away. Why were you running?"

His face had gone pale but he wasn't backing down. He said very carefully, "There's many things can make a man run. I tell you, I didn't touch the wench."

She saw again that flicker of fear, and suddenly she believed him. But if he was innocent, what was he afraid of? As a child at the fair she had once seen a jester wearing a two-faced mask, one pair of eyes looking forward, the pair at the back of his head looking backward, and the truth about Rigaud now struck her like that jester turning to flash his other face. It was not guilt that had made him run. "You *saw* something. That's it, isn't it?"

His face went hard, like a door closing. "I saw I had lost a chance to earn a living. So I left."

"Who did you see? The killer?"

He wiped his nose, red in the cold, and looked back at his door as though ready to go back inside. "I didn't do it, and now you know. I have nothing more to say."

"But you know more. You saw the killer, didn't you. Who is he? Someone you know? Someone you've seen before?"

A twitch of his eyes. "You'd best leave this alone, mistress. Get yourself back to your fine house. Around here there are dangers for a lady. Cutpurses and worse. Children, too, some very clever at getting the clothes off a lady's back."

She remembered the three children in his room picking the seams out of soiled clothing. Was he threatening her? She was now too hungry for an answer to be afraid. "Tell me, I beg you. Alice was my dearest friend. For pity's sake, man, tell me who you saw!"

A new light came into Rigaud's eyes. "It's worth something to you, then, is it?"

"Anything. Just *tell* me."

He studied her as if weighing the risk. He picked a scrap of bread from his teeth, thinking. "Ten pounds."

"What?"

"You're right, I saw the man who killed your friend. It'll cost you ten pounds."

Ten pounds! "Yes, all right. Who was it? Do you know his name?"

"I do," he said grimly.

"Tell me!"

He held out his palm. "Pay first."

It took her aback. "Now? But . . . I don't walk the streets with so much money."

"Ten pounds, or no name."

She was trembling with frustration. How could she get such a huge amount? The Thornleighs were her only source of funds—they paid for everything she'd ever needed or wanted—but she could not possibly go to them now. Who else, then? Wildly, she thought of her father. *My flesh and blood*. But she had no way to contact him. He was somewhere in Yorkshire, to serve Mary. Then it struck her: She had kin nearby. Her father's sister, Frances, in Chelsea. "All right," she told Rigaud. "I'll get it. I'll bring it."

"Good." He took a step toward his door. "Do it fast. Before the poxy churchmen hustle me onto a ship to France." He shot a wary look past the woman roasting chestnuts as if he expected to see the parish elders turning the corner, coming for him with manacles and chains. "Come back by Sunday, or it'll be too late for us both."

"Don't you see, Frances? This is our great chance." Christopher was so infuriated by his sister that he found it hard to keep his voice low. He did not trust her servants and had insisted that she bring him to this children's playroom at the back of her house where no one would see him. He wasn't sure he could trust Frances, for that matter, but he had told her too much to turn back now. "When Mary is on the throne, she will restore all that was taken from us. Our lands. Our name. Our religion."

"*Your* lands."

"Your religion."

She looked agonizingly torn. "*If* we succeed. But if we fail?" She was fidgeting with a child's rag doll, pinching its row of buttons. They clicked through her fingernails like rosary beads. Her voice was thin with fear. "All I see is failure and ruin."

"Because you have not allowed yourself to see victory." The room was hot. A child's tower of colored wooden blocks by the hearth seemed to waver in the heat, and the glass eyes of a rocking horse glowed red like a demon's. Yet there was no fire in the hearth and frost etched the windowpanes and Christopher knew that it was only he who was hot. A fever. Every word he spoke grated his throat like sandpaper. Every muscle ached. He had made a punishing ride north to Bolton to finalize with Mary the next crucial step in the plan, then galloped back here to Chelsea to put it into action. He craved sleep. Yet he could not rest, there was so much to do. Most urgently, he had to talk to Justine. He could not go to the Thornleighs' house, of course; he would have Frances invite her here. He had told his sister about Justine's conversion to Mary's cause, which had astonished her but stiffened her backbone, he hoped. His daughter's participation now was essential. Without her the whole plan would be stillborn.

Shouts outside made him flinch. He went to the window and parted the curtain a finger's width to investigate. In the snowy courtyard Frances's children, a tall girl and a younger boy, were laughing and pelting a burly young footman with snowballs. The grinning footman whipped a snowball back at them and it knocked off the girl's hat, making her shriek with laughter. Christopher scanned the area for other servants. Across the courtyard, past the snow-shrouded topiary, lay the unfinished three-story wing. Its unglazed windows were covered with snow-caked canvas. A couple of workers were carrying boards out through its entrance and loading them into a wagon.

Christopher tugged the curtain closed and turned back to Frances. When she had left the Spanish embassy cellar after meeting him and de Spes she had seemed aquiver with the thrill of removing Elizabeth, but after days to fret about it she was now faltering. He bit back his furious impatience and spoke in a tone to calm her. "Your part is so very simple. Once your home is suggested to Elizabeth as the meeting place, you simply agree to host the meeting. That is all. Then you are done."

"But when she is dead, who will they suspect? Me!"

"Why should they? You and your husband have excellent relations with her. A history of pure loyalty."

"Except for the connection with my brother, the traitor," she snapped.

"Who died eight years ago," he reminded her. "And back then no one suspected *you*."

She bit her lip, clutching the doll, looking unconvinced.

He stifled the urge to shake her. "Frances," he said soothingly, "there is nothing to connect you. Every step Elizabeth takes is whispered by dozens, even about her so-called secrets, so everyone will believe that word of the meeting simply leaked from court. It happens all the time. Then, once the deed is done, her officers will look for culprits who are known to hate her. And her enemies are legion. Every good Catholic in England, and all the Spaniards here whose goods she confiscated in retaliation for Philip freezing English assets. The two countries stand on the brink of war. Whole factions in both realms want Elizabeth's death. When it happens, no one will even give a thought to you. They are more likely to pity you as an innocent dupe, especially when you bewail the tragedy."

She stared at him as if wanting to believe him. A back door slammed. Christopher heard children's laughter and running footsteps. Frances looked at the door, distracted by the sound of the footsteps fading. "Katherine and Robert. I should go—"

"Never mind them. Frances, you must pledge me your help. What say you?"

She looked down at the doll in her hands, twisting one of its buttons, lost in an agony of indecision. Then she shook her head. "No. I cannot do it. The risk is too great."

He snatched the doll and tossed it across the room. "Then get your husband to do it."

"What?" she said horror. Cowed, she backed up toward the tower of blocks.

"All he has to do is agree to host the meeting."

"I would never put him in such jeopardy!"

"What jeopardy? The risk to him is nonexistent. He is known to be Elizabeth's staunch supporter, according to de Spes. People even say he's the pirate who captured Philip's gold and gave it to Elizabeth, that he is her favorite courtier—"

"People are ignorant fools," she snapped. "What they say is vile slander!"

He had struck a nerve, and it surprised him. So that was why she wanted Elizabeth gone, he suddenly realized. Not religion. Jealousy. It flared in her eyes and stamped angry red splotches high on her cheeks. And it gave him hope. "Where *is* your husband, by the way?"

"Portsmouth, seeing to his ship."

"Ah yes, seeing to the naval welfare of the lovely Elizabeth. She must be very grateful."

"All you need to know," she said with quiet bitterness as she bent to straighten the red block on top of the tower, "is that he is far away. Safe. Otherwise I would not even be listening to you."

Christopher kicked the tower and the blocks tumbled. Frances froze. "But you have listened. You are listening. Because you know it's the right thing to do. Elizabeth is a blight on my life and yours. Do you want your husband to be forever in her thrall?"

She looked as if he had slapped her. She swallowed, then answered with a new steadiness, "No."

"Then you know your part. Do this, Frances, or everything we want will be lost to us forever."

A child's muffled shout from inside the house: "Hooray! Justine's here!"

Frances's head jerked up. Christopher stared at his sister in astonishment. "Did you know she was coming?"

She looked so flustered it was clear she was as surprised as he was. "No."

They heard Justine's voice and a maid's coming toward them. Christopher had time only to turn his back to the door as it opened.

"Forgive me for this interruption," Justine said to her aunt, hurrying in. She sounded slightly out of breath.

"That is all," Frances tightly told the maid. "Leave us."

When the maid was gone, Christopher turned. A dart of happiness went through him at the sight of his daughter's pretty face, cheeks pink from the cold, eyes keen with some pent-up urgency. She stiffened when she saw him.

"Father . . ."

The two children came scrambling in, the girl exclaiming, "Mother, may we play with Justine?"

The boy bounced up and down in excitement, "Justine! Justine!"

"Get them out," Christopher told Frances, itching to talk to his daughter. The children regarded him with curiosity, having never seen him before, and flicked looks at their mother and Justine as though aware of the tension between all three adults.

"Off with you," Frances said, shooing them out of the room. "Find Master Rowan and see to your Latin."

"But Justine said—"

"Later, my pets," Justine promised. Her eyes were on her father.

"Run along," said Frances, closing the door on the children.

Christopher gazed at Justine, his heart almost too full to speak. She had come to him! "This is wonderful. I feared I might never see you again." He came to her, opening his arms, and embraced her. "God has brought us together, we three Grenvilles," he said. "I praise Him for it."

"Amen," Frances whispered in awe.

"Your aunt is amazed to see you, Justine." His daughter stood so stiffly in his embrace, he pulled away and saw her bewilderment.

"No more than I, sir, to see you in London. Is it not dangerous for you lest you be recognized?"

"But worth the danger, to see you." He laughed in delight at his luck, a delight sharpened by fever. The laugh made him cough.

"Sir, you are ill," she said with concern.

Frances said, very agitated, "Justine, does Lord Thornleigh know you've come to my house?"

Justine had a guilty look. "No. I have come . . . to ask your help."

"Of course, Frances is your aunt," Christopher said eagerly. "We are all Grenvilles here."

"Surely you will be missed," Frances said in alarm. "Christopher, she cannot stay." She turned to Justine. "It is not safe, you being here. Not safe for any of us. You must go."

"Wait, Frances, wait. Justine, how can we help you?"

She hesitated. "I need money. Ten pounds. Right away."

Frances stared at her. "What in heaven's name for?"

Justine said to her father, "It's about Alice. I told you I was searching for the man who killed her. I found a witness, here in London. He knows who the murderer is, but he won't tell me until I pay him. He wants ten pounds."

Christopher coughed. He found it hard to catch his breath. "A witness? Who?"

"I promised him I would not say." Her glance flicked between him and Frances. "Perhaps I have said too much already."

"Who is Alice?" Frances asked.

"From Yeavering Hall. Alice Boyer, my childhood friend. Father remembers her, don't you, sir?"

"Indeed, the gardener's daughter." Christopher nudged one of the fallen blocks with his boot. He was so shaken he did not dare look Justine in the eye. If the witness could identify him, if Justine found out that he had killed her friend, she could inform on him. Mary's words echoed in his mind: *"If they capture you, I am dead!"* Elizabeth would live . . . the plan to overthrow her would crumble . . . Christopher would be tortured and executed for treason. Everything he had struggled to accomplish—annihilated.

Reeling from the blow, he felt he was burning up from his fever. Frantically, he tried to think. Could he stop Justine, hold her back? *Should* he? No, no, he needed her. She was essential for getting Elizabeth to come here. The only way to survive this was to convince Justine to do his bidding now, immediately, before she could pay the witness. Mary's terrible words came back to him, the oath she had made him swear: *"If it comes to choosing your daughter or your queen, swear that you will choose your queen."* If he could strike quickly he would never have to make that hideous choice.

He forced himself look at Justine. "You haven't asked about Mary."

"I'm sorry . . . yes, how is she?"

"She misses you."

A sad nod. "She was kind to me."

"We know you were placed there to spy on her."

Justine flinched. "Pardon?"

"Thornleigh sent you as a spy for Elizabeth. I know it and Mary knows it."

"Sir, I only went to—"

"Come, come, child, there is no point in denying it." He took her hand. It was rigid. Christopher patted it gently. "Don't worry, we understand. They infected you with Elizabeth's mistrust for Mary. But Mary cured you by giving you *her* trust, and you came to love her. I was so proud to hear how you tried to help her. A pity you couldn't get the letters."

"I thought it only justice."

"Of course you did. You proved yourself her true friend. I know it has brought you Thornleigh's wrath, and I am sorry for that. But Mary thanks you for your brave attempt, and I thank you, too."

Her hand in his relaxed. A gleam of tears brightened her eyes. He gloried in it. *My flesh and blood.* And felt a clutch of relief.

"Justine, you asked me why I'm here. It is because of Mary. She needs your help."

"Me? I can do nothing for her now."

"You can. I will tell you how."

"No, it's impossible." She tugged her hand free. "My aunt is right, I cannot stay long away from Lord Thornleigh's house. I only came to ask her for the money."

"Oh, for heaven's sake," Frances said impatiently, "I'll go and fetch you the ten pounds, and then let's have done with this money business. There are urgent matters to discuss." She hurried out, saying, "Listen to your father."

Christopher could have struck her. He held his tongue until she was gone. "Justine—"

"You understand, don't you? This means so much to me. I may have failed Mary, but I mean to see justice done for Alice."

He managed to say, "And so you shall." *Make Mary queen . . . then I will be safe.* "But not just yet. I come with a far more important mission for you. You alone hold the key to success."

He had her attention now. "Success? At what?"

"Peace for Mary. She has fought well, but she knows she has lost. All she wants now is to retire with honor. She wants to give up her Scottish crown, to surrender all claim to any royal privileges. Yes, you heard me aright, Justine. She wants to abdicate."

The room was so quiet Christopher could hear the workmen far across the courtyard heave a load clattering into their wagon.

Justine looked fascinated, yet wary. "She signed Lord Moray's abdication paper once, then renounced it."

"They held a knife to her throat when she signed then. This time, she will abdicate of her own free will. She wants to leave England unburdened of all royal cares and live as a private person in France."

A smile lit her face. "This is wonderful! It's what I've wanted. It's best for everyone."

"But difficult to bring about. The process requires delicate diplomacy. Mary will not write openly to Elizabeth to offer abdication, partly for fear of further weakening her position, partly in anxiety about the reaction of her own supporters. Word of it might inflame them to take up arms while they can still call her queen. She has no wish to ignite a civil war in England. She will not even send Lord Herries to Elizabeth with this offer, lest tongues wag at his coming to court and word gets out. Once Mary has quietly retired to France, her supporters will have no choice but to accept the *fait accompli*. So, who *can* she send to Elizabeth with this extraordinary offer? A common porter or footman? No, Elizabeth would not take the word of a menial. It must be someone who stands high enough with her that she will give ear and believe. A person such as your guardian."

"Lord Thornleigh!"

"And you are the one with the credibility to convey the matter to him, for the very reason that made him recall you in disfavor. Because he knows you love Mary."

The wonder of it seemed to strike her with the force of a revelation. Her smile became radiant. "Father . . ." She threw her arms around his neck. "How they have misjudged you. They would call you peacemaker, if only they knew!"

❧ 22 ❧

Justine's Gift

In her eagerness, Justine stood up in the wherry as it reached the Westminster wharf. She could hardly wait to get out. "Whoa, mistress," the boatman at the oars warned. Justine almost lost her footing in the river's chop.

"I'm fine. Put in there." She pointed to a space opening up among the crowd of tilt boats and wherries taking on passengers and landing them. Her boatman expertly sculled the craft up to the wharf, a noisy stage of jostling lawyers and clerks, gentlemen and common petitioners, all with business at Westminster Hall, the hub of England's law courts. Men hailing wherries to take them back to the city shouted "Oars! Eastward, ho!" Below the wharf, along the riverbank, poor folk were scavenging fish. The tide, now at its ebb, had flooded so high it had left hundreds of fish flopping on the mudbanks, gasping, reeking, and people were scooping them into baskets.

Westminster Hall's massive bulk ran parallel to the river, and from the water stairs Justine looked up at its walls, which rose before her like a cliff. The snow had stopped and in the cold blue sky the sun shone, emblazoning victory over the fast-departing clouds. Justine hardly felt the cold. Her father's words had kindled an energy in her as irresistible as the sunshine. He had given her a gift—Mary's astounding offer to abdicate. Now she had the power to pass along that gift. Her father had said to take it to Lord Thornleigh, but that was not why Justine had come to Westminster. There was another way to get Mary's message to Elizabeth.

It came with a risk. She shouldn't even be out, should be sitting contritely in Lord Thornleigh's house accepting her disgrace. But she didn't feel she had done anything wrong, and this was a chance to vindicate herself. Excitement bubbled up in her. Her mission brought sunshine for *everyone*.

She had been inside Westminster Hall before, and the vastness of the place always awed her with its lofty hammer-beam roof echoing the din of people milling through its humming honeycomb of shops and stalls, and its crowded passages leading to courtrooms and offices and the House of Commons in St. Stephen's Chapel. She passed a rookery of black-robed lawyers conferring outside the Court of Queen's Bench. Soldiers of the palace guard patrolled. Judges ambled, trailed by clerks. Pie sellers and booksellers hawked their wares. Today the place was busier than ever with more officials, lawyers, clerks, retainers, and hangers-on, because the commissioners in the inquiry about Mary had reconvened here, joined by the lords of Elizabeth's entire council.

"The inquiry? In the Painted Chamber," an elderly clerk told Justine when she stopped him to ask the way. He pointed up a crowded staircase. "Fireworks there today," he added cryptically as he shuffled on.

Up she went, shouldering through the crowd on the stairs, and was directed to a closed double door where packs of men shouted and argued and pages scurried about with messages. She stopped a freckle-faced page about to go in with an armful of papers. "Do you know Will Croft? Sir William Cecil's assistant?"

"Master Croft, mistress? Aye, he's here every day."

She gave him her name and a penny and sent him in to seek Will. Waiting, giddily impatient, she was aware of the men's inquisitive glances. It tickled her. If only they knew the news she carried! Her heart thumped when the door opened and Will came out, scanning the crowd, looking for her. She pushed through to him. "Will!"

Astonishment flooded his face. "I thought I'd misheard the boy. What are you—"

"Not here." People were watching them. "Can you come outside?"

"No, Sir William's speaking. I must get back." His bewilderment at seeing her was clear, and so was his discomfort.

It rocked her. Would he never forgive her? Was she mad to have come? *No,* she thought, taking courage, *this is my chance to make everything right.* "Then I'll be quick."

She took his arm and led him to the edge of the packed staircase. The area was jammed, and raucous with so many people talking, some calling down to others on the lower floor, but between the stair railing and a pillar they found a pocket of privacy. As she let go his arm he caught her hand and held it tightly as though to help him get his bearings at seeing her. At his warm grip she felt blood fire her cheeks, remembering his room in York and the thrill of their lovemaking. She saw that he felt it, too, even in his bewilderment. It made him more flustered and he let go her hand. That she had stolen the letters—her crime, as he saw it—hung between them like a noxious vapor. Justine was torn between shame and a burning urge to defend herself. "I'm glad, at least, Sir William hasn't held it against you," she said, hoping they could meet on this common ground. "Being connected to me, I mean."

His pained look told her she was wrong, though he said nothing. She suddenly imagined what must have happened. Cecil, furious, threatening to discharge him. Lord Thornleigh coming to his defense. Will now working harder than ever to prove himself. "I'm so sorry," she said. "I never thought it would hurt *you.*"

"Why did you do it?" His voice was almost a plea, and in it she heard his deep need to understand. "Why undermine Elizabeth?"

"I thought I was *helping* Elizabeth. Helping everyone. If Mary could fight the letters, I thought she could save herself from ruin and Elizabeth would let her go to France with dignity. Problem solved. It might have been misguided, even foolish, but it was not disloyal."

His eyebrows lifted in surprise. "Actually, it's *not* foolish. But why not explain your reasoning to me? We could have discussed it. Did you think you couldn't trust me?"

She almost smiled. "Will, you live by the law. It's like a living thing to you, something to be protected. That's why you're such a fine advocate. Discuss it? Truly, would you ever have let me copy the letters?"

He didn't hesitate. "No."

It took her aback. She had hoped to raise a grudging glimmer of a smile, some acknowledgment that she had been right not to take him into her confidence, but there was none. She saw that he was miserably torn, loving her but struggling to accept what she had done. She felt a clutch of despair. Would they never get back the sweet harmony they had once shared?

"Master Croft!" A page reached Will and handed him a docket of papers. "From my lord Admiral Clinton. For Sir William Cecil." He flipped open the portable desk on a strap around his neck. "Will you sign, sir?"

Will slipped the docket under his arm, dipped the quill in ink, and scrawled his signature. The page hurried away, closing his desk. Will said to Justine, indicating the docket, "I have to get back."

"No, wait." She was bursting to tell him. "I've come with news. Please wait."

"Justine, I can't, Sir William needs me. Tempers are boiling in there. Mary's commissioners have withdrawn to protest Elizabeth not giving her an audience, and Elizabeth has sent word that Mary has one last chance to defend herself against the charges. And that's not all. Elizabeth summoned all her councilors to this final session, but two earls have not come, Northumberland and West-morland, powerful lords of the North. That worries Sir William. Especially since we're on the brink of war with Spain."

"War?" She was horrified. "Is it that bad?"

"Sir William has put Ambassador de Spes under house arrest. We learned that he's been urging his king to help Mary take Eliza-beth's throne by force." He gave Justine a probing look, almost suspicious. "You don't know anything about that, do you?"

His look chilled her. "No."

He winced as though ashamed his own misgivings. "Of course not. Sorry." He glanced toward the inquiry chamber doors. "I must go." He looked pained at leaving her, but started for the doors.

"Will, there's a solution. I've heard from Mary."

He stopped and turned. Men jostled past him. "What?"

"I bring an extraordinary offer from her. You must hear it." She beckoned him back to the quiet space behind the pillar. The moment he stood face-to-face with her she whispered, "She wants to abdicate."

He blinked in shock. Then frowned, disbelieving. Justine was ready for that. She tugged from her sleeve a thin scroll the length of her hand. Her father had given it to her. "Read," she said.

He unfurled the scroll. She waited, happily impatient, and so grateful to her father. When everyone else had mistrusted her—Lord and Lady Thornleigh, and Will, too—her father had entrusted this crucial mission to her. She felt she was only beginning to know him, and it saddened her that he would soon be gone. He would leave for France with Mary, and likely Justine would never see him again. It seemed cruel—just when she was proud, for the first time, of being his daughter. But she chided herself for that selfish thought. In England he was in danger; in France he would be safe.

Will looked up from reading, wide-eyed. Justine knew what Mary had written:

> *I authorize the bearer to convey my message of amity to*
> *my dear cousin Elizabeth and an invitation to meet*
> *with my envoy on an issue of grave importance to both*
> *our realms. I pray you, give ear to this bearer.*
> *Marie R.*

"Yes," she said quietly, eagerly. "The issue is her abdication."

He was stone still with amazement. "Good Lord."

Jubilant, she took the scroll from him before he dropped it.

"She makes three conditions. First and most vital, this invitation must be accepted before the inquiry brings down its conclusion."

He pulled himself together. "That may be only a matter of days."

"Then the meeting must be arranged immediately."

He said evenly, trying to mask the astonishment that still gripped him, "Seems a reasonable quid pro quo."

"Master Croft!" Another page was calling him as though in search, his voice thin beyond the milling men. Will didn't budge. "And the other two conditions?"

"That Elizabeth *herself* meet with Mary's envoy, Lord Herries. There is no time for protracted negotiations with some lord sent in Elizabeth's place. And finally, that the meeting take place in secret, because neither queen can risk the negotiation failing in public. I suggest Kilburn Manor, Sir Adam's home in Chelsea. I'll be glad to arrange the details with Lady Frances." Justine considered it brilliant of her father to have thought of this location. "It is neutral ground, away from court," she explained, "acceptable to Elizabeth because she holds Sir Adam in such high esteem, and acceptable to Mary because of her trust in me."

"Her trust in you," he repeated in wonder. He was utterly still, staring at her, dumbfounded.

Justine plowed on. "Lady Frances is willing, and she will be discreet. No one else will know of the meeting."

"Master Croft!" the searching page sang out. Justine saw him catch sight of Will and thread through the crowd toward them.

There was no time to lose. "Will, go in and take this," she said, quickly rolling up the scroll. She held it up for him. "Give the news to Sir William."

He didn't move. "Why bring this to me? Why not to Lord Thornleigh?"

"So you can reap the glory." Her heart swelled with the pleasure of bestowing the gift. She was so keyed up she found it hard to keep her voice low. "No one in London, no one in this whole realm, has the power you now hold, Will. A diplomatic triumph. Tell Sir William, and he shall praise you as the man who relieved

Elizabeth of the burden of Mary, the man who delivered peace."
She urged the scroll on him. "There will be little he can deny you."
A look of awe came over Will's face. He took the scroll. His eyes
were shining. "How skilful you've been . . . and I didn't see it until
now. I thought Mary had turned you onto a path away from Elizabeth, away from accord. But no, you just took a different route to
get there. You made a friend of Mary, won her trust . . . and look at
what you've achieved." He gave a quick laugh of delight. "My
Lord, Justine, what an astute diplomat you've proved."

Her heart sang with vindication. "You see? As loyal as even *you*
could hope."

His look turned sober. "Can you ever forgive me?" He sounded
almost choked with shame. "Reporting you was the hardest thing
I've ever done. I felt I had to, or . . ." He struggled to find the
words. "Or what's it all for? All the striving to protect Elizabeth
and build a strong England. It seemed essential, but . . . I hated in-
forming on you." He took her hand and held it tight. "I swear, if I
could choose again, duty or you, I would choose you."

"Never mind." Tears of joy pricked her eyes. "You did what you
had to. It's over."

He kissed her.

She pulled back. People could see! Though she was so happy
she wanted to hold him and kiss him forever. "Go in. Tell Sir William."

"Yes." He grinned. "Yes, I will. And then, come with me to see
my mother."

"What?"

"I want to marry you, Justine. I want everyone to know it. Come
with me to my mother's house and we'll finally get her blessing
and then post the banns. We'll go as soon as I've given this message to Sir William. Wait here. All right?"

She hesitated. Meet his mother who was so set against her? But
Will's eager look gave her courage. She nodded.

"Good." He kissed her again. "How I love you," he said. And then
he was gone.

As soon as she was alone in the crowd her misgivings rushed

back. Will believed that his mother's opposition to her was a general objection to his marrying at all, since he still had his way to make in the world, but Justine knew the real reason. She was a Grenville. Will still didn't know that. She had avoided telling him the truth for so long its significance had slipped to the back of her mind. And now that she *did* think of it, did it really matter anymore? They loved each other and nothing could change that now. It occurred to her that maybe his mother did not know the true depth of their love. If she did, surely she would reconsider and give them her blessing. Suddenly, meeting her seemed a positive step. Daunting, perhaps, but Justine longed to get her approval.

Lost in these thoughts, she was startled when the door swung open and Sir William Cecil marched out. The crowd parted with a hush to let him pass, the Queen's most trusted adviser. Will was at Cecil's side. Justine craned to see past the press of bodies as Cecil and Will hurried down the stairs, vanishing in the throng. What was happening? She pushed her way to the railing and was looking down to catch a last glimpse of Will when a page reached her and handed her a note. Will's handwriting—the scrawl showed his haste. It said he and Cecil were going to Whitehall to see Her Majesty and he would call on her at the Thornleighs' house first thing in the morning to take her to see his mother.

So her news had lit a fire! This was good. Yet she felt a stab of disappointment. Newly eager to meet Will's mother, she would now have to wait until tomorrow. She was so proud of him, though; it appeared he had become indispensible to Cecil.

She started down the stairs, then stopped at a sudden thought. Why not visit his mother herself? Alone with the lady she might win her over. Once, the prospect would have made her cower, but this day had wrought such wondrous things: the resolution of the two queens' standoff, the joyful reunion with Will, his leap forward in Cecil's esteem, all of which would bring Justine back into the Thornleighs' good graces. Why should she not try for one more marvel?

She went east into London, buoyed by hope.

The sun, misted by returning clouds, had slunk below the city's rooftops by the time she reached the narrow streets of Cripplegate

Ward, and people were trudging home for supper. On Silver Street, near the northwest angle of the city's wall, she found the house tucked into the crooked intersection with Monkwell Street. She paused at the front door. Lord Thornleigh had told her that the last time his sister had been to his house was when he'd brought Justine into it. After that she had refused his invitations so consistently the family had stopped expecting her. Justine took a deep breath, then knocked. Snow had begun falling.

An elderly, weary-looking housemaid opened the door. Justine asked for Mistress Croft and was led through the dim passage and into a small parlor at the back of the house. Shuffling back into the passage, the maid muttered that the mistress might be back or might not, and before Justine could ask what she meant the kitchen door groaned, closing behind the maid.

Justine looked around in the silence. She had come this far. May as well wait.

The room had a forlorn feeling and a musty smell. Its two small mullioned windows, cut into many panes, held thick glass opaque with dampness. The simple furnishings were of old oak, solid but scarred. Hewn oak beams supported the low ceiling where a cobweb in a corner snagged a ray of the lowering sun. A sound made Justine turn. In the cold hearth a draft whispered, sucking air from the chimney. Cold white ashes rose in a puff, then collapsed. Beside the hearth was a table on which a domed glass case held flowers that looked dead.

Death. Justine shivered, remembering Rigaud. He had seen the man strangling Alice and knew his name. Who was it? Frances had given her the money, so now at last she would find out. She glanced at the window. It would soon be dusk. Too late to return to Rigaud now. Tomorrow, first thing, she would go back and buy his information.

"Hello? I did not know we had visitors."

Justine spun around. A cloaked woman stood in the parlor doorway. She held a small posy of withered flowers. Justine's heart thumped as she curtsied. "Mistress Croft."

"Has Susan not taken your cloak? Do forgive us. She is forgetful. And I, well, I sometimes lose track of time when I am with my husband." She smiled sadly at the withered flowers she held. "These have done their office." She took them to the glass case. Separating one brittle bloom, she lifted the glass dome and laid the dead flower among the other desiccated ones arranged there. "My husband Geoffrey rests in St. Olav's churchyard," she explained, turning to Justine. "It is difficult to get flowers in January, but I do my best." She lowered her voice and added with a knowing smile, as though sharing a secret with a friend, "He cannot abide holly."

"Mistress Croft, I—"

"Yes, do forgive my manners." She glanced toward the kitchen. "Susan should have welcomed you. May I take your cloak?" She was shrugging off her own.

Justine whirled off her cloak. "I have just seen your son."

"Will?" She draped both cloaks over the back of a chair. Her courteous smile persisted, but with a mildly probing look. "Are you acquainted with my son?"

"I am." Justine's mouth felt as dry as the withered flowers. "Madam, I am Lord Thornleigh's ward. Justine."

She had never seen a person change so abruptly. The kind cordiality died. "I see." Her eyes were as cold as a grave. "Have you come to gloat?"

"I beg your pardon?"

"You ensnared him. Now that I see your face, I see how. Men are easily blinded."

Justine's anger flared. She squelched it, telling herself to be the diplomat Will thought she was. "It was he who ensnared me, madam, with his kindness and goodness. You should be very proud of such a son."

It was as if she had not spoken. "Even my brother is blinded. Richard says I must accept you." A shudder ran over her features. "That I cannot do."

There was something so strange in her look, her tone—something unbalanced. It drained Justine's anger, and she felt a tug of pity. The lady knew she was losing her son. "Madam, I know you have misgivings about me. I understand why. But Will and I have pledged to marry, as you know, and it would mean so much to him if you would give us your blessing. I promise you, nothing means more to me than his happiness."

"Liar."

This was too much. "Madam, I have come in good faith. If you think—" She stopped, pushed back the anger again. Trying one more time, she forced civility into her voice. "Will you not sit with me a moment and talk? We both love your son. With such affection in common, can we not be friends?"

"Love? Ha! You are a Grenville!"

The venom in her voice rocked Justine.

"If you really loved him, you would tell him the truth."

Lord Thornleigh's very words. It rankled Justine. She was tired of people telling her what to do. "Perhaps I *have* told him," she challenged.

"No. If he knew he would have turned his back on you."

"Yet you have not told him either. Why is that? Perhaps because you fear it would make no difference to him?"

"I made a vow to my brother to keep silent about you. A foolish vow, made years ago, and one I now bitterly regret. But a vow is a sacred thing, and I will not profane it. Poor deluded Richard, he thought if he raised you gently and no one knew the truth about you he could make you into a Thornleigh. Impossible. Can a crocodile be made a lion?"

This was madness. She would not stay and be abused. "Hear me, madam. I love Will and he loves me and we shall be married, and nothing you can do or say will make him change his mind. I came to offer my friendship. I see that I expected too much. I shall leave you to your morbid fantasies." She snatched her cloak off the chair. "I wish you a good day."

She was almost at the door when the woman said in a stunned tone, as though having a revelation, "You don't *know* the truth. That's it, isn't it? No one has told you."

"That I was born a Grenville?" What nonsense. "Of course I know it."

"Poor fool, you're rotten to the core and you don't even know it."

The insult was so gross it left Justine almost breathless. "Have a care, madam, or—"

"Let me tell you about the swamp that bred you. The crocodiles who whelped you. Your grandfather, Anthony Grenville, was Richard's neighbor in Essex where he and Honor first settled. Grenville was a foul-hearted papist, a mad dog in his religion. He heard of Honor's so-called heresy and one night he stalked into their home with a pistol and shot Honor. She lived in fevered agony for weeks and we thought she would surely die. It is God's mercy that she survived. Anthony Grenville was *your grandfather.*"

Justine stood in shock. Her father had said nothing about this. She had never met her grandfather.

"As wicked as the father were the sons. John Grenville, the eldest, hoarded his hatred for our family. Under cruel Queen Mary he rose to prominence, one of her papist lapdogs. But to us he bared his fangs. He captured Richard. Threw him into the Tower in a cell so small he could neither stand nor lie, and left him in his filth to starve. Then he captured Honor, and her fate was worse. He stretched her on the rack, ripped her sinews, a torture that would leave most people shrieking mad, but Honor endured the agony for the sake of her friend, Princess Elizabeth, now our queen. I nursed them both, Honor and Richard, when Grenville was made to let them go, and pitiful it was to see Honor broken, with a lifeless arm, and Richard as thin as if he were made of sticks. They recovered, and John Grenville went to Ireland on Queen Mary's business, but only to bide his time. Finally, he struck at us. Geoffrey was at Richard's house with Will. Speedwell House. Will was twelve. A drowsy Midsummer Day it was, the household folk at lazy chores in the courtyard when Grenville thundered in with his horsemen. They charged the men, hacking with swords, firing arrows. My Geoffrey tried to rally with Richard. Will grabbed a bow. But they were swarmed. Three arrows felled Geoffrey. Will saw his father writhing in the dirt, bleeding out his life. John Grenville burned Speedwell House to the ground. That was *your uncle.*"

Justine was riveted in horror. *Will saw his father murdered.*

The woman's eyes narrowed on her. "And then there was your

father, Christopher Grenville. A traitor. He used my niece, Isabel, to further his plot against our queen, and when Isabel tried to stop him he bound her and carried her to his millrace to drown her. Yes! He was about to hurl her, hands tethered, into the tumbling river before he was stopped. That was *your father*."

Justine blinked. *Father?* Impossible. The tale had leapt beyond belief. The woman was raving. Eaten up with hatred and grief, her mind deranged, she was spinning lies about anyone with the name of Grenville. Justine said as civilly as she could, "Madam, I am sorry you lost your husband. But this awful feud had nothing to do with me. I was a child. It is the past. If you keep Will chained to these ghosts—"

"It has everything to do with you! You Grenvilles are born wicked. Born bad. You may think you're different with your pretty face and your gentle ways learned from my brother and his wife, but you cannot escape your tainted blood. It is your destiny to be the worm in the apple, the canker in the rose. You are a bad seed, Justine Grenville. If you marry my son you will make him wretched, as wretched your aunt has made my nephew Adam. You will blight Will's life. You will spawn children to carry on the Grenville evil." She was short of breath, almost panting. A wild light leapt in her eyes. She snatched Justine's hand. "It is not too late! Release my son. Tell him you cannot marry him. Let him go. Let this end!"

Justine pulled back her hand, appalled. The woman was a lunatic. "Please understand. I love Will. He loves me. Nothing can stop us."

In the awful silence, footsteps sounded in the passage and a moment later the parlor door opened.

"Justine!"

She spun around. *Will.*

"Sir William is in conference with Her Majesty," he said, in high spirits, "won't need me until tomorrow. How wonderful that you came. Hello, Mother." He was grinning, dusting snow from his shoulder. "Even more wonderful to see you two together." He came to Justine's side and said to his mother, "I hope you've been discussing the wedding. As soon the inquiry ends we'll post the banns." He winked at Justine. "And the inquiry's end, I predict, is nigh."

She could not find words. He looked so happy, his mother so miserable. Rubbing his hands briskly to warm them, he insisted that Justine stay for supper. "We'll set a wedding date, we three, and discuss who to invite."

When he went to the kitchen to tell the cook, his mother regarded Justine with a look that sent a chill up her backbone. "You are wrong, girl," she said quietly. "There is something I can do to stop you."

It shook Justine so deeply that when Will came back she could scarcely put on a calm face. He was saying that after supper it would be too late for her to return to his uncle's house. "Stay the night, my love." She balked, saying Lord Thornleigh would expect her.

"I'll send a note. He'll be fine, knowing you're here. Besides, the snow is falling thick. It's hardly safe. Stay, and we'll make merry." His smile was warm, full of admiration. "Today we have good cause, God knows."

His mother pleaded a headache, ordered that supper be brought to her chamber, and left them. Justine was relieved to see her go, yet didn't know how she could put a rational sentence together for Will, let alone spend the evening with him in the parlor. She was saved when, after supper, a clerk came to the door and delivered an armload of documents from Sir William. Will winced, telling Justine he was sorry, but the papers required his immediate attention. She was secretly glad, and left him to go to her bed.

She lay on a narrow bed in the cold light of the moon, watching it dart through clouds as though in search of a hiding place. She could not sleep for thinking of Will's mother's words. *I can still stop you.* How? *By telling him about me?* Her vow to Lord Thornleigh was sacred, she had said, but people routinely broke their vows. If she did tell, would it devastate Will? That afternoon in the hubbub of Westminster, when they were both flushed with the thrill of Justine's message from Mary and the joy of being reunited, it had seemed that nothing could take Will from her. But now, shaken by the depth of his mother's derangement, she was no longer sure.

About anything. She could not beat back images of the atrocities her grandfather and her uncle had inflicted on the Thornleighs. Could such things be true? Her father had said nothing about it. *He told me only what our family suffered. But can I believe a woman who raves such lies about Father? No, she is truly mad.*

Did Will know his mother was mad? Was that why he was so solicitous about her? It gave Justine a desperate hope. *Maybe, then, he won't believe her if she tells him about me.* The thought made her cringe with shame. *I'm a coward. He's bound to find out some day. I should tell him myself, just as Lord Thornleigh has always said.*

A loud thump jarred her. She listened intently. Had an animal got into the room adjoining hers? All she could hear was a faint creaking. It sounded odd, rhythmic. Curious, she got up and opened her door. The passage was dark, no one in sight, human or animal. But the creaking was louder, definitely coming from the chamber next to hers. She tapped lightly on the door. "Hello?"

No answer.

She opened the door. A bedchamber, ghostly dark. She made out a chair fallen on its side. Above the chair a figure floated, all in white, like a ghost.

Justine's heart kicked. The figure was Will's mother. Head askew. The rope from the rafter, creaking.

She lurched forward. Grabbed the dangling legs. The creaking stopped. She looked up and saw the white face lazily swing to her, a result of the rope's final twist. The dead eyes stared down at her.

A form appeared at the doorway. Will, in shirtsleeves. He froze. Ink stains on his fingers.

❧ 23 ❧

Journeys

The gunpowder was hidden inside household goods being delivered by boat to Kilburn Manor: a keg of salt, two crates of candles, and five sacks of grain. Christopher, in workman's clothes, was aboard the boat as it reached his sister's jetty just east of Chelsea village. He rolled the salt keg down the ramp from the deck, keeping his head down as four porters from her house came down the jetty to pick up the cargo. He was relieved to see the area so quiet. The sun was up, a new workday beginning, but on this stretch of the Thames the only signs of life were a couple of fishing smacks, and ducks diving among the riverbank reeds. Kilburn Manor was the ideal place to lure Elizabeth. But would she take the bait? Christopher was on tenterhooks waiting to hear. He'd had no word from Justine since sending her with Mary's message yesterday.

A deeper fear had gnawed him all night. Had Justine gone back to pay the witness for his information? Frances, the fool, had given her the money. Did Justine now know that he had dispatched her friend Alice? His time was running out. Elizabeth *had* to take his bait.

He glanced up at the house. Frances was rushing down the steps. He was dismayed to see her coming straight toward him. Damn the woman, why hadn't she just sent her steward? Had she no sense?

"Where to, my lady?" one of the porters asked.

"What?" She looked as nervous as a caught felon.

Christopher hefted the keg up onto his shoulder and prompted her. "To the cellar, my lady?"

"Oh . . . yes." She went on with unnatural precision, raising her voice for her porters to hear, "That's right. Take everything down to the cellar."

Christopher stalked past her. She followed him and the porters as they carried the cargo around to the cellar door, trudged down the stairs, and deposited it. The space was dim, the morning light creeping through a single high slit of a window. Frances dismissed the porters, and Christopher pretended to wipe a cut on his hand, waiting as the men went up the steps. As soon as he was alone with her he said in a furious low voice, "I told you, everything must seem normal. Change nothing in your household routine. Nothing. Now, have you heard from Justine?"

She shook her head, looking distraught. "No."

So he still didn't know where he stood. Would Elizabeth come before Justine's witness could destroy him? There was nothing to do but prepare. He grabbed a crowbar to pry off the keg lid. "All right. Get upstairs and go about your day."

"No, Christopher, we cannot go on!"

He turned on her. "What?"

"We must abandon the scheme."

Dread gripped him. Had he been betrayed? "What's happened?"

She held out a paper. "Look!" The light was so poor Christopher could not make out the writing. "What is it?"

"From Adam. He has left Portsmouth. He's stopped in London." She wailed, "He'll be home tomorrow!"

"Shh!" He glanced up the stairs. Anyone might hear her. "Pull yourself together, Frances. We will deal with this. You know we cannot stop now."

Her mouth trembled. Fear strained her face. She shook her head. "No . . . not here. Not with Adam coming. You must find another place."

He wanted to shake her. Another place? The fool! He clamped

down his fury. "You're anxious, I understand that. But we have come too far to turn back now."

"But, Adam!"

"All you need to do is put him off." He forced gentleness into his voice. "Frances, we are so close to victory. I've heard from Northumberland. He has over five thousand men ready to ride, with more being mustered every hour. And they will be backed by battle-hardened Spanish troops ready to cross from Rotterdam at a day's notice. Now you and I must do our part. If Elizabeth agrees to meet Lord Herries here, your work is finished. I shall do the rest." He slapped his palm on the crate that held some of the gunpowder. "Just think, she'll be in your great hall, right above where you and I stand now."

"Put him off?" She said it as if she had heard nothing else. "How?"

"Send him a message. Forestall him." He wished her wretched husband *would* come; then he could rid the world of one more Thornleigh. But Frances would not go through with this if there was a chance of her husband being hurt. "You say he's in London. Where?"

"The Admiralty."

"Then send him word there's sickness here in the house. Tell him to stay where he is until he hears from you that the infection is past. Can you do that?" She still looked glassy-eyed with anxiety. "Frances, if Elizabeth agrees, this will soon be over. But until then you must stay strong. Now go, send the message. And then wait to hear from Elizabeth."

She closed her eyes as if it was all too much. But she nodded and whispered, "All right."

Like a sleepwalker fleeing a nightmare, Justine found herself at Kilburn Manor. She hardly knew how she had reached the place. Stumbling out of Will's house was the last thing she remembered clearly. She must have wandered London's streets for hours because she was vaguely aware of the sun being high as she sat numbly in the boat heading west. But the decision to come to Chelsea, and the conversation, if it could be called that, with her aunt in the parlor—a conversation in which Justine could scarcely hold a thought or hold herself upright on her trembling legs—was all a fog.

"Your father?" her aunt had said, looking oddly frightened and distant. "He is in the new wing." She had pointed to the empty building across the courtyard.

Now Justine found herself standing in a space that seemed like a huge cave. A cave on a cliff. That's how it felt, for she had come up a long flight of marble stairs, and all the way up she had glimpsed sky through gaps in canvas sheets hung over tall, unglazed windows that ran from the ground to the second-story ceiling. Her skirt hem had dragged over thin drifts of snow hiding in the stair corners. The cave was a vast empty chamber off the staircase. It was dark, the windows covered with boards that blotted the sunlight. As her eyes adjusted to the gloom she saw, at the far end, a small coal fire glowing in a grate in a marble fireplace that was taller than her. She walked toward it, her footsteps echoing up to the lofty ceiling. Her gaze drifted up to the ceiling's twitching shadows and she halted, pierced by the ghastly memory of the woman's body. The creaking rope. The dead eyes staring down at her.

"Justine?"

She gasped as a ghost stepped out of the gloom. A man. Firelight glinted off his blond hair.

"Father!" She ran to him and threw her arms around his neck and held on to him tightly with all the need of a child lost in a nightmare. From the warmth of him she realized she was cold to the bone.

"You're shaking. Justine, what has happened?"

"Take me with you! Please, Father. Take me with you to France."

He pried her away from him and took hold of her hands. "France? What are you talking about?"

"When you go with Mary. I beg you, let me go with you!"

"Child, you're making no sense. This isn't about . . . your friend Alice, is it? The man you mentioned?"

Rigaud. Oh God, she had forgotten. "No, no, I haven't been there."

"I see." He squeezed her hands with fresh energy. "But you did deliver the message to Thornleigh, didn't you?"

"No."

"What?" he cried in dismay.

"Not to him. To Sir William Cecil."

"Ah! Even better. And Cecil has taken it to Elizabeth?"

She nodded. It was difficult to think.

"You're sure?"

"Yes. He took the message to Whitehall. He is urging Her Majesty to agree. No, wait . . . was that yesterday? Yes, I saw him go yesterday." She could not force her mind onto the matter. Her thoughts were still snagged in the horror. Will's face, as white as his mother's corpse. His hoarse questions. She had blurted in shock, "It's my fault." Shock had heaved the confession out of her, about her family, herself: "I am a Grenville." And a cold grave of silence had opened between her and Will.

"Justine, you have done well," her father said.

He was smiling, but misery racked Justine. Done well? She had brought everything crashing down around her and was stumbling through the rubble of her life. Will hated her. It was over. *Just as his mother intended.*

"Oh, Father . . . Father." He was all she had now. The only person who loved her for herself. She clutched fistfuls of his shirt. "He hates me. *Hates* me." She could not hold back the tears.

"Who hates you? What are you talking about?"

It came out of her in a rush of wretchedness. How she loved Will but had kept secret her identity even as they took their betrothal vows. How his mother had hated her and hanged herself. How Justine finally told him, over his mother's body, and lost him forever.

"Good heavens," he murmured, holding her to comfort her. "I had no idea. Poor Justine."

His sympathy felt like balm. She sobbed in his embrace. He smelled faintly of smoke. Or was it just a fragment of memory? That night he had fled from Yeavering Hall. It sent a thought of Alice shuddering through her. *I must see Rigaud. Must do that, for Alice.* Two days, Rigaud had said. *When did he say that?* Her thoughts were a dark tangle, all thorns. She could not think straight. She clung to her father, adrift.

"Come, sit down." He led her to a scatter of cushions on the floor by the little fire. She kneeled, feeling suddenly so drained she could have laid down and gladly sunk into the oblivion of sleep. He poured her a cup of wine from a bottle amongst his few belongings, and she took several deep swallows. The liquor shot fire to her empty stomach and fuzziness to her head.

"I am sorry for this crude place with so little to comfort you," he said gently. "You know I cannot show my face in public. So I camp here as I wait."

She was so grateful for his love and understanding, it took a moment to pull her mind back to what he meant. She dried her eyes with her sleeve. "Wait?"

"For Elizabeth's reply. Whether she will come here to meet Lord Herries, aye or nay."

"Ah, yes." The rest of the world, beyond her private woe.

"She will send word to Frances."

Justine nodded. "I believe she will come." The wine, the warm little fire, the affection in her father's face—she had found a haven and longed to stay safe within it, with him. "And when Mary's abdication is settled you will return with her to France. You said so. All I want is to go with you." She tried to smile. "You and I, Father, we will lighten each other's exile." But she could not hold on to the smile. Hot tears brimmed. "There is nothing for me here."

Dusk was gathering when Christopher got the news. Frances beckoned him to the doorway to tell him. Justine lay asleep on the cushions by the small fire. Frances stood hugging herself, the fur trim on her cloak trembling in the draft. "Elizabeth has agreed," she whispered.

His heart jumped. "When?"

"Tomorrow."

So fast! He could not believe his luck. "What time?"

"Just after dark. Cecil sent word. She will come in a fishing boat with five men-at-arms dressed as sailors. There must be no special preparations here to give away her identity. Herries must come alone. She will stay no more than an hour. Those are Cecil's terms."

He smiled. The hour would be Elizabeth's last. As for Herries, Mary had agreed to sacrifice him. "You accepted, of course?"

She nodded. Now that it was arranged she seemed calmer, almost eager. Yet worry flitted across her face. "A pity to lose the old manor house."

"Frances, when Mary is queen you shall build as many grand new mansions as you wish."

A smile wobbled on her lips. She looked past him to the hearth where Justine lay sleeping. "Does she know?"

"Only what she needs to. Go now. And do not come back unless it's urgent."

He closed the door and came back to the hearth. He sat on a cushion beside Justine, feeling strangely empty. Now that victory was so near, he knew he should be elated. Or even feel the opposite, fear that something might yet go wrong. But he felt neither as he watched the fire's glow flicker over his daughter's face, her brow creasing in her fitful sleep. How relieved he had been to hear that she had not gone back to the witness. It meant he had time to finish his mission, thank God. But what a sad tale she had told about the young man she loved, and his mother hanging herself. He felt a deep pang of regret. *She loves a nephew of Richard Thornleigh, yet I, her father, knew nothing of it, played no part in advising her, guiding her.* He had not even seen her grow to womanhood. He felt cheated of the years spent apart from her. The puny fire cringed in a draft, and Christopher looked around the room in anger at being an outlaw, forced to camp here in the barren vastness of his sister's broken dream. The three of them—his daughter, his sister, and himself—had all been cheated of what was theirs. Yeavering Hall should be his. *He* should be baron, not Thornleigh.

A new thought reared up in his mind. Talking to Frances earlier to allay her fears about her husband, he had half wished Adam Thornleigh would indeed come home and die with Elizabeth. Rid the world of one more Thornleigh. But the member of that house that Christopher most wanted to see pay for his sins was the baron himself. Could he make that happen?

Justine awoke with a start. "What?" she cried, sitting bolt upright, looking about, disoriented.

"Shh. You're safe here, child. All is well."

She blinked, relaxing. "Father." She rubbed her neck, sore from the makeshift bed. "You should have woken me."

"You need sleep. And a proper bed. Go to your aunt now. She will see you are taken care of for the night."

"I would rather stay with you."

"I have some business to attend to. For Mary." He lowered his voice, though there was not another soul in the entire deserted building. "Justine, Elizabeth comes here tomorrow."

She brightened. "It's arranged? She sent word to my aunt?"

"Yes, tomorrow night. The feast day of Saint Thomas à Becket." He added, teasing, "You haven't forgotten your saints' days, I hope?"

"No, indeed." She mustered a smile. "Saint Thomas. I am glad. Mary going to France is best for both queens."

He wished he could tell her the truth. That the day after tomorrow one queen would be dead and the other would be awaiting Northumberland's forces to restore a panicked country and crown her Queen Mary. But there was something he *could* share with Justine. In fact, he needed her. To settle his score with Thornleigh. "You shall not come with me to France," he said.

She was about to protest, but he held up his hands to forestall her, though he was moved by the entreaty in her eyes. "Your place is in England, Justine. Your homeland. You should go back tomorrow morning to Thornleigh's house. It is where you belong."

"But why? They don't trust me anymore. I told you, Father, there is nothing now to keep me here."

"There is. A future. There is none for you in France. I cannot give you what Thornleigh can give you. A grand family name. A glittering match. You should marry an earl's son." It gave him pleasure to say so, for it was exactly what he intended for her. When Mary was queen of England she would raise Christopher to the peerage, and if he were made an earl his daughter deserved no lesser rank in her husband. But he could not tell her that. "No, I will not take you to France. You belong in England, and in England you shall stay."

She slumped, dejectedly accepting it.

"But there is something I want you to do," he said. "My name will always be a weight around your neck as long as the old feud festers between our families. I want to lift that weight."

She looked curious despite her disappointment.

"Oh, I'll admit, my kinfolk must bear their share of blame," he went on. "Mind you, more Grenvilles died than Thornleighs. But the feud has gone on too long and has hurt too many people, including you. I want to end the lethal rancor, once and for all. Will you help me? Will you be the peacemaker?"

Her look was full of wonder. "I? How?"

"By bringing me and Thornleigh together. I will make an apology to him. I will grovel, if that's what he wants. Whatever it takes I will do if it's in my power. I want peace between us, finally. For your sake, Justine. For your future."

"But he might hand you over to be hanged."

"I think he will not. He has raised you like a daughter, hiding your name, which a scandal about me might unmask. Clearly he, too, wants an unblemished future for you. Let us hope he also wants peace."

Her eyes brimmed. "You are such a good and generous man, Father. Tell me what I can do."

Morning mist drifted over Cripplegate Ward where mourners threaded into St. Olave's churchyard behind six pallbearers. Richard Thornleigh walked hand in hand with Honor at the head of the procession, preceded only by Will. Richard's eyes, scratchy with grief, were fixed on his sister's coffin. Poor, deranged Joan. He had never imagined her despair so deep that she would take her own life! To steady himself he wrapped his other hand around the hilt of his sword in its sheath. A memory flooded him of Joan as a child romping in their father's barley field, laughing as she stuck a feather in the cap of the scarecrow. She was younger than Richard. *She should not have died first.* The plodding group turned as they passed through the church gate, and it seemed to him the coffin floated, barely touching the pallbearers' shoulders. *An illusion,* he told himself. *Stay rational.*

His eyes fell again on Will ahead of him, Will's back rigid with anguish. And with wrath at Justine, Richard knew. Will held her responsible for Joan's death. That cut into Richard. What a tragic breach his sister had wrought between the two young people. What a heartbreaking, senseless tragedy. He heard a small sound of pain from Honor and suddenly realized he was crushing her hand. He let it go, the word *sorry* rising in him but not making it through his dry mouth. She took his hand again with a look of desolate but ardent solidarity. It moved him. He wanted to say *thank you* but could only nod, a feeble substitute.

He looked ahead down the path, and it pained him to see the freshly mounded earth beside the grave. Yet he was relieved that the procession was almost over. The walk from the house on Silver Street had been a trial, his right foot numb again. It occurred to him, with a pin-prick of bleak awareness, that no one noticed, since everyone was shuffling like him.

The black-robed vicar stood waiting at the grave. *Like a vulture,* was Richard's thought. The vicar opened his prayer book, looking sour. *My bribe should have sweetened him,* Richard thought. The churchman had pocketed the gold and agreed to allow the cause of death to be entered in the parish register as "a sickly heart," yet now he was barely hiding his disgust at a suicide being interred in hallowed ground. Richard didn't give a damn. Nothing and no one would stop him from burying Joan beside her husband.

Everyone grouped around the grave, then halted. For a moment, silence. The morning was unseasonably warm, humid. Melting snow dripped off the church eaves. It felt oddly like spring, Richard thought. But it was winter. No green buds on the barren branches. No birdsong. Just the damp silence of death. Wasn't this the feast day of Saint Thomas à Becket? He remembered Joan as a child asking in amazement how a king could order soldiers to murder an archbishop in his cathedral. She had whispered in awe, "That king must be in hell."

Will stood like a headstone, so rigid it seemed to Richard he was not even breathing. *Poor boy,* he thought. *Grief cannot be borne alone. Justine should be beside you.*

Where was the girl? They had not seen her since yesterday. His first thought was that she had gone to Adam's house in Chelsea, but Adam was in Portsmouth and Richard knew Justine had never warmed to Frances, so it seemed an unlikely place for her to seek comfort. He hoped she had gone to see a sympathetic friend. The Langly girl's house, perhaps. Or the Fosters. But why not send him word? Too shaken, he supposed. No wonder. It rocked him, remembering the awful scene he had found at Joan's house. Her manservant, Joseph, said he saw Justine stumbling out of the house soon after finding the body.

"She found Joan . . . hanging?"

"Aye, my lord." Joseph had shaken his head, overwhelmed. "I were in my bed in the attic and I heard her and Master Will exchange words. Couldn't tell what they said, just voices, edgy-like and fast speaking. Then a scream from Susan. I hurried down to see what was amiss, and there was Susan keening over the mistress's body where they'd laid on her bed, and Master Will staring at Mistress Thornleigh like she'd killed his mother with her bare hands."

Later, when Richard could get Will, still in shock, to talk, Will had told him about Justine's confession. Her deceit, as he put it. "A Grenville," he had said in a voice as tight as wire. "She's a *Grenville.*"

Sorrow had swept Richard. The feud had claimed another victim. Joan had laid up her hate for years, like so much kindling, until it finally blazed and consumed her. Justine was only the spark.

And now, where was the girl? *What hell must she be suffering? She is paying for our feud,* he thought. *Another victim.*

The prayers drifted past his ears, an indistinct drone. The coffin was lowered into the grave. Will took a shovel and cast on the first earth. The pebbled dirt pattered on the coffin lid. Richard swallowed a choke of grief and closed his eyes to say a silent farewell to his sister. He heard the mourners shuffle away. When he looked up, he was alone with Will. Honor was leading Joan's weeping servant, Susan, toward a bench by the church wall, Honor's arm around her. Two gravediggers slowly came forward, giving Richard an apologetic look that said the job had to be done. They began shoveling earth into the grave.

Richard turned to Will. "I don't know what's happened to Justine. We have to find her. Do you have any idea where she might have gone?"

"No." He watched the earth thudding onto the coffin. "Nor do I care."

"Will, she must be in a terrible state. She could be wandering somewhere. She could be hurt."

"What's that to me?"

"Don't talk nonsense. You love the girl."

"I loved *someone*. Not her. That's over."

Such exasperating self-pity. It lit a spark of fury in Richard. "Oh no, this feud isn't done with you yet, boy. Why not speed up its work? Cut your own throat and jump into that grave with your mother." He unsheathed his sword and said to the gravediggers, "Stop your work. Let him jump in."

They halted, stunned, their shovels stilled in midair. Will gaped at Richard.

"Go on, do it," Richard said, prodding him with the flat of his sword. "You're just a walking dead man. You might as well get it over with. Tumble right in beside Joan. There's plenty of room."

They all looked at him like he was a lunatic.

Richard sighed, his anger spent. He jerked his chin in a command to the gravediggers to leave them. They backed off, mumbling, "Yes, my lord," then turned and quickly walked away.

Richard raised the sword, touching the tip to Will's throat. "Hate kills, as surely as does this blade. Kills the spirit, Will. If you keep stoking your hate, the feud just claims another victim. You. Is that what you want? To let this thing kill you as it has killed your mother?"

"I'll live," he growled.

"No, you won't. There's only one way to save yourself. Forgive Justine."

"Forgive?" Rage flashed in Will's eyes. "She's a *liar*. Everything about her is a lie." He chopped the blade away with his arm. "And so are you. You knew about her. All these years."

Richard steadied the sword. "She didn't lie about her love for you. That's why she was so afraid of telling you."

"With good reason!"

"To reject love is to be a killer. So the damnable feud kills Justine, too. Listen to me, Will. Bury this madness along with your mother. Pardon Justine. And let yourself live."

The welfare of England was no respecter of Richard's grief. That very afternoon, back at his house, he was preparing to ride to Baynard's Castle for a meeting with the Earl of Pembroke about carrying out Elizabeth's orders to fortify the Cinque Ports. The threat of war with Spain was very real. Heading for the stable, dragging his numb foot, he felt weighted with weariness, almost despair. Joan was dead. Justine missing. Will intractable. Elizabeth faced the fury of Spain. *And this leg will soon drag me to my own grave.*

"My lord, a message for you." The footman had come from the house.

Richard unfolded the page. It read:

> *Dear my lord,*
> *I must see you. It is urgent. I am in sore difficulty. I*
> *pray you, come this evening to Kilburn Manor at*
> *Chelsea, but do not let Sir Adam's household see you.*
> *Meet me in the new building where we can be alone.*
> *Do not fail me, sir, or my life will be nothing.*
> *Justine*

"Gone?" Justine asked in dismay. She stood at the open door of Rigaud's room in the Martin's le Grand tenement, the pouch of money in her hand. The woman at the door, skinny but for the huge mound of her pregnancy, scowled.

"Gone." She started to shut the door.

"Wait!" Justine pushed it to keep it open. "Gone where?"

"To hell, for all I care. The poxy churchmen took him. Good riddance, say I. Now slog off." She slammed the door.

Justine turned away, trying to think. From dark cracks in door-
ways eyes peered at her. She slipped the purse she carried, bulging
with the money, back into the folds of her cloak. Someone upstairs
bawled a drunken song. Churchmen . . . did that mean the elders
of the French Church? They had chastised Rigaud for his lechery
and his chronic absence from services. They had warned him . . .
of what? What was the punishment?

The moment the answer came to her, she hurried down the
stairs. Her route took her straight across the city, eastward on
Cheapside, then south on Gracechurch Street as it led to London
Bridge. The seaweedy smell of the river rolled to meet her, and
just before the bridge she turned onto Thames Street. She hastened past the Billingsgate fishmongers hawking their catches to
housewives and kept on east to the Custom House Quay. The
church bells of All-Hallows-by-the-Tower were clanging, and the
Tower itself rose above the rooftops, its gray stone walls and tur-
rets glaring over the city and its river traffic.

She was almost out of breath from hurrying as she made her way
through the throng on the quay. Was she too late? The quay was a
noisy mass of merchants and their agents, pie sellers and pamphle-
teers, sailors and whores. Reaching the water's edge, she felt a rush
of panic. So many ships! Only low-masted vessels could go west
beyond the bridge, so here the big ships lay at anchor, crammed together in the Pool. Galleons, carracks, galleasses, caravels, all with
bright flags and pennons fluttering from their shrouds, the flags of
France, Portugal, Sweden, Poland. Seagulls wheeled and swooped,
screeching their impatient cries. She spotted a French ship with
several wherries nudging its side. Men in the wherries were loading crates, barrels, and sacks aboard the ship, and the French crew
were taking on the cargo and readying canvas and lines as though
preparing to embark. Justine pushed through to a spot where busy
clusters of men were carting and sorting more cargo to go out to the
ship. A man sat slumped on a barrel, his back to her, his hands
bound at his back. A prisoner. Justine's spirit soared. It was Rigaud.
She'd been right. He was being deported home to France. She
shouldered through to him.

"Monsieur Rigaud!"

He looked up, over his shoulder. His nose was bloody, his cheek scraped. His eyes went wide as he recognized her.

A pock-faced man stepped into her path. "Halt there. What business have you with the prisoner?"

"I . . . I owe him money."

Rigaud struggled to his feet.

The man pushed him down again, looking almost amused. "Your doxies pay *you*, do they, Frenchie? That's a twist." He chuckled, and so did another man standing guard over Rigaud.

"Please, may I have a word alone with him?" Justine handed the pock-faced man a half crown.

He took the coin and shrugged. "Why not?"

The two guards withdrew a few paces. It was enough for Justine.

"I have the money," she told Rigaud. "Look." She held up the fat purse. "Now, tell me who you saw with Alice in the church. You said you knew the man."

He scoffed. "What's the use? If you give me the money now, it'll go straight into their pockets." He jerked his blood-flecked chin at the two guards who were watching them, arms lazily crossed.

"I can send it to you," she urged. "In France."

"Ha. The devil alone knows where I'll be." He looked away as if done with her.

"Monsieur, please. Won't you tell me? I will give you all of this and more for just one word. Just the name of the man who killed my friend."

He regarded her for a long moment, a misty light coming into his eyes. "I'll tell you what. Give it to Nan."

"Who?"

"You saw her. Big with child."

The skinny woman at the door? It surprised her. The woman had spat his name.

"I'll miss her," he said. "Give the money to her."

"I shall." The lead guard was starting to look impatient. "The name, monsieur," she said. "Give me the name."

A wherryman shouted a last call for loading his boat to go out to the ship. "That's for me," Rigaud said, getting wearily to his feet.

"*Adieu* to Puritan-ridden England." Then, bitterly, "*Bonjour* to priest-ridden France."

It struck Justine that she had come for nothing. "You don't know," she said in dismay. "You don't know who killed her. You only wanted the money."

"Oh, I know," he said quietly. "I sold him wine for years. I saw him strangle that girl. I ran so he wouldn't see *me*. That was the last thing I needed, him looking to finish me off, too. He always was a prickly one. Liked a fine claret, but I never could sell him my Malmsey. Not good enough for the lord of Yeavering Hall."

"Did you say . . . Yeavering Hall?" The thought of Isabel's husband Carlos jolted her. Madness. Impossible.

"That's right. For that's the name. Sir Christopher Grenville. I'd heard he was dead. I'd been away so long. But Grenville is who I saw that day in Kirknewton church. He was very much alive. It was the girl who was dead." Rigaud looked at her. "See that you give that money to Nan, won't you?"

She heard no more words. Only clanging church bells. Shrieking gulls. In her head, in her horror, a roaring like the sea.

PART THREE

Elizabeth

❧ 24 ❧

The Children

I saw him strangle that girl. Rigaud's words thrashed in Justine's mind as the wherryman strained at his oars, making for Chelsea. The wind had kicked up choppy waves, and Justine gripped the gunwale for balance. The waves beat the boat and the Frenchman's words beat at her: *Sir Christopher Grenville . . . I saw him strangle that girl.*

Absurd, her rational mind told her. Rigaud, of course, had made a terrible mistake. He was simply wrong. Justine was coming to Kilburn Manor to see her father, and a few words with him would clear up the hideous error. *June fifth?* he would tell her. *I was sailing that day from France.*

The wherry rocked as it came alongside the Kilburn Manor jetty and she climbed out, shivering so much she fumbled at the coins in her purse to pay the wherryman. The wherryman tipped his cap to her and pushed off to row back to the city. She was alone on the jetty. Winter's late-afternoon shadows stretched across the river, trying to claim the land for dusk. She looked up at the old red brick manor house. She had spent the night there in a soft bed in a scented chamber and had not seen her father that morning before she'd set off to see Rigaud. Across the courtyard rose the new wing, imposing but deserted. Her father was camping there. Hiding out.

A crane startled her, lifting off the water with a noisy flapping of wings. She stared at the rings of ripples the bird left, breaking up as they met the confused waves. Kilburn Manor was such a solitary place here at the bend in the river where waterfowl fed among the reeds. It struck her that Elizabeth would be coming here tonight to discuss Mary's abdication. An excellent place for the secret meeting. No one to see Elizabeth arrive.

Father arranged that well. That was a happy thought. *He cares about Mary. Cares about me. Rigaud's accusation is absurd.*

Up the steps to the house she went, then across the muddy courtyard toward the new wing. The mild weather of the last days had melted the pristine Christmas snow. The lane of topiary felt like a tunnel rising out of the muck. She hastened through its shadows. *Absurd,* she told herself. Her father had barely remembered Alice when she had mentioned her murder. Besides, why would he have been anywhere near Yeavering Hall?

To simply see again the grand house that once was his? She remembered his anger: *"It was stolen from me."*

No, it was absurd and Rigaud was confused. He had not seen her father for over a decade. He only *thought* he saw him in Kirknewton church.

Yet Rigaud had been so sure. He had known her father well, had personally sold him wine at Yeavering Hall. For years.

No, *absurd.* Strangle Alice? What possible reason could he have for such a savage act? *Father will explain. He'll scoff and say that poor Rigaud has been drinking too much of his own wine.*

She reached the new building, cold inside, deserted, and climbed the wide staircase. Upstairs she opened the door to the lofty chamber where her father had comforted her yesterday beside the little coal fire. The room was abandoned. No sign of his makeshift camp at the hearth. His few belongings, the scatter of cushions, the coal fire, all had vanished. For a moment, standing in the chill darkness, it seemed to Justine that she might only have dreamed that he had been here.

No. She remembered his comforting words, his sympathetic embrace. Remembered him telling her Elizabeth was coming.

Back to the main house she went to seek Frances. *Aunt* Frances, she reminded herself. It was still hard to think of her as kin since she had avoided Frances for so long, not wanting any tie to another Grenville, wanting everyone to accept her as a Thornleigh. Now, with Will lost to her, everything was different. It gripped her like grief. She tried to take heart from the lesson she had learned, that her Grenville kin were the only people she could rely on. Her aunt. Her father.

She found Frances in her bedchamber. She had pushed open the green brocade bed curtains and stood sorting through a heap of objects dumped helter-skelter on the bed. Silver spoons, silver plates, ropes of pearls and jeweled rings, gem-studded goblets, silver candlesticks.

"Aunt, have you seen my father?"

Frances spun around, her hand flying to her heart. "Justine! Oh, you gave me a fright."

Justine was surprised by her appearance. A frantic look in her eyes, her hair in disarray. Perhaps it was the stress of preparing to welcome Her Majesty to her house. Frances had always been high-strung. "Has he left for Bolton already? My father?"

"Bolton?"

"In the north. To see Mary. Help her prepare."

"For what?"

"For going to France. I must see him before he leaves England."

"Leaves? Good heavens, Christopher will never leave England. No, no, he just rode to Kingston. He'll be back in time." She wiped a hand across her brow sheened with sweat and went back to sorting through the pile, hastily packing objects into a satchel on the foot of the bed.

Never leave England? Justine knew that was not true, but she hesitated to press the point, for her aunt looked so oddly distracted, her actions almost manic. Was she ill? She watched her cram a silver salt cellar into the satchel. "Are you going somewhere? After the Queen's visit?"

"After . . . ?" Frances started like a caught thief. She wrung her hands. "I know, Christopher said not to pack. Said it would look wrong. I understand. And of course gowns I can replace. But these precious things . . ." She caught sight of something on a table and cried, "Ah!" She hurried over to it and grabbed it, a jeweled casket. "My mother's." She tried to jam it into the satchel, but it was too large, the satchel too full. She threw up her hands in despair, then sank onto the bed. "So much to organize. I cannot keep it all in my head. The servants . . . well, nothing can be done about that. It's the children . . . the children . . . they are my life!" She looked frightened and was fighting tears. "They will go to my friend, Lady FitzAlan. It's all arranged. But not until later, Christopher says. Not until not until Elizabeth arrives. I promised him, no changes. But, oh dear God, to wait until the last moment . . ." She rubbed her brow. Her breathing was shallow. "Do I have time to take my little ones before he comes back? No . . . no, Christopher would be angry. And I know he's right, but—" She suddenly stopped and gaped up at Justine. "You!" She jumped up. "*You* can take them!"

Justine was trying to follow the incoherent babble. "Katherine and Robert? To see your friend?" A social visit for the children? How could she think about such things with Rigaud's words clanging in her mind! "I'm sorry but I cannot. I must see my father. You say he'll be back this evening?"

"Of course. Soon. But I want the children out before he comes. Please, you *must* take them."

"Perhaps your steward can take them. It's urgent that I stay and see—"

"I cannot trust him! Not him, not any servant."

"What? Why not?"

"Because he is not one of *us*. You are. Christopher says you are." She clutched Justine's hand. Frances's hand felt so icy, Justine flinched. "He wants the best for you, Justine. And we all must trust each other now. It will be worth it, you'll see. Once this is over and Mary is queen, our family will be restored. But for now, my children cannot stay here."

"Mary . . . queen?" What was she talking about?

"Good heavens, Justine, what else do you think all this is about?"

"The meeting tonight, you mean? It's because Mary is abdicating."

Frances shook her head, a sly light in her eyes. "No, she's not."

A cold finger scraped up Justine's backbone. *Why* was Frances sending the children away? Was there some impending danger? And why was she packing her silver? She slid her hand free of Frances's grip. "Aunt, what is going on?"

Frances spoke in a low voice that thrummed with excitement. "Plans are afoot."

"Yes. Elizabeth is coming. But if not to discuss Mary's abdication, then why?"

The sly look in Frances's eyes deepened to satisfaction. "Because after tonight there will be no Elizabeth."

Justine stared at her. Her mind emptied violently as if a plug had been pulled and everything she knew about herself flooded out. Will's mother's words rushed in. *"The swamp that bred you, the crocodiles who whelped you . . . you cannot escape your tainted blood . . . your father, Christopher Grenville, a traitor . . . He plotted against our queen."*

She felt her legs might give out. Treason. *Father.* She groped for the bed-curtain to steady herself.

He's going to kill Elizabeth.

"Justine? Are you all right?" Frances was regarding her warily, a frown creasing her brow, as if she suddenly realized she had said too much.

Justine's heart was banging so hard, so high in her chest, she could not find breath to speak. *Frances is his accomplice. They're going to kill Elizabeth. Here. Tonight.*

"Justine?" Frances stiffened.

Their eyes locked.

Justine saw that if she betrayed an inkling of her horror, Frances would see. Would know she was not one of them. *Get out,* she thought frantically. *Get away from here.* But if Frances suspected, she could call in servants to hold her.

She made herself let go of the curtain. There was only one way to get out. Pretend to go along.

"I had no idea," she said, forcing steadiness into her voice. "About . . . dispatching Elizabeth. I wish Father had told me."

Frances still seemed wary. "He thought it better that you didn't know. Safer for us all. Since you're so close to Lord and Lady Thornleigh."

Justine's heart bled. *Father used me.* The abdication message from Mary—a lie. His litany of the Thornleighs' crimes—lies.

And Rigaud? "I saw him strangle that girl."

That horror was too monstrous. If she thought about it now she would go mad.

"Still," she said, "I wish you had confided in me. I could have helped more."

"Well, I wasn't sure," Frances said, flustered.

"I got close to Mary, as you know. She is the monarch England needs. A monarch of the true faith. *Our* faith."

Frances relaxed a little. "Christopher brought you up well. Your soul is Catholic."

Justine's thoughts were charging ahead. She had to get away immediately, before her father came back. And Elizabeth—she would soon be on her way here. *How can I prevent the calamity?* "Aunt, we will work together and get this done. So please, keep nothing from me. Let me help. What can I do? Of course, the children! We must get them away, now."

Frances brightened. "You'll take them?"

"Right away. You are so right not to entrust their safety to servants. But we must leave without making a fuss, it must look like an ordinary outing."

"Exactly. To Arundel House. Lady FitzAlan is expecting them. A visit to her children, I told her."

"I know her ladyship. Call Katherine and Robert." She tugged Frances to the door. "Hurry, Aunt, call the children. I'll have them settled snugly with Lady FitzAlan before the sun goes down."

"Bless you, Justine."

Frances's boat had been brought around to the end the jetty, and a gray-haired footman with a sunken chest and a cough sat at the oars waiting for them. Justine held hands with Katherine and Robert, hurrying them toward the boat. Her father might be back at any moment.

"Off we go now," she told the children as merrily as she could. She turned to the footman, smiling. She needed to make a friend of him if she was to countermand the orders Frances had given him. Her destination was not Arundel House, but Lord Thornleigh's house. No one would believe a warning from her, but Elizabeth would listen to Lord Thornleigh. "What's your name?" she asked.

"He's Fletcher," said Robert as he hopped into the boat.

The footman nodded, suppressing a cough. "Aye, mistress. Fletcher." He did not look well.

"There's a half crown for you," she said, "if you'll row us faster than you've ever rowed."

"A race?" Katherine asked eagerly as she took the stern seat beside her brother.

"That's silly," Robert told her. "We're the only boat."

"I'll do me best," the footman muttered.

"What's wrong with Mother?" Katherine asked Justine.

"Wrong? Why, nothing."

"She was crying when she said good-bye."

"Ah, well, I warrant there's a lot on her mind." Justine stepped into the bow and sat, telling Fletcher to cast off. He was in the middle, his back to her. He hauled at the oars and the boat pulled away, and Justine looked back at the house. Sickness roiled in her stomach. How did her father plan to kill Elizabeth? *Like he killed Alice?* She took a deep breath of the cold river air. No time for sickness. She had to stop Elizabeth from coming.

They passed a fishing smack, its sails luffing as the men hauled in their catch. The river was broad, and near the far shore wherries and small sailboats beat against the wind and waves. She watched Fletcher labor at the oars. He did not look strong, and it was four miles to London. She wished she had a strapping oarsman to speed her all the way to the Old Swan Stairs by London Bridge. From there she could run to Lord Thornleigh's house on Bishopsgate Street.

A terrible new thought struck her. The note she had sent to Lord Thornleigh! *I pray you, come this evening to Kilburn Manor . . . Do not fail me, or my life will be nothing.* Her father had urged her to write it—to make peace with his lordship, he had said. She cursed herself for believing him. She dreaded what he really intended. He had murdered Alice—it choked her to face that, but she now felt it must be true. And he was preparing to murder the Queen. And Lord Thornleigh? Was that part of his grotesque plan? Wildly, she prayed that her note had miscarried, that his lordship had not received it. *Let it be so. Don't let him come.*

Finally they were abreast of Westminster. But there was still so far to go! "As fast as you can, Fletcher. *Please.*"

She looked at the children in the stern. Katherine had got hold of a rope and was making the end of it dance like a spirited snake to entertain Robert, who giggled. *They have no idea,* Justine thought. The girl had her father's lively dark eyes. A new fear cut into her. Was Sir Adam part of the treason plot? "Katherine, where is your father?"

"In Portsmouth," she said proudly. "With the fleet."

Robert grumbled, "He's *always* in Portsmouth."

Safely distant, Justine thought. Had Sir Adam planned it that way to prevent suspicion? She didn't know what to think. He used to be one of Elizabeth's most favored courtiers, but everyone knew he had fallen out with her over his attack on the Spanish ambassador's kinsman. Besides, he had married a Grenville. Where did Sir Adam's loyalty lie?

It didn't matter. All that mattered was keeping her father from getting near Elizabeth. How was he planning to do it? A knife? Poison? A garrote? *Oh, Alice, Alice . . .*

Past the river traffic she now could see the luxurious grounds of the noblemen's mansions that ran down to the river from the Strand. Leicester House, Somerset House, Durham House, Russell House, and the sheer walls of Arundel House rising straight out of the river. The home of Henry FitzAlan, Earl of Arundel, and his wife.

Fletcher began to turn the boat, heading for the water stairs of Arundel House.

"No, row on," Justine told him. She had no intention of stopping there. "Straight on toward the bridge. We'll stop at the Old Swan Stairs."

"What?" Katherine asked, curious. "Are we not to visit Lady FitzAlan?"

"No, we're going to see your grandfather." *I'll tell him everything. About Father. He will stop this.*

"Go on?" Fletcher repeated, frowning at her over his shoulder, his oars lifted in confusion. "Sorry, mistress, I cannot do that."

She put steel in her voice. "I beg your pardon? Row *on*, man."

He shook his head. "My orders are from Lady Frances."

"Lady Frances entrusted her children to me, and I am telling you, row on."

He lowered the oars, his mind made up. "My mistress is Lady Frances, and she said Arundel House. So Arundel House it is." He rowed for the earl's wharf.

Justine felt frantic. Arundel House was over a mile away from Lord Thornleigh's house. She had to get there before he left for Chelsea. There was not a moment to lose. "Stop," she ordered.

He grimly kept rowing. "Pardon me, mistress, I can do without your half crown. Cannot do with losing my post."

The children watched in surprised fascination, their eyes darting between the two adults.

Justine stood up. The boat rocked. "You are relieved. I will take the oars." She stepped toward him. The boat wallowed dangerously. Fletcher gaped over his shoulder at her, her balance so unsteady she swayed on her feet. "Move forward," she said. "I am rowing." She grabbed his sleeve and jerked him up off his seat. Unbalanced, he threw a leg over the seat but lost his footing. The boat rolled wildly. Icy water splashed Justine's leg. Fletcher grabbed for her to steady himself, pulling her down. She scrambled to avoid pitching into the river.

"Justine! Look out!" Katherine cried, pointing. The boat, unmanned, had slewed into the path of an oncoming fishing smack, its sails bellying in the wind. Justine thudded onto the midship seat and grabbed an oar. She plied it with desperate strokes, straining to right their course. The fishing boat skimmed past them, the fisherman at the tiller wide-eyed as he veered to miss them. Fletcher got his footing and stood, cursing Justine. He lunged for her to take back the oars. The fishing boat's stern quarter grated against the rowboat's beam, jostling Justine and the children and Fletcher so roughly he toppled overboard.

"Fletcher!" Robert cried.

Justine watched in horror as the footman thrashed in the water. "Help me!" he cried.

His struggle appalled her. She could not let him drown. Hauling on the oars, she forced the boat around and rowed back toward him. The current was against her and it took all her strength to make any way. A wherry, coming eastward with the current, reached Fletcher and the wherryman called out to him and threw him a line. Justine watched, panting, her oars lifted, as Fletcher was hauled aboard the wherry. *Thank heaven.*

The children looked to her, their eyes huge with amazement. She sat gripping the oars, catching her breath, sweat chilling her skin.

"Now, to your grandfather's house," she said, turning the boat again. She had almost got the bow around when she spotted another wherry in the distance beyond the scattered river traffic. It was coming from the west, moving fast under the power of two strong oarsmen. A man stood in the bow, his blond hair streaming in the wind. Even at this distance Justine felt his gaze locked on her. Her heart jolted, them seemed to stop. *Father.*

In one icy wave the knowledge washed over her. He had returned to Kilburn Manor and Frances had told him everything. That Justine had come. That she now knew about Elizabeth. That she had taken the children to safety.

His look was fierce. It terrified her. *He's coming for me.*

"Hold on," she told the children. She rowed with every shred of strength. Rowed so hard her back muscles felt they would snap and the oars burned her palms.

But her father's wherry was faster, the two rowers accustomed to the work. She struggled on, as fast as her shaking body could manage. They passed the Temple and she shot a glance over her shoulder. Ahead to the north the tower of St. Paul's loomed into the gray sky above the city rooftops. In the distance the bridge with its houses straddled the river. The Old Swan Stairs was just this side of the bridge, but there was still so far to go—past Blackfriars, Baynard's Castle, Paul's Stairs, Queenhithe, the Three Cranes. Her father's boat was gaining on her.

The children sat clutching the gunwales, frozen in dismay at her desperate effort. They did not know what she was fleeing from, but clearly they saw her terror. Looking at their frightened faces, concern for them swamped her. It was wrong of her to risk their lives. If she were by herself, she would keep rowing until her hands bled, but what if her father managed to grapple her boat and drag her off it? What if he hurt the children? He had proved his savagery in strangling Alice. Some madness drove him. She could not let Katherine and Robert fall into his hands. She had to get the children ashore, even if it meant risking herself.

The nearest wharf was Blackfriars. She turned and rowed hard for it. The old monastery buildings were a warren of shops and homes crowded together on the crooked streets that led down to the wharf. Boats nudged the water stairs, and wherrymen chatted among people packing their wares into handcarts, some already trudging for home, their workday over. Justine came in so fast her boat crunched alongside the stone steps, jostling her and the children. She tossed the bow line to Katherine. "Hop out. Both of you. I cannot take you to your grandfather's. You must go there on your own." She would row on by herself. She would reach Lord Thornleigh's house faster by water, much faster than the children would. But here in the crowded city they would be safe from her father. "You'll be fine at his house. Get out now, hurry."

"Where are *you* going?" Katherine asked anxiously as she climbed out onto the water stairs.

Justine didn't answer. She was watching over her shoulder. Her father's boat was racing toward her. "Off you go, now. I cannot stop."

Robert was climbing out. "But we don't know the way."

"That way." Justine pointed toward Fleet Street. "Ask as you go. Baron Thornleigh's house. Bishopsgate Street. Off with you. Hurry!"

Reluctantly, they backed away from her. A man pushing a wheelbarrow narrowly missed them. Katherine grabbed Robert's hand and pulled him out of the way. They both stared again at Justine.

"Go!" she called, pushing the boat off from the wharf.

She struggled to turn the boat in the confined space among other boats coming and going. Her oars splashed in frantic jabs at the water. A quick glance back at the wharf. The children had vanished. Thank God! But the glance cost her—she barely managed to avoid colliding with a lumbering tilt boat, and only by veering wildly. It put her on the wrong course. Again, she turned with choppy strokes, her head down with the effort, breathing so hard the cold air stung her throat. Open water lay ahead.

Finally free, she was starting to row in earnest when she raised her head and saw her father closing in on her, looming up on the bow of his boat, his oarsmen pulling hard. They were just an oar's length off, blocking her way. His boat crashed against her bow, knocking her off the seat. She cried out at the pain of her rib hitting the gunwale. She scrambled to her feet. Her father jumped aboard her boat. She lunged for an oar and wrenched it from the oarlock and raised it to swing it at him. He grabbed it in both hands and jerked it, pulling her off balance. She toppled to her knees on the floorboards.

One of his men jumped aboard. "Keep her still," her father said as he refitted the oar. The man clamped his thick hand on the back of Justine's neck and pushed head her down. She was bent over so low it was torture. Fighting for breath, her heart felt it would burst as she heard her father's hard breathing at the oars.

"This is the wrong way," Robert said, balking at the pull of his sister's hand. He pointed behind them. "Grandpapa lives that way."

Katherine kept pulling. "Come *on*." She was straining to keep her eyes on the two men flanking Justine as they marched her west on Fleet Street. "Look, they've made her their prisoner!" The street was busy with people coming and going under Temple Bar, and she lost sight of Justine's rose-colored cloak. She gave Robert a strong tug and got him moving.

"But we should tell that to Grandpapa," he protested as she dragged him.

"What's the good of that if we don't know where they're they taking her? We have to find out. Come *on*."

Past Temple Bar they caught up with the men who had Justine. "We'll follow them," Katherine said. But it was hard to keep the men and Justine in sight. People surged past the children, all taller than they were. Katherine felt she was walking through a moving forest. They didn't dare move into the middle of the street to get a better look for fear of being swallowed up among the wagons and carts and horsemen. When Fleet Street branched into the Strand, cows bellowed as a drove of cattle came south, squeezing all the traffic aside.

"Where is she? I can't see her anymore."

Robert jumped up and down, trying to see beyond people's backs. "There!" he cried, pointing. "I see her!"

"Come on, then."

They passed great houses of the nobility with their walled gardens running down to the river. Footmen in bright livery came and went, going about their masters' business. Katherine recognized the front gates of some of the mansions. She had often come with her mother to visit Lady FitzAlan at Arundel House, which lay a little farther along. Were the men talking Justine there? That didn't seem right. Justine had avoided that place.

She got her answer when the men turned, taking Justine into the sprawling buildings of the Savoy, which hulked between the mansions. "Stop." Katherine jerked Robert to a halt. "Mother said never to go near this place."

"Why not?"

"It's full of thieves. Master Rowan told me that in olden days it was a palace of the church. But there was a rebellion and it got burned and then vagabonds moved in."

They stood in silence, gazing through the Savoy's crumbling stone gates at the despoiled mass of tenements. "And murderers?" Robert asked in hushed awe.

"There she is," Katherine whispered watching Justine's rose-colored cloak disappear down a gloomy alley. She looked up at the high charred walls with gaping window holes. A rough face glared at her from a window. A bristling black beard, a dirty bandage wound around his head, a mad gleam in his eye.

They ran. It was so far to Bishopsgate Street they were out of breath by the time they passed St. Paul's. The rest of the way they went at a fast, breathless walk. Their grandparents' house was one of Katherine's favorite places, always busy with interesting things to do. Helping Grandmamma dig in her garden, playing chess with Grandpapa, throwing sticks for the dogs in the orchard, or goggling at the lords and ladies eating lavish suppers, the children watching from the musicians' gallery. This evening Katherine had never been so glad to run into the great hall. Now her grandfather would take charge and rescue Justine.

"Bless me, where have you little 'uns been mucking about?" said the old nursemaid, Meg, looking up from the end of the long table where she was playing patience, her deck of cards laid out in columns before her. She tsk-tsked at Katherine. "You look more mud than maid."

"Is my grandfather upstairs?" Katherine asked. The hall was empty except for the steward sitting at the other end of the table murmuring with the clerk over ale, and the dogs snoring at the hearth.

"Nay, you just missed his lordship. Rode off alone, so John at the stable said." She turned over the knave of spades, muttering, "John told his lordship he should take him along with darkness coming, but off he went alone."

"And my grandmother?" Katherine said. Lady Thornleigh could send men to rescue Justine. She could even call on help from her friend, the Queen. "Is she in her library?"

"Nay, child, she's been all day at Mistress Croft's house getting the poor dead lady's things in order. No one's here." She peered at the two of them as if realizing how odd their coming here was. "Where's your lady mother? Not with you? Does she know the pair of you are out running wild at this hour?"

Katherine turned to Robert. In his eyes she saw her own alarm. Who could they go to?

❧ 25 ❧

Den of Thieves

Torches on posts lit the Kilburn Manor jetty as Adam Thornleigh's wherry skimmed alongside. Adam was so anxious to see his children, he hopped out before the boat had stopped. *Sickness in the house,* Frances had written. He tossed the wherryman a sovereign for bringing him from the Admiralty, far too much money, but he had no time to poke in pockets for smaller coins. He was wealthy now since Elizabeth had given him a tenth of the Spanish gold. All he wanted was to see Katherine and Robert. Frances's note had been so brief, so abrupt, he had no idea what he was going to find. Who was sick? What kind of sickness? The very terseness of her warning made him think she'd been too upset to give details, and what could distress her that much except a terribly sick child?

Lost in these thoughts as he went down the jetty to the house, he didn't notice the fishing smack until he was abeam it. A weathered but worthy old craft. It was tethered in the shadows, away from the torchlight, its single sail lowered. Had the crew put in here to check on some damage aboard? Two men stood in the darkness at the rail. They wore fisherman's drab homespun garments but looked like no fishermen Adam had ever seen. Cleanshaven. Alert. And wearing polished swords. From the Admiralty? But why come in this guise?

"Are you looking for me?" He introduced himself. "Do you have business with me?"

"No, sir. Not you, sir," one of them said, concise as a soldier.

"Who, then?"

"I can't say, sir."

Adam was taken aback. What kind of answer was that? "Are you here to see my steward?"

"No, sir."

No, indeed. The hour was far too late for any manor business. Perhaps one of their fellows had gone inside for a romantic tryst with a housemaid? The servants' behavior was Frances's purview. He would have questioned them further, but his thoughts kept running back to his children. *Sickness*. He looked up at his house. Over half the windows were dark. "I'll talk to you men later."

He went up the steps to the building, thinking of Robert as a baby. Born weeks early, so tiny, so weak. And now, at six, still small for his age. If plague had struck the house, little Robin would have no chance. Nor Katherine. The thought of losing his daughter sent a shudder through him. *My Kate*. He would rather die himself. *No, stop imagining the worst*, he told himself. He was letting his fears run away with him. It could not be anything as terrible as plague. News of plague in Chelsea would have hit London like a squall; he would have heard.

Nevertheless, the moment he was inside the house, he went straight up to their room. The staircase was dimly lit by rushlights and all was quiet. A good sign, surely. If the servants had gone calmly to bed, the sickness could not be serious.

He reached the children's bedchamber door. It opened with a whisper of air. The room lay in darkness. He went to the bed the children shared. Empty. Neatly made. He looked around half expecting to hear giggling in the shadows, the two of them watching him, playing a trick. But there was silence.

He stared at the bed's neatly tucked covers and dread crept over him. Both dead? Taken away? That boat. Had it brought the undertaker?

Stop, he ordered himself again. He didn't know why such morbid fears were plaguing him. Something about the silence here. And that boat.

Where was Frances? Maybe the children were with her? He headed for her bedchamber.

The tenements in the ruined palace of the Savoy echoed with the barking of dogs. Justine could not stop shivering, and with every shiver the leather cord chafed her wrists bound at her back. She sat on a crumbled, fallen pillar in a dark corner. Across the room a fire spat and leapt inside a cauldron set on the stone floor. The charred walls rose to a ceiling where painted angels, once bright, were grimed with soot. Stars glinted through a jagged hole in the roof.

Justine's eyes flicked between the man who stood beside her, guarding her, and the boys sitting around the cauldron—nine boys, maybe fourteen or fifteen years old, but so stunted by poverty some looked like children. Thieves. They were engrossed in feasting on a roast goose one had stolen from a cookhouse. Their world was so foreign to Justine that she had no idea how much she had to fear from them. But the man beside her she did fear. A hulking, fleshy man like a wrestler. Gorm, her father had called him.

Father. He had brought her to this place. A prisoner. Had ordered Gorm to tie her hands behind her back.

"Forgive me, child. It pains me to have to do this," he had said as Gorm bound her wrists.

"Then don't." She could hardly bear to look at him. But she had to if there was any chance of stopping him. "Take flight for France. Sail away now and never come back, and no one will ever know about tonight. I promise you."

He looked at her sadly. "Would you not miss me just a little, now that we have found each other again?" He jerked his chin at Gorm, an order to step away. When they were alone he went on, "Justine, if anything goes wrong tonight . . . I mean, if I do not see you again—"

"So you're going back? To kill Elizabeth?"

"I want you to know," he said as if she had not spoken, "how happy it has made me to find you. I want you to understand why I am doing this. England is—"

"Your plan is madness. It's wrong. It's a sin!"

"Quite the opposite, child. In ridding the realm of a heretic tyrant, I am doing God's work. And I want you to know that I am doing it for *you*. For your future. The future of our house. Our people. The future of England."

A voice inside her wailed, *My house is the house of Thornleigh. They are my people!* She looked around, desperate for someone to help her. The boy thieves ignored her and her father. It struck her in dismay that they were used to seeing him come and go. This derelict mansion must be where he had hidden while running his mission for Mary. *Mary*, she thought suddenly. "Does Mary know?"

Again, he ignored her question. "I realize how much this troubles you now. Naturally, since Thornleigh has poisoned your mind and your heart. But later, after—"

"You used me to lure him to Chelsea. Why? What are you going to do to him?"

He flinched. "It grieves me to see you so distraught. Especially for *him*." He wrapped his arm around her shoulders and hugged her close. She froze, trying with all her might not to squirm at his touch. He rested his cheek on the top of her head. His voice was raw. "Justine, you cannot imagine the hell I have endured. An exile. Without family. Without home. Without you. It is a living death." He let her go to look at her, and hope stole over his face. "But after tonight everything will change. I will come back for you. We will attend the coronation of Queen Mary. Our house will be restored. Ennobled. Once you are the daughter of an earl, you will thank me."

She looked into his eyes and saw tears. It rocked her. His affection for her was real.

But so was her horror. How could she stop him? She didn't even know how he planned to execute his terrible scheme. Could she find out by dissembling? It seemed her only hope. "I know you have suffered . . . Father. I do understand. But what you are planning is too dangerous. You could die. Elizabeth is well guarded. They will kill you before you even get near her."

His look was sly. "I will not have to. When I served Mary in Edinburgh I attended Bothwell's trial for the murder of Lord Darnley, and I learned valuable facts. Exactly how much gunpowder is necessary to blow up a house."

It stunned her. Lord Darnley, assassinated at Kirk o' Field. It was said that most of Edinburgh had felt the explosion. Now her father was going to blow up Kilburn Manor? She was so horrified, further pretense was impossible. "Dear God," she whispered.

"Ah," he said with satisfaction, "you see that it is possible."

"I see that you are a monster. You killed Alice Boyer!"

He flinched again. "That was . . . an error. She recognized me. I am heartily sorry for it. I have done penance, Justine. But believe me, it had to be done."

"Why?" she wailed. "Why poor Alice?"

A door seemed to close in his eyes. "Enough talk. I must go." He beckoned Gorm. "I will come back for you, Justine. We will put all this unpleasantness behind us." Pulling out a purse, he paid Gorm, dropping coins into his palm. He turned back to Justine and stroked her cheek with sad fondness. "Pray for me, child."

And then he was gone, vanishing into the dark passageway.

Now she watched the boys. And Gorm. He stood near her, leaning against the crumbling stone wall, his arms crossed, his small eyes fixed with amusement on the boys' actions. He was the one she had to get past. If she could manage that, she would run. She had to warn them at Kilburn Manor. If she failed, Elizabeth would die. And Lord Thornleigh.

The boys had finished wolfing the stolen goose and were now busy at their work. Pickpockets and cutpurses, learning their trade. They sat watching a freckle-faced boy who was on his feet approaching a satin doublet that hung from a wire. Small hawks' bells had been sewn on the doublet's hem, and on the pocket flap a little sacring bell hung, the kind once used in church at the elevation of the host.

"Go on. Try it," a tall boy said. He was the instructor, teaching the younger ones.

The student circled the hanging doublet. He stopped and snaked his hand up toward the pocket. The tall boy walked past him and knocked him against the garment. All the bells all rang. Gorm laughed.

The tall boy cuffed the student's ear. "You'll get jostled like that in a crowd, so be ready for it." The others shook their heads, murmuring at the hapless student's error. The tall boy said, "Sit down, runt. Alf, come and show 'im how."

Gorm was enjoying the show, and Justine willed him to keep his attention there. The fallen pillar she sat on was at the end of a row of erect pillars, and beyond them lay a dark corridor. She didn't know where it led—she had been too terrified to take note when her father had Gorm drag her in through the warren of rooms. But there had to be several ways out of the ruined palace, and once she was free of Gorm she would find one. She would run.

"That's showing 'im," said the lead boy proudly as the expert, Alf, slipped his hand out of the doublet pocket without jangling a single bell. Grinning, Alf opened his hand and coin-sized lead disks spilled out, clattering over the broken stone floor. "Grab a counter, each of you," the instructor told the boys. "Anyone who can't, they don't eat tomorrow." They dove for the disks. Gorm laughed at their skirmishing. Justine kept her eyes fixed on him. *Just get to the corridor beyond the pillars.* Then maybe she could lose him. Gorm threw back his head, laughing.

Now.

She jumped up. She took two strides, about to break into a run, when Gorm stuck out his leg. She tripped on his foot and tumbled, hitting the floor on her shoulder. Stone scraped her cheek. Pain seared through her.

Gorm's boot came down on her back. She squirmed at the agony of her hip bones being ground against the floor. He called to the boys, "Why not try with a live one?" His tucked his boot toe under Justine's rib, pried her body up, and flipped her over onto her bound hands. Pain shot like fire to her shoulders.

She looked up in horror. The boys were crowding around her.

*   *   *

Adam swung open the door to the bedchamber. "Frances?"

The room was dark. The bed-curtains were open and on the bed gowns lay helter-skelter amid strewn linens, pewter goblets, papers. The clothes chest under the window stood open, its contents ransacked, leaving a wool stocking snagged on a corner. The strongbox that Adam kept under the bed had been pulled out and stood open, empty of its gold and silver coins.

We've been robbed. Adam turned back to the door. Had that boat outside brought the thieves? Were they still in the house? And where was his family?

He hurried back down the stairs, making the rushlights on the wall tremble in his wake. He turned toward the great hall, but stopped in the gloom when he saw that the doors were shut and four men stood guard. Seeing him, they drew their swords. They wore homespun clothes like the men in the boat but they stood rock still, watching him, ready to defend but not attack. *As disciplined as soldiers*, Adam thought. It made no sense to him. Thieves would not act this way. Who *were* these people? He thought of the Spanish ambassador, de Spes, and his fury at the death of his kinsman after Adam's attack. A fury fed by the pirate attack on the *Nuestra Señora* which gossip credited to Adam. Had de Spes sent these men to rob him in revenge? Worse, had they kidnapped Robin and Kate? Or were they holding his wife and children in the hall behind those doors?

He could not fight four men. He backed away. The guards made no move to stop him.

He considered running up to the servants' quarters on the third floor and rousing the footmen from their beds. But Frances had hired new men while he'd been in the Indies, and they were strangers to him. He didn't know if they could fight, or would.

The stable, then. He knew the grooms.

Down the passage he went and pushed out the back door. He was heading for the stable, trying to make sense of what he'd seen—why would thieves, even kidnappers, shut themselves up in the great hall?—when he heard a scraping and grunting. He stopped and made out a figure slowly dragging something across the courtyard. The darkness made it hard to see, but he could tell it was a woman, and she was struggling to pull a heavy sack that clanked over the flagstones. It was Frances.

He ran to her. "Frances, what's happened?"

"Adam!" She froze.

"Where are the children?"

She gaped at him, still hunched over the sack. "No! No, you cannot *be* here!"

"Who are those men in the house?"

"No . . . no," she gibbered. She looked almost terrorized, obsessively gripping the sack. He had to get her to speak rationally. He took hold of her shoulders, breaking her hold on the sack. Its contents shifted, clattering. "Tell me what's happening." He almost shook her. "Have they got Robert and Kate?"

"We must get away! Come, Adam. Come!" She was pointing at the door in the courtyard's west wall. She lunged for the sack. "Away to the river!"

"What are you talking about?" Beyond that door was nothing but the marshy banks of the River Westbourne, which fed the Thames. "Frances, *where are the children?*"

"Come with me." She began dragging the sack. "To safety!"

Will Croft had been at his mother's house when the children arrived. His friend John Stubbs, the newly ordained vicar, was helping him pack his mother's belongings, some things to go to friends, some to the poor in Stubbs's parish. It was a heartbreaking business and Will was carrying it out mindlessly, like a sleepwalker. Having spiraled through shock, anger, and grief, he had reached a state of drained acceptance that left him almost numb. Stubbs was in the parlor packing candlesticks and Will was coming downstairs from his mother's room with an armload of her books when the two children staggered in through the front door, out of breath and bedraggled. Will stopped on the staircase in surprise. His cousin Adam's little girl Katherine and his son Robert. The last time he'd seen them was months ago, the night of his uncle's fireworks for the Queen.

"Grandmamma!" Katherine called, looking around for her.

"She's gone home," Will said, coming down the steps. Lady Thornleigh had been helping him but had left about a half hour ago. The children's pale, frightened faces alarmed him. They looked exhausted, as if they'd been running for hours. What were they doing out at night, all alone? "Katherine, what's wrong?"

"Oh, Master Croft, it's Justine!" the girl cried. Her little brother burst into tears.

The story gushed out of Katherine. They had gone in their mother's boat with Justine, who had put them ashore at Blackfriars and told them to get to their grandfather's house, but two strange men jumped into the boat and dragged her out and forced her along Fleet Street. The children had followed them. "They took her into the Savoy! We did not dare go in. Mama says it's a wicked place. Oh, please, Master Croft, save her!" Katherine and her sobbing brother pressed against Will's leg for comfort.

He laid his hand on their heaving, hot little backs, his mind lurching. *Justine.* The terrible things he had said to her over his mother's body swarmed back, every vile word he had hurled at her in his shock at her confessing she was a Grenville. She had fled that morning in anguish, and Will, cruelly, had let her go. His uncle had tried to talk sense to him over his mother's grave, *"She hid the truth because she loves you,"* but Will had been immovable, too wounded, too angry. It was as if he had shut down his heart, as if he were dead. Now these two sobbing children shook him back to life. Justine was in danger, abducted, a prisoner in the Savoy. Nothing mattered except saving her.

"Your betrothed, Will?" Stubbs asked gravely. He stood in the doorway to the parlor, candlesticks in his hands. He had heard the children's tale.

"Can I take your horse, John?" Will was on his way to the front door.

"You can't do this alone," Stubbs said.

"I'm going to ask my neighbor if he'll come." The goldsmith's son, Thomas, was a strapping fellow two years younger than Will. Will had tutored him. "You two," he said to the children, "stay here."

"The Savoy's a rough place," Stubbs said. "I'll come, too."

＊　＊　＊

The three of them—Will, Stubbs, and Thomas Pierson—rode fast through the dark streets of London. Searching the echoing ruins of the Savoy, they skirted men in tatters slumped in corners asleep and dodged others squatting around puny fires who looked at them with dull, suspicious eyes. Will noticed the light of a large fire in a cauldron far down a columned passageway, and a murmur of chatter drew him toward it. When he was a stone's throw from the cauldron, he caught a glimpse of Justine that horrified him. She lay on the floor surrounded by a gang of young cutpurses who were chattering and laughing, one big man with them. Will halted his friends with a gesture that said, "Quiet!" and motioned for them to duck behind the columns.

Will listened, his back pressed against a column, sweat chilling his back. The thieves were engrossed in a noisy, merry contest over who could get into Justine's pockets the quickest and who could get her rings off. Will waited in agony, terrified their sport would end in rape, and then he knew he would charge them in blind rage and they would kill Justine, kill all of them. He didn't even have a sword. He'd never had one. Like every English boy he had done his training in archery, as was the law of the land, and had brought his mind to bear on it, but never his heart. Now he wished he had studied every martial art, had a sword, and knew how to use it. The dagger in his belt would not help him overcome the big fellow, nor even the young thieves if they proved vicious. Most were mere lads, but there were nine of them, and each appeared to have a knife. The big man had a sword on one hip, a long knife on the other, and the look of a hardened brute. Will glanced at his friends. Pierson had come armed with a sword. Stubbs had a dagger.

Suddenly, the big man stopped the game, ordering, "Rings back on 'er now. And keep your peckers in your breeches. My master wants her whole."

The boys dispersed, grumbling. Will heard them shuffling back to sit around the cauldron. He dared a glance around the pillar. The big man was guiding Justine to sit on a fallen pillar, shoving her down on it. How pale she looked! But defiant, too, sneering at the man. Her bravery snagged Will's heart.

He looked at Stubbs and Pierson. They were watching him, waiting. He whispered, "Go for the big one." They nodded. Will felt for the dagger at his belt. His fingers were cold as he slipped it from its sheath. He took a deep breath, then stepped out around the column, his heart banging. Pierson drew his sword. The three of them charged.

The big man spun around, his sword drawn in a heartbeat. Pierson attacked him, Will and Stubbs right beside him, daggers up. The big man was ferocious, hacking with his blade, but the three of them harried him and he backed away, slashing at them but on the defensive.

A few of the young thieves slunk forward, crouched like wolves, ready to pick off whichever of the three attackers might lag.

Stubbs turned to them, ran at them, and kicked over the cauldron. Flaming hunks of wood spilled. One thief wailed, his foot burned. The others froze. A blanket on the floor caught fire and flames leapt. The thieves scattered.

"Get the lady, Will!" Pierson shouted as he parried with the big man. "I've got this fellow!"

Will spun around and went straight for Justine. She was on her feet, her eyes wide in amazement, but she was alert, ready to run. With his dagger he sliced the leather tie binding her wrists. They shared a look of wonder—of joy—a look that lasted only a moment. No time! His two friends were keeping the big man at bay, blades clanging, feet scuffling, all three of them grunting. Will snatched Justine's hand. They ran.

Out through the pillars and down the corridor they ran. They passed men lounging against walls, men sprawled asleep in corners, men cooking over puny fires. Justine knocked over a tin cookpot and men's curses flew at their backs as she and Will ran on. He held her hand tightly, leading the way, around a corner, down a flight of stairs slippery with spilled ale. They reached a corridor, this one wider, darker, less crowded with people but more fetid. A stench of animals and dung and rubbish. A pig snorted in some far corner, rooting in the trash.

"There," Will told Justine, pointing at a smudge of light at the end of the corridor. "That's the street." They hurried toward it, skirting a trough of scummy water, then a heap of firewood. A dog sprang at them and Justine's hand flew free of Will's. They both halted, their way barred by the dog. It crouched, growling, fangs bared. Will took a step toward the dog, his dagger ready. The dog sprang and sank its teeth into his boot at the ankle. He toppled, groaning in pain. The dog's jaws around his ankle twisted. Will heard the bone snap. He gasped at the pain. Justine grabbed a chunk of firewood and hurled it at the dog, hitting its flank. It let go of Will's ankle with a snarl. She pitched another chunk, hitting the dog's head, and it yelped and slunk away.

"Will, can you walk?"

He struggled to his feet, but when he put his weight on the ankle, pain shot up his leg so fiercely it made him dizzy. He was afraid he would pass out.

"Lean on me," she said. He limped, hanging on to her.

Muffled shouting sounded behind them, up the stairs. Then a bellowing voice. "It's Gorm!" Justine cried. "The man you fought. Come, Will!"

He limped faster, his eyes watering at the excruciating pain.

"Almost there." Justine was breathing hard at the effort of dragging him. They trod over stinking refuse and tripped over scattered firewood, straining to get to the light.

Footsteps thudded behind them, getting louder, faster. A hand snatched Will's collar and yanked him backward. Will smelled Gorm's foul breath. "No!" Justine cried.

Dragged along the ground, Will wrenched free of Gorm's grip and fought to get to his feet. He made it, but his ankle would not hold him. In a surge of blinding pain he sank to his knees. Gorm loomed over him, his sword drawn. Will knew, in his fog of pain, that the sword could cut off his head. His fingers around his own dagger were slippery with sweat. He saw the massive black outline of the man, both hands on the sword hilt, twisting to position himself to scythe with the blade.

Will rammed his dagger up into the man's groin. Gorm let out a howl of shock. His arms, as if independent, swung the sword to lop off Will's head but Will twisted the blade inside the man's gut and Gorm swung diagonally. The sword blade hacked the edge of Will's shoulder. The force of it knocked him sideways.

"Will!" Justine cried.

He sprawled, dazed. He grabbed at the bleeding raw muscle of his shoulder.

Gorm shifted unsteadily on his feet, but bloodlust gleamed in his eyes and with a bellow he raised the sword again to hack Will. Justine snatched a hunk of firewood and hurled it at his face, striking his eye. Half-blinded, Gorm swung in wild confused slashes. He staggered, dropping the sword. He gripped the dagger hilt in his gut. He toppled.

Will felt the weight of the man thud onto his leg, crushing his broken ankle. White light blazed through his head. It dazzled his mind. His first thought was: *I'll get up now and we'll run.* But Justine's face, so close to his, made him wonder if she was well enough, for tears glistened on her cheeks. Her lips were moving but, oddly, he could hear no words. Her hand was stroking his face but her fingers were wet with blood. Then he knew: *my blood.* Her face was so close he could have kissed the tears that slid down to her lips.

His eyes flicked to the shadows behind her. A growing pool of light. A torch, bobbing toward them, getting closer. Thieves? He jerked in fear for her. He tried to warn her, but his tongue would not move. *He* could not move. His last thought was: *Run, Justine . . . run!*

❧ 26 ❧

Decision at Kilburn Manor

Justine groped in the gloom for something to stanch Will's blood. Kneeling over him, she was shaking. His eyes were closed and he lay as still as death, the gash in his shoulder dripping blood, his leg pinned beneath Gorm's dead body. *Will, don't die!* She snatched a rag from the floor, but flinched when she saw it was a filthy thing and flung it away. Use her clothes? She reached across him for his dagger in Gorm's abdomen. She took hold of the handle. Her hand, slippery with Will's blood, slid off. She wiped her hands on her skirt, gripped the dagger again, and yanked it out. With the blade she stabbed the hem of her cloak, ripping the wool until she had torn a wide strip. She bunched it and pressed it against Will's wound. She cut another strip and wound it tightly around his shoulder, under his arm, keeping the bunched wad in place. *Don't die . . . don't die!*

"Who's there?" a man shouted.

She looked up. A torch was bobbing toward her. Two men, coming for her. She snatched the dagger and scrambled to her feet and held it high, ready to stab. "Keep away!" she cried. She was shaking, but she forced her legs to hold her steady beside Will to protect him. "Stay back!"

"Mistress Thornleigh, do not fear!"

They reached her, panting. Will's friends! One was the vicar who had betrothed her and Will. She lowered the dagger and took breath again.

"Dear God," the vicar said, seeing Will and the dead man.

"Will!" the other said. "Is he—"

"He's alive," Justine said. "But grievously wounded. Help me, please." She dropped to her knees again and started to roll the dead man off Will's leg.

His friends took over, dragging the corpse off Will. "Are you hurt, mistress?" the vicar asked, eyeing the blood on her hands and clothes.

"No." She wiped her sweating forehead with the back of her arm. "Thank you. Both of you." Still on her knees, she laid her hand on Will's chest to make sure he was still breathing. *Yes, thank God!* The very fact that he had come here overwhelmed her. *He came for me.* She looked at his friends. "He needs help."

"Yes," the younger one said. "First we must get him out of this foul place."

"Can you carry him?"

"Yes," said the vicar. The two of them were already positioning themselves at Will's head and feet. Justine stared at Will's horrible wound, his blood soaking through the strips of her cloak wrapped around his shoulder. *So much blood.* It wrenched her mind to Chelsea. *Assassination.* She had come to get help to stop her father . . . and stop Lord Thornleigh from going there. Was she too late? Will's friends were talking quickly, urgently, but she heard nothing but her own pulse thudding in her ears. She could not stay with Will.

"I must leave you."

They stared at her. She felt their bewilderment, their eyes accusing her: *You're leaving Will?* Tears stung her. Impossible to explain. Her father . . . Queen Elizabeth. If there was still time, she had to warn the Queen. She shuddered, looking down at Will. The thought of him dying almost crushed the heart within her. Her tears choked her as she bent and touched her lips to his.

She stood up, trembling, and tugged her ripped and bloodied cloak about her and looked toward the door that led to the street.

She did not dare look again at Will for fear she would not be able to leave him. Her voice faltered as she told his friends, "Stay with him," as she hurried away.

At first, Christopher had been jubilant that his plan was going so well. That was before he saw Adam Thornleigh.

Everything had been proceeding perfectly. He had watched in tense excitement from an upstairs window in the dark new wing as the fishing boat arrived at the jetty. Four of the "fishermen" marched up to the house—Elizabeth's palace guards, obviously. They would sweep through the house as a security precaution before Elizabeth entered it. Christopher had expected that and had hidden everything behind a false wall in the cellar: the kegs of gunpowder and the reeds he had filled with gunpowder to lay as fuses. He watched the guards return to the boat, and only then did Elizabeth step out of it. She wore a plain gray cloak, and her guards quickly escorted her up to the house. She disappeared from Christopher's view. He knew that Frances would greet her at the door, without fanfare as befitted the meeting's secrecy, and bring her into the great hall to join Lord Herries. Frances would then leave the Queen and surreptitiously cross the courtyard and leave by the west gate. Christopher had felt a moment of exultation—everything was going as planned! All he had to do now was connect the fuses to the gunpowder kegs and run the reed fuses along the tunnel that connected the wing to the house. He had not felt nervous, just excited. Elizabeth's meeting was in progress. He had time.

He went downstairs heading for the cellar and passed a window that fronted the river, and that's when he saw Adam Thornleigh marching up the jetty to the house. Christopher froze. He had never met Richard Thornleigh's son, but the man had an air about him as if he owned the place, and who else would be arriving so late but the lord of the manor coming home? He silently cursed Frances—why had she not kept her damn husband away? His mind churned. Would Thornleigh speak to Frances inside? Of course he would. What would she tell him? She was already so dangerously nervous. Surprised to see her husband, would she blurt the truth?

There was not a moment to lose. He ran down to the wing's empty cellar, then through the tunnel that connected it to the house. Working in the dark—he had not dared bring even a rush-light with him, not with all the gunpowder here—he lifted from their hiding place the lengths of dried reeds he had previously packed with gunpowder. He left the three kegs of gunpowder be-hind the wall and connected a reed to each one. He glanced up at the ceiling. It was the floor of the great hall, and a faint sound touched him in the silence. Voices? Elizabeth's? *Perfect.* Spurred by excitement, he joined the ends of the three feeder reeds to one reed and began laying more reeds along the floor toward the tun-nel, carefully connecting them into one long fuse. His hands were slick with sweat as he worked, expecting at any moment to hear Eliz-abeth's guards charging down upon him led by Adam Thornleigh. If they caught him, Elizabeth would live. *And I will hang.*

Fumbling the reeds, he spilled a little gunpowder. He clenched his fists, told himself to stay calm. He forced control of the tremble in his hand and continued connecting the reeds. It was painstaking work as he made his way backward, foot by foot, his boots scuffling over the stone, laying the thin fuse of reeds all the way along the tunnel. The sound of voices startled him, raising the hair on the back of his neck. He halted, sweating. *Fool,* he told himself. He'd only imagined voices. The sound was wind humming down the tunnel, a tuneless dirge rushing from the barren wing.

Finally, he reached the far cellar. It was a hollow space, dark as a grave, for he had not dared light any part of the wing lest an alert guard should spot the glow. Christopher was breathing hard from the spasm of work, but he felt excited. Everything was now ready. Going down on hands and knees in the darkness, he groped at the base of a pillar for the cylindrical tinderbox he had put there be-neath a handful of straw. His fingers found the cold metal cylinder beneath. It contained a flint, a firesteel, and a charcloth, all he needed to create a tiny flame to light the straw. Had Frances got out yet? With her husband there, how could she? What excuse could she give him for leaving? She might not get out in time. Christopher was sorry about that, but his sister had served her purpose. And it was an unexpected bit of luck that her husband would die, too.

He turned back to the end of the reed fuse and opened the tinderbox.

"Tom, grab the pitchfork. Walter, the gelding shears. You other two see what's in the shed for weapons."

Adam gave these orders as he hurried down the stairs from the grooms' loft in the stable. The grooms were right behind him, two experienced men and two younger ones, all blinking sleep out of their eyes. The last one held a lantern. "We'll surprise them," Adam said. "And we have five to their four. But they look alert, so keep your wits about you." He didn't mention the two in the boat. The odds were bad enough without frightening his men.

He drew his sword as he led them out into the stable yard. If the men in the house had his children hostage, Adam was ready to cut them down by himself. He had kept his voice steady for the men, but he was still reeling from his encounter with Frances. Mute to his questions, gibbering words that made no sense, she had staggered on across the courtyard dragging that sack. It was as if she had gone mad.

"Ho! Sir Adam!" a groom at the rear cried, pointing.

Adam spun around and his men halted. A horse clomped into the stable yard heaving bellows breaths, hooves clattering on the cobbles. Under the pale moonlight its slim rider was a mere shadow. Adam raised his sword, expecting more horsemen to follow. None appeared. The lone rider called out, "Sir Adam, is that you?"

A woman. Breathless. It was clear she had ridden hard. She drew rein beside Adam and he beckoned one of the grooms to hold the horse and help her down. She struggled to dismount, half sliding off the saddle in fatigue or fear, or both. "Have you stopped him?" she cried. "Please, tell me you have stopped him!"

"Justine?" He stared at her, utterly bewildered. The Grenville girl his father had taken in years ago. He had not seen her since he'd sailed for the Indies. What on earth had brought her to his house this night? Her haggard face and disheveled state told him it was something dire. "Stopped who?" Was that blood on her clothes? "Justine, what's happened?"

She let out a thin cry of dismay. "So you do not *know!*" She looked at the house, clutching her side with a wince as she caught her breath. "At least I am not too late. Has your father come?"

"Father? Here?" What did she mean? "Too late for what? What in hell is going on?"

"Murder. Unless we can stop it."

He tensed. "My children?"

"No, sir. They are not here, they are safe away. The target is Her Majesty the Queen."

He listened, stunned, as the facts tumbled out of her. Elizabeth, lured to his house for a meeting. Her traitorous father, alive. The house, undermined with gunpowder. Her father's plan: to assassinate Elizabeth. "Sir," she finished, gulping air from the haste of her telling, "Her Majesty is in your great hall at this very moment!"

The grooms heard it all and instinctively shuffled back a step at the word *gunpowder*. Adam had not moved. His mind flew to Frances, so hell-bent on getting across the courtyard, a wild determination in her eyes . . . almost as if . . .

She knows?

The truth surged over him. *Grenville is her brother . . . she hates Elizabeth . . . she knows!* It was a monster wave crashing down on him. He could only hang on, hold to his course.

He turned to his men and took in their frightened faces as they awaited his command. He was grateful for their loyalty; they had not run away. But if the house was primed to explode, he could not lead them into certain death. "Back to the stable with you," he told them. "Take cover at the rear." He turned for the house, sword in hand.

"I'll come," said Walter.

"And I," said Tom. "There's folk abed in the house, sir—"

Adam understood. They had friends among the servants. He nodded his heartfelt thanks. "All right. You two are with me." He ordered the younger men back to the stable. "And take the lady with you." He said to Tom and Walter, "The gunpowder is likely hidden. There's no time to search. We have to get Her Majesty out. And the household folk."

He started for the house at a run. Justine called something after him. Only when he and his two men pounded into the house did he realize the girl had said, "I'm coming!" and was right behind them.

A long line of black ash charred the tunnel's stone floor as the fuse burned, slow but steady, the flame eating the gunpowder-packed dried reeds that stretched toward the house. Satisfied, Christopher turned and walked through the wing's echoing cellar toward the stairs. He didn't hurry. Sweat chilled his skin from his labor, but he felt newly calm. The thing was done. Nothing could stop it now.

It left an odd emptiness inside him. For months he had worked and planned and maneuvered for this supreme moment, and now that it was upon him he felt bereft. The excitement was gone, that tiny flame of tinder that had smoldered inside him, keeping his hopes alive through his wretched years as an outcast. He felt almost cheated as he climbed the steps to safety, reached the first floor, and closed the thick door behind him.

So it was with a deeply satisfying spark of new energy that he turned his thoughts to Richard Thornleigh. He had pushed that matter to the back of his mind during his labors, but now it leapt forward. Justine had sent Thornleigh her note yesterday, entreating him to come here tonight. Had Thornleigh taken the bait? *Is he already here?* Excitement surged afresh in Christopher and he picked up his pace as he crossed the long reception corridor, looking for a sign of his enemy. Moonlight shone through the cavernous unglazed windows. On the lofty ceiling, the gilt and blue paint of half-completed scenes of cherubs glimmered in a cloudless sky.

He heard voices and halted. Real voices this time. Men shouting. The sound was faint, coming from the direction opposite the grand window vista. It came from the area of stables and outbuildings. Christopher turned sharply down a passageway and reached a trio of modest, multipaned windows that overlooked the stable yard, and looked out. His heart slammed up in his throat at what he saw. Adam Thornleigh, sword drawn, was running across the stable yard toward the house. Two men followed at his heels. And a fourth figure. A woman. The floor of Christopher's stomach plummeted. *Justine.*

He pushed his face as close as he could to the windowpane to make sure. His breath on the cold glass came back at him like smoke. Even in the fog he was sure—it was his daughter! He watched in horror as she ran with the three men, crossing the stable yard, and vanished inside the house.

He twisted around, groping for support, but there was only the cold stone wall. He pressed his back against it, wanting its coldness to steady him. The fuse in the cellar tunnel would soon reach the gunpowder under the house. *But she is in the house!*

Heart banging painfully, he faced the horrifying fact: To save Justine, he had two choices. Run down to the cellar and snuff out the burning fuse. Or run across the courtyard to the house and shout a warning for everyone to get out.

If he warned them he would give himself away. They would capture him. He would hang.

He had to stop the fuses. Then flee.

But that meant Elizabeth would live. He would never get back what was his—his lands, his property, his *life.* Never rise to become a peer of England, a nobleman. He would slink back to France in penniless exile again, condemned to insignificance and poverty for the rest of his days.

The decision shook him with an icy jolt. A third choice.

He could let the fuses burn.

Shaky, his back against the wall, he slid down it. He dropped forward onto his knees. He felt with frigid fingers for the thin chain around his neck and lifted the crucifix from inside his shirt. *Justine . . .*

He closed his eyes and bowed his head. *My darling Justine . . .*

He was clutching the crucifix so tightly it dug painfully into his palm. He wanted the pain as he whispered a hoarse prayer into the silence. "Dear Lord . . . take the soul of my dear daughter to your rest."

She ran with Sir Adam and the grooms. In through the back door, along the dim passage past the kitchen. The three men pounded toward the great hall, and Justine stayed on their heels. How much time did they have? Fear sawed her nerves, expecting the blast any moment to rip her head from her body, tear her limbs apart. They had to get Elizabeth out . . . and rouse the sleeping servants . . . it would all take precious time.

She knew Sir Adam was going for Elizabeth. His men would stick with him. *It's up to me to spread the alarm to the servants' quarters. And Lord Thornleigh? Perhaps he has not come. Please, God, let it be so.*

They reached the closed doors of the hall where four men stood guard. Seeing them come, the guards drew their swords and took stances of grim-faced defense. It flashed over Justine how they must appear, the half-dressed grooms with pitchfork and shears, she in ripped and bloodstained clothes. Adam lowered his sword and raised his free hand in a gesture of peace. "I am Sir Adam Thornleigh, lord of this house, and I must get inside to Her Majesty."

Justine hurried for the staircase to race up to rouse the servants as Adam went on to the guards, "There is a plot against Her Majesty's life. The house is undermined and will explode. Open the doors and help me take her to safety."

The guards' faces remained stony. "Sir," one said, "I am authorized to let no one in."

"I tell you, this is my house."

"My orders include you."

Justine froze on the steps. The guards would not let Adam in! Adam raised his sword. "Stand aside. I will enter."

The guards stood firm.

Adam charged the leader. Swords clanged. The two grooms lunged for two other guards, jabbing with pitchfork and shears.

The fourth guard came at Adam with his sword. Adam fought off the two, hacking at their blades.

Justine watched, her heart in her throat. By attacking, Adam had drawn the guards a few paces away from the doors. If she could skirt the fray, she might get in.

Down the stairs she ran. The grim-faced guards hacked and slashed at their opponents. The grooms, though brave, were no match, and Walter fell with a cry, blood gushing from his side. His attacker turned on Adam. Adam spun to fend off the man, then lunged to keep fighting the other two. But the three of them were backing him away under earsplitting clashes of steel. Justine reached the doors and flung them open.

"Your Majesty!"

Queen Elizabeth stood at the far end of the hall, too far away to have heard the fighting. She stood with Lord Herries at the hearth, and both their startled faces turned to Justine as she ran toward them. She heard a guard pound in after her, so close to her she heard the air whistle over his raised sword. "Your Majesty!" she cried, "You must flee!"

❧ 27 ❧

The Feud

Richard paced. His footsteps sounded hollowly through the long reception hall like echoes of the words running through his head: *Where is Justine?* The new building, she had told him in her note. *Do not fail me*, she had written. Well, here he was in Kilburn's new wing. Where was she?

Wind moaned at the casements of the tall, unglazed windows, and the canvas tacked over them flogged like sails on a crewless ship. The place was barren in its unfinished state, cold, smelling of musty wet sawdust. Gloomy, too; the only light was the moonlight that flitted in when the canvas flapped, then fled again. There was not a stick of furniture to rest on. Richard didn't want to rest, he wanted to see Justine and find out what trouble she was in. Nevertheless, the ride to Chelsea on the frost-hard roads had jarred his bones, and he felt it keenly in this cold place. *Old bones*, he thought. Years ago he could have ridden all day and enjoyed the exercise, the sights, the fresh air. Now the only thing good about being on horseback was that it took the weight off his painful left foot. Pacing, he favored the right.

His boots scuffed through the sawdust. *Where is the girl?*

A sound made him halt. A bat skimmed past his head. Silvered by moonlight, it shot by him, swift as a blink.

He looked toward the shadowy main doors. They led to the

courtyard, and across it stood the manor house. Should he go over there to find Justine? When she left his house so abruptly days ago she obviously had come here to Adam's. That had hurt Richard, her leaving without a word. But he soon had realized that she had cause. He had railed at her fiercely for being disloyal to Elizabeth, had been furious at her wrongheaded attempt to get copies of the casket letters for Mary. But after all, she had failed, and no harm was done, and he knew she had acted for reasons that she *thought* were loyal. Besides, she had paid for it later, God knew, coming upon the body of poor Joan, at which point the girl's secret, so carefully kept from Will, had spilled out, and Will had cruelly spurned her, the young fool. Richard heaved a sigh. He had longed to put right the feud's past miseries with the happy union of these two young people, but it was not to be. Given Justine's broken heart, he wasn't surprised that she had taken refuge here at Adam's house. She must feel quite alone, and Frances, after all, was her blood kin, both Grenvilles. It gave him an odd shiver. *Blood always wins out.*

Well, should he go to the house to look for her? But everyone over there would be abed. And she had specifically told him to come to the new building.

He looked in the opposite direction, up the broad staircase. A long gallery lay up there in the darkness. And rooms just as barren, no doubt. Could she be there?

He started up the steps, worried about her. Why such hole-in-corner secrecy? What kind of trouble was she in? Pregnant? By God, if Will had compromised her he would prod his nephew to the altar at the end of his sword.

The staircase was treacherous, the cold marble filmed with moisture. He reached the top and stopped. The long gallery ahead was a tunnel of darkness. He called out, "Justine?"

Silence. Just his own voice echoing off the bare walls.

This was pointless. She was not here. A prickle of alarm touched him. Perhaps she could not come because her trouble had worsened. She was too ill. Or too frightened. He turned on the step to go back down, get over to the house, wake Frances and get to the bottom of this. The girl might be in real danger somewhere.

From the corner of his eye he caught a light down the long gallery. He stopped and peered into the darkness. It was no more than a faint glow, a band of light at the bottom of a door. He reached the door and opened it. A vast room stretched before him, with a high ceiling and a massive marble hearth at the far end. The room was vacant like everywhere else in the place, but aglow with a dozen or more rushlights in wall sconces. He walked in. The flickering flames revealed boarded-up windows, linen-shrouded chandeliers, flooring that was a parquet pattern of rare woods filmed with sawdust.

"Baron Thornleigh, I think?"

The voice started Richard and he turned. A man stood at the door, closing it. He wore simple black clothes and offered a relaxed smile. One of Adam's servants?

"Yes, I'm Thornleigh. Who are you?" The fellow wore a sword. No servant, then. He was lean, perhaps forty, with blond hair that fell below his ears.

"My lord." The man made a courtly bow. "It is a great pleasure to make your acquaintance. A moment I have looked forward to with the happiest of expectations."

His tone grated Richard. Servile yet intimate. "I'm here to meet someone. Have you seen a young lady?"

"Look about you, my lord. Do you see any such?"

He had already seen. The room was empty. "No. So I'll be on my way." He took a step toward the door to leave.

"Oh, do look carefully, sir," the man said, moving in front of the door. "Corners can reveal surprises."

Richard was irked by the fellow's unctuous manner, but he turned to look one last time around the room, make sure he hadn't missed Justine standing quietly in a shadowed corner. Though why she would do such a thing made no real sense.

He heard the man's sword scrape from its sheath and before he could turn the blade slashed the back of his thigh, gashing fabric, severing muscle. Richard gasped in shock. He staggered around, stunned by the attack. "What the devil!" The man was insane! The searing pain in his thigh made Richard stumble backward. The man was smiling, blade poised to fight like an expert swordsman. Richard groped for his own sword. Pulled it free. Stood as firmly as he could to take on the madman. "Whoever you are, you've made a grave mistake."

"Oh, I think not, my lord. Do forgive me for not introducing myself." He strolled in a wide circle around Richard, sword at the ready. "Though we have never met, you have heard of me, I dare say. I could tell you my name, but perhaps you might enjoy guessing. Would that amuse you, my lord?"

Richard knew the taunt of an aggressor when he heard it. The only defense was attack. He raised his sword and lunged. The man swiftly and easily blocked the thrust with a clang of steel on steel. Richard staggered back, catching his breath, his gashed right leg weak with pain, his left as feeble as ever. He tottered like a bear wounded by dogs.

"I know it would amuse *me*." The man made a lightning strike. His blade sliced Richard's sword wrist. In shock Richard let go the weapon and it clattered to the floor. He lunged and picked it up, his feet slewing like a drunkard's as he righted himself. Blood streamed from his wrist over his fingers, making them too slippery to keep hold of the sword. He switched it to his left hand. Impossibly awkward. He could not fight effectively with his left even if he were not wounded.

He lurched backward, looking for another way out. Boarded-up windows. Hearth. No other door.

The man followed him at a stroll, his outstretched sword tip making small circles, air-drawing on Richard's forehead for amusement. "So, shall we begin the guessing game?" He lunged, and his sword tip cut the leather tie that held Richard's eye patch in place. The patch flew up in the air. "Here is your first clue. *This* is for my father, Anthony Grenville." His blade sliced off the top of Richard's ear.

Richard gasped at the pain. Blood gushed, pooling in his ear, streaming down his neck. He cupped the torn ear in shock, his mind tripping over itself to grasp the madman's meaning. "You're . . . a Grenville?" His right leg, drenched in blood from his thigh, was so weak he could barely stand. He rocked on his feet.

"Ah, but you must guess my *Christian* name, my lord. Here is another clue. *This* is for my brother John." His blade whistled with its swiftness, slashing an *X* that ripped through the fabric on Richard's chest and etched the *X* on his skin.

Richard winced in anguish . . . in impotent fury. The oncoming sword suddenly hacked his sword with a clang of ferocity that numbed his arm. He lost his grip. His weapon went sliding across the floor.

"Still in the dark, your lordship?" The man's smile had vanished. His face was a sneer. He lifted his free hand to his scalp and tore off his hair. A wig! He hurled it at Richard's feet, and Richard saw the burned, scarred ridges of flesh that ran from his ear down his neck. His mind reeled. *Christopher Grenville . . . alive?*

"*This* is for stealing my house and my land." His blade speared Richard's knee.

He howled in agony. He collapsed. Sprawling on his back, he looked toward the closed door . . . the only way out. He hauled himself onto hands and knees, crawling. Every inch was agony. His blood-slick palms slipped on the floor.

"And *this* is for stealing my daughter!"

Steel sliced the small of Richard's back. He collapsed again. "Justine . . ." The name came out half breath, half pain.

"She hates you, you know. She and I spent time together while she served Mary, and we became as close as father and daughter can be. I told her all about you Thornleighs, the murders you've committed. So she hates *you* above all. She lured you here so I could finish you."

Justine? Impossible. Lying on his cheek, gasping at the pain, Richard blinked through the blood that ran into his one good eye. Every fiber in him yearned to fight, but he was so gored he had no strength. His left arm, next to Grenville's foot, was pinned under his own body. He could barely move his right, the wrist still gushing blood. He could not move beyond writhing at the pain. The curse that rose in his throat came out as a moan.

Grenville's boots moved lazily past his face. The boots stopped. "Now roll over, *my lord*." He spat the last two words. "Roll over so I can cut out your tongue." His boot toe prodded Richard's belly. "I must leave you, you see, and you might scream. But no one will

hear you with your tongue rammed down your throat." He grunted
at the effort of trying to flip Richard over with his foot, enjoying
the challenge of doing it without using his hands. "No one will
even know you're here. Except Justine, and she would be glad to
know you're dead. Ah, my pretty Justine. She could live had she
not become ensnared by you. You will pay for her death, Thornleigh. Pay in hellfire. But first, you must die. How many days do
you think it will take you to bleed to death? One? Two? Soon
they'll all be gone, everyone in the house, and those who come afterward will have more on their minds than poking through this
uninhabited building. You have a strong constitution, old man, so
you might last for days." Giving up on using his foot, he crouched
by Richard's side. "I really must go. Just the one final task. Your
tongue."

He set down his sword to use both hands to turn him over.

A *boom!* So thunderous it stabbed Richard's ears, hollowed his
chest, lifted his body. The floor shuddered and walls rattled. He
gasped for air as he thudded back down on his side, his vision all
blackness. Was he at sea? Earsplitting thunder . . . seas pitching
him high . . . hurling him back to the deck. Dust rained on him.
Dust? Not at sea . . . He writhed, coughing.

The blast had knocked Grenville over. "Aha!" he cried in ec-
stasy, scrambling onto hands and knees. Coughing, he pushed
himself to his feet. His eyes were shining. "Aha!" he crowed again.
He raised his arms in jubilation as he stood over Richard. "It is
done! It is *done!*"

Richard saw Grenville's sword on the floor. A jolt of energy
coursed through him. Grenville had no weapon! With a surge of
fresh strength Richard swung his arm and snatched Grenville's
ankle. Yanked it. Grenville toppled. He thudded on his back.

Richard staggered to his feet and lunged for the sword. Grenville pushed himself up on his elbow, about to leap up. Richard
stomped on his forearm. Grenville grunted in pain. He looked up
at Richard, fury blazing in his eyes. He started to heave himself up
with his other hand. Richard stabbed the sword through his palm,
pinning his hand to the wood floor. Grenville screamed, collapsing
on his back.

Richard planted his foot on Grenville's other arm and stood over him, legs wide to hold himself up, his blood dripping onto Grenville's face. Disoriented by the booming blast, tortured by his wounds, Richard's strength was ebbing. He did not think he could stand much longer. Was this what dying was? Despair surged over him. He did not want his last act on earth to be murder. He had seen enough of death.

"I only want peace," he said, his voice a rasp. "For the love of God, Grenville . . . *peace.*"

If there was a hell, Justine knew she was stumbling through it. Flames licked the night sky. Broken walls loomed jagged in a fog of dust. In the rubble of stone and splintered wood and glass, bodies lay bleeding and blackened. Coughing, her throat choked with dust and smoke, Justine shuffled past a lump of charred meat that was a torso . . . saw the raw stump of a man's foot in its shoe . . . an old woman sitting on the ground, her wrinkled mouth an *O*, one hand to her head, the other hand gone, wrist spurting blood.

Justine staggered on, the screams that reached her sounding underwater. Her ears felt packed with mud. The silent flames writhed. The acrid smell of gunpowder almost made her retch.

Tripping over clumps of stone, she clawed at the insect that stung the back of her neck. She drew back her hand and saw bright blood wetting her palm, and felt her neck again. A dart of glass impaled in her skin. She tugged it out, the sting like cat's teeth. Men ran past her. She followed them. Ahead, the moon! She lurched toward its clean brightness.

She halted when she felt spongy dead grass under her feet. She sucked in fresh air, swaying on her feet. Shivering, she groped the edges of her cloak, ripped and blood-spattered. and tugged it tight around her, trying to think. Men dashed by her, swords raised. One banged her shoulder as he charged past. She turned to look at the hell she had come from. The house . . . the blast had left it a smoldering shell.

Reality crashed over her. *Elizabeth!* She twisted back to look for the men who had run past with swords—Elizabeth's guards. She saw only servants, men and women in nightdress, dazed and wandering, bleeding. A man carried another man slung over his shoulder. Two women crouched over a bloodied body that jerked in spasms. Men ran with buckets of water. Where was Elizabeth? Had her guards got her out alive?

Where was Sir Adam? She started after the guards, burning to question them, and tripped over a hook of metal. She looked down. A sword hilt, the blade plowed diagonally into the earth. She dropped to her knees and felt the hilt. She recognized its swirls of silver and bronze. Sir Adam's. Horror froze her. Was he among the dead? She got up, scanning the frenzy of people in their misery. Smoke from the house ribboned over her head, carried on the breeze across the courtyard toward the wing. Her gaze fell on the dark new building. Untouched, immaculate, it seemed to stand in mockery of the wounded house that gasped in its flames.

A tremor jerked her. *Father.*

Lord Thornleigh!

She ran. Past the people, down the alley of night-black yews, up the entry stairs and into the building. Inside, darkness engulfed her. Tingles of sound from across the courtyard reached her ears, her hearing returning. Shards of screams and shouts. Here, though, there was silence. She thought with a rush of relief, *He did not get my note! He did not come!*

A thump. Upstairs. Her eyes snapped to the broad staircase. A deeper darkness lay up there, shot through with flashes of moonlight when the breeze stirred the canvas at the windows. A muffled crash. Justine went up the stairs, ears straining to pinpoint the sound's location. At the top of the staircase she stopped, one foot still on the lower stair, listening, her eyes straining to see down the gloom of the long gallery. Another thump. To the left. She hastened toward it. Faint light glowed under the closed door—the very room where she had sat by the hearth with her father and poured out her grief. The memory was painful, her eyes now wide open to his crimes. Yet a feeble ray remained of the intimacy with him, the afterglow of a dead fire. She pushed open the door.

In the rushlights' glow she saw them, and froze. Her father on the floor on his back, squirming, his bloodied hand impaled by a sword. Lord Thornleigh standing over him gripping the sword hilt, his boot on her father's other arm. Like some monster who had fed, Lord Thornleigh's face and neck glistened with blood. The naked socket of his ruined eye dribbled blood. His clothes dripped blood.

Her father saw her. "Justine!" he cried out. "Thank God!" His face was contorted in agony. "Help me!"

She rushed forward. Lord Thornleigh wrenched his sword out of her father's hand, a move so violent the hand jerked up and her father screamed at the pain. Lord Thornleigh gripped the sword with both hands. His wild look stunned Justine. Her father lay helpless. She was sure Lord Thornleigh meant to strike a death blow.

"Don't!" she cried.

He turned to her, panting, swaying on his feet. "I want—"

"You cannot! It would be murder!" She ran for him, twisting as she reached him so that she was between the two of them, her back to her father, shielding him.

"Justine!" Her father staggered to his feet, clutching her skirts to right himself. "My child!"

Lord Thornleigh blinked at her in shock. "I only—"

"Enough!" she cried. She pushed him away. He stumbled back a step. He swayed. His sword arm drooped in surrender. The blade tip scraped the floor.

Justine heard her father grunt behind her but she had no time even to turn, so swiftly did he move. Instantly on his feet, he chopped Lord Thornleigh's sword arm with his hand. The weapon fell and her father caught the hilt before it hit the floor. In a flash he brandished the sword.

Lord Thornleigh grabbed Justine's arm. A glance at his anguished face told her he was trying to pull her clear of the dangerous blade, but there was no strength in his grip. It was the grope of a sleeper in a nightmare, purposeful but powerless. "Justine . . . go," he breathed. He let go of her, shuffling to stay on his feet. But he could not. He dropped to his knees.

Her father took two slow, victorious steps toward him. His free hand bled from the wound in his palm, but his sword hand was strong.

Lord Thornleigh looked up at Justine, and she saw the ghastly truth. He was half-dead. His look of desolation cut into her. *I've killed him*. His struggle to stay on his knees, to not topple, was ferocious, as though he knew that the moment he fell would be the end. His voice was a croak. "Only . . . wanted . . . peace."

"You won't find it in hell." Her father raised the sword, poised to plunge it into his enemy's heart.

Justine opened her mouth to cry *No!* but knew as surely as she had killed Lord Thornleigh that no word would stop her father. She moved before she could think. Grabbed the blade, wrapped her hands around it as it plunged. It sliced her palms. Pain like fire! Gushing blood. It did not stop her father's lunge, but was enough to deflect the blade. It slid past Lord Thornleigh's shoulder into the air. Unbalanced, her father staggered. Justine snatched the sword hilt from him. She hurled the weapon, sending it skittering across the floor.

Lord Thornleigh gaped at her bleeding hands. So did her father. He had quickly righted himself, and he looked at her with horror at her betrayal. "Traitor," he said, his voice choked with feeling. "My own daughter."

"Not yours." Stunned at the pain, her heart wailing for Lord Thornleigh, she cried, "His!"

Her father slapped her so hard she sprawled.

He strode around his enemy, Lord Thornleigh still on his knees. Standing at his back, he whipped his arm around Lord Thornleigh's neck. His elbow like a vise, he crushed him against his thigh with a savage wrench. Choking, Lord Thornleigh clawed at the arm.

Justine struggled to her feet. She staggered over to the fallen sword. She gripped the handle in both bleeding, raw hands. She lurched back to the men and stood facing her father, Lord Thornleigh between them. "Stop . . ." She was breathless. "Let him go . . ." She raised the sword. "Stop . . . or I will stop you."

Her father looked at her in surprise. His face, contorted with his labor, was a sneer. "Your own flesh and blood? No. You would not."

He squeezed Lord Thornleigh's neck with a vicious jerk.

"Stop!" she screamed. She rammed the blade up under Lord Thornleigh's raised arm and deep into her father's heart.

❧ 28 ❧

Rosethorn House

The children, too young to be heartbroken, were the only mourners at the funeral whose hands stayed calmly at their sides. The adults—and there were many, Sir William Cecil among the high-ranking—all sought some activity for their hands: pockets and sleeves to take refuge in, cloak edges to grip, tears to wipe. The vicar fingered his prayer book as he intoned the psalm. A gravedigger rested his hand on his upright shovel as though on the shoulder of a friend.

Justine noted all these hands. It engrossed her. She *made* it engross her, wanting anything that would keep her eyes off the coffin about to be lowered into the grave. If there had been a thick falling snow to huddle from, or rain to cringe from, or even wind to listen to as it rode through the trees, she would have seized the distraction. Anything to keep her from looking at the polished wood box that enclosed him, the pit waiting to swallow him. Keep her from hearing the voice in her head that keened night and day: *I killed him.*

Instead, the air was still and the sun shone bright and strong. She could hear melting snow dribble off the church roof onto the stone path below. A thread of chimney smoke rose from Rosethorn House, the Thornleighs' grand residence that lay beyond the village woods.

Justine's own hands, wrapped with linen bandages, were as still as the children's, but her stillness was a façade as thin as the bandages. Inside, she longed to spring forward and paw the earth back into the pit. Longed to keep him here. To have him back, alive. Her palms, sliced by her father's sword, throbbed dully, but her wounds were nothing compared to the savagery she had witnessed that night. She had not succumbed from loss of blood. Not like Will. His horrifying wound. His shoulder hacked . . . raw muscle and bone. So much blood . . .

She forced herself to concentrate on the Thornleighs' daughter Isabel and her husband Carlos, who stood across the grave gripping each other's hands, Isabel's smaller, white at the knuckles from pressing his, which were roughened and brown from his life in the saddle. Their three children stood with them. Though their eldest, Nicolas, was not really a child anymore; at thirteen he was facing manhood. His dark eyes revealed a deeper understanding of life and loss than his little brother and sister could grasp, as though today he had closed the door on the innocence of childhood. Justine felt a bond with him; it was not so long ago that she had closed that door. Yet she and Nicolas were worlds apart. In the last weeks she had been cast into a dark netherworld that he could not even imagine. Nicolas had not lured Lord Thornleigh to his death. Nicolas had not murdered his own father.

Blood. So much blood that night . . .

Her own blood, streaming from her sliced palms. Her father's blood, bubbling from his ribs around his own sword, which she had rammed into him. Lord Thornleigh's blood, dripping from his ravaged ear, soaking his clothes from the gashes her father had inflicted. Her father stood, his eyes wide in shock, his arm still crooked around Lord Thornleigh's neck. Lord Thornleigh, on his knees between them, stared at Justine in dazed wonder. She still gripped the sword hilt, stunned by her own act.

Her father dropped his arm from Lord Thornleigh's neck. His look at Justine was utter, wild surprise. "How could you . . . ?" Blood spilled over his lips. "How . . . ?"

Shaking, she let go of the sword hilt. Her father's eyes clouded over. She saw death in them. He slumped backward. His body thudded to the floor. The sword quivered, a foot of steel buried inside him.

"Justine . . ." Lord Thornleigh's voice was a reed through his crushed throat. He struggled to get to his feet. He was so gored, his effort was a shambling, pitiful sight. A heroic effort. It tore Justine's heart.

"Don't," she cried, her mouth so dry the word grated her throat. "Don't try."

He swayed halfway to standing, giving up the struggle. "You're right." He fell back down to his knees. He made a feeble motion with his hand as if to calm her. "You're right." He collapsed, sprawled on his back.

"My lord!" She dropped to her knees and lifted his head onto her lap as gently as she could with her ravaged hands. "I only meant you should rest," she said, desperate. "Rest before you get up."

The faintest shake of his head. "I'm finished."

Justine's heart felt torn from her chest. She could not hold back the sobs. He groped for her hand. She grabbed his and held tight, willing her strength into him.

"Don't cry," he said, wheezing through his crushed windpipe. "I was finished . . . before. Bad leg . . . arm. Not much time . . ." He strained to look back at the corpse. He rasped, "Your father . . ."

"You are wrong!" she said, sobbing. "So wrong. *You*, sir . . ." She pressed her cheek to his. "*You* are my father."

A ghost of a smile. "Good." He squeezed her hand. "You're free now . . . to live."

A wail threatened from deep inside her.

"Tell Honor . . ." He coughed. He could not get his breath.

"Yes?" Justine strained to hear his thin voice. "Tell her ladyship what?"

"Tell . . . she is . . . my love . . ." He stiffened in agony. "Take care of her!" Breath rattled from his throat. His head lolled. His eyes closed.

She rocked him, sobbing. "Father . . . Father . . . Father . . ."

* * *

The sun was a hand on her back gently urging to lift her head and bear witness to the funeral ceremony. She felt Lady Thornleigh beside her tremble. Justine pitied the lady's struggle to stay strong, and hooked her arm around hers as a support. Lady Thornleigh pressed closer for comfort. Justine hardly knew why the lady did not despise her. *I killed him.* Instead, she had thrown herself into Justine's arms at the horrible moment of hearing the news. And in the days that followed, even after Justine had confessed her father's machinations and her own part in luring Lord Thornleigh to the rendezvous, Lady Thornleigh had not cursed her. "You were with him at the end," she had said from the depths of her sorrow. "You tried to save him."

No one blamed Justine. She was left to blame herself. She had told her story to officials of Elizabeth's court and eventually to Sir William Cecil himself, and everyone accepted that her father had abominably used her. What everyone really wanted to know was whether Mary had been complicit in Christopher Grenville's assassination plot. The only person who could tell them was dead.

I have done murder, Justine thought. It was a hard thing to live with, to murder your own father. Yet she did not blame herself for his death, only for the death she had not been able to prevent, the father of her heart.

"Yea, though I walk through the valley of the shadow of death, I will fear no evil . . ." The vicar finished the psalm, closed his prayer book, and made a slight bow to Baron Thornleigh to indicate that the service was concluded. Inheritor of his father's title, Adam stood by himself at the head of the grave, the head of the family now. His hands at his sides were balled into fists. He bore no wounds. His house had blown up around him and eleven servants had lost their lives, but Adam had rushed Queen Elizabeth out before the gunpowder had exploded. Elizabeth was unharmed. Adam had suffered scarcely a scratch.

Still, Justine knew the wounds he suffered inside. Returning to his father's house for his children, he had found they were not there. "Your lady wife has come and gone, sir," the old nursemaid Meg had told him, unaware of Frances's treason. "She took the children with her. I reckoned she was taking them home." But there was no home. Kilburn Manor was rubble. And Adam's wife, with his children, had disappeared.

The vicar stepped aside to make way for the pallbearers who were shuffling forward with Lord Thornleigh's coffin. Still, Justine could not make herself look at it. She glanced at Lady Thornleigh, whose gaze was fixed on her husband's coffin as it went down into the pit, fixed on it as though nothing could make her tear her eyes from it. Her arm hooked around Justine's was shaking. Justine squeezed with her elbow to give what comfort she could. She silently vowed, *Yes, Father, I will take care of her.* It was an aching, bittersweet love that swelled her heart. Never had she felt so much like a Thornleigh.

She turned her head away from the pit. Bare winter trees skirted the churchyard, and through a break in their trunks she saw a swath of bulrushes. They were tall, obscuring what lay beyond them, but a glint now and then gave it away: the sparkle of sun on water. A pond. Water birds warbled in the rushes, busy with the work of their lives. An oak tree kept watch over the pond and Justine spotted a hawk perched on a high branch, motionless, alert. Something in the sky caught the bird's attention and it lifted to life, wings slowly beating, taking it up into the blue. It soared above the church, then flew on across the winter-drab fields, over the low hills that rose to Rosethorn House. There it disappeared, a vanishing speck in the vastness of blue.

"Lord Thornleigh, with your leave . . ."

Startled by the voice, Justine turned back. It was Will, just arrived, speaking to Adam. She had been told Will was too weak to attend the funeral, and her heart lurched at the sight of him, his bandaged arm in a sling, his face pale. She had not seen him since leaving him wounded at the Savoy. Lady Thornleigh, in her grief, had left London for Rosethorn House, and Justine had accompanied her to help in any way she could, while Will's friends had taken him to the Thornleighs' London house. She had longed to see him but was told he could have no visitors, so severe was his wound. She had lived on scraps of news as he convalesced. Now, as he stepped forward from the rest of the family, his arm in the sling, he limped from his injured ankle, but there was a determined glint in his eyes. He bowed across the grave to Lady Thornleigh, then looked straight at Justine. A piercing look. A shiver touched her scalp. He had loved his uncle. *And I killed him.*

His eulogy for Lord Thornleigh was eloquent, respectful, heartfelt. But there was a ragged edge in his voice that clipped the comfort his listeners might have taken from his words. Justine was not imagining it; she saw tension in many faces.

"Baron Thornleigh died a victim of a feud," Will declared, his final word a harsh indictment. "For years the house of Grenville has been the sworn enemy of the house of Thornleigh." There were agitated murmurs from the mourners. Justine felt a cold needle of dread.

"A feud is a demon," Will plowed on. "It lusts to feed on flesh. It lays waste to everyone and everything in its path. Blind in its hunger, deaf in its purpose, it is insensible to the sorrow it inflicts. We, though, we feel the sorrow deeply today. The demon took your husband, your ladyship. It took my father. That demon even took my mother."

He fixed his eyes on Justine. She thought her heart would stop.

"Dear friends," he went on, "today we will move past our sorrow, for the demon is dead. It is dead because of the extraordinary bravery of one person." He stretched out his arm to indicate her. "Justine Grenville."

Every face turned to her. She was so astonished she could not breathe.

"This brave lady saved the life of our Queen. It was she whose warning thwarted the traitor's plot. All of England owes her an everlasting debt. But this family owes her even more, for with her courage Justine Grenville killed the demon."

The people's muttering grew louder. Justine was barely aware of it. All she knew was that Will's eyes, locked on hers, were shining.

"I have long loved this lady," he said, "and months ago I asked her to marry me. She accepted and we became betrothed. But we kept our betrothal a secret, for she is of the house of Grenville and I am of the house of Thornleigh. In her wisdom, she did not want to feed the demon. Now, thanks to her, its rancorous power is vanquished." He looked around, taking in all the people. They were quiet, waiting.

"Lady Thornleigh, my lords, friends. Lord Thornleigh wanted peace, finally, between the two houses. Today, I want to honor his wish." He looked at Justine with a tentative, hopeful smile. "But I want something far more selfish, too. The woman I love, the woman who has taught me what true loyalty is. I want Justine Grenville to be my wife."

He started toward her, limping, along the edge of the grave. People stepped back to make way for him in a hush. When he reached Justine he bowed to Lady Thornleigh, who gave him a sad smile and a nod. He held out his hand to Justine.

"Mistress Grenville, you alone have the power to transform this melancholy day into one of joy. Will you stand with me before all these witnesses and have the good vicar, here and now, join us together as man and wife?"

Until that moment she would not have believed that sorrow could flash in an instant into joy. "Oh yes, Will," she said, smiling, a smile born in the glowing heart of her. "Yes."

The murmuring around her rose to an excited hum. *A wedding?* people asked. *Now? A wedding!* others answered. *Yes, now!*

Justine looked down at the coffin in the pit. It brought her no pain. Lord Thornleigh now was at peace.

She put her hand in Will's. He clasped it.

Winter came roaring back with January. Freezing rain lashed the windows, and the men who tramped in all day with reports to Adam shook ice pellets off their hats. He was alone for the moment, standing over the map of England spread out on the desk at his father's house on Bishopsgate Street. *My house,* he thought. Hard to get used to that. He didn't think he would ever get used to the thought of his father lying dead in his grave. The sight of his gored body, when Justine had led him to it, had shaken Adam to his core.

"Begging your pardon, my lord."

Adam looked up. Another agent, one he had sent to the north coast. "Yes? What word from Scarborough?"

"No sign of her, my lord. The harbormaster swore she did not take ship from his port. Leastways no woman with two children in tow."

Adam shoved aside the map, galled by the failure. *My wife, the traitor.* He had agents searching for traces of Frances in every harbor from Newcastle to Norwich to Plymouth, but no one had seen her take ship. There was a possibility, of course, that she had gone to ground in England. If so he would find her. He had sent word to every mayor to declare a general lookout for the fugitive, and orders from Baron Thornleigh were obeyed. Every time he thought of Frances scheming behind his back to murder Elizabeth, lying to him while plotting with her brother, setting enough gunpowder to tear Elizabeth to pieces, rage surged through him. But deeper still ran his fury that she had stolen his children. It made him wild with desperation to think of Kate and Robin being wrenched from their homeland, confused and frightened, or worse, suffering harm. If Frances were brought before him he felt he might strangle her with his bare hands.

First, he had to find her. He called in his steward. "Get some men across to France. An Englishwoman with two children cannot hide long."

The steward acknowledged the order, then urged him again to see the estate people who oversaw the Thornleigh mines, timber lands, glassworks, and weaving operations. Once his father's, now Adam's. "They have been waiting all morning, your lordship. They are eager to acquaint you with the details of your properties."

Adam groaned inside. He had little interest in such matters. His father had managed all of this so well. *Father...* the thought weighed him down with sadness. He agreed to discuss the timber operation now, the rest later. Supplying oak masts to Elizabeth's navy was a priority, and he would not let that slide. "And send some men to the Low Countries, too, to look for my wife. Amsterdam, Rotterdam. Antwerp." He doubted that Frances would seek refuge in the Protestant German lands. She was a Catholic to her bones.

"My lord, news!" It was Curry, his longtime first mate, marching in with a man Adam had not seen before. Barrel-chested, with a lumbering gait and a face like aged oak, the fellow paid no mind to the ice crystals that clumped his beard. Adam knew an old salt when he saw one.

"This man captains a brigantine out of Cardiff," Curry reported. "He gave passage ten days ago to a woman and two children."

The seaman bowed. "M'lord."

"Her name, man," Adam demanded.

"She gave none, m'lord. Her silver was name enough for me."

"A girl and boy with her?"

"Aye. And the name of the girl I did hear, from the lady's own lips. Katherine, it was."

My Kate. "Where did you take them?"

"Waterford, m'lord."

Ireland!

Adam rode all day and reached Portsmouth in the dark, his hands raw from the cold as he boarded the *Elizabeth*. Refitted and rerigged, with fresh caulking, a new bowsprit, new canvas, and eight big demi-cannons in the gun ports, she was in fighting shape. At dawn he set sail for Ireland, Curry at the helm. They were passing Milford Haven, heading into St. George's Channel, when Adam spotted a pinnace racing toward them from the east. English flags. The pinnace hailed them. Adam ordered Curry to heave to, and they took on a messenger. He had come from the Admiralty, he said as he bowed to Adam. "Your lordship, Admiral Wynter sends his regards and condolences on the death of your father."

"You haven't tracked me out here to tell me that."

"No, my lord. There is word of a fleet of Spanish men-of-war sailing for the Norfolk coast. Her Majesty has ordered Admiral Wynter to send ships to intercept them." He handed Adam sealed papers. Adam broke the seal and read. He was to take on archers and handgunners immediately at Plymouth and rendezvous with Admiral Wynter off Dover.

He looked astern, eastward across the gray, heaving seas. Spanish ships were carving those frigid waters. On their way to attack England? Attack Elizabeth? He looked westward across the gray, heaving channel he was bound for. Ireland was so near. Frances was there. Kate and Robin were there. Where would his children live? *How* would they live?

It was the hardest order he had ever given. "Hoist sail, Master Curry," he said, crushing the admiral's letter in his hand, "And set a course for Plymouth."

The *Elizabeth* reared as she turned as though spoiling for the fight with Spain. Adam did not look back. But he made a silent vow that he would hunt down his wife, and soon. He would retrieve his son and daughter. And he would see that Frances paid the full, terrible penalty for her treason.

Their lovemaking was slow, gentle, careful, for Will's wound was still painful. It wasn't pain that Justine saw on his face, though, his eyes on hers as she caressed him, careful not to jostle his arm. She savored every moment of it. The slide of warm skin on skin, the sweetness of touched tongues, the caress of fingertips on cheeks, necks, arms, bellies. The fire inside her as she took him into her. *My husband. My love.*

After, they lay together, letting their breathing settle, their hearts return to a calm cadence. Rain clattered on the windows. A cold rain, Justine thought with a slight shiver, for winter was not quite done with them yet. A month from now it would be a soft spring rain. Justine imagined it pattering on Lady Thornleigh's dormant rose garden below this very window. Would a month be long enough to heal the worst of her ladyship's sorrow? Enough, at least, to draw her out one morning to smell the dew and notice the rosebuds?

"Sir William is looking out for a house for us," Will said, stroking her hair as it fell across his chest.

"Ah, good," she sighed. A house in London—*their* house. It gave her a small thrill. Her home had been with the Thornleighs since she was ten, and Rosethorn House was Will's home, too, for a while at least. Neither wanted to live in his mother's house. Justine nestled closer to him. Right now, there was no place she wanted to be except here.

They murmured on in the candlelight. Sir William Cecil wanted

Will back at work as soon as possible. Elizabeth had terminated the inquiry at the end of January. What a strange moment that had been. No fanfare. No drama. And no verdict. Justine thought it very shrewd of Elizabeth, for a guilty verdict against Mary might have inflamed those Englishmen who supported her in their desire to restore the Catholic Church; it might even have incited the Catholic kings of France and Spain to move against Her Majesty. Yet the inquiry, in laying before public view the facts of Mary's unsavory adventures in Scotland, had grievously undermined her reputation. Had that been Elizabeth's intention all along? Justine wondered. She felt she was only beginning to understand this queen she had risked her life to save. She did know, however, that as Justine Croft of the house of Thornleigh she would now and forever be loyal to Elizabeth.

The one thing no one knew was whether Mary had abetted the assassination attempt. Many of Elizabeth's people said she did, citing the letter signed by Mary that Justine's father had brought Justine to arrange the abdication meeting. Mary, under questioning, swore with much weeping that she had no knowledge of the plot and that Justine's father had forged the letter. Justine herself did not know the truth of it, but it gave her an odd chill to see how quickly Mary distanced herself from the man who had been her secret agent. Elizabeth, in any case, was taking no chances. She had moved Mary from Bolton farther south to Tutbury Castle in Staffordshire, a bleak old bastion of the Earl of Shrewsbury in whose custody she now was held, and her retinue of servants was reduced. The Scottish delegation led by the Earl of Moray had returned to Edinburgh. "The status quo is unchanged," Will had commented to Justine, pleased with Elizabeth's wise handling of the matter. "Scotland will remain our bulwark against France."

Will's breathing became slower, steadier as he drifted into sleep. *Sleep, nature's nurse,* Justine thought, happy to have Will so nearly restored to full health. She lay close to him and listened to the rain spatter the windows like pebbles flung by an angry god. Will made a sound in his sleep, a faint grunt of pain. His shoulder? A nightmare? In Justine's mind the two were one: Will's brush with death was a nightmare that still troubled her sleep. How near she had come to losing him that night. She thought of it as the night she had killed both her fathers. One had caused so much misery, she hoped she would soon forget him. The other she knew she would mourn forever.

They were both asleep when the messenger arrived at the front gates.

"He is waiting in the long gallery, mistress," the maid with her candle whispered to Justine from the bedchamber doorway. "From Sir William Cecil."

Justine woke Will. They both threw on robes and met the messenger in the gallery. He was bundled up against the rain and his garments glistened wet in the candlelight. Sir William had sent orders for Will. He was to leave in the morning and ride to Leicester to meet the Earl of Sussex, and from there proceed to Leeds to assist Sussex in investigating rumors of trouble brewing in the north. Rumors of an incipient rebellion.

"I'll be the earl's right hand man," Will said when he and Justine were alone again. Though the message hinted at danger, he was far from displeased. "This could make our fortune, my love."

She tried to see it that way. Certainly, the advancement for Will was thrilling, and she was proud that he had Sir William's trust. But all she saw was separation.

He smiled at her. "Come with me."

"To Leicester?"

"All the way north. It will be weeks. Maybe months. I want you with me."

She thought of the northern moors. Of Yeavering Hall. Of Alice. It was a place that held no joy for her. But neither did she want to be apart from Will. "I cannot leave her ladyship, not right away. She needs me now."

"So do I," he said gently. "But you're right. She will mend better with you nearby."

"I'll come later. As soon as I feel I can leave her."

"Easter?"

Three weeks. She smiled. How easily she and Will settled things. How perfectly matched they were. "Yes," she said.

The next morning the wind was a cold blade scything the courtyard, but the rain had stopped and the sun was struggling to shine through the clouds, and Justine took heart from Will's cheerful face as she saw him to horse with his servant. He leaned down from the saddle to kiss her one last time, and she went up on her toes, and their lips met. "Easter," he whispered.

"Easter," she whispered in return.

She watched him trot away, her eyes on him until he and his servant were small figures taking the bend in the road northward. She tugged her shawl around her in the wind and turned and looked up at Rosethorn House, casting her mind to the gardening book that she would read to Lady Thornleigh. Roses. Spring was not so far away.

AUTHOR'S NOTES

Fact and fiction are intertwined in *Blood Between Queens*. The characters in the two feuding families—the Thornleighs and the Grenvilles—are purely my creation, but their lives weave through actual historical events and around real historical personalities. Among the latter are Elizabeth I of England and Mary Queen of Scots, the cousins whose dramatic rivalry has enthralled the world for over four hundred years, generating plays, an opera, biographies, novels, and films.

Here are some of the real historical events, with notes on how I have sometimes shaped them for the dramatic purposes of my novel.

First is the inquiry that Elizabeth convened to examine the Scottish confederate lords' charges that Mary was complicit in her husband's murder. My general depiction of the inquiry is accurate: the composition of its commissioners on both sides; the fact that Mary refused to attend; the venues, first at York, then at Westminster; the introduction of the famous "casket letters"; and the withdrawal of Mary's commissioners in protest. However, I have altered a detail about the ambassadors of Spain and France. Both were replaced in the middle of the inquiry. The Spanish Ambassador was Guzman da Silva for most of 1568, but he left on September 12 and was replaced by Guerau de Spes, while France's ambassador Bodutel de la Forest was replaced by Bertrand de la Mothe Fenelon. For the sake of simplicity I have used the replacements' names throughout.

Elizabeth adjourned the inquiry without delivering a verdict. She didn't need to; the damage to Mary's reputation was done, thanks to the casket letters. These letters, eight in all, have fueled passionate discussion for centuries and still do. The Earl of Moray, Mary's half brother, delivered them in private to the inquiry panel led by the Duke of Norfolk, as is depicted in *Blood Between Queens*, though I have invented the details of the scene in which he did so. The letters showed that Mary had conspired in her husband's murder with her alleged lover, the Earl of Bothwell, and this damning evidence shattered her reputation at the time and for posterity. Mary insisted to her dying day that the letters were forged by her enemies. Did she write them or not? Sadly, they were destroyed by her son, James VI of England, and with them was lost the chance to study their authenticity. Any reader interested in delving more deeply into the complexities of these events will enjoy Alison Weir's splendid book *Mary, Queen of Scots, and the Murder of Lord Darnley.*

Adam Thornleigh's adventure in pirating King Philip's gold and delivering it to Elizabeth is my invention, but is based on a fascinating true event. In November 1568 French Huguenot rovers chased four small Spanish ships into port in southern England, where customs officers found that the ships carried treasure to pay the troops in the Spanish-occupied Low Countries—a staggering 85,000 pounds in gold (about 30 million dollars today). The Italian merchant banker Benedict Spinola, living in London, advised Elizabeth that the gold was his loan to the Spanish king, but assured her that he would consider a loan to the Queen of England just as advantageous as one to Philip of Spain. So Elizabeth worked out good terms with Spinola and borrowed the money, making herself richer and leaving her cold-war enemy, Spain, unable to pay its army. The Spanish were furious and ordered all English property in the Low Countries confiscated. Elizabeth retaliated by impounding Spanish assets in England, which were worth far more. It worked out well for Elizabeth.

Adam's part in the expedition led by John Hawkins to the Spanish Caribbean is based on Hawkins's true-life expedition. His six ships left Plymouth in October 1567, one of them, the *Judith*, captained by Francis Drake. In July 1568, near Veracruz, Mexico, they were attacked by the Spanish—the battle of San Juan de Ulúa—and some of Hawkins's ships were sunk, including the *Jesus of Lubeck* carrying the expedition's profit in treasure. Drake on the *Judith* got away, and so did Hawkins on the *Minion*, with two hundred men aboard but insufficient food. In January 1569 the *Judith* limped into Plymouth harbor with just fifteen survivors, and five days later Hawkins and his starving crew on the *Minion* reached port in Cornwall. I added Adam Thornleigh to this ill-fated expedition as captain of his ship, the *Elizabeth*.

In *Blood Between Queens* Grenville's plot to incite an uprising under the banner of the Earl of Northumberland is fiction but is based on truth, for in 1569, just months after the novel ends, the Earls of Northumberland and Westmorland raised the northern Catholics in a massive armed revolt. Leading five thousand men they took Durham Cathedral and were preparing to march on London to depose Elizabeth. She sent a force under the Earl of Sussex to put down the uprising, which he did with great brutality, hanging over six hundred rebels. Westmorland fled to the Netherlands. Elizabeth executed Northumberland.

The fate of Mary Queen of Scots following the inquiry is a sad and well-known tale. Of all the ill-judged decisions she made during her unstable seven-year reign in Scotland, her flight into England to escape her enemies was the worst. She asked Elizabeth to help her crush the Scottish confederate lords who had deposed her, and to restore her to her throne, and this put Elizabeth in an untenable situation. She sympathized, for Mary was her cousin, and Mary's status as a fellow sovereign was something Elizabeth took very seriously. But she could not afford to antagonize England's ally, the Scottish lords, by backing Mary. Yet neither could she allow Mary to move freely around England because Mary had a dangerous appeal to militant English Catholics who wanted her on the English throne. So Elizabeth kept Mary under house arrest—a captivity that lasted for nineteen years. It was a comfortable captivity as befitted Mary's rank, but she never again gained her freedom.

During those nineteen years Mary plotted ceaselessly via smuggled letters to overthrow Elizabeth with the help of Catholic supporters both foreign and domestic. Elizabeth waited, uneasy but unwilling to act against her, until in 1586 the final plot, known as the Babington Plot, proved beyond doubt Mary's guilt in conniving to bring about Elizabeth's assassination. That winter, in the hardest decision Elizabeth ever made, she signed her cousin's death warrant. Mary was executed on February 7, 1587, at Fotheringhay Castle.

One of the most surprising facts about these two queens is that they never met. All their communication was done through letters and representatives.

In researching the complex rivalry between them I am indebted to Jane Dunn's masterly book *Elizabeth & Mary: Cousins, Rivals, Queens* and recommend it to any reader eager to understand what drove these two women.

Fact and fiction are intertwined in all my "Thornleigh" novels. The first, *The Queen's Lady,* features young Honor Larke, a fictional ward of Sir Thomas More and lady-in-waiting to Catherine of Aragon, Henry VIII's first wife, and follows Honor's stormy love affair with Richard Thornleigh as she works to rescue heretics from the Church's fires. *The King's Daughter* introduces their daughter Isabel, who joins the Wyatt rebellion, a true event, to oust Queen Mary and hires mercenary Carlos Valverde to help her rescue her father from prison. *The Queen's Captive* brings Honor and Richard back from exile with their seafaring son Adam to help the young Princess Elizabeth, who has been imprisoned by her half sister, Queen Mary, another true event. *The Queen's Gamble* is set during the fledgling reign of Elizabeth, who fears that the massive buildup of French troops on her Scottish border will lead to an invasion, so she entrusts Isabel Thornleigh to take money to aid the Scottish rebellion led by firebrand preacher John Knox, to oust the French.

Readers have sent me wonderfully astute comments and questions about the characters, real and invented, in my books and I always enjoy replying. This partnership with you, the reader, makes my work a joy. If you'd like to write to me, I'd love to hear from you. Contact me at bkyle@barbarakyle.com and follow me on Twitter @BKyleAuthor. And if you'd like to receive my occasional newsletters, just sign up via my website at www.barabarakyle.com.

ACKNOWLEDGMENTS

I've been fortunate to work with the gifted Audrey LaFehr as my editor at Kensington Books in New York for five books in my "Thornleigh" series. No author could ask for a more dedicated champion. I'm also grateful to the team of splendid professionals at Kensington who shepherd my books so skillfully through the production process, including Production Editor Paula Reedy and Assistant Editor Martin Biro. Special thanks go to John Rosenberg, whose indefatigable work has made my books so successful in Canada. My agent, Al Zuckerman, of Writers House, has been a mainstay for many years, and I continue to appreciate his literary advice and steady counsel. My deepest thanks go to my husband, Stephen Best, who sees the heart of everything I write and helps me shape it.

It's a great pleasure to acknowledge some wonderful input from my readers. While I was writing *Blood Between Queens* I ran a contest—the "Name the Thornleighs' House" contest—and scores of readers sent in suggestions. Everyone who participated has my sincere thanks. Here are the results. Fourth runner-up: Col. Elmer Follis of Tennessee for "Haven Hall." Third runner-up: Lynne Deragon of Ontario for "Larkston Place." Second runner-up: Linda Lefler of Nova Scotia for "Thornbloom." First runner-up: Hollye Patterson of Tennessee for "Larkeleigh." And the winner: Pat Larke of Indiana for "Rosethorn Manor." Thank you, Pat, for so elegantly grafting Honor's love of roses onto Richard's surname. I was delighted to call the Thornleighs' home "Rosethorn" throughout the novel.

BLOOD BETWEEN QUEENS

Barbara Kyle

ABOUT THIS GUIDE

The suggested questions are included to
enhance your group's reading of Barbara Kyle's
Blood Between Queens.

DISCUSSION QUESTIONS

1. Secrets figure prominently in *Blood Between Queens*. Richard and Honor Thornleigh have kept Justine's identity as a Grenville secret to spare her the stigma of being known as a traitor's child. Were they right in making this decision?

2. Justine has hidden from the Thornleighs the fact that her traitorous father is alive because she believes that he will never come back to England. Was she wise in hiding this crucial information from them?

3. Justine doesn't tell Will about her Grenville background for fear of losing him, convincing herself that the feud between their families is long past and best forgotten. Do you, like Justine, think that secrets are sometimes necessary?

4. Several characters in *Blood Between Queens* have to make hard choices. Queen Elizabeth must decide what to do with her cousin Mary, Queen of Scots, who has fled to England asking for Elizabeth's protection and an army to rout her enemies in Scotland. But Elizabeth dare not antagonize her ally, the Scottish Protestant government, by helping restore Mary to her throne. Neither, though, can she allow Mary to move freely around England because of Mary's dangerous appeal to English Catholics who want her on the English throne. Given this dilemma, do you think Elizabeth was justified in keeping Mary under house arrest?

5. When Christopher Grenville fled England, he lost everything: his lands, his grand house, and even his daughter Justine, who has been brought up by his enemies, the Thornleighs. Do you feel any sympathy for Grenville in using Justine to get revenge on Richard Thornleigh?

6. Mary, Queen of Scots refuses to attend the inquiry to answer questions about her involvement in the murder of

her husband. Was she right to refuse to appear and refute the charges of her subjects? Do you think she was innocent or guilty of complicity in the murder?

7. Hoping to help Mary clear her name, Justine tells Mary that the casket letters have been introduced in private at the inquiry as damning evidence against her. Did you think Justine was right to try to help Mary?

8. Justine deceives Will in order to get his copies of Mary's letters, hoping it will bring an end to the inquiry, and she seduces him to accomplish this. Do you think Justine's deception was valid?

9. Frances Thornleigh's overwhelming love for her husband Adam makes her irrationally jealous of Elizabeth, so she helps her brother conspire against Elizabeth. Do you sympathize with Frances? Is love ever a justifiable motive for a crime?